THE WANDERERS

Books by Paul Stutzman

The Wandering Home Series
Book One: The Wanderers
Book Two: Wandering Home
Book Three (Coming Soon): Wander No More

Adventure Memoir
Hiking Through
 One Man's Journey to Peace and Freedom on the Appalachian Trail
Biking Across America
 My Coast-to-Coast Adventure and the People I Met Along the Way
Stuck in the Weeds
 A Pilgrim on the Mississippi River and the Camino de Santiago

With Author Serena Miller
More Than Happy: The Wisdom of Amish Parenting

Contact
www.paulstutzman.com
www.facebook.com/pvstutzman
pstutzman@roadrunner.com

The Wanderers

Paul Stutzman

Not all who wander are lost.
-- J.R.R. Tolkien.

All who are lost wander.
-- Johnny Miller

Wandering Home Books
Berlin, Ohio

With admiration and appreciation, I dedicate *The Wanderers* to teachers who left an enduring imprint on this student's wandering mind:

Sevilla Jaberg, Eva Crilow, John "Bunny John" Miller, Loil Brown, James Mast, Glen Mast, Sturgis Miller, Orpha Troyer, Abe Mast, Merele Kinsey, Roy R. Miller, Tim Miller, Oscar Miller, Roger Dunn, John Maxwell, and Robert Smailes.

The results of your work and dedication cannot be measured semester to semester, but require a lifetime to come to fruition.

Author's Note

This is a work of fiction. All characters were fabricated by my imagination, and any resemblance you may see to anyone, either living or dead, is coincidental. This is not a treatise on the Amish lifestyle; the story just happens to be set in an Amish community. Although I was born into an Amish family and understand that world, this book is not intended to make me a spokesman for the Amish way of life. There are many other books written attempting to describe and explain the Amish community, some even nibbling at the edges of truth. Yes, there were several seeds of truth in my story; but upon sprouting, they were quickly pounced on, wrestled to the ground, and suffocated by fiction.

You will, however, find truths here that cannot be denied or ignored or fictionalized. Those are the truths of Scripture.

I am quite aware that butterflies don't talk as we humans do, but I have taken the liberty of pretending to know how butterflies think. I did, after all, have one hatch in my house one night shortly after my wife passed away. I awoke and it was flying circles above me. Perhaps it was relaying this story to me. I am also aware that Jim Hogg is buried in Austin, not in Hebbronville, and that Sun Dancer was nowhere near Louisville on the day Secretariat won the Kentucky Derby.

Thanks to Elaine Starner for her assistance with this book.

Enjoy the story a wandering butterfly told to me late one night, once upon a time.

In Hebbronville, a rancher leaves Frank's Diner and climbs into his cattle truck. The door slams shut and the engine roars to life. He is late, and he hurries along well beyond the posted limit.

Twenty miles east of town, the speeding vehicle creates a maelstrom of air currents that picks up bits of detritus and scatters them at will. Two dried out butterfly carcasses are swept from the roadside and tossed and turned violently in the midst of the whirlwind. Wings separate from fragile bodies, and the tattered pieces slowly drift to rest in a neighboring field. On a milkweed plant nearby, over one hundred little larvae devour milkweed leaves as if their existence depends on it. It does.

Another wandering awaits. And so it continues, the cycle of life. Death stalks life while life attempts to remain one heartbeat ahead. The dead return to the earth; the living continue to seek.

They seek a place of safety, a place called home.

I

The Wanderers

1

Before dawn, Annie's groans woke him. He was out of bed and by her side in seconds. How could he have let himself doze off? She clutched her head, mumbling unintelligible sounds. Her eyes, wide open, did not see her husband.

Johnny ran to the big house. A light was on in the kitchen, and Mandy jumped as he burst through the door.

"Mom! Annie's much worse! We need help!"

Mandy moved the kettle off the stove and ran out the door. Johnny raced up the road on his old bike. At the pay phone near the sawmill, he started dialing the numbers of drivers the family frequently used. Finally he rousted someone who said he would be at the Miller house in fifteen minutes.

Naomi had joined Mandy in the small house, and both knelt at Annie's side.

"Our driver will be here soon."

Headlights swung into the driveway. Johnny carefully lifted Annie, still bundled in the blanket, and carried her to the car. As he placed her gently in the back seat, the blanket fell away and he noticed she was clutching the notebook she had asked for the night before. Mandy peeled her fingers from it, and mother and son wrapped the blanket tightly around the slight figure. Then they climbed in, one on each side of her. She seemed asleep and would have toppled over if they had not held her steady.

Naomi wanted to go along, but she would need to stay and help Dad with the chores. She stood in the driveway and watched forlornly as the car drove away.

The ride to Stevenson seemed to take hours. In the emergency room, the doctor did not take long in his assessment and decision that Annie would be rushed off to a larger hospital better equipped to deal with head injuries.

Head injuries! She was in grave danger, the doctor said.

Johnny climbed into the ambulance. The pale, unresponsive body on the stretcher did not look like his wife. She seemed more fragile than ever. Mandy followed the ambulance in the car they had hired. For an hour, Johnny Miller listened to the wailing siren and prayed for his Annie as they sped through the gray dawn.

In the ambulance, the paramedics monitored her constantly. By the time they pulled into the emergency entrance at the hospital, Johnny could see that Annie was having trouble breathing. Doctors rushed her off into surgery. Numb, Johnny and his mother were ushered to a nearby waiting area.

"The best thing we can do for her is pray," Mandy said. She must have known how helpless Johnny felt. *I am her husband. It's my job to protect her. How could I let this happen?*

A terrible thought lurked at the edges of his mind. *Could God be punishing us?*

He had thought he had settled this matter. He and Annie were forgiven. They were new creatures, transformed from the people they had once been. God had given them the gift of new life and each other. Would He still demand that they *pay* for things they had done? He believed in the forgiveness and mercy of God, but ... Johnny Miller knew he deserved a settling up, a day of reckoning when he would have to account to a holy God for the things he'd done in his life.

Was this God's day of reckoning with them?

2

He was ten when he had his first taste of beer. A late start, to be sure, but he was never bothered much by peer pressure. His friends had all sampled the stuff two or three years before, but Johnny Miller had felt no desire or need. There was only one reason he drank on that hot August day. He was thirsty.

Finished with his morning chores, the boy started across the hayfield with an armful of boards ripped from the old wash house. Previous generations had scrubbed and soaked and steamed in the one-room shack in front of their farmhouse; John and Mandy Miller, though, had upgraded to a new kerosene washer, and now the women worked in the coolness under the long front porch. An old kettle still hung above the brick fire pit, but the wash house sagged like a tired old work horse.

John, Johnny's father, had assigned the boy the task of dismantling the old building. That was fine with Johnny; he had plans for that scrap lumber. He wanted to enlarge the deer stand. *His* deer stand.

Years ago, Johnny's grandfather had secured several boards across two gnarled branches of a stately oak that stood sentinel at the edge of the Millers' woods. Ten feet off the ground, the rough platform was accessed by short slabs nailed up the oak's trunk, creating a ladder. Over time, the trunk had swallowed up most of the rungs, but edges still protruded far enough for deer hunters to clamber up and lie in wait for the quarry.

Johnny's first hunt with his dad and his brother, Jonas, was also his last. Finally, he was deemed old enough to go hunting with the men. His excitement rose as he climbed the ladder and settled into waiting, tense with anticipation. Very soon, a doe came through the woods, paused at the spring to drink, then walked slowly down the side of the ravine. One shot echoed through the quiet morning. The three scampered down the ladder rungs and approached the deer, lying bleeding on the hillside. It struggled to its feet, took another tumble, and lay still.

The boy's excitement vanished. He felt only sadness and pangs of remorse. The doe's brown eye was open, staring at the hunters, asking, "Why? What did I do to deserve this?"

John had a knife in his hands; the boy knew what must come next. Backtracking, he was violently sick behind a bush. Johnny Miller was not meant to be a hunter, and if he had any say at all, no one would ever shoot another deer from that stand.

He did have his say. That is, Mandy did. Although John was the authority and power in the Miller house, Mandy often held the reins. The children knew this. With tears streaming down his face, Johnny unloaded his sad description of the dying deer. "We can't shoot them anymore. We just can't," he told his mother.

Soon the NO HUNTING signs were posted, and the woods, deer stand, and all of God's nature on the Millers' 120 acres became Johnny's kingdom. The platform in the oak tree on the hill overlooked the fields that the Miller family had owned for generations, and Johnny claimed it as his hideout, where he spent countless hours dreaming and contemplating life. It was a haven for his wondering mind that did wander to many places.

Now he had been given the means to enlarge and build a much grander hideout. Johnny had the sharp business sense of his father; he saw an opportunity in the chore his father had given him. When he tackled the job of taking down the old wash house with much gusto, Mandy watched from her kitchen window, amused, accurately guessing the reason for her son's enthusiasm.

His usual route from the wash house to the deer stand followed the cow path leading from the barn to the pasture field. Twice a day, their herd traveled the path. On this day, though, the hayfield between the house and the woods had been mowed and Johnny took advantage of the shorter route. Even if the route through the hayfield were longer, he might have chosen it on this day. As a ten-year-old, he drank in the sensory gifts of summer: the aroma of new mown hay, the sweetness of warm strawberries, the smell of an August rain on dusty ground.

"Johnny, go get us some Stroh's!" his older brother Jonas called. He and his friend Andrew were in the field, making hay. Andrew had been recruited to help Jonas today because John was away on a lumber-buying trip, and the clouds warned there would be rain by tomorrow.

Johnny dropped his boards reluctantly and retraced his steps back to the farmhouse.

His great-grandparents had built their house over a spring, and the cool waters flowed through the basement, filling a concrete trough where Mandy stored crocks of butter, fresh milk and cream, eggs, watermelon, and dishes prepared for the next meal. The amber bottles of Stroh's were chilling in the trough just inside the door. Johnny grabbed two by the necks and rushed back outside, leaving a wet trail of spring water.

The Stroh's stash belonged to Jonas. Johnny's father was bishop of their Amish church, and Johnny had never seen him drink beer. As a church leader, John was very much aware that anything misused, misread, or mistaken could affect his reputation and influence in the community.

Big brother Jonas, on the other hand, had no such reputation to protect. At sixteen, he had recently concluded his formal education and knew exactly where his future lay. He was not yet a member of the church, but he would join in a few years, get married, and settle down right here in the valley. He had big plans to take over the sawmill that John ran as a part-time operation. Johnny was the younger of John and Mandy's sons; he knew his father hoped that he would someday be farming the Millers' family land.

"You thirsty?" Jonas handed his half-empty bottle to Johnny. The boy was thirsty. But that first taste was not good.

Still, that swallow in the hayfield meant that now he was one of the men. He may have been a Miller boy, but now he was a Stroh's man.

Yes, many bottles of Stroh's beer would find their way to the deer stand in the years to come. Stroh's would bring much trouble to Johnny's life, but it would also lead to meeting Annie.

And then, for a short time, he would have it all. He would be the Amish man, living the dream.

.

3

Earlier that same year, in March, as melting ice dripped from the roofs and bare ground began to green and young boys were afflicted with spring fever, Johnny had approached his father with an urgent appeal.

"Dad, I need a new bicycle."

"We already have two; why another one?"

"The one the big sisters used to ride is a girl's bike. And boys don't ride girls' bikes; it's embarrassing."

"You could use Jonas's old Schwinn."

"That's too old, and it's never here when I want it."

The youngster plunged ahead with his sales pitch. "I saw the perfect bike advertised in the paper. It's a Schwinn Mark IV Jaguar. It's a beauty, Dad. It has two speeds, a light, and a carrier on both wheels. It's got a horn and stainless steel fenders." And here was the line to clinch the deal: "I could use it to run errands for you and Mom."

John's train-up-a-child expertise was even sharper than his son's sales pitch.

"Son, here's what I'm thinking. I could, of course, buy you that bike. On the other hand, wouldn't it be more rewarding to earn the money and buy it yourself?"

Before the boy could debate that, John rolled out his proposal.

"Out behind the woodshed is that old chicken house where Grandma used to raise her pullets. The Milford Feed and Supply has a deal where they supply the chicks free to anyone wishing to raise laying hens. You buy the feed from them, collect your eggs, and they'll pick up whatever you have to sell. They'll even supply the egg cartons.

"There's some work to be done first; the henhouse has boards missing and the chicken netting needs to be tacked up again. But I know you can do it. You've helped with enough jobs in the furniture shop; a few repairs on a chicken house should be easy."

The deal sounded too good to be true. His very own egg business at age ten! And thus, Johnny launched his poultry operation.

Every day after school, he flew through his chores and then worked feverishly to build his financial empire. He assessed the work needed in the old chicken house, with its rounded roof and two small, wood walkways leading in and out of the coop. The laying boxes were still intact; two rows of twenty-five, one atop the other, stretched the length of two facing walls. Johnny pounded up boards, stretched the fencing, and even yanked out weeds that marred his entrepreneurial landscape.

Finally, the weathered building was ready, with neat fencing around the perimeter and one hundred cozy cubicles filled with straw, awaiting his moneymakers.

The golden balls of fluff arrived in a cardboard box. For one week, the peeps were kept corralled in an area of the Millers' basement. Then Johnny moved them to their new home. In the morning, he'd unlatch the flap releasing the chickens into the fenced area; and at night, he was careful to raise and latch the two walkways again, securing the chicken house against predators. The chicks ate a mash that he made by mixing feed with water.

There really wasn't much to raising chickens, he thought. He was starting his days an hour earlier, tending to his birds before the school bus pulled up by the mailbox. Of course, no eggs had arrived yet to collect, sort, wash, and stack in cartons.

In his dreams, the shiny new bike was already parked outside the big farmhouse, ready for long summer days of adventure. Johnny visualized the egg money piling up in the bank, and he was busy composing his side of another conversation with his dad. In six years, he would be eligible for a driver's license—if his father would sign for him; and after six years of eggs, surely there would be enough money for a car. Convincing John to sign would take some persuasion; that would be a conversation for another day, a conversation that in all likelihood stood no chance of success. Nonetheless, Johnny was certain it would be worth the effort.

It would be five months, though, before any eggs would appear; and the young entrepreneur soon realized that the money flow was going in only one direction. He accumulated quite a debt, since his dad was paying the feed until his own money started to come in from the sale of eggs.

Even though all his dreams were pinned on the arrival of those eggs, he was still startled one morning when he carried a bucket of pellets to his charges and caught sight of a white orb in one cubicle. At last! The money train had finally pulled into the station. He would pay his debt to John, and the bike would soon be here.

For several days, the egg production was just enough for the Miller family's breakfast; but the morning arrived when Johnny realized he would have to buy another wire egg basket, or else make two trips to the house with his bounty.

Then the pullets started to lay eggs with a vengeance. They no longer left the boxes when he entered the coop. A mothering instinct seized their pea-sized brains and they remained on their nests, protecting their eggs and believing they were starting a family. Every morning Johnny reached in and slid his arm beneath those pullets to rob them of their dreams. Then there was the cleaning and sorting and packing. And the job he came to dread the most—cleaning out the chicken house.

The work required soon dulled his dreams. In a few weeks, school would be in session again. He had begun his deer stand project earlier that summer, but once the eggs started coming, he had less and less time in the woods. The summer was almost gone; and the shiny new bike rolled only through his dreams and not down their country road.

Johnny did the calculations and realized that saving the $84.95 needed for the new bicycle would take more time than his dreams had allocated. The pullets would lay eggs for two years. Eggs were quite cheap, and he would only realize the bulk of his needed funds when he sold the birds for chicken dinners. His natural aversion to killing any living thing rose up in protest at this thought, but money was now involved, and those chickens had pecked his arms enough to warrant a death penalty.

He did begin to question whether the poultry operation was worth all the effort and sacrifice. His creative mind began to shape a plan. He would need to implement the plan discreetly; he had some idea what his parents would say if they happened to get wind of it, and that was a situation he most definitely wanted to avoid.

4

Up to that summer, Johnny and his little sister, Naomi, had spent all their free time together. The family called them "the little ones." The Millers' three older daughters were "the big sisters," and Jonas, six years older than Johnny, was just "Jonas."

Johnny knew Naomi missed her playmate, but this summer he had a business to run and his own private sanctuary to construct up in the woods. Sometimes, he sneaked off to work on the deer stand, slipping away before Naomi had a chance to ask him to share some adventure with her. He did not want to see the disappointment in her eyes when he declined her invitation.

On one August afternoon, while he pulled the final remnants of siding from the wash house, Naomi helped Mom in the garden, stripping plump ears of corn from their stalks. When Mandy picked up the basket and headed toward the house, Naomi ambled over to watch her big brother's progress.

"Looks like you're almost done with that."

"Yup," he said, laying another board on the neat pile he already had and not looking at his sister.

"Are you taking those boards up to the woods?"

"Yup."

"What are you building up there?"

"It's sort of a clubhouse," Johnny replied. "It's private, for boys only, no girls allowed." He actually had no intention of inviting other boys, since most of his friends didn't understand the concept of allowing deer to roam freely and unthreatened.

Naomi stood silently, and Johnny fiddled at straightening the pile of wood.

"Can I come up to see it? Just once?"

Her brother frowned a bit, stared at his boards, and pretended to think about that.

"Naomi, I have an idea. Do you like treasure?" Of course she did. Hunting treasure used to be one of their favorite adventures. "When I go out to get the eggs, it's like finding buried treasure. If I allowed you to help gather eggs in exchange for being allowed to come up to the deer stand, would you do it?"

"You would let me do that?"

"We also have to wash the eggs and pack them in the cartons and get them ready for the mill to pick up."

"Okay! Okay! And can I help you carry this pile up to the woods right now?"

"I'm not quite ready for company up there. But soon. You'll be my first guest. And you probably shouldn't mention to Mom that you'll be helping me, or she might decide to give you more chores of your own."

Naomi skipped back to the house, delighted to be included in such a special venture.

The two established a routine, each taking one side of the coop. Naomi copied her brother's approach, talking to the chickens by name. Johnny had named almost every animal on the Miller farm. That included four Clydesdale work horses, three buggy horses, two cats, four kittens, twenty-four pigs, more than a dozen cows, calves, and one dog. The process of assigning names to all the chickens, though, had been a bit more complicated. At the beginning, all those little peeps chirping and scuttling about had made identifying each one more difficult. As they had grown, they took on more distinct characteristics and even different behaviors. Johnny had found that once the hens were in the coop, the same two or three birds always shared the same box.

So the naming was by nest. In the first nest, Alice and Abby clucked and scolded. Betty and Barbara and Brenda settled into the second box, Clara and Cindy in the third. And so on through the alphabet, although Johnny never needed the *X, Y,* or *Z* names. Thus all the pullets were named. Naomi helped supply some of the monikers. Johnny had been stumped by the *Q.* And over the weeks, Naomi remembered the names even better than he did.

The little sister, so industrious and eager to please her big brother, gradually did more and more of the work. Soon, all Johnny was doing was helping to gather the eggs and clean the chicken house, and Naomi did the rest.

The days were growing shorter, and in a few weeks all scholars would be back in school. Johnny wanted to finish his building project; and with the bulk of the egg operation subbed out, he once again had more time for the deer stand. For a few weeks, everything was working great.

* * *

"Johnny!" He had run in from the bus, changed into work clothes, and was on his way out again when Mandy's call stopped him. "Naomi tells me she is being *allowed* to help with the eggs in exchange for visiting your hideout in the woods."

"Uh … yes. It's a business deal."

He couldn't look at her.

"Aren't you a little ashamed of yourself for tricking her? Doesn't it disturb you that you are taking advantage of a sister who just wants to be with you?"

Yes, it had bothered him a little, but the twinges of conscience had passed fairly quickly.

"Naomi is my helper, and you're taking her away from me to

do your work," Mandy went on. "So here's what will happen. You will either pay Naomi to help you, or I will see that Dad charges you rent for his chicken house. And the rent payment will then come to me for the loss of my little helper."

That meant John would hear about the slave labor operation. Johnny was sure of his father's reaction to that. But he liked the way things were going; and since he didn't want to lose his help, he was open to adjusting his business plan.

That evening after the milk had been poured and strained and the milk cans all were cooling in the water trough, John clamped a hand on his son's shoulder.

"Son, we need to talk."

Johnny knew his father already knew.

John propped one leg up on the top of the trough, leaned an elbow on his knee, and looked at his boy sternly. "Mom tells me you've brought on some extra help in the egg business."

"Well, she wanted to help … it was taking so much of my time, and … she …"

"Listen," said John. "I admire your powers of persuasion, but taking advantage of anyone is wrong. If you treat others fairly, it will be returned to you. You can do ten things right, but one misstep can taint your reputation or your relationships forever. Our family has a reputation for being good business people, but also for being fair and honest. I'm suggesting rather strongly that you start paying your help."

Johnny put on his best forlorn look and pretended to be chastised, but his new plan was already taking shape. He also caught a grin on his father's face, even though the elder Miller had turned away quickly, hoping to hide his amusement. John was not happy his daughter had been deceived and that it was his son who had done the deceiving. Still, Johnny suspected his father was also encouraged that his son had shown some signs of entrepreneurship, and he hoped his father was thinking that he might someday have what it took to run the farm, after all.

As the two youngsters gathered eggs the next morning, Naomi was thrilled when Johnny informed her she would be added to the payroll. "I'll give you one dollar a week to be my helper. Depending how things go, it could be even more."

"Wow! I get paid, plus I get to see your clubhouse!"

"Well, about that clubhouse. I've been thinking about making that a private clubhouse for members only. There would, of course, be dues to pay if anyone wants to join. It was intended to be boys only, but I might consider an exception for little sisters."

"Can I? Can I please join?" she begged.

"The dues will probably be close to one dollar a week."

"But if you pay me that much each week, I can use that money to pay my dues."

"You probably shouldn't say anything to Mom or Dad, or they might want to join and then it won't even be a clubhouse; it won't be any different than being here at the house."

"I'll keep the secret. And if I have any money left over, could you hide it for me somewhere in your room? I want to use it to buy everybody Christmas presents."

Johnny's conscience cringed. What an innocent, pure-hearted girl she was, and what a cruel trickster he had become! His father's words finally squirmed past his devious plans and took root in his mind. Treat others right, and they will treat you right. He was treating his sister poorly, but she was still treating him right.

He heard her singing as she trudged off to the house with a heavy basket of eggs.

He was only ten years old, but that day he decided if he ever got married (which seemed only remotely possible), he wanted a girl as kind, pure-hearted, and trusting as his little sister. From what he knew of girls, though, he didn't think that would be possible.

5

"What's wrong?" Naomi could read her brother's disgust in the way he glared at the fence around the chicken house.

Biff had made quite a commotion in the middle of the night. His barking had summoned Johnny from his dreams, but instead, the boy had wiggled deeper under the quilt.

Now here was another burrowed hole. That fox had been back, trying to get at the chickens. It looked like Biff had chased him off before he got under the fence. Johnny had always been very careful to close up the chicken coop at night; he'd heard stories about how a fox in the chicken house would often kill all the birds, even though he'd take only one.

"It looks like another visit from that fox."

"Are you going to hunt him down?" Naomi sounded almost eager for the critter's demise. Johnny shrugged and shook his head.

"No. I can't really blame him. Foxes are born foxes. They do foxy things."

Besides, he had only one thing on his mind on this clear October Saturday. One or two small touches, and his deer stand would be perfect.

"Tell you what, after you finish washing and sorting the eggs, I'll take you up to the deer stand and give you a tour." For the last two months, Naomi had worked hard while waiting patiently for his invitation.

"It's ready? You're done?" Naomi bounced with excitement, but then the bounce died. "Do I have enough money for the dues?"

Weeks ago, Johnny's conscience had prompted him to change his plan to charge admission to the private woodsy retreat. The little chats with Mom and Dad had assisted his conscience in making the decision; but he had not yet told his sister.

"Naomi, I've changed my mind about that. You won't have to pay dues. You can come up, but there will be one rule. You can only be there when I'm there, too."

"Really? You're the best brother ever, Johnny! I'll hurry …"

She almost ran to the house, the full basket swinging precariously.

"Not too many Humpty Dumptys today," he called after her.

* * *

The egg chores were finally done, and Naomi chattered happily as she trailed her brother up the cow path toward the woods, past the blackberry bushes, through the field dotted with grazing cows. The two large gnarled oak branches extended out over the edge of the pasture, and Naomi gasped in delight when she spied the structure held securely in the tree's embrace.

When the pasture had been fenced many years ago, the trunk of the tree had anchored this stretch of barbed wire. Now the wire strands were deeply embedded in the trunk, with bark growing over them like a wound healing. Johnny had nailed up a new series of rungs on the pasture side. The remnants of the old ladder remained on the woods side of the trunk. If Johnny ever need to escape lawmen or assorted villains approaching from the south, he could scamper down the north side and disappear into the woods.

Johnny ascended first, and Naomi admired from below. "It looks like our old wash house climbed up the tree," she said.

The deer stand did bear a resemblance to the recently departed wash house. The few boards positioned in the tree's branches years ago now held aloft a boy's dream. Four walls supported a roof that slanted back toward the woods. The gray-green slate roof and weathered-board walls blended nicely with the surrounding branches. On all four sides, floor boards extended beyond the walls, creating a narrow deck on which to sit, a front row seat for everything that happened in the valley below.

Two windows and a door from the wash house had survived. Johnny had positioned the windows carefully. One faced north, looking into the woods where a spring bubbled cool, fresh water that spilled down into a little creek in the ravine. Johnny never knew what surprising scene that window might frame. All kinds of woodland life stopped at the spring, raccoons and rabbits, deer and fox, and—once, and only once, but he was certain of what he'd seen—a bobcat.

The second window gave a view to the west, where a narrow dirt road the locals called Strawberry Lane climbed and then descended Strawberry Patch Hill. Grandma Miller had planted strawberries in a large patch near the top of the hill many years ago, and neighbors had paid a small fee to pick the red summertime treasure. At the crest of the hill and across Strawberry Lane, a small family cemetery rested under the western sky, its white fence always painted and tidy. Inside that white fence, John had buried both of his parents within the past two years. Beyond the cemetery, farmlands rolled to the horizon. Young Johnny witnessed many sunsets from what he called his thinking stand.

Naomi stood at the door, admiring the kingdom. Johnny felt a swell of ownership and accomplishment.

"This is perfect. I could live up here. We need to have Mom make some curtains, and I'll bring up a rug ..." Naomi began.

Whoa. This conversation was going in the wrong direction.

"No. No curtains. No rugs. This is exactly the way I want it."

A tiny frown flitted across Naomi's face as she appraised the rustic retreat. All she saw was a pair of binoculars hanging on a nail beside a shelf holding assorted books and magazines, a rough wood floor, no chair or stool, and a large spider web across one window. But she decided to keep her thoughts on décor and furnishings to herself.

The two went outside, and Johnny sat on the narrow deck, with legs dangling. Naomi stood on tiptoe, steadying herself against the wall.

"I can see all the way down to the sawmill. And I think I can even see Jonas's bike parked out front."

She was right. From here, Johnny could watch all the comings and goings of the valley.

To the east, three miles distant, the water tower stood guard over the hilltop town of Milford, a cluster of houses and small businesses that anchored the farming community. The Millers hauled their grain to the mill, they shopped at the old general store for everything from shovels to sugar, and Johnny deposited egg money at the bank. Milford even had a doctor's office, squeezed into one corner of the brick building housing the post office. Naomi and Johnny attended school in town. Sometimes, during a baseball game at recess, the boy looked across the hills toward the Miller woods, trying to spy his hideaway at the edge of the trees.

His favorite view was south, overlooking the big farmhouse, the road, pasture land, and acres of rippling grain and corn stalks stretching toward the sun. He watched seasons come and go in the valley, the fields changing colors every day, every week. Even up on the hill, he was certain he could smell the aromas of the farm, freshly plowed ground, mowed alfalfa, and the smoke of wood fires on crisp fall days. He never tired of the valley panorama.

But as he watched his dad walk behind the plow, questions buzzed around the boy's head like annoying mosquitoes. Was the scene spread out below him his future? Would he fit into that picture? Was he cut out to be a farmer? And the biggest question of all: Was this the way he wanted to live?

6

Most of the farmers in the valley were Amish. Johnny knew the old stories about his ancestors coming from Pennsylvania and finding prime farming country here. They settled in and multiplied, and over generations the Amish community had expanded and covered thousands of acres of the hills and valleys. "This is a good place for our people," John had often said, "a good place to farm, a good place to live."

But Johnny knew that people sometimes left their way of life. Even in their church, led by John, every now and then a person chose to no longer be a part of them. That meant also leaving their families behind. To a child's eyes, it seemed those people simply disappeared. What had happened to them? And why had they gone? Johnny did not know why they went, or where, or even how.

While working on his deer stand, he was constantly distracted by all of the interesting things going on in nature around him. He marveled at the variety of wildflowers, their shapes and colors and light preferences; and he had started a list of all the trees in the Miller woods. He carried the binoculars to the deer stand because he wanted to study the hawk soaring above the valley and find the secretive catbird darting among the branches of the oak tree and mimicking every other sound in the woods.

It seemed to him that in nature every animal, insect, or plant was born and, in most cases, did what God intended it to do. Foxes ate chickens. The doe hid her fawn. Each goose took its place in those flying formations. He wondered how the knowledge of generations was imprinted somewhere in those geese, knowledge that directed a flight over thousands of miles in migration. Even the fragile butterflies undertook long journeys, begun by one generation and carried on throughout succeeding generations.

Humans, although supposedly created with a higher purpose than the animals, did not always follow their Creator's intentions. Nor is knowledge or wisdom always passed from one generation to the next. What had he been created to do? What had, or had not, been passed on to him?

He was Jonas's John's Johnny. Boys were often identified in the Amish community by referencing their father and grandfather. But Johnny wondered many times how he would fit into the history of this lineage and the traditions of the Miller generations.

He was the fourth generation to live in the big farmhouse. Back in the early 1800s, five Amish families had emigrated from Pennsylvania and settled in the Milford area. His ancestor, Simon Miller, had built a log cabin and cleared this land for farming. After a few years, a new, timber-framed house was added to the farm. That house was built incorporating a spring in the basement. From a sandstone quarry a few miles away, large blocks of stone were hand-cut and used in the foundations of houses and barns.

Years later, the family of his great-grandfather outgrew the house, and a larger farmhouse and a bigger barn were constructed. The old log cabin was converted into a shop, where Great-grandfather Simon had built furniture for local families. Bed frames and dressers were his specialties, and he always signed and dated his pieces. Several of his pieces still held their places in the Miller farmhouse, and collectors who stumbled across Simon Miller's work from the 1800s willingly paid high prices to own such a piece. As another side business, Simon had also built coffins when the need arose, but of course none of those could be found in circulation and available.

Simon's son Jonas, Johnny's grandfather, grew up in the big farmhouse, took over the farm, and also became an experienced woodworker. His parents moved to the smaller house when Jonas married and had a family. Jonas's sons—John and his brothers—learned to farm and spent many hours in the log-cabin furniture shop alongside their father.

Eventually, John Miller married and took over the farming. The grandparents moved to the smaller house, as was the custom, and John and Mandy raised their family in the big farmhouse. Grandma and Grandpa were assured of being looked after for the rest of their lives.

John's siblings had been quite happy when he purchased the farm. Even though the price he paid was a bargain, his siblings were ready to leave the farm and start their own ventures. One brother built a small sawmill down the road, where folks brought logs to be sawed into lumber for furniture or home building.

John farmed, milked, and worked in the furniture shop. When his brother's sawmill failed to support a family, John bought the mill and ran it as a part-time business. John Miller, Johnny's father, was a keen businessman and was doing well.

He had two sons. The elder, Jonas, had begun working at the sawmill as soon as Mandy could be convinced he was old enough to work with the machines. Jonas much preferred the mill to farming. Soon, he would be taking over that operation and making it a full-time business.

John Miller had hopes that his younger son, Johnny, would be the next one to farm the family's land. Already at ten, the boy knew that. Still, he wondered. Was he really Jonas's John's Johnny? Would he fit in this line of Miller farmers?

7

"Too late," Mandy muttered to herself. "There go those two again. I probably won't see them until suppertime."

She had caught a glimpse of Johnny and Naomi trotting up the hill beyond the barn. Probably up to that deer stand. Mandy had hoped that Naomi could help with the tomatoes once she was back in the house, and she knew John wanted Johnny to clean out stalls that day. But their two youngest were off on another one of their adventures.

"Oh, well. I'm glad they're doing it together. Won't be too many more years for that, I'm guessing." Mandy spoke aloud but didn't expect any kind of answering comment. She was alone in the big house; but since it seemed so empty of late, she had been having more conversations with herself.

The big sisters were already gone, married, with homes of their own. Jonas still lived at home, although Mandy saw precious little of him. He was sixteen, and he had big plans that included a wife and that sawmill down the road. Mandy joked that only his dirty laundry proved he still lived in the Miller house.

"I wonder if we're too easy on the young ones. Seems they have much more free time, like they aren't working nearly as much as the big sisters and Jonas did at their age," Mandy mused. Johnny was six years younger than Jonas, and Naomi was the baby.

No, John wasn't too easy on Johnny; she knew that. They had always been careful to teach their children how to work hard and carry responsibility. That was a good thing about farm life; from the time they were toddlers and could do simple chores, the children worked with the adults, doing whatever jobs they could handle. John and Mandy had six children and were determined that all of them would be trained up in the way they should go, and that included learning how to work.

Learning how to work was simply one part of learning the best way to live. Most of their Amish lifestyle was prescribed by church traditions, and ever since John had been ordained in the spring, he had walked even more cautiously and required his family to do the same. John had always been very careful of the church's traditions; but after the lot fell on him that day, Mandy's husband sometimes seemed to have picked up a heavier burden than she'd ever before seen him carry.

Not that he would ever say such a thing to her. And there was nothing wrong with tradition. They were convinced this was the best way to live, the best way to raise a family, the best way to be Christian. There was a time, when John and Mandy were much younger, that they could have rejected this life; but they chose it and were determined to do their best at it and to teach their children as well as they could.

Mandy's husband was a good man and a sharp businessman who was fair and honest. He had a solid reputation in the community, and Amish and English alike sought him out for farming and business advice. So it did not surprise her that day after communion when the books were opened and John Miller was the new bishop of their church.

The children walked home that afternoon, and John and Mandy rode alone in the buggy. John was silent, unusual for him. His wife reached over and touched his arm.

"You'll do well. I believe in you. And now I'll pray extra for you, every day."

John smiled. That was all.

The church felt solid under John's leadership, and his wisdom was respected by all. Sometimes, when quilting with neighbors or shopping at the general store, Mandy would hear stories about her husband's business dealings. Of course, they were complimentary. She doubted anyone would tell her the scandalous stories—but then again, there would likely never be any scandals whispered about John Miller.

As a businessman, John was never about what was best for him alone or what would get him ahead. His rule was always to consider what was best for the other person. How many times his wife had heard him tell his boys, "Treat others well, and it will come back to you."

And the Millers did well. John was farming, milking, buying trees, and occasionally helping his dad in the furniture shop.

When his father died, John had no desire to run the furniture shop. By then the oldest daughter, Martha, was married. Levi Troyer had come to work for Grandpa Jonas in the furniture shop when he was sixteen. It wasn't long until he and Martha were quite taken with each other, and they were married a few years later. They built a house a half mile down the road, and Levi took over the furniture business, a relief to John.

In what seemed like too short a time, the next two girls were also married. The big house was emptying of children. John and Mandy were already Grandma and Grandpa to several toddlers and babies, and she was looking forward to waves of grandchildren running in and out of her house. Her three oldest daughters were all settled, with their own lives and families.

Her two boys were so different. Jonas was dark-headed and in many other ways a mirror of the young John she had married. Johnny, though, had her fair complexion and hair streaked with a reddish tint that became almost blond in the summer sun.

By the time her second son arrived, Mandy knew that there might be no more children. They had only five, a relatively small family. The second son would be John J. Miller. His English friends called him J.J. The family called him Johnny. Except when his father said, in that stern voice, "Come here, John Miller." Then everyone within hearing knew the boy was in trouble.

Johnny was named after his father, but in many ways he took after his mother. As a child, he had an eye for the gifts of God's creation, an interest in nature that soaked up knowledge other children ignored. He studied flights of birds and intricacies of blossoms. Sometimes Mandy would see him on his stomach in the grass, watching an insect. He read like a growing boy eats, always needing more and more. His cheerfulness and grin helped him get along with nearly everyone, but sometimes he disappeared, off by himself for hours. Every now and then, his mother would catch a look on his face as though he were watching their family life, like a spectator. She could not guess, then, what her son was thinking.

At an early age, Jonas had made it clear that he would follow his father's path in life. As a toddler, he trailed after his dad around the farm, mimicking all of John's moves, learning everything. And when he was older, he was eager to carve his own way in business, starting with managing the sawmill.

But Johnny ... Johnny would have to think about things awhile. John's dream was to have his youngest son someday take over the farm, but already at ten, Mandy saw something in her boy, some unspoken and undefined questioning, that had not been in any of the four older children.

One more baby had come after Johnny, and then Dr. Brown finally persuaded Mandy to be content with six. For the sake of her body, he said; and she knew he was right.

Naomi, the last, and her brother had a special bond. Those two, the "little ones," were still here. But like this morning, they would disappear down their own paths all too soon.

8

The egg business finally turned a profit; and early in the following spring, freedom arrived for Johnny. After the chores were finished one Saturday morning, John hitched the horse up to the road cart and he and his son headed first to the Milford Savings Bank where Johnny withdrew money for his new bicycle. Then they were off on the twelve-mile excursion westward to the county seat.

Trips to Stevenson fed the boy's imagination and watered his daydreams. A drugstore, a grocery, and a furniture store stood shoulder to shoulder along Main Street, enticing shoppers with all sorts of goods displayed in wide front windows. Johnny always stopped at the window of the clothing and dry goods store, fascinated by the posed plastic people—a man, a woman, and a child, changing outfits according to the season, but always with the same expressions on their faces.

The old stone courthouse anchored one corner of the square. John turned the horse into the side street along this landmark building and pulled up at the long hitching rail. He had business here at the tax map office, wanting to check several property lines between adjoining timber tracts. Some border dispute was brewing, and the more information he had, the better he would be able to tread where others feared to go. If he could assist in settling the argument, a big payday could be realized, not only for himself but also for both landowners.

He had tried to explain the details to Johnny on the ride to Stevenson, but only one ear listened to his voice. Johnny was wiggling in anticipation, dreaming of what waited for him at Kauffman's Five and Dime. A few days earlier, he had ripped open the envelope that came addressed to him with Kauffman's return address in the upper corner. His bike had arrived. He could pick it up at his convenience.

Unfortunately, the trip must be made at his dad's convenience. Or, rather, the farm's convenience. And Johnny could not skip school, so that left only Saturday for a trip to town. Even on that day, Johnny was well aware that Dad would have rather been home planting corn instead of coming to town for a bicycle. The boy fretted and fidgeted for four days until that morning when his father said, "I think we'll go to town today."

Finally in Stevenson, one more delay appeared. Mose Yutzy, the deacon in their church, pulled up to the hitching rail before John had even tied up the horse. John and Mose greeted each other, and it was obvious to Johnny that his father did not understand the urgency of hurrying down to Kauffman's. The two men stood on the sidewalk and began one of those conversations that the boy knew could easily stretch to an hour. He shuffled, fiddling with his suspenders, and kept his eyes on John's face.

John finally felt the boy's gaze and understood. A slight nod from him, and Johnny went trotting down the sidewalk.

Kauffman's was two blocks from the courthouse. Like any child, he knew exactly where to find the toy department. And there it was. A shiny red bike with chrome wheel covers.

Dangling from the handlebar, a tag proclaimed to all the world: SOLD. JOHNNY MILLER. It was his. He had earned every penny by himself. (Well, almost by himself. He had also hired some help.) As he wheeled it out of the store, he realized his father had been right. He appreciated this red beauty all the more because he had worked for it.

On any other trip to Stevenson, Johnny would have wanted time to roam the streets, gawking into store windows, wishing and dreaming. No daydreaming today. As he pushed the bike along the sidewalk, he barely glanced at the revolving barber pole that usually intrigued and hypnotized him. He did not imagine he'd ever sit in a barber's chair. Mandy was the family barber.

Entranced by the light flashing from the spokes revolving in the sun, he jumped when a bus roared by and enveloped him in a cloud of exhaust smoke. The Greyhound bus pulled up at the corner below the courthouse. A picture of a sleek dog leaping forward promised speed, and the line "Go Greyhound, and leave the driving to us," spoke of ease and comfort for travelers.

Johnny had no interest that day in leaving the driving to anyone but himself. He did wonder, though, what was out there, out beyond their farming community, where those hound dog buses delivered anyone who climbed the steps and settled into a seat. Maybe someday he'd step through the door onto one of those magic carpets and discover what "out there" looked like.

Mose Yutzy was walking down the sidewalk as Johnny approached the courthouse. He nodded to the grinning boy.

"That's quite a bike you've got there, Johnny."

The boy beamed.

His father saw him coming and waited in front of the courthouse. John was finally ready to go into the tax office. On most days, wandering through that ornate old building with his father was a treat for Johnny, but not today. Today, a shiny red and chrome bicycle waited for adventure.

"Can I start toward home, and you pick me up when you catch up with me?"

John hesitated a moment; his eager young son was, after all, only eleven. He had never ridden more than five miles before, and never on a paved state highway. Today, though, he saw that his son had grown a bit taller. He had run a successful business. He had paid for his own bicycle. John gave his blessing.

With great excitement and much pride, Johnny mounted the prized bike. Up Main Street he rode, merging with the mainstream of humanity, moving along on a mode of transportation other than his own two feet. The red bike shared the road with cars, trucks, and an occasional buggy. Rolling along on this gleaming contraption that he had paid for himself, he felt adult and free.

He shifted into low gear to climb the grade leading out of town and didn't even have to stand up to crest the hill. On the downhill, he experimented with the hand brakes. This bike seemed made for him, to carry him into adventure, free and unhindered.

He hoped his father would spend at least an hour at the courthouse and then meet more friends on the street to talk with and maybe find one or two other things to do in town. But too soon, he heard a clip-clop behind him and John calling his name. He was already more than halfway home, but the eight miles had flowed quickly under the streak of red and chrome.

"Go ahead. I'll ride all the way," he shouted and waved his father on. He had never before enjoyed a bike ride like that ride home from Stevenson.

Johnny could not wait to show this beauty to his friends. He wanted to attach a wire carrier to the front. The bike already had a rack, but he had convinced his dad he needed a carrier for heavier loads. He had promised to deliver strawberries and eggs or ride to the store when necessary. Of course, he was looking forward to camping trips with his friends, and that carrier would hold his tent and sleeping gear and perhaps a radio. And maybe even a certain brand of beer.

9

Johnny's closest friends were four other Amish boys who lived within a three-mile radius of the Miller farm. Over the next few years, the boys did pitch their tents occasionally in someone's woods or up by the quarry. Around the campfire, they spent hours dreaming of adventures outside their Amish world. They had grandiose plans for their lives.

The first step would be to get their driver's licenses. They would have to wait until they were eighteen, unless they could convince their dads to sign for them when they were sixteen. That conversation with John was still several years away, but already Johnny was rehearsing it.

The new bike did keep him from his tree house for a while, although he still spent many evenings up there. His little sister understood him; after that first time in the deer stand, she never asked to come again, and it remained his inviolate retreat. Besides, Naomi was growing up, too, and she no longer tagged so closely on her big brother's heels. Johnny wasn't sure what all she was up to; girl stuff, he supposed.

He faced the spring of his fourteenth year with sadness. Soon, his eight years at Milford Elementary School would be at an end. Jonas was working every day and all day at the sawmill, and

Johnny knew his parents expected their younger son to take on even more of the farm duties as soon as the school year had ended.

On that last day of school in May, others were laughing and happy and looking forward to summer vacation. Instead, Johnny grieved. The remainder of his youth was being taken away. Even though the English students had sometimes mocked the Amish as backwards farmers, Johnny had enjoyed school, excelled in sports, and had the gift of gab. He had many friends, and he could talk himself into or out of anything. He was known as something of a "charmer." He never liked that word. He was, he reasoned, only making the most of whatever talents God had given him.

He wanted so much to join his English friends that fall in high school. But it was not to be. At the end of eight years at Milford Elementary, he boarded the school bus for home on that last day with a great sense of sorrow and loss.

That spring, he had started his third set of birds for his egg business. In the summer, he took on additional farm duties; and so the time came to pass this generation of pullets over to his twelve-year-old sister. Naomi was ecstatic when he informed her she would get the business free and clear.

The money from the eggs had bought a bicycle, some books, and a transistor radio that he had secreted away in the deer stand to listen to the Cleveland Indians and country music. John had allowed him to keep several hogs to fatten and sell. For about half the work, he made twice the money. And he did want to make money faster; a car cost much more than a bicycle.

In the fall, on the morning that would have been his first day of high school, he plodded up the hill to his deer stand. The milking was finished; the hogs were slopped. His task before lunch was to clean out the gutters in the barn and haul manure, but he needed one hour of higher learning before slinging cow manure.

While his English buddies would be meeting new teachers and new students from surrounding towns, he would be stuck on the farm. It didn't seem right. It seemed as if learning and knowledge were good things. Eight years of school had not satisfied his curiosity. There was so much he did not yet know. Why should there be boundaries and limits on what a person could know?

His tree stand became his place of higher learning. While his friends were opening new books, discovering new ideas, and seeing new things, he pored over the few books he had squirreled away up in his tree stand. He had a National Geographic guide to birds and a twenty-five page booklet identifying many of Ohio's one hundred species of trees. He'd roam the woods with his notebook, sketching leaves and drawing a map that marked locations of all the trees he could identify. Maple, oak, cherry, hickory, walnut, ash.

The single shelf in the tree stand also held the loose pages of an article torn from a farming magazine, including illustrations identifying foliage and wild flowers indigenous to the area. Stacked at one end were several back issues of *Grit,* delivered to the Miller house every Saturday by a young boy from Milford. The magazine ran a series of western stories that Johnny anticipated each week.

Tucked behind the stack of magazines was the transistor radio. The golden voice of Jimmy Dudley would fill the deer stand, telling him, "It's a beautiful day for baseball." He'd try to imagine the scene in a stadium somewhere, as his heroes broke the terrible bats of the Bronx Bombers, those dreaded New York Yankees.

But he had never been to a baseball stadium. He could only imagine what it would be like to be part of the clamoring crowd he could hear on the transistor radio behind the voice of announcers describing the game.

Why was he born Amish? Why couldn't he have been born into one of the privileged Mennonite homes? Those kids clicked on a television and watched "Mr. Ed," a show about a talking horse, while he followed horses all day making sounds other than talk. They watched the Indians play in a sunny stadium while he sat on the floor of his deer stand next to the transistor radio. They played basketball and baseball in uniforms and organized teams against other schools; he ran the bases in the pasture field and dodged cow patties and fished the ball out of the creek. They talked of vacations in the mountains or at the lake; he had never been out of the county. Johnny was certain he was missing out on a great deal of life because his family was Amish.

It was not that he disliked working the land. It was just that there were many other things he also wanted to see and do.

* * *

On the September morning that should have been Johnny's first day in high school, he dangled his legs from the deck of his deer stand and surveyed life in the valley. A tide of melancholy rose up within, swelled, and engulfed him as he watched the school bus come to a stop in front of the Miller house and swallow Naomi. For eight years, that had been his ride to an escape from farm life. Now the yellow bus rolled east, leaving him behind.

As he looked eastward toward the school on top of the hill in Milford, he realized that the schoolyard bursting with childhood and the classroom full of the smells of books and chalk dust were now only memories in his past. To the south lay rolling farmland— neat, predictable, fenced fields of his present and perhaps all the seasons and years of his future. To the west was, for a certainty, his final end, within the small family graveyard.

Behind him, to the north, was the woods, where wandering paths led through rich, unspoiled nature that offered refreshment and surprises. The woods always beckoned to Johnny, and he hoped to spend a great deal of time there before resting inside the white fence to the west.

10

John and Mandy must have had their suspicions about the habit their son was developing. The ice man knew, for sure.

Tormented with doubts about his future as a farmer and carrying the burden of his family's expectations, Johnny retreated to the deer stand whenever he could steal an hour. Often, he'd grab a cold bottle of Stroh's from the basement water trough and take it with him. It seemed to quiet some of the turmoil and make it easier to accept, for one more day, his farm fate.

Once a week, a truck delivered ice to the Amish folks. The only refrigeration in Mandy's kitchen was an old Kelvinator icebox. When the ice man was due to arrive, she posted a cardboard sign in the window, indicating how many pounds of ice were needed that week. Johnny had always been fascinated by the big truck filled with frost and its driver, who wore leather chaps to protect his legs. The ice man took his pick and perforated a large block of ice to chop off the desired amount. When Johnny was younger, he lingered at the truck, watching every move, and the driver always offered the boy a small ice chip. It was a special treat for a hot, dusty, barefoot farm boy on a summer day.

The ice man also supplied the Stroh's beer. Atop the pile of ice blocks rested several cases of the brew, and thus, it arrived at the house already chilled. The driver would make a quick trip into the Millers' basement and check the small ledge beside the water trough. If money lay there, he would deposit the bottles in the cold spring water.

Whenever Johnny ventured up to his deer stand, he was accompanied by a bottle of Stroh's. It started out slowly, like so many habits do; but before he knew it, he considered himself an experienced and accomplished beer drinker.

A short distance to the west of the stand, beyond the woods and along the fence line, grew a thicket of multiflora rose. In his quest to identify everything around him, Johnny had found that this was an invasive plant brought over from Asia with the best of intentions. Originally used for soil conservation and as a natural border hedge, it quickly became uncontrollable. Birds ate the little red berries and then excreted the seeds, spreading the nuisance plant around the countryside.

He started the ritual of finishing his beer and then tossing the empty bottle in a high arching shot into the prickly thicket. It was a game; the goal was to hit the bushes in such a way that the bottle would bounce down through the vines and be dropped gently from the lowest branches, unbroken. Most throws were successful, but an occasional errant toss shattered on the ever-growing amber mound under the roses.

* * *

He was fifteen, going on sixteen, thinking and drinking in the deer stand on a beautiful summer evening. That day he and John had started in the fields before sunup, coming in only for barn chores and supper. Naomi had brought dinner to them in the fields. Finally, shortly before sunset, John called a halt and declared the work day ended, giving them enough time to get a good night's sleep so that they could start again early the next day.

But Johnny needed more than a good night's sleep. He needed

time in his drinking stand. He needed time to watch the sunset. He needed … something … other than cutting hay and milking cows. He climbed the hill to the deer stand.

As the sun slipped toward the cemetery, he leaned against the outside wall and surveyed the fields. The golden orb was just above the horizon when a small explosion of light glittered about the stand. Rays from the sun hit the cast-off amber bottles and the shards of glass, and he was caught in a sparkling shower of color and brightness. He watched in awe as the rays of light flickered and shimmered, changing and then disappearing as the sun slipped lower. For a few brief moments, he had been given a glimpse into a sphere normally unseen by the eye.

It was the tree stand's own show of northern lights. He called it "the shimmering," and whenever he could manage to be in his hideaway at sunset, he hoped for another such moment, when the sun was at just the right place in the sky. He told no one. The shimmering was part of his retreat, part of his secret life.

Now the game of beer bottles had a new objective. Every additional bottle changed the pattern of light. Additional broken pieces added more prisms. Rain filling a bottle changed the dynamics of the shimmering. Just because he was no longer in school didn't mean he couldn't do his own science projects, he observed grimly. He guessed that none of his English friends were doing such experiments in high school.

There was one privilege, though, that Johnny would have that his English buddies would not. He had even bragged about it, and those English friends were in disbelief and expressed great envy.

Amish boys went scouting.

* * *

What the boys jokingly called "scouting" was formally known as bed courtship or bundling. The traditions of the Amish included the practice of courting couples sharing a bed when the young man visited. Long ago, when houses were great distances apart, this practice supposedly arose from necessity and convenience. The ride home from a sweetheart's house might take hours, and it seemed practical for the suitor to stay the night.

Now, going scouting meant Johnny and his friends would cruise the countryside on buggies or bicycles, seeking available dates. A girl eligible and available put a lit lamp in her upstairs bedroom window; it was an invitation for guests to come on up.

Although he would never voice his thoughts to his friends, Johnny sometimes stood back and questioned this tradition. Traditions began because they made sense for a certain time and place. But Johnny had begun to wonder if some traditions should be abandoned as situations change. The death of a tradition, though, is often slow and painful. Yet it seemed to him that his community was keeping alive some traditions that no longer made sense and should be allowed to die.

For one thing, when he was sixteen and finally noticing the fairer sex, he also could not help but notice that Naomi, who was almost fourteen, had already caught the attention of some of his friends. Sometimes a friend stopped by, and Johnny suspected that the visit was a sly excuse to see his sister. The thought of anyone coming up the stairs to her bedroom disgusted him. He imagined that he would probably spend her maturing years standing sentry at her door. The path to Naomi's heart would run through her big brother, and that might be rough traveling for some fellow.

Granted, as a young man, he was fascinated with the idea of spending a date in bed with someone of the opposite gender. But when he was honest with himself, he admitted that something about this tradition didn't ring true to him.

In the Amish community, when a boy turned sixteen, he was given a horse and buggy. Two months before Johnny's sixteenth birthday, he decided to plunge into the conversation with his dad that he had practiced for years. His strategy was to appeal to the businessman. He would save his father money.

"Dad, I've been thinking about that buggy you're planning to get for me. I've saved up a good amount toward the car I want to buy when I'm eighteen. Why not sign off for my license at sixteen, and save the money you would spend on a horse and buggy?"

John looked at his son, and the teenager felt certain that his father could read all his thoughts.

"Son, I know you can get a license without my approval once you're eighteen, but you know I cannot sign for you before that. I would be signing an approval of something we teach against, and it would be wrong to ask others to follow a rule and then not enforce it with my own son."

"But you can change the rules. You're a church leader; you could do that."

"Many of our rules baffle those outside our life. Many things we teach against may not be wrong in themselves; but if we allow them, they will detract from our peaceful existence."

"But Jonas bought a car."

"Without my blessing, yes. And I did, too, when I was young and I went against my father's wishes. Some feel compelled to go out and taste life outside the Amish community. I have been there, Johnny, and I can assure you, you will find nothing out there in the English world that will satisfy better than our Amish life. If you go looking, you're taking a great chance of being lost to the world. I realize you may decide to do things your way, but I'm still hoping you will not."

"I guess that's a no, then."

"That's a no, Son."

So he could not drive at sixteen, but he could spend the night in bed with a girl. It was the way they had always done things.

11

Since he was destined to several more years of bike transportation, he determined to make the most of it.

The gang of five Amish boys who hung out together were all farm boys with dreams and goals bigger than their buttoned-up pants. They called themselves the cowboys. They were not going to be boys with cows. Instead, they had visions of someday riding the western range with horses beneath them, not pulling their buggies and plows. They wanted to drive cattle, not milk them. Several more years of this farm life, they promised each other, would only season them for the range.

The sixteenth birthday did arrive and with it, a new mode of transportation. John made a trip to a horse auction and purchased a Standardbred mare. She was a retired trotter that had made some money for her owner but was no longer winning enough to pay for her keep. The horse, Joyce, still created a fine picture, trotting down the road and outfitted with a fancy harness.

Sometimes, coming home in the early morning from dates, Johnny and his friend Paul, tired and talked out, would prop their legs up on the buggy's dashboard and let Joyce find the way home.

In the group of cowboys, Paul Troyer was Johnny's best friend. Whether sober or inebriated, they understood each other.

Paul was a bit taller than Johnny, with dark eyes and hair—the embodiment of tall, dark, and handsome. Johnny thought of him as a more attractive version of Abe Lincoln.

Paul's personality complemented Johnny's; in a group, Paul was the quiet, steady one; Johnny was the talker and entertainer. Whether on their bicycles or in their buggies, the two were completely at ease with each other. They matched wits and sharpened each other. They talked about baseball, politics, farming, and, of course, girls. No subject was off limits between these two friends. And on quiet buggy rides home, silence was simply another form of their communication.

On many Saturday evenings, the gang would meet at the quarry to discuss plans for the evening. Other young people from the area drifted in and out. The quarry was the local meeting place. Sometimes, youths from neighboring communities were invited. Sometimes, they pitched tents and built a campfire. Once a year, an Ohio-Indiana weekend gathering rocked the quarry. This was not a night for the timid. With a generator supplying power for the amplifier, guitars wailed long into the night and the supply of alcohol was never exhausted.

Most weekends, though, the gathering at the quarry was local Amish boys having fun, swimming and taking a break from a week in the barns and fields. Granted, a considerable amount of brew was always consumed. Only a draining of the quarry could accurately tell how many bottles were tossed into the depths over the years—or rather, over the generations. The quarry, too, was a tradition of teenage Amish boys.

It was on such a Saturday night of partying, when they had taken Joyce and the buggy to the quarry with no particular plans, that Johnny first noticed hints of change in his friend Paul.

When they arrived that evening, one of the cowboys was already atop a large rock formation, belting out country music hits. Mel Weaver was short and stocky, with a hairline that was already receding. Paul and Johnny called him Little Napoleon, a nickname no one else understood. Mel was usually a quiet fellow, but when inspired by enough beer, he'd climb up on one of the rocks, stretch to his full 4'11", and become a singing legend.

Sober, Mel was a worker. Whenever the neighborhood got together to thrash, he volunteered for the dirtiest job. He wanted to do the shoveling back in the granary, where the dust hung heavy and choked and blinded.

"I love to see the finished product," he explained. "I plant it, I watch it grow, and I help shock it. Now I want to see the results." Although Johnny was more than happy to let Mel do the dirtiest jobs, he could understand his friend's reasoning. He had collected eggs all those years with only the goal in mind.

That night, Mel had already done away with too much of his favorite, Rolling Rock. He finished one rendition of a Buck Owens song and gave a shout, "Let's go scouting!"

Johnny punched Paul's arm.

"Need some spice in your life?"

"Sure do."

And off they went in the direction of the Erb farm. Sara and Clara Erb were identical twins, both ornery and fun to be with. A visit to the Erb farm usually added spice to any Saturday night.

While most young men either rushed upstairs or tried to creep up undetected by the rest of the family, Johnny often spent time in the Erbs' kitchen, conversing with Sara and Clara's mom and dad. He especially enjoyed the twins' father, Eli. John Miller had cut out Eli's woods years before when Johnny was still a young boy, tagging along. He had learned to know the Erbs then and had grown quite fond of the family, most of whom seemed to share Sara's and Clara's fun-loving nature.

Although never spoken publicly, in the privacy of many homes the subject of a daughter getting serious with Johnny Miller was discussed. It was not necessarily Johnny Miller that gained parents' approval. Instead, they looked at the family tree and believed it would be a good tree to have a daughter grafted into.

Paul had gone upstairs, but Johnny lingered in the kitchen, discussing with Eli the weather, the price of milk, and where the Cleveland Indians stood in the league.

"Say, Johnny, when is your family having another singing?"

Several times a year, Mandy invited neighbors and friends for an evening of singing together. Over popcorn and freshly picked spearmint tea, the fellowship and music flowed. Fiddle Bill provided the highlight of the evening when he opened up his case and pulled out his violin.

Fiddle Bill knew every country song written since 1930. He had never married, and his violin might have been frowned on by many Amish preachers. But the instrument had been a part of Fiddle Bill for almost fifty years, so long that most people simply looked on it as a part of the man himself. At the Millers' singings, the country music gave way to well-loved hymns.

One evening, Bill played "Will the Circle Be Unbroken." Johnny was across the room from his family, and he took in the scene of Mandy and Naomi standing on either side of John, who sat in his favorite rocking chair. The moment became sacred.

Mandy and Naomi sang in pleasant harmony, but John's scale never varied. When a note should have been sung a little higher, he simply sang louder.

The final song of the evening was always "Amazing Grace." As the first notes filled the living room, John would join in with everyone. Then, without fail, the man folks knew as stoic and strong suddenly crumpled. Tremors shook his strong voice. Looking toward the floor, he'd grasp his beard and tug gently, nodding. Always, a tear or two slipped down his weathered cheek.

Johnny often wondered why that song had such a powerful effect on his father. Much of their Amish tradition meant they followed rules set down by man; an understanding of God's grace was not often taught. However, that song certainly struck a chord with John Miller.

Drawn in by the friendly chit-chat of the Erb kitchen, Johnny had almost forgotten Paul was also in the house. When he remembered his friend upstairs, he also hoped that Paul had determined who was who. Sara was usually Johnny's date, but the twins were ornery; sometimes they switched identities.

Johnny felt a twinge of guilt. Perhaps that was another reason he was in no hurry to go upstairs. The twins obviously had dreams of landing both Paul and Johnny. Although the young men did not blatantly lead them on, they also did not discourage the girls' dreams. But Johnny was all too aware that a steady Amish girlfriend meant a probable Amish wedding and Amish in-laws and Amish babies and an Amish house and, in his case, an Amish farm. He still wasn't convinced he wanted all that.

For most of the night, he and Paul sat on the edge of the beds entertaining each other. While their dates had gone to sleep hours earlier, they were still in animated conversation. Johnny also detected a distinct lack of interest from Paul toward Clara, and he began to wonder about his friend. The picture soon became clear.

Paul had five younger brothers. Since there was plenty of help on the farm, his father had permitted Paul to join a carpenter crew and thus Paul brought home additional money to help support his family. Most of the young Amish men who worked away turned their paychecks over to their dads. John Miller had been an exception, allowing Johnny to keep his egg and hog profits.

Because he worked long days off the farm, Paul was usually excused from the barn chores. No such luck for Johnny; he was his father's primary farm hand, and it meant being in the barn early to milk the cows. Even though he had been up all night, he was expected to help with the Sunday morning milking.

He did not have to wonder long about Paul's disinterest in Clara that night.

"Hey, why don't I come home with you and help with the milking?" Paul offered. Johnny looked at his friend in surprise. Paul was watching Joyce's rump. "I miss going out to the barn in the mornings. I always liked milking. Can I help you today?"

Johnny knew his friend too well, and he saw the truth. Paul's motives were a wee bit less than honorable. He was not simply being a friend and generously helping with chores. He had taken a liking to Johnny's fourteen-year-old sister. Helping Johnny to milk meant helping Naomi to milk.

Johnny had three older sisters who were married and had children and were sometimes more of mothers to him than sisters. Naomi was his other best friend, his confidant. He trusted her completely. He had never thought of his sisters as beautiful; they were, after all, just his sisters. Now, as he detected Paul's interest, he also saw Naomi in a new light. She had poise and confidence that most girls her age lacked. At school, she had as many English friends as Amish friends. She was intelligent and observant. He was sure that, in an English world, his little sister would have been the prom queen.

Naomi, of course, would not be permitted to date for several more years, years in which Johnny had hoped to convince John to discourage or even demand that bed courtship stop. But that Sunday morning, he saw that Naomi was already enjoying the attention his friend showered her way.

Paul was the proverbial camel that had stuck its nose under the tent and was now completely inside the Miller compound. Johnny did believe he would be a great brother-in-law many years down the road—perhaps, after they had returned from roaming the West. But maybe Paul was no longer interested in going cowboying? If that was the case, then Johnny would likely need to stay home, too, and guard the kingdom.

12

The year of freedom and joy finally arrived. Johnny's eighteenth birthday promised adventures unknown to bike or buggy riders. At last, he could expand his horizons beyond the valley that had contained him for all of his youthful years.

The move west to be a real cowboy would be possible once he owned a car; but, sadly, possibility was now meeting the reality of other emotions. Mel Weaver could not and would not leave his beloved farm. He was a real barnyard philosopher, loquaciously describing the beauty of young blades of corn emerging from their slumber in underground seed pods. In his eyes, wheat shocks dotting the landscape were little Indian villages. His rendition made even the life cycle of manure intriguing. Mel and his affections weren't going anywhere.

Johnny also saw his best friend, Paul, wavering on the execution of their plans. Naomi had turned sixteen, and Paul's affection for her constrained his impulse for western progression.

Johnny's hopes rested on the two remaining cowboys. Yost and Henry Mast lived several miles beyond Paul's and Mel's properties, west of the quarry. Henry was a half year older and Yost that much younger than Johnny. The brothers were as different as two people can be.

Yost was tall and gangly, with an introverted personality. Occasionally he pedaled past the Millers' farm, and his long, churning legs and thin arms made him look like a praying mantis moving down the road. In school, children had laughed and called him Yost the Post. Although most of them genuinely liked Yost and the ribbing was good-natured, he could not see the humor and withdrew from most interaction with other students. Yost never stepped forward to lead; he always followed.

Yost was as content on the farm as Mel was and had no desire to ever leave the Amish life. While Henry and Johnny counted the days to their eighteenth birthdays and a car, Yost knew he would never drive himself. He was content to stay where he was and let his brother blaze new trails. Johnny's only hope for companionship on his flight west now rested solely on Henry.

He was greatly relieved that one worry had never materialized. Naomi and Paul were, without a doubt, in love. Johnny had eventually realized that his anxiety had failed to consider Naomi's character. She was not only a very attractive girl, she was also very prudent. There was no need for her brother or anyone else to speak to her against the practice of bed courtship. Her decision, made independently of her family, was that she would not participate in this tradition.

"I'll share a bed with a man only when, or if, I get married," she had said, and Johnny had seen Mandy's spunky expression on his sister's face. Anyone wishing Naomi's hand in marriage would follow her rules. At midnight, when many youths were starting their courting, her dates ended. Paul realized this was a special girl and honored her commitment to courtship.

Johnny had thought his father had held the key to changing the rules. As he watched his baby sister grow up, he realized that true change comes from personal conviction, not dictates of laws or rules and traditions.

He wondered if he would be so fortunate as to find such a girl.

***

Henry was the first to purchase a vehicle, a large, four-door Pontiac capable of hauling all five of the cowboys to adventures previously only imagined. They journeyed at last to the shore of Lake Erie to watch their beloved Indians play, and the cavernous Cleveland stadium took Johnny's breath away the first time he walked through the towering grandstand and saw the green field laid out below him, a perfect blue sky overhead, and the lake glittering on the horizon. He had not imagined how endless that lake would look.

Although Johnny had ridden with his brother Jonas during the time he owned a car, he had been too young to attempt more than sitting behind the wheel and pretending to drive. Jonas had sold that car when he and his girlfriend joined the Amish church and married. He was working full time at the sawmill now and had fully embraced the Amish lifestyle. Johnny knew this same path was also expected of him, after he'd had his time of dabbling in the world's ways.

One evening, Henry picked Johnny up in his big Pontiac, which they had dubbed "The Chief," and they toured the countryside. With no particular mission or goal, they were out looking for an evening of fun.

"Do you want to drive?"

Of course! That first experience behind the wheel was magical. The power available at the touch of his foot intoxicated Johnny. However, since he did not wish to ruin his chances at driving privileges of his own, he maintained a speed barely above a crawl. Joyce in full trot could have passed him. His Schwinn bike could have kept up. But even creeping along the dirt road, he felt the surge of freedom and promise of adventure bestowed by a car.

He counted the days until his birthday and spent hours debating what vehicle might fill his heart's desires. There was the popular and powerful Mustang. It certainly represented what he wanted in a car, but too many were already on the road. Johnny wanted a vehicle that stood apart from the crowd, one that not many others owned. He also already had one horse named Joyce, and the only mustangs he wanted to see were the real ones when he took off for the West.

Chevrolet had recently released a car in response to Ford's Mustang. The Camaro intrigued him. He had read somewhere that the word was French for *friend* or *little companion.* That sounded good. His car was definitely going to be his friend and companion in life's adventures. And not everyone was driving a Camaro; he'd only seen one other such car in the county.

Debates between Ford lovers and Chevy admirers raged hotly among Johnny's circle of friends. He cared not a whit about the rivalry; he wanted a car that was a bit different, with lots of power and the magic to transport him from a mundane life on the farm to distant quests. A Camaro would be the perfect choice.

The birthday finally arrived, and he wasted no time in getting licensed to drive. Then he prowled the car lots.

He found a 1968 blue Camaro with two white stripes across the hood. Packed into this marvel of acceleration was a 350 Joycepower power plant. The motor was rated at 396 cubic inches. That really meant nothing to Johnny, but he understood 350 horsepower. Wherever he was headed, he would get there fast.

The little blue marvel weighed a bit over 3,700 pounds. White numbers on the windshield asked for $3,800. At slightly over $1 a pound, the price sounded reasonable. The final cost with tax, title and dealer prep (whatever that meant) was right at $4,000.

A great deal of money. He did, however, have that amount available. Years of listening to his father talk about the power of saved money finally paid off.

He told the salesman at Stevenson Motors that he would need to go to the bank and get a cashier's check.

"Unless you prefer cash."

That stunned the salesman; he was dealing with an eighteen-year-old cash customer.

"Did you rob a bank?" he joked. Had he known the hard work and dedication that $4,000 represented, he would not have been so flippant. All those early morning egg gatherings and years of slopping hogs now brought their reward. Realizing he had a serious buyer, the salesman offered the car to Johnny for $3,900, out the door.

"I'll be back in one hour with the money."

Henry and The Chief had brought Johnny to the dealership.

"Take me to Milford, Henry, and hurry." They were back at the car lot, with cash in hand, in less than an hour.

Paperwork done, money exchanged. Johnny sank into the blue vinyl seat, gripped the wheel, and took a deep breath. Grinning, he slid the key into the ignition.

His little blue friend took the same route home that the red and chrome streak had traveled seven years before. But this power was 350 horses, not Johnny's two feet. He wondered what so much horsepower would do when asked.

Incredible. Beyond belief. The little blue car came to life, surging forward and pressing him back against the seat with no warning. He knew this blue Camaro would catapult him into new worlds.

13

At last, Johnny had the freedom he had so long sought. With his little blue companion, he explored an expanding world, sometimes with his friend Paul, but often alone. The car did take him away from time in his thinking stand. The time he had spent daydreaming up a tree was now spent living out those daydreams.

He tried many of the worldly things forbidden by the church and his father's teachings. His social circles changed. He dated English girls and caught up on all he had missed in four years.

But where he gained, he also lost. His two brother friends, Yost and Henry, swooped in and took advantage of his and Paul's absence at the Erb farm. Henry and Sara seemed destined to stay together. Gangly Yost the Post obligingly went along and found love in the arms of Clara. The Erb twins effectively ended all Johnny's dreams of leading the cowboys on a charge westward.

And something was still missing. Johnny had arrived at the intersection of boyhood and manhood surrounded by uncertainties. Why couldn't he, like Mel, be contented with farming? Here was the family farm, ready for his taking, but he didn't want it. Amish girls were a bit wary of his unsettledness, and English girls liked his company but weren't too sure about losing their hearts to a boy with one foot in their world and one foot on the Amish farm.

It seemed he had only one choice. It was time to make a break for it and leave the farm. His four buddies appeared to have settled into the Amish lifestyle so easily. They were driving cars (with the exception of Yost) and all of them still palled around, but it was clear that their lives were already charted out.

Johnny's path, though, was still undiscovered and unknown.

***

This would be a two-bottle visit. Two dripping bottles of Stroh's in hand, Johnny meandered up the cow path toward his thinking and drinking stand. All around him were the fields he and his father had plowed, planted, and harvested. This was his world; these fields and cows and pigs were his life. But he was certain there was more to living than tending plants and animals.

Taking in the panorama laid out below him, he once again determined to break free. He would leave the farm and discover the mysteries awaiting elsewhere. He had no idea where that elsewhere was, but he believed it was many miles westward. He felt he *must* leave the farm if he was ever to find what his life was meant to be.

He had nailed up several more boards and filled the new shelves with his research on plants, trees, birds, and insects. The notebooks and piles of loose papers represented a collection of life in nature on these 120 acres.

How to leave? It would be inconsiderate and hurtful to disappear without talking with his parents, but he would rather avoid that conversation. The best thing might be to go without warning or fanfare. Leave a note behind. Gathering pencil and paper, he tried to also gather his thoughts.

> *Dear Mom and Dad,*
> *You have been the best parents a son could have, but I think you know that I have never been certain of my place in this life on the farm and in our community. I*

need to get away for a while to see what's out there. By the time you read this, I will be on my way.

I will write as soon as possible to let you know I'm all right.

Johnny

He reread his words. A poor good-bye, but what else could he tell them? He knew that they could see how unsettled he was. Even though they had hoped for a different outcome, this would not surprise them. He tried not to think of his mother's face when she read the note.

And Naomi. He could not leave without a note of explanation to his sister.

Dear Naomi,

I so badly want the joy I see in you and Paul. But for me, it is not here. Something is missing, and I must go find it. Why is it this hard to know where I want to be? I will write you soon.

Johnny

He read both letters again, and shame flooded through him. He was a coward. His father had always taught him to do the honorable thing. Now he was writing short notes and planning to slip away. No, he would tell them face to face. He ripped both letters from the tablet; and with no better place to dispose of them, he stuffed them into the one Stroh's bottle that was already empty.

Then came a bizarre impulse. *Write a letter to God.* Johnny had no idea what triggered that thought. John always prayed at the supper table, and Johnny mumbled a short prayer in the morning and before going to bed; but he had never given much thought to an almighty God, much less one that he could approach to voice his intimate thoughts. But he was in a letter-writing mood. He felt as though someone *had* to hear him. *It can't hurt,* he thought.

Dear God,
  Johnny here.

This seemed a rather strange way to start talking to God, but merely writing the words on paper felt comforting.

> *I need help. My friends all seem to have life figured out, but I am so confused about so many things. Does it really matter whether or not I stay Amish? I don't seem to fit here. Will I still be able to get to Heaven if I leave? I don't know what you could possibly do to help me, but I sure would appreciate you sending someone who could give me some direction and advice.*
>
> *I'm not sure when the heavenly mail pickup is, so I'll just stuff this letter into my other beer bottle. Sorry, God, if my letter holder is offensive. It's a bad habit I have acquired. If drinking sends a person to hell, it looks like I'll be there.*
>
> *John's Johnny*
> *P.S. I'd even accept help to quit this drinking.*

He stuffed the letter into the second empty bottle and set the two on one of the new shelves. The letter to God had somehow calmed his spirit. Maybe there was something to communing with God after all. Forays into the woods, surrounded by flowers, trees and nature, had a similar impact on him. Perhaps he had been worshiping a creator all along and didn't realize it.

With his spirit calmed, he decided to postpone the discussion with John and Mandy for at least another week. The following weekend was the big Fourth of July party at the quarry. Many Amish youths from Indiana would be coming to Ohio for a bash that promised to surpass any party ever held there in the past. Festivities started on Thursday evening of the Fourth and lasted into the wee hours of Sunday morning. Perhaps he could find some unsettled Indiana boys to join him in a quest of the West. Perhaps he'd meet some Indiana beauty. He'd wait one more week to leave.

On Thursday evening, carloads from Indiana found their way up the dirt road to the quarry. Bikes, buggies and vehicles all assembled in one amalgamation of transportation. Tents went up, reminding Mel of a field of shocked wheat. A generator electrified a band from Indiana. It would be a weekend of Amish bliss.

Until it all went wrong.

14

Every car brought more cases of brew. Arguments broke out. Boasting of adventures and conquests reached new heights. The Ford and Chevy camps were in heated debate. Johnny listened with little interest. He knew his little blue companion could blow the doors off any Ford parked in the nearby field, but he had no more desire to debate the issue than he wanted to prove that Joyce was a faster horse than any tied to yonder tree.

Mel, the Mast brothers, and Johnny shared two tents side by side in the encampment. Each morning and evening, the four left to do chores at home, but returned to the party as soon as possible.

In Johnny's estimation, it was not turning out to be much of a party. He wasn't in a partying mood. He was present. He drank and he debated and he joked. But he was waiting. He desperately wanted a sober discussion with someone who could help him sort out the merits of the life he was now living in comparison to what might be *out there.* Or he wanted to meet a kindred spirit who shared his wanderlust. At the very least, he had hoped to find a girl with whom he could interact on an intelligent level.

He had even wondered if it might be possible to find a girl here who could talk about spiritual things. That seemed too bizarre to hope for. No decent, self-respecting Amish girl would be anywhere near this party. Naomi had flatly refused Paul's offer to join him there, and so he had the decency to not attend himself.

Johnny was at a beer party, where everyone was too drunk to talk about anything serious. He was downing his own Stroh's, but he watched the drunken antics and knew he would gain no knowledge or answers this weekend. The quarry had never before seen such an assortment of misfits, rowdies, and lost youths.

Nevertheless, he did learn a few things. New words floated around, terms like *acid trip* and *speed.* Drugs were completely foreign to his circle of friends. The Indiana folks were far advanced in that culture, and they were more than willing to share what they knew. Johnny could take a trip, they said, without even leaving the county.

Someone handed him a white pill, and he washed it down with one gulp of Stroh's. He wondered if there was a little white pill that would transport him to a western ranch.

A huge bonfire leapt up and lit the night sky. Watching the blaze, Johnny saw demons dancing among the flames. Dark, evil, and ... exultant. A horror gripped him. Was he peering into hell itself? Is this what awaited him if he broke with his Amish heritage? Was this a warning, an omen? Or was the glimpse merely a result of the mingling of beer and pill?

He wanted only to survive the weekend and spend time alone in his thinking stand. He wanted the calmness that had come when he wrote that first letter to God.

***

Events sometimes converge and obliterate life's planned pathway. Choices must be made. Actions have consequences.

Johnny had started the weekend with hopes of finding kindred spirits or a lovely lady or ... *something.* But he had only stared deeper into his misery.

In the early hours of Sunday morning, he awoke in his tent

with a headache. People were straggling out to their cars and leaving for home. Some had left during the night. The buggy riders were the fortunate ones, since the horses knew the way home and drivers could remain in the zombie zone.

On a clear-minded morning, he would have taken pleasure in the beauty of the early dawn. The sun was peeking over the horizon, awaking the countryside, when those still at the encampment heard a crunching sound break the morning stillness. A car horn sounded for what seemed like thirty seconds, then silence fell.

Dread chilled him, and he shivered. Many had left the party under the heavy influence of drugs and alcohol, and the Indiana guests especially were not acquainted with the road. One mile east of the quarry, near Jonas's sawmill, the road turned sharply to the right. Across from the curve, a large butternut tree bore the scars of several entanglements with vehicles. Locals knew this was a dangerous spot. At sunrise, that became a blind curve for several seconds when the sun shone directly into a driver's eyes.

The dread within Johnny warned that the curve and butternut tree had claimed another victim. He and Mel lay tense and silent. He saw his own fear reflected in Mel's eyes, and knew that Mel was thinking of that curve, too. For one minute, they hoped they had imagined the sounds or that the crash was nothing more than an ordinary noise from a nearby farm.

Then came a low, plaintive wail. A hard knot filled Johnny's stomach, and he and Mel jumped up. Others were running from tents to cars. Vehicles sped from the quarry, toward the sawmill. Most parked at the mill, and people tumbled out, toward the mangled car smashed against the immovable butternut tree.

Johnny walked in a nightmare, the images burning into him. Screams came from the car. The driver moaned, caught between seat and steering wheel, face twisted with pain. One girl sat on the road, arm bent at a strange angle. Two others, crouched beside her, held each other, sobbing, wailing. Blood trickled through blond hair, down along a thin neck, soaking a blue blouse.

In the front passenger's seat sat a fifteen-year-old Johnny had seen earlier that weekend. He had wondered why someone so young was at the party. Now the boy's head lay serenely on the dashboard, eyes open, calm, quiet. Johnny recoiled from the horror; there was no life in those eyes.

The dead boy was the brother of the driver.

Johnny was conscious then that the police had arrived. The emergency vehicles screamed up to the chaos. An angry officer demanded that everyone leave the area immediately or be arrested. Confused and dazed by the scene and the days of drinking and drugs, most ignored the order and continued to stumble around aimlessly. A third patrol car arrived. The officer in charge ordered all driver's licenses confiscated. He wrote up a dozen tickets for DWI, and the weekend of misery and horror now ripped away Johnny's freedom.

He and Mel began the walk home. Mel's farm was close to the quarry, and as he turned into his long driveway, Johnny watched him walk away, dejected, his entire body drooping. Johnny continued down the road toward home, feeling more alone than he had ever felt in his life.

15

John and Mandy were already milking when their youngest son entered the barn and picked up his milking stool without a word.

"I didn't hear you drive in, Son. What's all the commotion going on with sirens and emergency vehicles?"

"Please, Dad, let me think a while. It's bad, it's very bad."

"But you're all right? There was an accident? Who was it? Where's your car?" Mandy's worry gushed up and burst out of her. Johnny turned his back and set the stool down beside the first cow. He could feel his father's eyes on him.

"Yes, there was an accident. At the butternut tree. No one we know." It was enough for them. They would have liked more information, but they left him to his milking. The grapevine would bring them all the details soon enough.

All he wanted to do was run up to his room, stick his head under the pillow, and escape the world. He wanted the horror to go away. The minutes dragged by until the milking and chores were done and he at last made his escape.

By that time, he had decided the deer stand was a better retreat than under his pillow in his bedroom.

Everything was just as he had left it; the two amber bottles on the shelf still held his letters. Grabbing pad and pencil, he wrote,

Dear God,

Remember me? Things did not go well this weekend, but I suspect you already know that. God, help the poor family that will soon receive the news about their son. We should have warned everyone about that curve in the road. I will also lose my driving privileges. Now what, God? I'm stuck here. I'm so lost and lonely, and would welcome any help you could send my way.

Johnny

P.S. Those Indiana girls were nothing special.

He stuffed the note into the same bottle that held the first letter to God, and stretched out on the floor to collect his thoughts.

***

Johnny had disappeared as soon as his chores were done. He didn't come to the house for breakfast. The family knew he wasn't up in his room. Mandy suspected he was out roaming the woods or up in that deer stand. Still, it was not like Johnny to miss a meal.

There was no church that day, but everyone in the neighborhood soon knew about the terrible accident. Mandy grieved for some unknown mother, getting the news that her son had died hundreds of miles away from home.

When Johnny did not appear at the noon meal, Mandy and Naomi were both concerned about him, and by mid-afternoon, they could wait no longer. Naomi was the first to make a suggestion.

"Mom, I know he's up in that tree stand. I'm going up there." The two were out the door. John silently watched them go.

Naomi started off at a quick pace, determined to find her brother and make certain he was all right. Mandy puffed a little, trying to keep up as they went up the hill.

Naomi stopped under the oak tree at the edge of the woods.

Mandy had never been to Johnny's hideaway, and standing

under the spreading branches and peering up through the leaves, she saw her old wash house. She looked around. No wonder Johnny loved this place; from here, he had a view of most of their world, but you had to look at the right place to see his tree house.

"I can't go up there, just barging in," said Naomi. Of course, she *could*; she was more than able to scramble up that little ladder. But she would not intrude on Johnny's sanctuary.

"Johnny! Are you up there?"

They heard only bird calls, a buggy rattling over Strawberry Lane, and old Biff barking at something down in the barn.

"Johnny? Are you all right?"

"I'm all right," came the answer.

Mandy could tell from his voice that he had been sleeping. She was relieved to hear him answer, but she did not believe he was all right.

"Johnny, what happened last night? Were you at the accident?" Naomi was looking upward, talking to the floor of the tree house. The grapevine had given them details, and they knew Johnny had not been involved in the accident, but what had he seen? Did he know the boy who had died? Had something happened before the crash? Why was he hiding from them?

More silence. And then Mandy heard her son give a great sob.

"It was horrible. The music and the drinking and fighting and demons dancing in the bonfire. There was an awful accident this morning. And I was cited for drinking and driving and my license was taken away. A whole group of us will have to appear in court in two weeks. I've embarrassed the family, the church, the community. And myself. I'm going to leave, try to figure out my life somewhere else. Take the shame out of your house."

No! Mandy had feared this, suspected it might come. But to hear her son say it now … Fear flashed through her. Her throat closed and the tears stung.

"No, Johnny," Naomi's voice was firm. She was suddenly the older sister, and Johnny the little boy. "You need us all now, more than ever. You'll stay right here. We'll get through this together."

Only silence in the tree house.

"Johnny? I'm going to pray, for all of us."

That startled Mandy. She blinked away the tears and watched as her daughter placed her hands on the tree trunk. Naomi's voice was strong and sure, and she talked to a God she knew well.

How did my daughter learn to pray like that? Mandy wondered. She had said little bedtime prayers with all her children. Traditionally, Amish families had silent prayers even at meals, but in their house, John had broken with tradition. As head of the home, he thought it important to lead his family in prayers. His prayers were filled with *thees* and *thous*, and his rich voice intoning lofty phrases sounded majestic to his wife. Mandy's private prayers were just that—private thoughts and talk with a God she had learned to know, a God she knew heard her.

But she had never before heard Naomi pray aloud, and she was astonished at the power in the girl's supplications as she talked with Someone right there under the tree with them.

After the *Amen,* there was only silence above them.

Then, "Naomi? Would you write down that prayer for my prayer bottle?"

"What do you mean?"

"Nothing. Never mind."

"Johnny," Mandy called. "Come down to the house. I'll warm up some lunch for you."

"I'll be down soon." His voice was even now, calmed.

Mother and daughter looked at each other and then turned back toward the cow path and started down the hill.

"I'm glad you prayed, Naomi. Johnny needs our prayers. He's at a crossroads. Whatever he chooses to do now may change the direction of the rest of his life."

16

Even in his despair, Johnny saw one thing clearly. The accident had been a terrible and tragic story, but the partying, drinking, wild Amish boys who lost their licenses made an even bigger story for the newspapers to pick apart and feast on for weeks.

On the day that twelve Amish youths appeared before the judge, the courthouse buzzed with activity. The Amish families walked in the spotlight; and try as they might, they could not avoid it. Television reporters wanted to talk with them. They tried to ignore the microphones and cameras, but the reporters pushed in close and almost blocked their way. The Amish youths were the entertainment of the day.

Most of the mothers were happy to stay home, away from the scandal. Mandy went with John. Yes, it was a scandal; but one of those twelve was her son. Outside the courthouse, many parents shielded their faces with hats or hands. Mandy caught snippets of conversations. *We thought the Amish had no such problems.* One long-bearded old man stood watching and proclaimed loudly that these youths were caught in evil and wrongdoing because they had rejected the Amish way of life.

Fortunately, the judge kept proceedings inside the courtroom under his control. He forbade photographs, whether from respect of the Amish beliefs or as standard protocol, Mandy could not tell. This was foreign territory to her.

The Amish prefer to have no dealing with court matters, and so none of the families had hired a lawyer. Twelve "no contests" were offered and the decision was left to the mercy of the judge. One by one, each boy stood before him as he dispensed his justice.

Mandy kept her eyes on her son. He had not come to the breakfast table, and Henry had driven him to town. He looked strained, tired, and pale in spite of his deep tan.

She knew her son deserved to be here. She suspected Johnny was drinking far more than his family knew, and of course he should not be driving when he was intoxicated. That was the law, for everyone's safety.

The drinking, though, was not the only thing that worried Mandy. She had also been grieving over the places that car took him and over the English girls and over the look in his eyes as he mechanically went about the farm chores. Johnny was drifting away from the church, from God, from the farm, and from his family. She did not want to think about how far away this drifting might take her son.

Some of the young men had been in trouble before and were dealt with harshly. Johnny had only been driving a few months and had not had so much as a parking ticket. The judge suspended his license for ninety days and imposed a fine. He gave Johnny a stern warning about any further misdeeds.

Mandy prayed that they would be spared from ever having to do this again.

***

"Son, if I see you in here again, I will suspend your driving privileges for one full year."

The judge's warning haunted Johnny, since the possibility of his appearing again before the judge was increasing every week.

Just a week after the party and the accident, Johnny had been back at the quarry. The gathering was subdued, but everyone had brought their beer. In fact, most had brought more beer than usual. Joyce knew the way home, so he did not need to worry that night about getting caught for BDWI—buggy driving while intoxicated.

Then a week later, at the court hearing, he was sober and disgusted with himself. The dead eyes of the fifteen-year-old still stared at him from his nightmares, but he had continued to drink.

He left the courthouse in The Chief. Henry had gone home in a different direction on the morning of the accident, and his license was now safely tucked away in his wallet.

The circus at the courthouse left Johnny deeply frustrated and humiliated. Not only had he embarrassed himself, but he had also brought shame to his family, the Amish church, and the Amish community. John did not have to say a word to him; Johnny knew what he was and what he had brought upon them all. He knew he was just a drunken Amish loser.

And he was without driving privileges. Ninety days would extend into the fall. He would miss all of the remaining summer. The dates with English girls evaporated. Cleveland Indians games, over. Movies, impossible. Even his Amish girl acquaintances were being snatched up by others. Johnny was once again back to riding his old bicycle or driving the buggy or hitching a ride with Henry. He was regressing instead of advancing in life.

The only upside to the situation was that he once again spent evenings up in the deer stand. On many of those evenings, he wrote notes to God. The God bottle was stuffed almost to the neck with his thoughts and pleas.

He still carried a full bottle or two with him when he walked up the hill, and he often hurled the empty into the prickly bush. Sometimes he caught the shimmering, and he marveled at the transformation every time the setting sun touched the pile of trash and showered him with light and color.

Dear God,

That's me you see on the road, pedaling my bicycle again. I thought I was done with that bike, but I can't drive my car for three months. Protect me from drivers like myself who are foolish enough to drink and drive.

I am so sorry I embarrassed my parents. I wish I could wipe the hurt and shame out of their lives. If there's a way to do that, tell me how. I'll do it!

My life is like that pile of trashed bottles, tossed away and broken up. Useless. Doing no one any good. I need help. Is there any help for me? Will it ever come?

Johnny

In the middle of this valley and family that had always felt so peaceful and secure, he was lost and confused. The only thing he felt good about was those letters to God.

17

"Mom, I've found just the girl for Johnny!" Naomi was beaming, and Mandy was reminded of the little girl who had hunted treasure with her brother. Johnny would hide a trinket or treat, then draw a map to the secret spot. Now Naomi looked like she had found one of those treasures.

"A girl for Johnny?"

"Yes. You said you wished he would meet a good Christian girl who would help him settle down. Well, she's here. She's from Indiana, but she's living here now. She's the new teacher over at Valley View School."

"Miss Yoder?" Mandy had heard about the new teacher. Martha's children had been absolutely bubbling in their admiration and excitement about Miss Yoder.

Mandy had wondered whether this new school would be a good thing. John was one of the Amish bishops who felt that the worldly influences at the Milford School were growing too strong, and he was much in favor of the new parochial school that two neighboring church districts had built. All eight grades would be taught in one room, by one teacher. Education by one of their own people might be a good idea, but Mandy felt sorry for the teacher who must handle all those students alone.

The Millers' oldest daughter, Martha, and her husband lived close to the school, and the three oldest children were now attending there. Whenever Mandy saw her grandchildren, they talked constantly about Miss Yoder.

"We had two butterflies flying around the classroom today. Miss Yoder collected the worms from milkweed ..."

"Larvae, she said they're called larvae," the oldest interrupted.

"Larvae. But they sure looked like worms to me. Miss Yoder told us they eat milkweed leaves and then make a chrysalis."

"And when they come out of the chrysalis, the worms have turned into butterflies!"

The children were captivated by the story, and their voices tumbled over each other in the telling.

"She says it's a miracle from God!"

Naomi had looked at Mandy, over the tops of little heads, and grinned with an I-told-you-so delight.

Mandy had not met Anna Yoder, although she had seen the young woman walking over Strawberry Lane on her way to the school. Naomi had spent time with the newcomer on several occasions and was already convinced that this young lady was something special.

And so mother and daughter started plotting. There's no other honest word for it. Mandy and Naomi plotted, with the help of several enthusiastic grandchildren.

Johnny needed a miracle. A good Christian girl might turn his life down another path. And could there be any harm in helping God with His miracle?

***

At breakfast, Johnny sensed something was afoot. Unspoken conversations were glanced about the room. Johnny prided himself on always being several steps ahead of everything, but this silent communication between Mandy and Naomi had him baffled. John pretended to be unaware of any unusual goings-on.

There had been whispering and giggling the night before, too. Martha had stopped in with her brood of six children. The three oldest were six, seven, and eight and were enrolled in the new parochial school. Johnny had his doubts about Martha and Levi's decision to send their children to this school; he remembered how he had longed to go on to high school and thought privately that his nieces and nephews would be limited and even handicapped in dealing with life if they did not attend the local public schools.

As he left the house that evening, headed for the woods, he had heard Naomi say something to Martha's children about watching and being ready the next day. About two o'clock, she had said. The children giggled as if something was quite hilarious, but it made no sense to Johnny.

The next afternoon, Johnny and his father were working at repairing a barn door wedged in the sliding track. A roller was loose and now ruined beyond repair. Naomi came around the corner of the barn to ask if Johnny could ride to town and pick up jar lids. The women were canning and had come up short of lids.

"Go ahead, Son. Looks like we need a new roller for this door, too. Pick one up at the hardware," said John.

Johnny relished a ride to Milford. He wanted to stop at the bank, and perhaps if he lingered long enough, the high school would dismiss and he could visit with old friends.

The old Schwinn that had given him so much pleasure had not seen much use since the blue Camaro had roared into Johnny's life. It did feel good, though, to pedal slowly down the road on this warm autumn day.

On past sister Martha's house was the new Valley View School. As he approached, a commotion spilled out onto the lawn and spread toward the road. Apparently this was the last recess of the day; but not all the students headed out back to the ball field. Instead, a knot of children stood along the edge of the road.

"Here he comes!" squeaked a young voice that Johnny was

fairly certain belonged to his niece.

As he neared the group, Martha's two oldest children and six cohorts jumped out onto the road with arms spread wide and grins almost as wide. Johnny braked and put a foot down on the asphalt.

"Come see our butterflies," the children begged. "We have two new ones, just this afternoon, and we're going to set them free. Please come, please."

Johnny wondered if the teacher knew these children were out here on the road.

"Are you sure your teacher won't object to me dropping in?"

His niece giggled. "Oh, no. We don't think so."

They were so excited that Johnny yielded.

He followed the chattering children around the corner. The new teacher had come down the steps from the back door. She was carrying two jars, each holding a butterfly that slowly moved its wings up and down, as though testing the fragile flags of color.

"Miss Yoder, it's Johnny." "My uncle's here." Johnny was introduced by a cacophony of young voices.

For a brief moment, he glanced at the captive butterflies; but he himself had already been captivated by the blue eyes above the jars. His gaze went back to those shining eyes and the smile on Miss Yoder's face.

"I'm ... I'm sorry," he sputtered. "The children ... they insisted I take a look at those butterflies."

"We're about to release them for their first flight. You're welcome to watch." She gave him another smile, and the excited children, the jar of butterflies, and the fine day all faded away. He saw only those blue eyes, and for one of the very few times in his life, Johnny Miller had no idea what to say next.

18

The teacher bent her dark head over the jars and her voice took on a tone of awe. "I think these Monarchs are the most amazing of God's creatures."

Miss Yoder's delight in the fragile creatures was refreshing. She carefully withdrew one twig with a clinging butterfly and held it aloft. The brilliant orange and black wings quivered as though nudged by an encouraging breeze. Lifting from the twig, the Monarch drifted a few feet and settled on the black cap covering the red hair of his oldest niece. He had never seen that little eight-year-old stand so quiet, breathlessly still.

The children were fascinated by the butterflies. Johnny was fascinated by Miss Yoder. She looked familiar, but he was certain they had never met before. If their paths had crossed before, he would have remembered. Attractive, yes, indeed; *that* he could not miss. She moved gracefully, with a certain poise, and ...

That was it. She reminded him of Naomi. Not in appearance, but in demeanor. Her face, slightly flushed, seemed lit by some radiance that was more than excitement about the butterflies. She looked serene and unblemished; apparently her life had never known anything as traumatic as the events of his life.

The butterflies looped across the schoolyard, the children

chasing their darting flights and leaving Johnny standing alone with the teacher. She turned to him again with that smile, and he still did not know what to say. But he needed to say something; he was not yet ready for this encounter to end.

"I'm Anna Yoder. My friends call me Annie, although I'm new here, so there aren't too many people here who call me that. You're Johnny Miller, Naomi's brother?"

"My friends call me J.J." So, Naomi had already met Anna Yoder. *Annie.*

"I'm from Indiana, but I'm staying up over Strawberry Hill, at Mervin Klein's. Mervin's wife, Lizzie, is my dad's sister. Lizzie came to Ohio many years ago to a party they had around here somewhere, and she met and fell in love with Mervin. It wasn't long until she moved to Ohio."

"Yes, parties at the quarry have been going on for decades. Have you ever been to one of those?"

"Not here," said Annie. "But, yes, I've had my share of parties. Now, though, I have no desire for that kind of party. When I found Jesus, He changed my heart, and I lost all interest."

Now not only was his tongue tied, but his mind was reeling. No Amish girl had ever talked to him like this.

He tried to think. How could he see her again? He had never had trouble asking out any girl, but his heart was beating so furiously he could not think. He wasn't sure he could breathe, either. What might impress her?

"That bicycle isn't my usual mode of transportation. I do have a horse and buggy, and even better, I have a car. Would you … umm … that is, could I … could we go out sometime?"

He was forgetting something, wasn't he? Oh. Maybe there was already a boyfriend?

"That is, if you don't have a boyfriend?"

She smiled.

"I don't, and yes, I will."

He had heard right … he hoped. She did say yes, didn't she?

"How about this Saturday night? I can't drive right now, my license is suspended," (*why did he tell her that?*) "so we can't go to a movie or anything, but …"

"Johnny, I could not go to a movie with you. Remember that Jesus I told you about? He's taught me that I'm better off without movies. Do you have a Plan B?"

Do I have a Plan B? No. I didn't even come here with a Plan A, he thought.

The thought that came was so foreign that he couldn't believe he heard himself saying it.

"The young people are playing volleyball over at Pine Creek. We could go there." He had never been to one of those volleyball evenings. Too tame, he had always thought. He did admit there were far more Amish young people who followed the dictates of the church than the ones who ran wild, like himself. But if Annie was interested in that kind of "party," it couldn't hurt to see what— if anything—he had been missing.

He didn't care where they went. He would be happy to let Joyce trot wherever she desired as long as Annie would be beside him in the buggy.

"I'll pick you up around seven, after chores."

"That sounds good to me."

He mounted the bicycle and pedaled away. Halfway home, he realized he had not yet been to town, and he sheepishly turned around and pedaled back toward the schoolhouse. Some of the children were already walking home, and as he passed them, their grins and laughter confirmed what he suspected as soon as he'd heard Annie mention Naomi's name. He had been set up.

Still, he had to give Naomi credit. She'd pulled off a great plan. Now, he hoped for a very successful outcome. Because Annie had looked him in the eye, and he saw peace.

"And can you believe it?" he said, voicing his surprise to no one but himself. "She's from Indiana!"

***

Although this little plot of Naomi's was quite to his liking, he couldn't let the opportunity go by for a payback prank. He would play ignorant for a while. He took the jar lids to Mandy's kitchen and went back to work on the barn door. Later, he dug into supper and said nothing other than casual talk about the day's work.

He enjoyed knowing that his mother and his sister were again engaged in a silent conversation.

"How was your trip to town?" Mandy finally asked.

"I saw a few people I knew, but nothing very exciting to report." Johnny took some satisfaction in the questioning look on his mother's face and the stifled gasp from his sister.

"Nothing interesting happened today?"

"No, nothing."

"Did you stop at Valley View School?" Mandy could not contain her curiosity.

"Oh," he said, as though just remembering that he had indeed stopped there. "Yes. Some of the children were out playing and stopped me to talk."

He saw them both droop as they despaired that their plan had somehow gone awry.

"I'm kidding!" he shouted. "Yes, I met her, and she's incredible!"

19

Saturday night finally arrived and Johnny pulled his buggy out of the shed, wishing he could take, instead, the blue Camaro that was parked and waiting for the day it could once again roam the country roads.

Temptation whispered a thought. The sheriff and his deputies never patrolled their quiet roads; the only time their community saw a police car was if there was an accident. And the road to Pine Creek was even less traveled. The chances of getting caught were remote. Pine Creek was only five miles away. What would be the harm of impressing Annie with his little companion rather than horse and buggy?

He pushed the buggy back into the shed, ran into the house for his keys, and headed over Strawberry Hill toward the Klein farm. The excitement of seeing Annie again was soon tempered by her reaction when she saw the Camaro. Her blue eyes widened.

"Johnny, didn't you tell me your license was suspended?"

Why had he blurted that out?

"Well, yes, but I thought since we ..."

"No," she interrupted, shaking her head. "You broke the law, and now we'll have to live with the consequences. Please go home and get the buggy. And then we'll start over."

Chastised and embarrassed, he headed back over Strawberry Lane. No girl had ever talked to him that way. Most of them were happy enough to go along with whatever he suggested. Although he felt shame, he also knew this was one very special lady he was dealing with—or attempting to deal with.

A half hour later, Johnny made his second appearance.

"Annie, your chariot awaits. And I'm sorry I put you in such a situation with my car."

"I'll gladly drive with you once you have your license again. It does look like a really nice car."

And with that, their date began again, and Johnny, who had often scoffed at the idea of love at first sight, was beginning to reconsider that opinion. When he had first seen Annie in the schoolyard, her poise and natural beauty had swept him up and taken him in. His immediate response had been to her outward beauty. Petite, dark-haired, and with those amazing blue eyes, she carried an aura of energy. The package was very appealing. Given what he was feeling, he would have to rethink his disbelief in love at first sight.

On the drive to Pine Creek, the conversation flowed easily, and Johnny began to see the simplicity of Annie's beauty. Her loveliness was clean and fresh. She did not wear the makeup or earrings or teased hair that his English girlfriends employed to enhance their appearance. Annie looked … the word *unblemished* came to mind again.

Granted, her beauty was covered modestly from neck to ankle with a plain dress and cape, and her hair was pulled back, pinned up, and covered with a cap. He wondered if, when he could court Annie in his car, she would change to English garb. Many of his Amish girlfriends had done that; away from home, they attempted the transformation from Amish to English by slipping into jeans and sweaters and letting hair fall to shoulders. What would Annie look like in English clothes? He did not dwell on the question; he was already certain that he would never know the answer.

The volleyball games had already started when Joyce trotted up the lane. Johnny knew most of the young people there, but he had not had much association with them. They had run in different circles. He and Annie were welcomed, though, and quickly drawn into the easy, friendly atmosphere.

Johnny watched Annie as she introduced herself to other girls, laughed with them, and seemed to slip right into the social fabric of the group. He was aware, too, that he was not the only young man who was impressed with Anna Yoder.

Afterward, they rode toward Strawberry Lane as a fingernail moon rose in the east. Only good memories rode with them; the nagging conscience that had often tormented Johnny on the drive home after a date or party was banished on this night. He was happy. He reached over and took Annie's hand. She did not draw away, but she did set her boundaries immediately.

"Johnny, I want you to know that I don't believe in bed courtship. At midnight, you'll have to leave."

She would not ride in the car with him as long as he didn't have a license; and he would need another license before he could place one foot in her bedroom. He felt an exhilaration greater than any he had ever felt when welcomed into a girl's room. Annie really was different from anyone he had ever been with.

"Believe it or not, I'm glad to hear you say that. But you will go out with me again?"

"Yes, Johnny, I will. And I can't wait to ride around with you in that car of yours. I've been wanting to tour the community and get acquainted here."

She paused. Then, in a quieter voice, she said, "But there are some things you need to know about me. And after I've told you my story, you may not want to be with me."

Johnny was certain nothing she could say would change the way he already felt.

"I want to hear whatever you want to tell me. I can't imagine anything that would change my mind. But you're right, I've only known you for several hours. You haven't killed anyone, have you? Is the law looking for you? If you're on the run, I do have a hideout, a tree house up in the woods. I'll be glad to harbor a fugitive there."

She laughed.

"No, I'm not a murderer and I'm not in trouble with the law. But I have broken some laws. God's laws. And there have been consequences. It's a long story, and it's nearly midnight. It will have to wait until another day."

Whatever she had to tell him, Johnny was certain it could not be too serious.

"What if we started your getting-acquainted tour in the buggy? Could I pick you up tomorrow afternoon and bring you home to meet Mom and Dad? I guess you've already met Naomi. And, in case you someday need a hideout, I'll show you that tree house if you like."

She said yes.

It was a good thing that Joyce knew her way home; Johnny certainly did not remember driving. He was too dazzled by the shimmering that had exploded in his life.

20

Never before had he felt so free and happy after a date. He had also never before returned home this early. Paul was leaving the house as Johnny's buggy rattled up to the barn. They unhitched Joyce, and Paul led the mare to her stall while Johnny wheeled the buggy into the shop.

The two friends leaned up against Paul's car, side by side, rehashing recent events. It was almost like old times. But now, instead of double-dating into the wee hours of the morning in someone's upstairs bedroom, they laughed at the irony of both being barred from their dates' homes once the clock struck twelve.

I could get used to this, Johnny thought. *A pleasant evening with a lovely lady, then conversation with my best friend.* He wondered if this would become the norm. Had he finally found for himself what Paul and Naomi shared?

Early Sunday afternoon, as he prepared to hitch up Joyce, another brilliant idea popped into his head. Leading Joyce back into the barn, he contemplated the merits of the plan. The idea had great potential, he decided.

The shortest way to Annie's house was not over Strawberry Lane. The most direct route was through the woods behind the deer stand. The back corner of the Millers' property jutted up against the lower end of Strawberry Hill. Johnny started up the cow path.

Lizzie Klein answered his knock and was surprised to see that he was on foot.

"Tell Annie to wear walking shoes."

When Annie came downstairs, she was smiling.

"You're full of surprises, aren't you?" she said.

"It's a nice day for a stroll in the woods. Down the hill a ways is the corner of our property. If you cut through our woods on your walk to school, you can save yourself a lot of steps and some time. You're welcome to use that shortcut any time you wish. I thought we could walk today, and I'll show you the path."

Granted, the route *happened* to run within yards of his stand, a happy coincidence.

They crossed the end of Strawberry Lane, went through a gate in the wood fence, and followed a field lane that had been used when logs were brought out of the woods. That old road bisected the northernmost acreage of the Millers' woods, so they soon left it, turned south, and Johnny showed Annie a trail he had blazed, a passage from his tree house to the back end of their farm. Cow paths and animal trails crisscrossed the canopied and sun-dappled ground. The thick undergrowth of summer was dying off and taking on autumn colors.

They stopped at the gate at the edge of the woods, standing at the top of the hill and looking out over the valley. At their feet, the cow path led along the fence line, down to the barn. Annie had not seen the deer stand. Johnny would have liked to think that was due to her fascination with him and their conversation, but he knew the deer stand blended so well into the leaves and branches of the oak that she had missed it.

"See? Follow the path down the hill to the road. You will have cut off the whole corner of Strawberry Hill. But before we do that … let's make a stop here."

"Where? Johnny, what … Oh!" She caught sight of the ladder climbing into the branches, as she squinted up through the leaves.

"Did you build this?"

He told her the story of taking down the old wash house when he was ten years old.

"After you," he said chivalrously.

"Thanks, but it's probably better if you go first."

"Oh, right." Slightly embarrassed, he agreed that would be the proper order for them to ascend.

Annie was suitably impressed with his hideout. She touched his books lightly, read each title, took in his drawings and newspaper clippings, and grinned at the radio.

"This is incredible, Johnny. You did a great job."

Then she drifted to another shelf, and he cringed. At the same time, he almost burst with the desire to tell her everything about the prayer bottles.

"What are the beer bottles doing here? They're stuffed with … why is there paper stuffed in them?"

"Those are my prayer bottles. I come up here sometimes to think and write letters to God. For some reason, I started stuffing the notes into my empty bottles, because I didn't know what else to do with them."

She said nothing for a moment. He tried to read her face. Was she shocked?

"Writing those letters calms my spirit."

"But … a beer bottle." She was smiling, and to Johnny's relief, she did not look horrified. "Stuffed with letters to God. Such a contradictory combination."

He had no desire to turn on the charm and wave off the complicated circumstance with a joke, as he often did. He only wanted to tell her the truth.

"I drink too much, and I know it. I've wanted to quit, but can't seem to do it. I don't like my life right now; and these letters come from me, trying to figure out who I am and how I can change."

She looked at him, her blue eyes deep and thoughtful. Were there tears there?

"Johnny, on your own, you can't and won't change, no matter how many letters you write. I've learned that the hard way. But I've also learned a secret about new lives. Can we sit outside on your deck? You wanted to know my story. I'll tell you how I was changed from a worm into a butterfly."

They settled on the deck on the south side of the tree house, their backs against the wall. Below, at the house, Paul's car was turning into the driveway. Annie began in a quiet but firm voice.

21

"Not too long ago, I pretty much lived from one drinking party to the next. Even before I was allowed to date, I was 'running wild,' as they say. The day I turned sixteen, I had a date with Joe. He was older, a real charmer."

Johnny winced. He knew some people would use that word to describe him. And he had a feeling this Joe-charmer was not the hero of Annie's story.

"I had been warned that Joe was just looking for a good time, that he had many other girlfriends. But I was flattered by his attention. He took me to parties and ... well, it wasn't long before I was pregnant. At sixteen. Mom and Dad were devastated. They tried to keep me hidden as much as possible, but of course that didn't work for very long. They reminded me constantly that I had brought shame and reproach on my family.

"I'll leave out some of the horrible details, but Joe was soon gone. We hated each other and went our separate ways. And at seventeen, I was mother to a little girl I named Christine."

Annie looked at him, her clear blue eyes now brimming with tears, but her voice was still strong.

"Do you want me to go on?"

He reached over and took her hand.

"Please. I want to know how you can have any happiness now, after all of that. Yet you seem to be at peace. And where's Christine?" he asked.

"I was too young to raise a child; and, of course, I had no way to support her. My oldest sister was married and unable to have children, so I agreed to give Christine to them. I know it was the right thing to do; she has brought them great joy. But it was so very painful for me.

"After Christine was born, I was bitter and angry. Angry at Joe. Angry at the church, because I felt only condemnation from them. Angry at my parents; they seemed to think that having to give up my baby was punishment I deserved. Maybe I was even angry at my sister, because she now had the child she had always wanted, but it was at my expense.

"I tried to shut off my sorrow with alcohol and drugs. I partied with the best, or worst, of them. I cared not a bit what my parents or the church thought. I told myself I was having a good time, but alone in the dark of night, I was overwhelmed by grief and shame.

"I had a job cleaning houses. One of the ladies I worked for was an older Mennonite lady, a widow. I don't think she knew about my partying and the baby, but she would often talk with me about God. She spoke of grace and mercy from a God that loves me. That concept was foreign to me, but I wanted so much to find some peace and relief from my burden of guilt. So I would listen.

"An evangelist was holding meetings at her church, and she invited me to go with her one evening. My parents would not have approved attending such meetings, but by now I was completely outside their control. That night I heard about a man called Jesus that could love me, even as sinful as I was.

"I had heard the gospel of Jesus explained before, in many of our Amish church services, but that evening I really began to see what grace and forgiveness are. Jesus could wipe away all my sins. He actually does love me, and His grace and mercy assure me of an everlasting life in Heaven. It's all *real*, Johnny.

"Perhaps I was just at the right place at the right time, because that night I felt the power of God's love. And I believed in His forgiveness. The preacher invited all who wanted to lay down their burdens to come to the front of the church and pray. I'll never forget his words: 'Come, however you are, and Jesus will meet you and transform your life into a life of peace and joy. The burden from your past can be lifted tonight.'

"I had heard enough. Before the devil could stop me, I jumped to my feet and literally ran to the altar. I wasn't taking any chances of arriving too late. I knelt there and sobbed. I could not quit crying. All the pain and remorse and sorrow came pouring out.

"Now I liken that experience to a butterfly struggling to remove itself from its chrysalis and then finally emerging as a new creature. 'Old things are passed away, and all things become new.' That's how the Bible describes it. I was a worm, Johnny; I can't even describe what a disgusting worm I was. But now, I'm a new creature.

"That night, I fell in love with a new man, a man called Jesus. And I knew He forgave all of that ugliness in my life. That's the reason I can no longer do those hurtful things I used to do. I refuse to let them in my life, not because they would hurt me, but because they would hurt Jesus." Her voice was soft. "I never want to hurt anyone who loves me as much as He does."

For the second time in a week (and maybe only the second time in his life), Johnny was speechless. He could only watch her face, as she gazed at white clouds drifting over the far hills, those blue eyes seeing something he could not see.

"I won't tell you it was easy; in many ways, life became even more difficult. My relationship with my parents was badly damaged. Jesus changed my attitude toward them, and I tried to be a respectful and obedient daughter. In spite of that, they were uncertain whether or not they could trust this change in me.

"I knew, though, that what I had discovered was real. I have never regretted my choice that night to give up my will and follow

Jesus and let Him guide my life; and now, when I rest my head on my pillow, I feel peace. And I'm free, Johnny. I gave my will to Jesus, but it's not a slavery. He set me free from so many things, and I'm going to follow Him because I love Him."

She paused, and Johnny saw a shadow of pain cross her face.

"Christine was right there, in my life almost every week. I saw them at church and at family gatherings. She started to walk and talk and call my sister 'Mommy.' The sorrow and loss I felt grew so intense, that when I saw the notice for a schoolteacher in Milford, I decided to apply. I needed to remove myself. And now here I am."

She turned to him.

"That, Johnny Miller, is the short version of who I was and Whose I now am. Do you still want to be my friend, knowing what lies back there in my past?"

22

Mandy couldn't help but notice that Miss Yoder sat down at supper with them and immediately slipped into the easy and comfortable conversation between the young people around the table.

It's as though she's my own daughter, come home after a long absence, Mandy thought as she watched the young folks. Annie and Naomi were already on the road to becoming good friends, but this was the first time the new teacher had met Paul.

Johnny had introduced Annie to his father and mother politely and properly, but with a grin that Mandy had not seen often enough of late. The older woman's welcome to Annie was heartfelt—more than the schoolteacher could have guessed. John, too, seemed to approve completely; Annie was a gracious young lady, and while she helped Mandy to serve the pie and ice cream, she caught the approving wink John sent toward his son.

Too soon, goodbyes were exchanged and Johnny and Annie set out for the Kleins'. In the September dusk, the woods quickly filled with darkness, so the two took Strawberry Lane over the hill. That route was longer, but Mandy suspected Johnny was happy with the additional time he would have with Annie.

Mandy wanted more time with Annie, too. She had not had a chance to talk with the young woman privately on that first

Sunday, and she had no intention of being the nosy mother who ferreted out everything about her son's girlfriend. But she had sensed something in their guest, something that prompted her heart to reach out to Annie. So young…and so alone, it seemed. So far from home. Annie and Naomi had laughed together and shared many understanding looks, but Mandy was certain there was some depth to Annie that even Naomi had not yet grasped.

So as they said goodbye, Mandy invited Annie to stop in some afternoon on her way home from school. They'd have conversation minus the men. Annie readily agreed, and Mandy hoped they could build a friendship, not so much for Johnny's sake, but for her own and Annie's.

Several weeks went by. Johnny brought Annie to Sunday suppers, but then the house was full of chatter. Sometimes Mandy was outside in the garden or hanging up the wash and she'd catch sight of Annie walking by. They waved and called hello to each other. But that was all.

Mandy waited.

On one of those rare November days that makes everyone forget December is lurking around the corner, Mandy raked up the leaves from one stubborn maple that always clung to its fall glory much later than most maples. Some of the dead leaves would be spread on the garden to be tilled under in the spring. The rest would be burned, filling the valley with one of those scents of the season that Mandy loved. She often said that she could sleep like Rip Van Winkle, and no matter when she woke up, without opening her eyes she would be able to tell from the smells of the farm and the earth exactly what month of the year it was.

She was thinking about those smells and wondering how folks in cities stayed close to the marvels of nature and the majesty of the One who created it all when Annie suddenly stood beside her.

"Hi, Mandy."

"Oh, you startled me. I didn't see you coming."

Good. Annie had come into the yard. Usually she waved and

walked on by. Maybe she would spend a few minutes chatting.

"Johnny said something about coming here for Thanksgiving next Thursday. Can I bring something or help you in any way?"

"Wonderful! I'm so glad you can come. All the children and their families will be here, so it will be a good time to meet everyone. Do you have a few minutes? I baked bread this morning and have several extra loaves. Let me fix one or two for you to take along for the Kleins."

They walked into the kitchen, still filled with the aroma of fresh bread. Annie stopped on the threshold.

"Oh! This smells like home."

"Are you homesick, Annie?"

"There are times I would like to be back in the safety of home. Home wasn't always comfortable and safe, though. It only seems that way in my memories." Annie gave a soft sigh. "And when I'm feeling alone."

Mandy remembered days of loneliness as a young wife, moving to a new house in a new church district with her new husband. She had only moved from one county to another, and after the move, she was surrounded by her husband's family. Annie had moved to a new state, to the home of someone she barely knew. And she was alone.

What else had Annie said?

"Home wasn't always safe, Annie?"

A sigh escaped before Annie could stop it, and a veil of sadness dropped over her face.

"The last few years at home were … there was a lot of pain. I caused my parents much embarrassment and grief. But old things are passed away; all things are new."

She said the last in almost a whisper.

"Annie, I don't know all of your story. But I do know that whatever happened back then, you have now made things right with God and He's forgiven you. But if you ever do want to talk about what you went through, I'm a good listener."

Annie smiled, a small, tender smile.

"Your son's a good listener, too. I've told him most of the story, but some parts are so painful that I've never spoken of them to anyone."

Her head dropped, and she caught her breath. It sounded to Mandy like a sob.

"Oh, Mandy, it was so horrible."

"Tell me. I will understand."

"How can I explain what it's like to be sixteen and pregnant and all alone? When I knew without a doubt that I was pregnant, I was so scared, Mandy. Joe had seemed so kind and friendly. I knew he'd had plenty of girlfriends. All kinds of rumors floated around, but I told myself it was only gossip because he was popular and others were jealous. I enjoyed the attention. And so I paid the price."

She gulped for air. Once started, the words came pouring out. She had opened the door, just a crack, to let Mandy in, and now the pain crashed through.

23

When Annie told Joe that she was certain she was pregnant and hoped he would go with her to tell her parents, he had other plans. There was a place in Indianapolis, he said, that would make the problem go away.

"You can't mean it," Annie told him. "You think I should have an abortion?"

"Do you want to make your problem go away or do you want to be stuck with raising a child? Do you really want to face your parents with this mess? Have you thought what your life will be like in this community if you have that baby?"

Annie had never thought much about abortion. Things like that never happened to people she knew. It was wrong. It was even illegal. But it was a way out, and she didn't have to imagine the ugly whispering and scandal—she had seen it happen to other girls. She was sixteen and scared—and Joe had said he was going to help her. She would not have to handle the problem alone. So she agreed to his plan.

Joe would take a day off work to drive her to Indianapolis.

"But don't you chicken out on me. I can't afford to take the day off for nothing."

Annie concocted an excuse to go to town that day. She didn't give a second thought to lying to her parents; she had done it so often that her conscience did not raise even a feeble whisper of protest. Joe met her there, and the two-hour trip to Indianapolis was spent in unspoken thoughts and apprehension. Joe kept the radio blaring, a good excuse not to talk.

In the city, Joe drove directly to a brick house in a quiet, residential part of town. No sign stood outside. The place looked like an ordinary home in an ordinary neighborhood.

"How did you find this place?"

His grin confirmed her suspicion. The fun and excitement of being with this man was gone. That grin was looking more evil to her with every hour.

"You've brought someone else here? How many times? How many others?" Annie was almost shouting and felt herself sinking into hysteria.

"Let's just say this isn't the first time," replied Joe.

"You really are a dog, a lowdown, dirty dog!" she screamed, unable to contain her rage and fear and frustration.

Joe rolled back his head and let out a long imitation of a howl, then sang his own rendition of an Elvis hit song.

"I ain't nothin' but a hound dog."

Annie's fury boiled. She was about to kill her child, and he was singing.

"Now get in there and get it done. Tell the lady that Joe sent you. They're expecting you." He gave her shoulder a push.

Annie was trembling and unsure her legs would support her. A lady in a white uniform greeted her and tried to make her feel welcome and at ease.

"Have a seat here. I'll be with you shortly."

She sat down across the room from a young girl whose cheeks were wet with tears.

"Follow me," the woman in white said to the weeping girl.

Annie clutched the armrest of the chair, her nails clawing into the material, and looked around the room, trying to think of something, anything else except what was going to happen to that weeping girl. *And to her.*

The walls were painted a dark, gloomy gray-blue, and the shag carpet was matted and old. The only window had no curtain, but a torn shade was pulled down almost to the floor. The ceiling fan squeaked, squeaked, squeaked; every squeak and rotation seemed to tighten her muscles and take more of her air.

A sliver of light came through a tear in the shade and fell on the carpet like a tiny spotlight. The air current from the fan moved the shade enough that the spotlight danced in patterns on the ugly floor. Annie sat there, numb, mesmerized by the dancing light. It was almost as if that light were alive.

Like a flood, a thought swept away all other thoughts. The light dancing on the carpet was like the gift of life; and somewhere inside her body was a tiny bit of life, already alive, that she was about to end forever. The recognition burst through her mind and drove out all the fear and rage and embarrassment.

Her stomach was churning; she rushed down the hall to the restroom and gasped and retched over the lavatory, her body shuddering with convulsions.

She heard a voice behind her. She looked up, but saw no one.

The voice said, "Annie, you must make a choice now."

And then she felt a gentle fluttering in her stomach.

It was too early for the baby to be moving, wasn't it? She thought so. But then, Christine made the decision for her.

She did not go back to the awful blue room. She fled the house, jumped into the car, and slammed the door.

"That sure didn't take long," Joe said. He gave her a strange look and sneered. "You chickened out, didn't you? You backed out; you couldn't do it, could you?"

"Take me home, now!" she said coldly.

His face turned into something so ugly she had to look away. She braced herself, afraid he would hit her.

"Don't ever come to me for any support; I don't want anything to do with a kid. I was good enough to bring you here, not even knowing for sure that I'm the father."

Annie had not known she could feel such rage and hatred as she felt toward Joe at that moment. She shook her fists at him and screamed, "I would never take a penny from you. I never want to see you after today."

Joe simply reached over, turned up the volume on the radio, and drove her home.

24

Annie's dark head lay on her arms on the kitchen table. She wept softly, spent from the wrenching of secrets from dark places. She had buried those horrible memories and feelings so deeply that the telling of them had torn her open. Mandy put her arms around the young woman and cried with her.

"Mandy, what if I had gone through with it?"

"But you didn't, you made the right choice." Mandy thought for a moment. "Do your parents know?"

Annie shook her head as she wiped tears off her cheeks.

"I never told them about Indianapolis. Breaking the news about the baby was as terrible as I expected. My dad was the one person I could lean on. Mom was so embarrassed and disappointed in me. She kept reminding me how much I'd shamed the family. And she was so concerned about what everyone would say. She wanted to keep me out of sight, but of course word spreads fast in our community." Annie's voice was tired now. "Yes, I had been rebellious and wild, but the rumors and half-truths turned into stories that exaggerated everything. In no time, I was turned into a hopelessly bad girl.

"Several weeks before the baby was due, we had church at our house. Of course, Mom wanted me upstairs and out of sight.

Everyone knew why I was absent from the services. While songs were sung and sermons preached, I sat in my rocking chair and rocked and rocked, visualizing everything that was happening downstairs, imagining what they were probably thinking about me and all the stories they had heard. I wished for someone to come and sit beside me and tell me everything would be all right. My younger sister brought a plate of food, but no one brought me comfort. No one ever tried."

Mandy tightened her arm around the slim shoulders.

"What happened to the baby?"

"My oldest sister and her husband took the baby as their own. I knew she would be loved and … I thought … I thought … if she grew up close to me … and I thought … maybe this would be better than having her adopted by complete strangers and never seeing her again. It seemed like a good decision.

John had come into the living room and was searching for something in his desk in the far corner of the living room. He'd caught sight of the two women at the kitchen table.

"You ladies seem to be having a serious discussion out there," he called across the room.

"Mmm-hmm. We'll give you a call if we need a man's input," Mandy shot back lightheartedly. John knew her language. He wouldn't be coming into the kitchen to visit with Annie.

"Oh, Mandy, there's something else. After Christine was born, a nurse came into the room and asked about the name of the father. She was filling out the birth certificate," said Annie. "I was bad."

"What did you do?"

"I gave a fictitious name. I sort of regret it, now that I'm a Christian. I'm almost embarrassed to tell you." Annie glanced toward the living room and leaned over and whispered a name.

"You didn't!" Mandy couldn't help but giggle.

"I did," replied Annie.

They heard the door close behind John, and Annie went on with her story.

"The day I left the hospital and handed Christine to my sister was the saddest day of my life. It also was the day I started partying and drinking. After hearing the stories and lies told about me during my pregnancy, I decided that if everyone thought those things about me, I might as well be that person.

"That's what I told myself. But I was really trying to forget everything, numb my feelings, stop hurting. I couldn't forgive myself. For a year, I tried to blot out my anger and sorrow with parties and drugs and alcohol." Annie looked directly into Mandy's eyes, "Mandy, I was a hard, bitter person."

"You aren't now," said Mandy gently. "Something happened."

Annie smiled gently, and Mandy saw a great peace settle over the girl's face.

"Yes." They were both quiet for a moment, and the only sound was the grandfather clock ticking in the living room.

"You know," Annie began again, "when I was a little girl, I would often dream that I died. I was never an old or sick woman in the dreams. Always, I was young and happy, but then something terrible would happen and …"

She hunched her shoulders, as though a cold breeze had blown through the room.

"Looking back now, I wonder if during that year of drugs and drinking and riding with wild drivers, God protected me from an early death. I know I put myself in many situations that could have turned out badly.

"Johnny may have told you the rest of the story. At the lowest ebb of my life, a kind lady took me to a revival meeting and I realized Jesus had taken my punishment … for everything I had done! And He loved me, in spite of the mess I had made of my life. That was incredible to me. But He gave me an assurance of His forgiveness and that I had a new beginning, a new life. That's what changed me, Mandy. Only the power of Jesus."

Mandy squeezed Annie's hand and said nothing.

"But life was still difficult. My parents did not trust the change in me. They doubted it would last. My friends were all partygoers, and one by one they dropped me. I quit drinking and doing drugs. I cleaned up my language. I wasn't *fun* in their eyes. Of course, it was a good thing to lose those friends, but I had no friends at all. No one else stepped up to be my friend. I think they were afraid.

"The final straw came one Sunday in church."

25

"I went back to the Amish church I grew up in," continued Annie, "and now I wanted to listen to the words preached. I had always found church almost unbearable, sitting for hours on those hard, wooden benches and listening to the preachers going over the same Scriptures again and again. It had seemed so foolish to me.

"But now the sermons and Scriptures held new meaning. What had previously been only words and phrases preached in German now inspired me and refreshed my spirit. I soaked it all up.

"Our church was like any other Amish church. The men sit on one side of the room, the women on the other. Women remain silent and take no part in the service. I never had any intention of being a rebel. I would never even think of speaking against that tradition. I'm quite content to be silent and listen.

"One day we had a guest minister; he must have been, oh, eighty years old. He rambled on and on. But he was preaching the Word of God, and the whole message of the Bible is God's love for the world. That's water for my soul, Mandy. I took it all in.

"The preacher started the New Testament and talked about God sending His son Jesus into the world so I could be forgiven for everything I'd done. I had such a feeling of freedom that before my brain could stop my mouth, I called out, 'Praise the Lord!'

"Well, you can imagine what happened. No woman's ever done such a thing in my church. I heard gasps among the women, and snickers from some of the boys. I wanted to sink through the floor when I thought of what my mother's face must look like at that moment.

"I was so ashamed. I kept my head down the rest of the service. The old preacher was completely thrown off his stride. The poor fellow abruptly finished his sermon and lunch was served a good half hour earlier than usual.

"Really, Mandy, I wasn't intending to do that, but I was so overcome with the Holy Spirit, I had to let it out."

Mandy chuckled.

"So how did your mom and dad react?" she asked, although she had a pretty good idea.

"Of course, Mom was appalled. I listened to her fume about how I had embarrassed her *yet again.* Dad simply said that it was nice to get to the dinner table earlier than usual."

Mandy thought to herself that she would like Annie's father. Her mother, though, might require patience and much forgiveness.

"So there I was, a new Christian rejected by my old friends and now looked on as a misfit in my own church. All I wanted to do was repair the damage I had already done. I did not regret becoming a Christian, but things were not going well.

"When I saw the advertisement for the teaching position at your school, I hoped that might be the answer. I'd move away from home for a year. Let things settle down in Indiana. Then decide if I could or should go home. I wanted to prove to my parents and church that I had indeed changed and wanted to be a good little Amish girl.

"The folks in the valley here have been so kind and welcoming. The church services are inspiring, too. I still shout 'Amen' and 'Praise the Lord!' during church, I do it silently, to myself and to God."

Annie looked spent, exhausted, like the sunflowers in Mandy's garden when they turned autumn brown and dropped their heavy heads. She did not know it yet, but telling her long story had purged some of the pain and broken more of the chains. Her blue eyes met Mandy's.

"That's it. That's my story."

"God did forgive it all, Annie." Mandy smiled at her. "Except for that 'Praise the Lord.' I'm not certain that needs forgiveness. I think that might have made Him glad. But all the sins, He has forgotten. He made you into a new creature. Your story is about your misdeeds and sadness, yes. But more importantly, it is about your transformation."

"Yes! It is all a miracle, Mandy. A miracle. Old things are passed away; all things are new, just like the Bible says. I am so grateful, and it gives me great peace to know that. Only … sometimes, the scars still ache."

She began to gather her bag and coat that were lying on the table next to her.

"I've kept you so long. Thank you for listening. It means so much that you have listened and not judged me harshly. It feels good to get those secrets out, even if you could never understand how it feels to be pregnant and so alone."

She rose from her chair and reached for the bread loaves Mandy had wrapped for the Kleins. Mandy touched Annie's arm.

"Annie, sit for one more minute."

Do I have to do this? Now? Mandy asked herself.

Yes. She did.

"This may surprise you, Annie, but I do understand what it was like for you to be young, pregnant, and unmarried. I understand better than you might think, because I, too, was pregnant before I was married."

Annie had never expected this.

"But you're a preacher's wife," she gasped.

Mandy laughed.

"John wasn't always a preacher. And I wasn't always a

Christian. And even after we're Christians, we still make mistakes. But, Annie, God can make good things come out of our mistakes. Do you have time to hear my messy story?"

Annie sat down again.

"Nothing will pry me from this chair now!"

***

Mandy's story was different than Annie's. John and Mandy had also been a young couple who were thinking only of dating and having fun. That changed with the pregnancy. John resolved to take responsibility for his wrong decisions and ask forgiveness of God and the people he had harmed. He had wanted to bring good from a bad situation, he had said. Their parents had offered them grace and forgiveness. It had not been easy for the young couple or their families, but God had transformed the lives of John and Mandy, too.

"I believe God has blessed our family because of John's determination to honor God and do what's right," said Mandy. "You see the leader and preacher he has become. His wisdom and calming advice have helped many people that come to him for counsel. But no, Annie, we weren't always the people you see today. God gave us new lives, too."

"I wish my story had ended so well," said Annie quietly.

"My dear, your story is not yet ended!"

Mandy was suddenly Johnny's mother again, thinking as mothers do. Had God led this girl to John's Johnny? Could she be the answer to their prayers? Was this the good that God would bring to both these young souls?

"Dare I dream of a storybook ending, Mandy?"

Naomi came up the sidewalk, back from helping Martha get ready for church the next Sunday. She was delighted to find Annie in the kitchen, and the chatter turned to teenage girl matters as Mandy started peeling potatoes for supper.

From her kitchen window, Mandy watched Annie walk up over Strawberry Lane. At the crest of the hill, the slender silhouette moved against the pink evening sky. Mandy saw arms raised upwards, and she was certain she caught a shout of "Praise the Lord!"

26

God had given Annie a new life in Ohio and was changing her into a new person. She had come to Ohio alone and suffering. The Millers opened their door and hearts and took her in as though she were family. She and Naomi were becoming good friends, and Johnny knew that even if he were not dating Annie, his family would have treated her with the same love and kindness. He was happy, though, that they *were* dating, and Annie already seemed to be a part of the Miller family.

He found that he could hold nothing back from her. Somehow, she compelled his honesty. It may have been the way she had told him about her own past that opened the way for him to voice his own dreams and doubts. There was no dancing around each other, as he and other girls had done.

The shortcut from the Kleins' house to school led through a red and orange autumn woods. On crisp fall afternoons, the low sun touched dried leaves and underbrush and filled the woods with a golden glow. Of course, Annie knew that if she took the shortcut, Johnny might possibly be up in that deer stand when she walked by; and Johnny knew that she knew. She always accepted his earnest invitations to climb up and join him.

He showed her his sketches and maps, his way of intimately

knowing the land he farmed. They discussed the books he read and what he tuned into on the radio dial. The beer bottles fascinated her; she wondered what was on all those small scraps of paper he had slipped down the narrow necks. Letters to God, Johnny had told her. He admitted with a grin that one paper held only two words: THANK YOU. He had written that note the day after her first supper with his family.

One afternoon, as the school day drew to a close, the little blue Camaro turned into the school driveway. Johnny caught sight of Annie through a window, and smiled when the children streamed out of the schoolhouse a few minutes earlier than usual. Solemnly reminding Annie of her promise to go riding with him again when he could legally drive, Johnny waved his license like a magic wand and whisked the schoolteacher off for a tour of the community.

She expressed her admiration of the little Camaro as they drove a country road close to Pine Creek that she had not traveled before. Blazing trees lined the route, and they drove through showers of fluttering leaves.

"A car certainly can take us places that Joyce can't," Johnny agreed. He looked across the console at her. "But riding in a car … well, you're so far away."

She blushed.

"And I kind of like moseying along behind a horse's rump with my feet propped up on the buggy dashboard. Can't prop up my feet in this car. There's something pleasing about holding those reins in the palm, controlling that one horsepower. I miss that, too. But buggy or car, either way is good if you're with me, Annie." He paused for only a minute, then said firmly, "Yes, I think we'll take the buggy next time."

The best days were Sundays, when long afternoons and no farm work made it possible to spend more time together. Sometimes they took a picnic basket, even though they also wore coats and gloves. When the first light snowflakes of the season fell on a November day, they were standing on top of Strawberry Hill in the small cemetery and Johnny was telling Annie stories about his grandparents.

Yes, the entire valley knew there was more than a little romance between Johnny Miller and the new school teacher.

Thanksgiving at the big Miller house was a delightful event for Annie. For the first time, she met the entire family. No one looked at her with doubtful eyes; she felt no clouds of the past hanging over that enjoyable day.

Naomi had been the first girl in the community to offer her friendship; and in those lonely early weeks, she had stayed by Annie's side at church and social functions. Annie talked more freely to Naomi than she had ever talked with her own sisters. The two had decided they would be friends always, no matter what happened between Johnny and Annie.

***

"Annie! We're in Indiana! Only forty-eight more states, and I will have seen the entire country."

Johnny liked the sound of Annie's laugh.

When they had made plans to go to Indiana for Christmas, he had told her of his boyhood dream to go cowboying. Now, he was finally headed west, even if it was only one state westward. He would leave Ohio for the first time in his life. Annie laughed at his excitement as they planned, and she laughed again at the enthusiasm bursting from him as they passed a big sign saying WELCOME TO INDIANA.

"It's Christmas Eve, Johnny," she said softly. "And here you are, traveling *west*. Your dream is just beginning." She paused. "Is this a dream? Is this dream too good to last? It's not going to end, is it, Johnny?"

He took his eyes from the road to glance over at her.

"No. Definitely no."

She sat silently for a few minutes. Johnny had become accustomed to her habit of thinking things through before she let any of her words slip out of her mouth. But he wondered what thoughts seemed to be troubling her.

"It's that … well, you're about to meet my family. I'm the prodigal daughter coming home. I have no idea what kind of reception we'll get."

Letters had gone between Ohio and Indiana for the last few months. Annie had written mostly of the small details of school days and the friendship of the Millers. She had mentioned that she had met someone who would be coming home with her at Christmas. There was never a return letter from either of her sisters, and she never expected her father to take pen in hand. So it was always her mother's voice that spoke when she opened the letters with Indiana postmarks.

"Didn't your mother write that I'd be welcome?"

"Yes, but I'm never sure how to read her statements. So often there's an underlying motive or accusation behind her words. I don't know if I can trust simple words on paper. I imagine the look she might have on her face that I know so well. And I imagine that even as she writes kind words, she is really thinking, *Oh, no, not another man. Has she not had enough problems with men already? But we'll be good Christians and be hospitable.* I'm sorry to be so suspicious of her intentions, but … Or maybe she's already fashioning her statement to her friends about Annie's new Ohio boyfriend. I don't know what she's told people about my reasons for being in Ohio.

"And you'll see Christine. I'll see Christine. I don't know what that will be like. I don't know what to expect. I don't know if I can bear to see her."

Johnny reached over and squeezed her hand. She clung to his.

27

They arrived in the twilight of Christmas Eve, and Annie's parents greeted them warmly. Only the four of them were in the house that night. Johnny talked with Mr. Yoder while Annie helped her mother prepare food for the Christmas meal. No hints of reproof or chastisement hung in the air; instead, the Christmas spirit seemed to have filled and transformed the house. Annie was grateful for Johnny's easy way of making everyone feel comfortable; her parents seemed to enjoy his presence.

Annie's sisters and their husbands—and Christine—would arrive at noon the next day. In the morning, Johnny noticed Annie's apprehension and saw it growing as she watched the clock and listened for the crunch of buggy wheels on the gravel driveway. He tried to send her many smiles and looks of understanding and encouragement, but he could feel the tension rising.

Then everyone arrived at once. Annie's younger sister, with her new husband came in first, then Henry and Betty with Christine. The two-year-old who bounced through the door took Johnny by surprise. For some reason, he was expecting a baby. This little girl was no longer a baby. Johnny's eyes went immediately to Annie's face, and he saw the rush of joy, then a shadow of fear.

Annie managed to introduce Johnny to everyone. Scooping up Christine, she gave the little one a hug.

"And this is Christine," she said to Johnny.

"I'm glad to meet you, Christine," Johnny somberly shook the child's small hand.

The little girl pulled back her hand and turned her face away from him. She wiggled out of Annie's arms, saying, "I want my Mommy." Annie put her down.

Was Annie going to burst into tears right then and there?

"Everything's ready!" called Mrs. Yoder, and while everyone turned to the table, Johnny leaned over and whispered to Annie, "She's beautiful. You sure did your part well."

Annie's smile was frozen in place.

***

They started home the day after Christmas. Johnny thought the visit had gone well. But something had happened to Annie, and the house had been full of people and he had had no chance to find out what was wrong.

As they drove out of Indiana, Annie was unusually quiet. Knowing he could not push her, Johnny instead told her about a conversation between him and her dad.

"I've never known anything but farm life, but your life here was different. You lived in the country, but not on a farm. And your father has always worked away."

"Yes, he grew up on a farm, but he's worked at that factory since he was sixteen. One of my uncles took over the family farm."

"I asked him if he missed farm life. He said he missed the closeness of family life on a farm. Eating meals together three times a day. Everyone in the barn at milking and chore time. I never really gave much thought to those things, but I'm glad we do have that life at home. I never thought I'd say this, Annie, but I miss my cows, the horses, Biff, the chickens. And especially

Naomi and my mom and dad. It feels as though we've been too far from our valley for too long. It will be good to be home. I'll be happy to be getting up tomorrow and going to the barn to milk."

"I've only been gone a few months, but it already felt strange for me to be back there," said Annie. "My parents do have a different life than yours."

"They have more freedom in their schedules," said Johnny.

Annie smiled.

"Yes, those cows of yours always have to be milked; chores always must be done. Dad works at the factory, then goes home and has his evenings free. We weren't chained to milking and planting and harvesting, so our family even took vacations when we girls were little." She was remembering the earlier years, before her teenage rebellion.

"Our family has never taken a vacation. Nothing more than a day trip to the zoo," Johnny said.

"There are three large factories in town. Jobs are always available and pay well. Many of our Amish work in the factories."

Johnny was thoughtful. "Our community is not yet at the point of your parents' town. But I can understand what your dad is saying—there aren't enough farms for the next generation of Amish boys. Factories do provide another way to support a family. But your father expressed his fear that families may be paying a price for the loss of the farming life."

"Do you think that time's coming soon to your valley, Johnny? And how about you? You're farming now; the home farm is yours if you want it. Do you want it?"

Whatever had been burdening Annie's mind seemed to be pushed into the background. Now she was waiting intently for Johnny's answer.

"I guess I'll have to make that decision soon. Leaving the farm does seem to have some desirable freedoms. But what would we be giving up in return?"

Annie caught the *we*. She knew that much would depend on

her. On whether or not she would marry him. Johnny had not yet said it, straight out. He had said enough, though, to assure Annie that he could easily give up his car and make a life as an Amish farmer if she would share that life with him.

They had talked about his restlessness one day while they sat on the deck of the deer stand. Johnny had also made it clear that as long as Annie was at the other end of Strawberry Lane, he would go nowhere.

Without Annie, though, he would be adrift. Wandering. His family was doing well with their farm and furniture shop and sawmill; everyone was waiting for the youngest son to step into his place. But Johnny still needed to find Home.

During that conversation on the deck that day, Annie could hold her tongue no longer.

"Johnny, you're still looking for something. I don't think it's life outside the Amish community or a ranch out west or a job that would give you more freedom. I don't even think it's me."

He had looked at her, startled, and opened his mouth, but she held up her hand and continued.

"You want to keep one foot in the world and the other foot at the entrance to Heaven. But you know you can't serve two masters. You want God's best for your life, but you can't quite give up your worldly interests. The day will come when you must choose one or the other pathway."

She knew Johnny's thoughts always came back to this … he would have to make a choice.

"I still wonder if I made the right choice," Annie voiced her own question now as they drove back toward home. "About Christine. Did I do the right thing? I haven't been able to think about much else these last two days."

Johnny wanted to reassure her, but he had seen the disquiet that had settled over Annie on Christmas Day, and he did not know how to comfort her.

"Betty's pregnant. I saw it as soon as she took off her coat yesterday morning. While we were washing dishes afterward, I asked her about it, because no one had told me anything.

"She was so evasive, Johnny. She shrugged and said they were waiting to tell me until they were … sure. But even though she's had two miscarriages before and they thought she couldn't have children, I knew she was only looking for an excuse to postpone telling me. Do you suppose she's afraid I will want to raise Christine myself now? If they have their own child, will that affect how she treats my little girl? Will this change everything?"

28

Johnny and his father were busy with spring plowing and planting, but the young man's mind wasn't always on the line he was plowing. In the afternoon, especially, as he caught sight of school children walking toward home, his mind wandered to the path through the woods, and he wondered if Annie had stopped at the tree house.

When he could be there, he always invited her up to his sanctuary. But for weeks he and John had been in the fields all day, and he had little time for the deer stand or even to see Annie. Their hours together usually came on Sunday, and as the snow melted and days grew warmer, both realized that decisions lay ahead for her. The school year was almost ended. She had enjoyed teaching more than she had expected. Would she agree to teach another year? The school board had asked and requested an answer by mid-July. Would it be wise to return to Indiana for the summer to work at mending relationships? The turmoil and pain inflamed by the Christmas visit had quieted somewhat, and Annie was not sure it was yet time to make another visit.

Of course, Johnny was hoping that her dreams for the future included him. He was not only hoping, he was counting on it. He felt confident that this was the case, but he had not yet voiced how strongly he felt about this. Could Annie be a farmer's wife? She had never milked a cow. He had tried to teach her once, and Naomi was still giggling about that scene. But Johnny was convinced that he and Annie could do anything together. She would learn. He would help her.

As he plowed and planted, he thought about these fields being his and Annie's. Perhaps she wouldn't have to learn to milk. She was already helping occasionally with other chores. She would be working in the garden, and the rows of canned goods in the fruit cellar would be a product of her hard work. Her meals would cover the table when Johnny came in from the fields. They would have a happy life. Mandy and John would move to the small house, and the big house would fill with Johnny and Annie Miller's little ones.

***

Annie came to supper one evening during the last week of school. Mandy had invited her. Johnny had been busy in the fields, and Annie was occupied with closing out the year with her students. They had not seen each other for a few days, but both were unusually quiet during the meal. The family's conversation flowed around them. Annie had little to say, and her eyes often seemed to be looking at a scene that no one else could see. Johnny was tired; he and John worked every day until dark and then were up early in the mornings.

After supper, Johnny walked Annie to the end of Strawberry Lane; he would have to be back in the field again until darkness stopped the work.

"Johnny, Mervin and Lizzie are leaving Friday night for a family reunion in Indiana. I need to go with them."

"All right. When will you be back?"

She took a deep breath.

"I ... don't know."

The uncertainty in her voice told him there was much more,

but that was all his tired mind could comprehend. He could not even guess at the unspoken heaviness behind it. He waited for her to go on. She took a deep sigh and spoke reluctantly.

"I had a letter this week. From Joe. He wants me to come back to Indiana and marry him, and we'll raise Christine together ..."

Johnny stopped walking and looked at her, shaking his head.

"What? Why would he think you would agree to that?"

"He tried to apologize. He wants us to start over. We do have a child together."

Johnny winced.

"You would think of resuming a relationship with *him*? Why? How could you trust him?" Unbelievable. How could this happen?

Annie looked miserable, and, now that his numb mind had awakened and he looked at her more closely, he realized her eyes were very tired and she was paler than he had ever seen her. He could not understand why she would even consider a proposal from someone who had treated her so despicably.

"Maybe that's why I have to go. Because I can't trust him. I have to find out what's going on. For one thing, he knows Christine's name. How does he know that? Does he know where she is? Would he try to claim her and take her from Henry and Betty? How much more does he know about us?

"I told him I hated him and never wanted to see him again. But he's found me. How did he know where I am?

"Or what if ... what if this is all good news? What if God saved him and changed him, like He changed me? What if God is giving me another chance to make things right? Maybe Joe has settled down and wants to be a good husband and father. What if this is a miracle to heal past hurts?"

"You mean ... you would actually do this?" He shook his head. How could she? Johnny had been sure that Annie was in love with him, that she could never feel an ounce of affection for that worm of a man in Indiana.

"As much as I dislike Joe, I have to talk with him. Only a

miracle could have changed him. But if he has changed …"

She looked away from him, toward the sun slipping down toward the white fence around the cemetery on Strawberry Hill.

"Maybe there's a way to right the wrongs I've done."

The heaviness was now sitting on his chest.

"Sounds to me like you're planning to do several wrongs that will undo all the good choices you've made." It was the harshest thing he had ever said to her. His voice was getting louder.

"This is something I must do, Johnny. You have been the best thing that's ever happened to me, but you know I want more than anything to understand what God would have me do. I want to put my spirit at rest once and for all on the question of Christine and Joe. Please, please help me do that by trusting me to make the right decision. Please, Johnny."

He was silent for a long moment. Her blue eyes were on his face, trying to look into his heart and soul.

"And you don't know when—or if—you'll be back?" he asked, more quietly.

"The church leaders want to know if I'll teach again next year. I promised them an answer by the middle of July."

"But that's almost two months. You really plan to stay in Indiana that long?"

"I think I need the time, Johnny."

29

Rain poured down all of the following week. In the fields, work was impossible, and the men suspended their planting. Johnny had too much time to imagine what might be going on in Indiana.

He wondered at times if he remembered their last conversation correctly. He had been exhausted that evening when Annie had told him about Joe's letter and her plans to leave. And he had been stunned and hurt. He replayed her words, but they seemed to be set in a fog, where lines are blurred and things appear to be something they are not. Had she really gone back to try to mend a relationship with Joe? Is that what she had said?

Trudging up to the deer stand almost every evening, he carried at least two cold bottles with him on every trip. While Annie had been there, the habit had tapered off, lessened, and almost died. Now he was back on a steady Stroh's diet.

A week dragged by. Only one week, and she did not plan to come home for at least six more weeks. *If* she came home. *Home.* He had thought this valley was becoming home for Annie, but now he wondered. Where was home for Annie? Had he been wrong about everything? As he finished his chores one evening, he decided it was a two-bottle night.

He was again writing letters to God and stuffing them into the empty bottles. Every night, he poured out his heart and soul to the Creator, lamenting Annie's decision to leave.

Dear God,

   I was so sure you had sent Annie to me, why take her away? Why send her back to Joe? Why would he be more suited to her than I am? I love her and Joe does not.

At last he admitted what he had known for a while but had never said: He did love Annie. And that, he thought, was what made him different from Joe. He loved Annie and she deserved God's best for her life. The best was surely not Joe.

Johnny recognized one truth: In God's eyes, he was no different from Joe. They were both sinners. Johnny saw a picture of himself that disgusted him: he was once again feeling sorry for himself and trying to ease pain with alcohol. Was this the only way he could face difficult times? And in reality he wasn't facing the problem, he was only trying to run away from a hard part of life.

The calmness and peace on Annie's face when they had first met had been a powerful attraction; only later had he learned about the troubled times she had endured. Peace in spite of difficulty, she had said, comes from having a relationship with Jesus.

Now Annie was gone. He could no longer bear the loneliness and despair. Falling to his knees on the worn wood floor, he begged God's mercy and forgiveness. And help. He needed help.

"God, I can't bear this on my own. I want the peace You gave Annie. Whatever it takes, I want that. Tonight I give up my life to you. Do with it whatever You think is best. Make of me whatever You will. I don't even know what the proper words or phrases are. The only thing I know for sure is that I give up. I've tried to do this myself, and it's not working. I need Your help."

Past transgressions loomed up in the hallways of his memory, and he saw how willful and stubborn he had been, how he had thought he had no need or room for God and had ignored Him.

Over and over, he pleaded, *I'm sorry, forgive me.*

As Johnny asked forgiveness, a peace spread through his body and spirit. The certainty that he was loved flowed over him like refreshing water. He could not explain what was happening, but he knew the old Johnny was gone and he was free ... and clean.

He picked up the pencil and notepad and scribbled, *God, did You really plan for Annie to leave me so I had to turn to You for help and hope?*

For the first time in a week, rays from the setting sun reached through the rain-streaked window. The clouds had broken, and prisms of light danced on the wall. Twilight, gloaming time to poets, signaled the ending of another day. As light splashed and splattered about him, Johnny reveled in the thought of new light in his life. He mused that the setting sun also represented the ending of the life he had lived. A new day and a new life was coming.

For one thing, no more bottles would be added to that amber pile along the fence row. He would clean up that mess somehow.

He remained in the tree stand long after the sun fell behind the headstones in the cemetery. Scrawling another message, he hung the paper on the same nail that held the binoculars.

Tonight my prayers were answered.
Jesus gave me a new life.
I am a new creature.
And I am going to follow Jesus.

He tried to recall the exact words Annie had used. *The old things are gone and I am going to follow Jesus.* That wasn't quite how Annie had described it, but it was close.

The moon glowed softly from behind a lingering cloud and rimmed its curves with shimmering silver as he climbed down from his thinking stand. He was determined about one thing: this would no longer be a drinking stand.

***

Johnny could see the unspoken questions besetting his family the next day. He had spent the last week sinking ever deeper into despondency, and now he went about his business as if he hadn't a care in the world. He hummed, he whistled, and occasionally he even broke into a tune. He knew his family well and understood that all day their looks and quick, quiet conversations were asking, "What happened to Johnny?"

He let them wonder until supper.

John stood, ready to say the prayer for their evening meal.

"Dad, is it okay if I lead the prayer tonight?"

This had never happened before. Throughout four generations of Millers, no one except the head of the family had prayed at the supper table.

"Ah … yes, I suppose so," said John. Naomi and Mandy exchanged looks as Johnny stood, cleared his throat, and began.

"God, thank you for my family, for a mom and dad who care for me and love me, and for a great sister, too. Thank you, Jesus, for coming into my heart last night and giving me such peace."

A sniffle came from Mandy's chair.

"God, give Annie peace too as she contemplates her future. You know I love her and want her back, but I also want what is best for her; and You alone know what that is."

He blessed the food and sat down. A tear glistened on Mandy's cheek. Naomi was sniffling now, too. No one moved.

Finally, Mandy broke the silence.

"You Miller men sure know how to make good decisions in hard times."

John was doing excessive beard tugging, an action usually reserved for emotional times like singing "Amazing Grace." That said far more to Johnny than any words his father might have uttered right then.

"Johnny, we've been so worried about you," said Naomi. He had told them why Annie had gone back to Indiana.

He had never before felt the calmness that now enabled him to say, "Annie will make the right decision. I have complete peace about that."

***

That calmness and peace was tested in the coming weeks. Johnny had agreed to give Annie the time she needed to clear her mind. He would wait until he received word from her about her decision. Not a day went by, though, that he didn't ask his father if the school officials had heard anything from Annie about her intentions. She had promised to notify them by the middle of July; Johnny knew he needed to be patient.

He started a new ritual, making daily trips to his thinking stand without the bottles of relaxation. The desire for alcohol had completely left him. His prayers had brought a peace that could not be delivered by a bottle. He would pause at the pile by the fence and take one unbroken bottle with him on high. Notes of praise and thankfulness, encouraging Scripture, and prayers for wisdom for Annie were stuffed into an ever-increasing array of bottles that had been trash. Questions still filled some of the letters, but he was learning to search for answers in the small Bible that had joined the other books on the shelf.

He hoped Annie would return soon. If not, he would have to build more shelves to hold the growing library of letters in bottles up in the tree stand.

But what if she did not return? What if there would be only a letter, saying she was staying in Indiana?

30

Annie wondered what she was doing back in Indiana. She had left the most considerate man she had ever known and a family who cared about her. She had left a job she loved. She was in Indiana, but it seemed everything she wanted or needed was back in Ohio. Why? Because a man who had hurt her terribly had asked her to give him a second chance?

Joe's letter had tumbled her into a maelstrom of emotions and questions. She had wanted to wipe Joe from all her memories, to put that old life behind her completely. Yet … if he had changed … what was the right thing to do? What was the best for Christine? When she had told Johnny that she was going back to Indiana, she had been so confused that she was afraid she had bungled the conversation completely. She tried replaying it over and over, but she could not remember what she had told him. What was he thinking now?

The one thing she did see clearly—now that she was in Indiana—was that everything she wanted was in Ohio. Everything, except Christine.

Betty had given birth to a little girl, and Christine was chattering to everyone about her new little sister. Wouldn't it be a terrible thing to take the little girl from the only home and family she had ever known? Or would it be setting things right again?

Dear Lord, why must this be so complicated? I have already hurt so many people. Can you give me any simple answers? Are there any answers?

Betty and Annie never discussed the reasons for Annie's return to Indiana, and Annie did not even know if her sister was aware of Joe's proposal. The two women carefully kept their conversations light and trivial—small talk about how the garden was doing and who had been to visit the new baby. Annie noticed that although mothers *always* talk about their children, Christine was never the subject of their conversation, even when the little girl was bouncing nearby. It was as though Betty never wanted to call attention to her older child, as though she didn't want Annie to think too much about Christine.

Annie sent Joe a note telling him she needed some time before they met. Several letters from him came to the Yoders' house, urging Annie to remember the good times and insisting that he needed an answer soon.

For three years, Joe had never tried to contact Annie or see Christine. Now, he suddenly had decided he wanted to marry her. His parents had promised to give him the family farm, and he and his wife could build a life there. But what was he up to?

Annie tried to discuss the situation with her mother and father. Mrs. Yoder expressed emphatic approval of the plan Joe's parents had set in place; Annie's father, however, said little.

One evening while preparing to leave for town, he asked Annie to join him. She tried to remember the last time that only she and her dad had ridden together in the buggy. It must have been when she was a young child, without a care in the world. She couldn't remember spending any time with her father since she had entered her teenage years.

"Annie, I invited you along to give you some fatherly advice," her dad began before they were very far down the road. He had been shifting the reins and moving his feet and adjusting his hat.

"It's hard being a dad sometimes, and I admit I have not always been there when you needed your father."

Annie felt tears spring up. Her father's eyes were focused on some point between the horse's ears.

"This may seem wrong, but I must contradict your mother in this matter about Joe. She wants things to be right with you and Joe and Christine. But in reality, what she really wants is for things to look good to other folks. I'm afraid sometimes we in our community are more worried about what other folks think of our choices than what God thinks.

"I realize you have a good relationship with God, but right now your reasoning ability has been compromised. I do not believe God would want you to be in a relationship with Joe."

"I thought … maybe he had changed."

"Unfortunately, Joe was bad news when you met him years ago; and no, nothing much has changed. Sadly, his folks have coddled him and covered for him his entire life. He's recently been in jail for stealing. His parents blame the boys he runs around with and refuse to see that their son has gone wrong."

"Sounds like the same old Joe," Annie said. "I wonder why he claims to want me now?"

"Here is what I've heard. At eighteen, all men need to register with the draft board. I'm sure your Johnny back in Ohio did that. A young man can file as a conscientious objector if he is Amish and the bishops sign a paper attesting to that. That means he won't have to perform military service. Since Joe was too irresponsible to take care of this, he is now in trouble. The draft board held a lottery to determine who would be drafted, and Joe's number was drawn. Uncle Sam ordered him to join the armed services and he's faced with the possibility of going to Vietnam."

"That certainly explains why he wants me to make a quick decision. How does he think he can avoid service now, if he didn't register as a conscientious objector in the first place?"

"Apparently there are people who help boys evade the draft.

His parents are offering him the entire farm if he gets married and joins the Amish Church. So I'm guessing he's going to try to prove that he has authentic religious objections. And if you marry him, he'll have a wife and the picture will be complete."

"So I'm worth the price of a farm," Annie said, and she thought, *Dad did not say "He'll have a wife and child."*

"Joe has no intention of remaining Amish," said her father. And can you imagine him farming? I doubt he even knows how to throw hay to the horses. He'll stay for several years and then sell the property and leave the Amish, disregarding your wishes completely. It wouldn't surprise me if he also leaves you or if he sells that rich farmland for commercial development. Land is getting scarce; people and businesses are paying a lot of money for acreage to build on."

"But I thought this was what you and Mom wanted."

"Mom thinks this is what she wants. She thinks if you're married and settled on that big farm, people will see a perfect picture of your life put back together. I'm sorry to say this, but she is thinking only of how our family will look to others, not of what is the best for you."

Her father paused a moment, taking a deep breath.

"Annie, I've been doing a lot of thinking and praying lately. When you accepted Christ and changed your life, I admit I was skeptical. However, your decision influenced me to really get serious about my relationship with God, and I started studying the Scriptures myself.

"Jesus said a good tree won't bear bad fruit and a bad tree cannot grow good fruit. In Galatians, Paul writes about the fruit of a spirit-filled man or woman. I see that fruit in your life now. Galatians also speaks of the results of a sinful nature. From what I have seen of Joe's life, he exhibits many of those characteristics. These are two conflicting spirits. I don't know your friend Johnny too well, but it seems he might offer fruit more acceptable than Joe. The same kind of fruit you want to bear in your life."

"Yes, they are two completely different trees." The thought of trees and fruit reminded Annie of Johnny's tree house. She doubted that Joe had ever taken on a project that showed such initiative and diligence. Now that she thought about it, she could not remember ever seeing him work. But she'd heard him lie to get his own way.

"Oh, Dad, this explains so much. I've been so confused. If Joe has not changed, my answer is clear. My future is not here with him or, I'm sad to say, not even with Christine. Thank you so much for your advice; there were so many days I felt all alone."

Her father put an arm across her shoulders and gave her a gentle hug.

"I do love you and admire you so much," he said in a low voice. Annie's dad had never hugged her or said those words before. "It's hard being a father at times. But now I see how important it is that our children know how much they mean to us."

"I hope you and Mom will be happy about my decision."

"The decision that will make me the happiest is the one that will make you the happiest," said her father.

"How about Mom? Won't she be disappointed?"

"Let me take care of that. I have too often stood back and not asserted myself as I should have. That is not your mother's fault; it is mine. Someone had to be a leader and too often by doing or saying nothing, I abdicated my responsibilities as a husband. I'm hoping your mother will like the new husband I want to be. And that, too, is because of you, Annie. My search of the Scriptures changed how I view my responsibilities in our home."

Annie was astonished. This was a new man indeed.

"When were you planning to meet with Joe?"

"We're meeting tomorrow evening at six, by the fountain in the park." The fountain had been a meeting place for her former friends, in what seemed like another lifetime.

"I'll take you there, and I'll wait nearby. I do not trust Joe at all. Do not get into his car, regardless of how persuasive he is."

"Don't worry, Dad. I trust him even less than you do."

31

Nothing had changed in the park. Obviously still a local hangout, the scene brought back memories of years she had wasted. Teenaged Amish girls in hip-hugging jeans or mini-skirts let their hair hang loose down their backs and tried to look "hip" and "cool" as they experimented with the English lifestyle. Annie remembered it all too well.

She chose a bench at the edge of the pavilion and sat down to wait. A motorcycle roared down the paved path. Motorized vehicles were prohibited in this area. The driver, a long-haired hippie, obviously didn't care about rules. A peace sign dangled from the gold chain around his neck.

"Hey, Annie. It's been a while. You sure look great, even wrapped up in those Amish duds."

"Joe, is that you under all that hair? I thought jailbirds had to cut their hair."

"How do you know about that?" He shrugged. "It wasn't my fault anyhow."

"Yes, I'm sure you were completely innocent."

Joe grinned wryly. He looked much older than she remembered. And hardened. Whatever living he'd been doing had left its mark on him.

"It wasn't so bad in jail. We had television and decent food. I made good friends in there, too. Some Vietnam vets in on drug charges had interesting stories to tell.

He sat down beside her, his eyes meeting hers. Long ago, that look in his eyes had always melted her resistance. She pulled her arms closer to her body, and clasped her hands firmly in her lap.

"We did have good times, Annie. Remember? So what do you think about us getting Christine back and being Amish farmers? We could be a happy Amish family."

"Are you really serious about that or are you only trying to avoid Vietnam? I hear Uncle Sam is breathing down your neck."

She saw that she had taken him by surprise and jarred his usual arrogance. He recovered quickly, though.

"Well, I didn't register as a conscientious objector when I was supposed to. Mom must have thrown away my paperwork before I ever saw it."

"Oh, so that wasn't your fault either?" Surely he heard the contempt in her voice. "Why me, Joe? I know you want to get married and join the Amish just to avoid military service, but why come after me? Why not any other Amish girl you might manage to charm into marrying you?"

"Well, think about it, Annie. Most girls my age are already married; and besides, starting over with someone else would take some time. You and I have a history; we even have a child. So, in some ways, I already have a family, even though there's no legal paperwork yet to prove it."

She felt a stab of panic. Even if she refused him, would he still attempt to use Christine to accomplish his purpose? The family farm, the Amish church, and even a little child—all would be his pawns to avoid the consequences of his own irresponsibility and laziness. Was there any way to stop his plan?

"Christine has a good home. She's well-cared for and happy where she is now. It would be cruel to move her." She heard her own voice give an answer she had prayed for.

Joe shrugged. "I really don't care whether we have her or not. If you marry me and I'm a farmer and belong to the Amish church, we don't really need her. Just thought it would add the final touch. Come on, Annie, let's give it a chance."

Her panic turned to loathing.

"My answer is no. No! Not now, not ever! One thousand times no and then an endless No after that. I'm not going to be part of your plan, and neither is Christine. Leave us both alone." She jumped up.

Joe's jaw clenched and his fist punched the back of the bench.

"Why not tell me no to begin with? A letter would have done the trick. Why the insults now?"

"I needed to see you face to face. I thought maybe you'd changed, and even if you hadn't, I needed to prove to myself that I harbored no ill will toward you. Maybe I've pushed up against the boundaries on that, but I will let the past go, Joe. I must. Today has finally convinced me of that.

"Here is a truth, Joe. It's simple: I want to produce good fruit in my life. You are a bad tree; you produce bad fruit. No farm is big enough or rich enough to buy us a future together."

She turned to leave and noticed the peace signs on Joe's motorcycle. She knew there was yet one more thing she must say.

"Joe, I can't and won't help you with your predicament. But there is an answer to your problems. It's not in those peace signs you wear so proudly. Instead of a broken cross, the answer is in a Man who was broken on the cross. I know you've heard this all your life, Joe, but believe me, He's real. He does amazing things. Jesus died for you, whether you care about that or not. And you might laugh at that now, but someday you will meet Him to give an account of your life. And your mom and dad won't be able to protect you then."

The Spirit astonished her once again. Hatred and fear and loathing were replaced by compassion for this man. Old feelings were gone, new mercy filled her.

"Jesus loves you, Joe. It's not too late. There is still hope. God is waiting and willing and able to change your life."

He rolled his eyes, shook his head, and turned away.

***

"How did it go?" asked her father.

"Quite well. Actually, it was amazing. I might have given in to a bit of sarcasm, but I almost pity him. Have you seen him lately, Dad? He looks like a hippie; if he does join the church, a little trim, and his hair will be quite acceptable." She stopped joking. "Changing his heart will be more difficult. Only God can do that."

"So, ready to go home?"

She grinned at her dad and felt a giddy freedom.

"Define home."

32

Annie went to the barn with her father and waited as he unhitched the horse, unwilling to break the special time the two had shared that evening. She knew her mother would pounce on her as soon as they went back to the house.

"How did it go?" Her mother opened the door before Annie was up the steps.

"Absolutely wonderful," Annie said, with her biggest smile. "I need to write a letter. Dad can give you the details."

Mrs. Yoder's eyes were wide; father and daughter were returning in great spirits. Annie could imagine her mother's thoughts. Everything must have worked out. Annie was finally getting married, all would be well. Her mother was probably already preparing the story she would tell her friends about her prodigal daughter's upcoming marriage and the big farm Annie's husband would own.

Mr. Yoder came through the door, cleared his throat, and said firmly, "Mom, we need to talk. Join me on the porch swing."

An hour later, Annie carried the precious letter to the gray galvanized mailbox at the end of the drive.

Her dad grinned and winked at her as she came back up the porch steps. He was holding his wife's hand; and while his was the look of a man at peace with the world, Mrs. Yoder's face still showed signs of agitation. Annie was certain her father had the situation well in hand, though.

She tumbled into bed feeling unburdened and free and fell asleep listening to the creaks of the porch swing.

***

"Hey, Johnny, there's a letter here for you from someone in Indiana." Naomi waved the envelope in the air.

The men had come into the house for lunch, after working all morning in the barn. At the sight of the white square in Naomi's hand, Johnny's heart jumped and he forgot his hunger. He grabbed the envelope from his grinning sister.

"Open it up; see what she says," said Naomi.

"I'm not sure I want to know."

Annie had been gone over a month, and he had not heard a word from her. He really didn't want to read this letter in front of his family's curious eyes, but he could not wait. He turned his back to them and ripped open the envelope. It took only seconds to scan Annie's familiar handwriting.

Then his shoulders drooped, and in a dejected voice he said, "She's staying."

Behind him came a small *Oh!* from Mandy and a squeaked *What?* from Naomi.

He swung around and flung out his arms in celebration.

"Here! She's staying here with all of us!"

He was grinning at them, almost silly with happiness. Naomi glared at him, and Mandy said, "Johnny, enough of your pranks! That was almost more than we can take!"

He ignored them both and went back to reading the letter.

"She's coming home in a month, to get ready for school in the fall." He grinned. "Unless, she says, I want to come and get her sometime before then."

"If my math is correct," John said with a twinkle in his eye, "you could leave here around one o'clock and surprise Annie this evening. If there were only a few hours separating me from Mandy and I had the means to go see her, I wouldn't hesitate."

"Paul and I will help with the milking and chores," offered Naomi. "Although I shouldn't, after what you just did to us. I'll go over this afternoon and tell Paul. He'll gladly help."

"Perhaps you should ask him, rather than tell him."

"He'll do it, to spend time with me," said Naomi confidently. "Now go get Annie and bring her home."

As the miles rolled under the wheels of the Camaro that afternoon, Johnny knew he would soon be separated from his little blue companion. He would have no regrets. Other new adventures lay ahead. He also noticed that driving a road previously traveled did not hold the excitement of a new road. The unknown, waiting around the next corner, beckoned and intrigued him.

He was certain that his life was now going down a new road and a great adventure awaited beyond the next bend.

***

The startled look on Mrs. Yoder's face when she opened the door told Johnny that no one had expected to see him on the front porch that night. Annie's mom stammered a greeting.

"Johnny! I ... we didn't expect you quite this soon."

"I received Annie's letter today, and I've come to take her home with me. You do approve of that, don't you?" Johnny gave her his most sincere and winning smile as he stepped into the house. "I came immediately because I didn't want to take the chance that she would change her mind."

Mrs. Yoder surprised him with a mischievous grin.

"Oh, her mind is definitely made up."

Johnny heard a gasp from the living room, and then Annie ran through the doorway and into his arms.

"I missed you so much!" they both said at the same time.

Mrs. Yoder stood there, watching the reunion, but Johnny held his Annie tightly and whispered to her, "I have so much to tell you. Jesus is changing me, too."

"I already know," she said, her face glowing with her smile. "Naomi's been writing me. Come, let's sit on the porch and catch up on everything that's happened."

Annie's mother shuffled away to the living room.

The two sat on the porch swing long after Annie's parents had gone to bed. The weeks of separation, filled with frustration for Johnny and confusion for Annie, quickly faded away. No awkwardness kept them from telling each other everything that had happened; they talked as if there had never been that time of silence between them.

In his haste to arrive in Indiana, Johnny had not given thought to the drive home or to the fact that if he surprised Annie, she would not be prepared to leave immediately. After midnight, Annie finally ended the evening with practical suggestions.

"Let's go to church tomorrow with my parents; I'll only need an hour or so to gather my things; and then I'm ready to go home!"

Johnny did not tell her how good that sounded to him.

33

Annie's mom had given him a warm and friendly welcome, but the next morning she seemed nervous and uneasy.

"I think this may be awkward for Mom," Annie said to Johnny as they walked to church. Her parents would come in the buggy. "She told some of her friends that there was a possibility Joe and I would get back together. And you know how that goes; tell a few, and the whole community soon knows. Now here I am, coming to church with another handsome man. I'm sure Mom is trying to decide how to explain this twist in the plot."

No anger tinged Annie's voice. She seemed amused by her mother's predicament. Johnny sensed that she held a new attitude toward her mom, one of understanding and forgiveness.

By the end of the morning, though, he felt right at home with the folks he met. Several of them knew his father or had known his grandfather. One family was related to the husband of one of his older sisters. He put all thoughts of gossip about Joe and Annie out of his mind and behaved as a proper prospective son-in-law. Someday soon, he hoped to be exactly that.

Lunch at Annie's house was a pleasant time of fellowship. The atmosphere in the house had changed, and it was almost as if he were meeting Annie's parents for the first time. Annie helped her mother with the dishes, and Johnny asked Mr. Yoder about his shop at the back end of the property.

"I'd love to see your tools and shop. Our family has a furniture business, and I do some woodworking in my spare time."

Annie's father was eager to give Johnny a tour, but Johnny had more on his mind than woodworking.

While Annie went upstairs to pack and her mother still bustled about the kitchen, the two men walked back to the large, light-filled building that smelled of wood and stain. The shop was meticulously clean and the lineup of equipment impressive. But Johnny wasted no time in bringing up his true reason for leaving the house with Annie's father.

"Annie told me how much she appreciated your help in the Joe matter," he began.

"It was time to step up and be a dad. It sure felt great to know I did what was right," Mr. Yoder said.

Johnny forged ahead.

"I've given this a lot of thought while Annie was here. I love your daughter, and my desire is to propose to her by the end of the year. How would you and Annie's mom feel about that?"

Without hesitation, Annie's father grabbed Johnny's hand and shook it heartily. "Johnny, you absolutely have our blessing! And I pray God's blessing on both your lives."

"Please don't say anything to Annie; I'm planning an unusual surprise for her."

On the ride to Indiana, he had spent the hours formulating the when and how of a proposal. The idea that had popped into his head seemed bizarre at first; but the more he pondered and planned, the more he realized how appropriate it would be.

***

Sometimes Annie would think back to that night Johnny Miller stood on her parents' porch and said, "I've come to take

Annie home." She would never forget the thrill that went through her, the absolute knowing then that home was in Ohio with Johnny. That was the moment she knew for certain that she would marry this man the very minute he asked her.

The months flew by. More than once that summer, one of them would look at the other and grin and say, "This is the best time of my life." And with each passing day, life seemed to be getting better and better.

In all her growing up years, Annie had never paid much attention to the changing seasons. Summer was green and hot. Winter brought cold and snow. Fall was colorful, and spring was welcome. That's about all she had noticed. Now, suddenly, Johnny's fields became living things, changing shape and color and smell as summer melted away, crops ripened, and harvesting changed every scene. Even the pungent smell of freshly spread manure was now simply a part of the place she called home.

Johnny amazed her; or, rather, his knowledge amazed her. In spite of all his doubts about this way of life, he had learned much from his father and grandfather. He always sought to understand more, and investigated the whys and hows of everything from fertilizer to Scriptures. He had taken on more of the farm responsibilities and tended his land with a zest she had not seen before. One day in September, she realized that since she had returned, Johnny had not once talked about leaving the farm.

Whenever possible, Annie helped Mandy in her garden or the big kitchen. The younger woman wanted to absorb as much as she could about canning and cooking. Mandy was a good teacher, and she never looked at Annie reproachfully when she confessed she did not know how to do something. Mandy was the mother-teacher Annie had never had; but Annie admitted, to her shame, that when she could have been learning these things from her own mother, she was instead running around in her mini-skirts, absent from home most days and many nights.

Now she felt an urgency; she wanted to learn as much as she

could. Not only did Mandy's home run smoothly, this woman gave her family steady, safe shelter and was an anchor for her children, grandchildren, and husband. How Annie admired her and hoped to learn much more than cooking from Mandy.

Johnny gave Annie the keys to his kingdom. He generously offered her his hideaway up in the oak tree, knowing that she loved sitting there on the deck and watching the valley below. At first, she hesitated to visit the tree house without Johnny. The stand was his retreat, and she felt like an intruder. Then she saw it pleased him to share it with her; he was happy knowing that she enjoyed what he had created. So she began to visit often, even when he was busy in the fields.

She marveled at the rows of amber glass bottles, many more bottles than that first day Johnny had taken her to the deer stand. The trash pile along the fence row had dwindled, but the notes held in glass had multiplied. What messages did those scraps of paper hold? What might all those notes to God tell her about this man she had fallen in love with? Would Johnny someday break open the bottles and let her read his story, contained in those letters?

Annie always breathed a prayerful "thank you" when she read the sign he had posted on the wall that night he had decided to follow Christ. Jesus was changing Johnny, as surely as the striped caterpillars she had brought into the tree house transformed into beautiful Monarch butterflies. The butterfly miracle fascinated her; but, even more, it kindled thankfulness in her. Every time one of those beautiful creatures emerged, she remembered that she, too, had been a worm; now God was changing her into something much more beautiful.

Following Johnny's example, she sometimes wrote notes to God while she sat on the tree house deck. Many times she recorded simple little stories about valley life; sometimes her page held more serious reflections about the great miracle of her changed life. She filled two notebooks that summer as her thoughts and thankfulness sprang out onto the paper.

Back in the schoolroom in September, she found she had really missed the children. The uncertainty of her first year was gone; she looked forward to the coming school year and made many plans for new ways to help energetic young minds learn.

Always, in the back of her mind, she knew this would be her last year of teaching. Johnny would propose. They would join that long line of Millers who had been happy in this valley. She could finally call Mandy "Mom." She and Johnny would live on this farm for all of their lives, together forever. And every day, life would continue to grow sweeter and sweeter.

Johnny would propose. He had not, yet. But she knew he would. She didn't know when or how. Knowing Johnny, though, she was sure he would spring some surprise and propose as only Johnny Miller could propose.

34

Living with a nosy sister and a mom who knew everything going on in her house, Johnny found it difficult to keep any secrets or conceal any planned surprise. Everyone expected that he and Annie would soon be engaged, but he was determined no one would know about the proposal before Annie herself heard it.

Mandy caught him bringing home a set of paints and small brushes. He tried to sound convincing when he explained that he thought he might try his hand at painting. It wasn't a total untruth. Mandy never asked how the painting experiments were going, but he was certain she was suspicious of his nonchalant answer.

Young and old alike looked forward to Christmas Eve at the Miller house. Popcorn was strung in long chains and the kitchen decorated with the garlands of white puffs. Christmas trees were part of the world's tradition, not the Millers', but they tramped through the woods and cut fragrant boughs that Mandy used in winter arrangements. The house smelled of pine and of Mandy's pies and cookies.

After the evening meal, they would listen for the arrival of the carolers. Young folks from the surrounding area hitched up a team, threw hay bales on a wagon for comfortable seating, and sang their way around the countryside, spreading tidings of hope and joy.

Johnny seemed distracted and restless. In the lull between supper and carolers, he could wait no longer.

"Annie and I are going to take a walk up to the stand," he said before the dishes were even put away. "Then I'll walk her home, but I don't expect to be home late." Annie's face showed her surprise. He could not look at her.

A moon almost full rose above the fields dusted with snow. Johnny carried a lantern, but it wasn't necessary for the walk up the hill. In the dark woods, he might light it. Now, though, the bright moon showed the path through the field, the soft light reflecting off the new snow. Tracks in the snow stitched a web across the hillside; apparently the rabbits were also out celebrating this special night.

"Johnny, please, slow down!" He had been marching up the hill too fast for Annie. His mind was only on his goal.

They climbed up the ladder, more slowly with heavy coats and gloves. At the door to his retreat, Johnny turned to Annie.

"Wait here. It's really dark in there. Let me go inside and light the lamp first."

Annie waited. This was not how Christmas Eve was supposed to go. For weeks, she had looked forward to Christmas with the Millers. Listening to them reminisce about previous Christmases and plan for this family time, she knew that Christmas would still be observed as a sacred time in their house, and she had wanted so much to be a part of all of it.

But soon after supper, Johnny had jumped up and announced he would walk her home. Why so early? He had been absent from the house most of the day, while Annie helped the grandchildren string popcorn and made pies with Mandy. When he did appear late that afternoon, his mind did not appear with him. His thoughts were somewhere else, not with Annie at the supper table.

She had tried not to let her disappointment show. Johnny was seldom thoughtless or inattentive; so while she ate, she wondered what thoughts had made Johnny forget Christmas Eve. And her.

35

No, this wasn't how she had imagined Christmas Eve with Johnny and his family. Would tomorrow be better? Tomorrow, when the entire family gathered at the big farmhouse for the noon meal and John would read the Christmas story and gifts would be opened and the afternoon would be spent playing games and eating the popcorn garlands? Would the Christmas Day she had looked forward to with such eagerness be better than Christmas Eve?

She hoped so.

From the dark interior came the sound of rhythmic pumping as Johnny pressurized the lamp he had hung in the tree house. Annie turned her back to the door and looked out over the valley, all aglitter in silver and white light.

Tiny streams of light came through the rough boards of the wall and she heard the hissing of the lit mantle.

"Okay, Annie, you can come in now."

After walking in the moonlight, she squinted against the brightness. This was the first time she had seen the deer stand illuminated by artificial light. Her eyes soon adjusted and fixed first on Johnny standing in the center of the room. Then she saw his Christmas decorations.

On the shelves lining the wall, the Stroh's bottles were barely recognizable in their new winter garb. The glass library containing Johnny's prayers and thoughts had all been painted in bright colors. Some bottles had been decorated further with hearts, butterflies, and leaves.

"It's beautiful," she said. "I'd give you an A + for creativity."

Her breath caught. In one row, every bottle wore a bold white letter. The letters spelled her name and ...

ANNIE, WILL YOU MARRY ME?

"Oh, Johnny, yes! I will! I will!"

The lump in her throat prevented more words. She moved closer to him and took both his hands in hers. Tears blurred everything, but she could not miss the love in his brown eyes.

"I want nothing more than to be your wife, Johnny. I love you so much." She giggled. "But beer bottles! I can't believe you proposed to me on beer bottles!"

"But it's fitting, isn't it, Annie? Changing those unpleasant things into something beautiful? Those bottles were like our lives before Jesus cleaned us up. And now look at the beauty He is bringing us."

For a moment, Annie could do nothing but close her eyes against the tears.

"You're crying? My wanting to marry you makes you cry?" Johnny was teasing her again, but she heard the huskiness in his voice, too.

"No, Silly." She blinked away the last tears and smiled at him. "I have not been this happy since the night I came to Jesus. Oh, Johnny, thank you so much for trusting me and waiting on me while I tried to sort out what God wanted me to do."

"If you remember," he said soberly, "God had some work He wanted to do with me during that time, too."

"Can I have a minute alone in here?"

Annie gave him a gentle push out the door.

On one shelf she found a tablet and pencils. Ripping off a page, she wrote her own note of thanks to God, rolled it tightly, and slipped it into a bottle decorated with butterflies. Then, picking up the small artist's brush and what was left of the paint, she brushed YES! YES! YES! below Johnny's proposal.

"Annie, come out here. You can finish your project later, but this moment can't wait."

Outside, the air was crisp, the stillness broken only by faint voices from below.

"Listen," Johnny whispered. "The carolers are here."

The soft melody of *Silent Night* drifted up from the Miller homestead. *Holy infant, so tender and mild.*

"Annie, it really happened, didn't it? Almighty God sent a baby, His Son, to this world. He did that for us, knowing we needed redemption."

Johnny's arm went around her.

"Yes, He knew how much we needed Him."

Over the frozen fields came *Joy to the world, the Lord is come.* He had come to their lives. And heaven and nature and their hearts were singing.

"A sacred night," whispered Johnny.

Laughter floated above the clatter of steel wheels and the jangle of harness as the carolers moved away.

"I've been thinking of how important this tree has been in my life. The big project I took on as a little kid. The reading and writing and pleading with God. Coming to Jesus that night. And now, giving my life to you—all here, in this stand. I could almost live up here in this tree, as long as you're with me.

"Look," he nodded over the valley. "Everything is here, Annie, right in front of us: the past, the present, our future. With God inside me and you beside me, I'll never want to leave this place."

As Johnny talked, Annie saw a picture, unmistakable and as clear as if it were painted on the sky in front of them. Her skin tightened and shivers ran down her back; she could barely speak what she saw.

"Johnny Miller, you are going to be a strong leader, a wise and kind Christian man that God uses in many ways. I can see it, Johnny! I don't know what troubles or joys lie ahead, but I see God working through you to bring peace and healing to many people."

"And you'll be there beside me," he murmured, tightening his arm around her waist.

***

Johnny and Annie walked through the woods in a circle of light falling from the lantern. The next day at the family Christmas lunch, they would announce their engagement.

Annie giggled.

"Do you suppose your family can keep the secret until we have it announced in church?" she wondered.

"If you care about that, you're the only one of us that does." Johnny was too happy to think about restrictive traditions. "We'll need to set a date quickly. Let's decide that tomorrow."

The only thing that pulled him away from Annie that night was knowing that the sooner he was home and in bed, the sooner morning would come and the sooner they could share the good news with the family. On an impulse, Johnny took the long way home over Strawberry Lane. At the top of the hill, he paused by the cemetery and leaned up against the white fence encircling the entombed members of the Miller family.

"Folks," he said to the shadowy silhouettes of gravestones. "I have an announcement to make. I'm getting married! Her name is Annie, and she is an incredible lady. You've probably seen her walking by. I wanted you folks to be the first to know. We are telling the rest of the family tomorrow, so don't be blabbing this secret to anyone."

He was feeling silly and funny; and he was so deliriously joyful, he couldn't be sure how his announcement was received.

36

The young couple had already decided they wanted to be married in the Miller house. Johnny was more than willing to go to Indiana for the wedding, but Annie insisted on getting married *at home.* John would perform the ceremony.

"One request," Johnny told him. "Keep it as short as possible. I've given Annie permission to shout *Amen* if you talk too long."

The wedding date was set for the last week of May. Annie and Johnny both joined the Amish church. The Camaro sold immediately, and Johnny declared he didn't even miss it that much. Annie said his beard made him even more handsome.

They would be moving to the small house previously occupied by Johnny's grandparents, right next door to the big farmhouse.

"When you fill that house with grandchildren, we will switch houses," said Mandy with a grin. Johnny would not have been surprised to find her already sewing baby quilts.

Annie, Naomi, and Mandy spent many joyous hours together planning every detail of the Thursday wedding. When the day finally arrived, Johnny walked through it as though in a dream, and many of those meticulously planned details went completely unnoticed by the very happy Mr. and Mrs. Johnny Miller.

The men were up early to do the milking, like any other

morning. The ladies were too busy in the house to join them. Jonas and Paul arrived, and in short order the chores were completed.

Many of the Yoder family had traveled from Indiana for the wedding, but Henry and Betty had left their daughters with friends, saying Christine and her sister were too young for the trip. Johnny considered briefly that this might only be an excuse, but then he was relieved that Annie would not be troubled by the sight of Christine on their wedding day.

The service was conducted in the barn, as was the custom for many of their weddings, and, in spite of Johnny's plea, it seemed much too long. The main area of the barn had been cleared of all wagons and implements and it had been swept almost as clean as Mandy's kitchen.

Annie looked radiant in her simple Amish wedding dress. She had no need to say anything except "I do" and "I will."

Together they walked to the main house after the service and sat at the bridal table in the living room where family and friends greeted them. Annie Miller sat by her husband's side. Mrs. Johnny Miller. Johnny said that name to himself many times that day.

Johnny dwelt, for a few somber moments, in reflection. His mind journeyed back through the years of his youth. The egg business, the building of the tree stand, the family singings, the friends he had grown up with. He was no longer that carefree young boy. Then came the darker years of restlessness and questions and drinking; he was no longer that aimless rebel, either. Now he had an anchor. Now he had responsibilities. What lay ahead? With Annie by his side, he believed he could conquer whatever came his way.

***

It was an amazing summer. Annie gardened with Naomi and Mandy while Johnny and his father spent hours together in the fields. Annie learned to sew clothes and to can vegetables, and

Johnny learned the nuances of successful farming.

His father was teaching Johnny far more than farming. As a boy, he had known his dad as a kind and generous person; but now they communicated as men, and the son saw an entirely new facet of his dad's character.

"Son, all we have comes from God," John said one day. "We are only stewards of this farm. Sure, we plow the fields and plant the seed; but without rain and sunshine, we have nothing." His quiet intellectual streak surfaced daily in their conversations, and now his son Johnny was ready to listen.

Who would ever imagine an Amish man could have so much fun without a car, electricity, and those other conveniences touted as so necessary to modern happiness? Johnny had Annie, and that was all he needed.

Chore time, especially milking, turned from work into a delight. Annie was determined to be a farmer's wife, and by summer's end, she was quite a milk maid. A new voice joined the choir during milking. If there wasn't singing, there was usually laughter. Some of the best times that summer were when the five Millers—sometimes six, if Paul was there—gathered around the supper table and laughed and enjoyed each other's company.

Annie worked hard at becoming a farmer's wife, but the farm also was her playground. She wandered everywhere, basking in the glory of fields, animals, and insects. Their small house was the launching pad for Monarch butterflies that September. While Johnny taught her about farming, she taught him about the amazing flight of the butterflies she released from their porch.

"Johnny, you must not cut the milkweed along the fence rows and ditches! Monarch butterflies can only survive where milkweed grows." She had collected almost a dozen of the striped caterpillars, put them in jars with twigs and leaves, and watched over those worms as though they were children.

"The Monarch is one of God's most amazing creatures. Once these caterpillars are transformed into butterflies, they'll fly to

Mexico on an incredible journey. They spend the winter on a mountainside with millions of fellow Monarchs, and then begin the journey back toward our farm. They'll never make it back, though.

"Somewhere in southern Texas, they will lay eggs and die. The first generation produced from those eggs will continue the journey back here, but they will live only a few weeks after also mating and laying eggs. The second generation continues the journey, and also lives only a few weeks. It is the third generation that arrives here in our fields, lays eggs that hatch into these caterpillars, and then dies.

"Something special happens to the generation that emerges here. This fourth generation lives up to seven months, finds its way again back to that mountain in Mexico, and the next spring begins the journey back home to us.

"Sometimes the Monarch is called *The Wanderer*, not only because it seems to wander about, flitting from plant to plant, but also because of those long journeys that are part of its life cycle, journeys that take four generations to complete.

"It's all so amazing, Johnny. Only God could take a creepy crawly worm and turn it into something as beautiful as a butterfly. It reminds me of us; we were worms, but God transformed us into something special."

Annie reminded him of a butterfly herself, wandering everywhere and enjoying all of God's creation, bringing beauty and happiness wherever she went on the Miller farm.

Even the tree stand was touched by transformation. What he had denied Naomi so many years ago, Annie had accomplished. Curtains hung from the windows and a rug softened the floor. His deer stand had been desecrated, or at least feminized, and he did not care one bit.

Johnny would always remember this time as the summer of joy, a time when none of them could have imagined the coming September of anguish.

37

For that one summer, life with Annie was like a fairy tale. As a young boy, Johnny had read those stories in which the prince wins his princess and the two live happily ever after. But the brothers Grimm had not written Johnny and Annie's story. Their story should have read, *Johnny married Annie and they lived a charmed life on their farm. They raised many happy children, and in their golden years they sat in rocking chairs until Johnny's beard grew so long it reached the ground and the little grandchildren climbed up his beard and sat on his lap.*

Why had the narrative gone so wrong? Was it his fault? What could he have done differently?

She wasn't a farm girl. Annie either didn't know, or she had forgotten. He should have warned her, reminded her, to give those Clydesdale hooves a wide berth when walking behind the horse stalls.

She was humming that evening as she went back the walkway, past the stalls, intending to say hello to Frank, the bull.

They all heard the thud, her sharp cry. Engulfed with fear, Johnny rushed back the alley. Annie was crumpled on the floor, holding her side and moaning in pain.

"Annie!"

She groaned and mumbled, "Too close ... got kicked ..."

An ugly purple bruise had already appeared on the right side of her forehead.

"Can you get up?" He gently put his arm under her shoulders.

"Oh, my side hurts so much. He kicked me in the ribs, and I think I hit my head when I fell."

With John on one side and Johnny on the other, Annie slowly got to her feet and they half-carried her into the house and settled her in a big chair in the living room.

"I'll call for a ride to take you to the hospital."

"No, I'll just sit for a while and see if the pain goes away."

Mandy and Naomi mothered over Annie, holding ice on the huge bump on her forehead, gently tucking pillows around her body, and covering her with the soft green blanket from the bed.

"Those ribs will heal," said Mandy, "but I'm worried about your head."

"Yes, I've worried about that myself for many years," replied Annie in a hoarse whisper. "I'm sorry for creating such a commotion. I'll rest and sleep tonight; and I believe I'll be better in the morning."

"Johnny, come get us if you need any help."

"Thanks, Mom, Naomi," Annie said softly, "you have been so good to me. I'll be better tomorrow."

Johnny knelt beside the chair, and gripped Annie's hand.

"My side really hurts, Johnny. Every time I breathe. And my head feels numb."

"Are you sure you don't want to go to the hospital?"

"Yes, I'm sure. Let's see how things feel in the morning. I don't think I can lie down, though. I'll have to stay here in the chair. Would you bring me the jar with the chrysalis inside?"

Butterflies had been launching from their front porch for the last few weeks. Only one more remained. A week ago, Annie had called Johnny to witness the spinning maneuver as the worm wriggled around, shedding its final skin. Over the course of a

Monarch worm's life cycle, she said, it sheds its skin four times.

"We're going to have another baby soon. Looks like another ten days or so. This butterfly will probably be the last one leaving here, and it will soon be on its way to Mexico."

Johnny knew that Annie, in spite of her pain, did not want to miss the birth of this last Monarch. He took the jar and placed it gently in her hands. Her eyes were closed and her eyebrows pulled together in a frown of pain, but she smiled when she felt the jar in her hands.

"Thank you, Johnny. One more thing. Could you put a notebook and pen on this stand? If I can't sleep tonight, perhaps I'll write some notes. You'd better get back to the barn and finish your chores."

"No, Dad and Naomi will take care of things in the barn. I'm not going anywhere."

He arranged the items she asked for, set a glass and pitcher of water within her reach, and tucked the blanket around her.

For the rest of the evening, Johnny watched over his wife. She seemed to sleep, and her soft whimpers tore at him. Later, she must have been aware of the darkening room. She opened her eyes and looked for him.

"Johnny, go to bed. I'll be okay as long as I don't move too much. If I can't sleep, I'll watch my chrysalis and maybe write a few things."

How many times would he replay that evening? How long would he be hounded by regret that they did not go to the hospital immediately? She would feel better in the morning, she had said. But he should have insisted.

38

In the hospital waiting room, Johnny sat for a long time, not speaking or moving. Mandy walked back and forth, from the couch to the window to the hallway, looking out, then coming back to the window. Finally, she sat down again.

"Johnny, here's that notebook Annie was holding onto this morning. I wondered what was in it; but when I flipped it open, I saw notes addressed to you, so I didn't want to read it."

Annie must have been awake a good part of the night. She had written several little poems about worms and butterflies. He had heard her sing some of them in the last few weeks.

> *Grow, little wormy, grow your wings.*
> *You're going to do incredible things.*

She had another little rhyme for the ceremony of release.

> *Fly little butterfly, spread your wings.*
> *You're going to see incredible things.*

One page was almost filled with wavering script that sometimes drifted above or below the faint blue lines. Her normally neat and precise handwriting was almost illegible. He could scarcely breathe as he read.

Dearest Johnny,

It is after two o'clock, and I'm afraid that soon I won't be able to think very clearly. I can hear you breathing in the next room and want so much to come in and hold you and tell you how much I love you.

Don't ever lament that we didn't seek help last night. It would not have made any difference. Things are as they are supposed to be. I never told you this, but when I was a child, I often dreamed I would die at an early age. Lately, those dreams have returned. It's as if God has been telling me it's about time to go home. I do love you with all my heart, but I love Jesus more. If He calls, I must go.

I have had it all. The most wonderful man in the world accepted me and loved me unconditionally, just as Jesus accepted me.

I am so sorry for the pain you will go through now, but always remember how very happy I will be. I will look for you every day and will meet you at the gates when you come home, too.

You have my blessing to remarry. You need a good wife, dearest. Someday, you will be ready, and a special lady will be very fortunate to share life with you.

I can hear angels singing. They will soon be here for me. Don't forget to release this last butterfly when it hatches.

Oh, Johnny, one last thing, Christine will need

The words trailed off into unreadable squiggles.

Mandy was watching him. Tears streamed down his face as he turned to her.

"Annie's not going to make it."

"Johnny, we don't know that …"

"She is dead. She is already in heaven."

"No, Johnny, that's not possible. Why would you say that?"

"Mom, listen to me. In several minutes the doctor is going to walk in and tell us what I just told you."

"No, not Annie. She's my daughter. She can't die."

"Mom, I'm telling you—she's gone."

The doctor was at the door, a somber expression on his face.

"She's gone, isn't she?" Johnny asked.

"Without the surgery, she would have lasted only several hours. We had to try, but we lost her during the surgery. I am so sorry we couldn't save her."

***

They rode home without speaking, the silence interrupted only by sounds of grief and weeping. Johnny tried to imagine what Annie was seeing and what she might be doing, but it was beyond his comprehension.

On that bright September afternoon, Naomi sobbed as she pulled the long rope to ring the brass bell hanging on the side of the barn. The clanging reverberated over the countryside, telling the valley that tragedy had come to the Miller house. Neighbors dropped whatever they were doing and came to help in any way they could and to participate in some way in the pain and sadness that had descended on Annie's family.

The house was soon a beehive of activity. Neighbors planned meals and set up a schedule to help with chores and milking. A group immediately started mowing the lawn and raking up the few leaves that had already fallen.

Johnny went through whatever motions were required of him and sat like a quiet spectator while plans were made to dig the grave up on Strawberry Patch Hill.

39

Questions and choices bombarded him. What dress to put on Annie? Where in the cemetery would he like to have Annie buried? He did not care about these details, as long as there was room for him beside his wife. He should have been thinking about their first Christmas, their first anniversary, their first child—not their first night apart and Annie's resting place in the cemetery.

The finality of all the plans sent his mind reeling. Fortunately, Mandy and Naomi gently guided him through the decisions and sometimes stepped in and made the choices for him.

He had been to a few English viewings and funerals. Traditions of grief in that world seem designed to shield the living from the harshness of death. In the midst of a mound of plants and flowers, a dead body suddenly appears, unexpected and out of place. The body rests in a funeral home until time for the burial service. At the cemetery, the crowd disperses while the body remains suspended between heaven and earth. Then the casket is lowered into the waiting pit once the eyes of loved ones have turned away.

The starkness of Amish funerals makes it impossible to avoid the reality of death. The body is brought into the home for the viewing. At the cemetery, the open grave waits; and, in full view of everyone, the earth swallows the body as the casket is lowered into the dark hole and dirt is immediately shoveled over it.

The intent is to warn the living of the inevitability of an end to every living person. *Dust to dust,* as John had often preached. Yet each action is harsh and final, squeezing every drop of emotion from body, soul, and spirit.

Thinking about what lay ahead, Johnny's mind flailed about as though in a bad dream from which he could not awaken. This was not just another funeral; this was Annie; this was his wife they were talking about burying. Could he not simply open his eyes and have this nightmare end?

One part of his mind tried to understand the reality of the nightmare, the other part refused to believe any of this was real. Caught between the two, his spirit was gripped in paralysis.

Annie's body would be brought to the main house the following afternoon, and his wife would be on view in the living room corner where John's desk normally reigned. The viewing would be that evening and the following day, followed by the funeral service in three days.

***

The Miller family gathered in the living room, awaiting the arrival of Annie. The mantle clock ticked away the seconds, moving toward the dreaded moment. Tick, tock, tick, tock. Time had changed dimensions. It had slowed, and now unmeasured time hung between each tick and tock. Would it forever move this slowly? Could he possibly grab those hands and fast forward them? Could he take the calendar and rip off twelve pages to move forward one year? If that were possible, could he not reverse time and dictate a different outcome to Annie's walk down the alley in the barn?

What could relieve the awful pain in his soul?

"I'll be back," he said to no one and to everyone as he rose from his chair. Perhaps a quick trip up to the old wash house would cleanse his soul. Perhaps he could find remnants of Annie's spirit still resting there. That stand had always been a refuge from emotional storms in the past.

Indeed, he was right. Annie was everywhere in the tree stand. He had spent most of the summer working the farm; Annie had spent time in the stand, taking ownership herself. He fingered the curtains and rubbed his foot over the carpet. The bottles still stood in line on the shelf, shouting out his proposal. Annie's YES! YES! YES! glowed in happy colors. Her notebooks were filled with observations of farm life and reflections from her vantage point above the countryside.

He would keep this spot as his comfort in the days and weeks to come. It was as if this was a sanctuary he had been willed to build for a time like this. Annie's notebooks of thoughts would be a balm to his pained spirit. He would read them, and hear her voice.

Surveying the landscape from his perch, he noticed the fresh mound of dirt in the cemetery on Strawberry Hill. How strange to think it was the grave dug for his wife. Compelled by the desire to visit that opening in the earth, he crossed the pasture and climbed a fence. His shoes stirred up little clouds of dust on Strawberry Lane, and he swung open the white gate to the silent garden of rest.

He stood over the gaping hole. This was the receptacle waiting to hold his dear Annie until such a time as God reunites body and spirit. The rough box constructed at the bottom of the hole was a rectangular wooden container similar to a vault. Annie's coffin would be lowered into this wooden box, and then a number of smaller boards would be laid atop the container.

What had happened to Annie's spirit when she died? What was she seeing and doing right now? Did she know he was standing above a hole where her body would rest? He was sure Annie was in Heaven, but he had more questions. He would ask his father at some future time.

In their Amish funeral services, Johnny had often heard John and other preachers talk about hope for a place in heaven for loved ones who had died. Before he had asked for God's mercy and come to Jesus, there was no question of where he would go after death; that message had been clear and unyielding. But now that he was saved, he wanted to be equally certain of his destination. Was it possible to be fully confident of heaven? And if so, how could he ever find such confidence?

Filled with hurt and dismay and questions, he stood at the open grave and wondered why God had allowed this to happen to him and Annie. Nearby lay his grandpa and grandma. Their passing had been sad, but it was in the normal way. They lived, they aged, and they died. Life goes on. How could life possibly go on without Annie?

Such thoughts raced back and forth at a frenzied pace. Some made sense, others did not. Johnny acted on one thought that did not make sense: He needed to be where Annie would be. Even in the haze of his deep sorrow, he knew that this impulse was too bizarre to act upon. However, he needed to do it.

Bracing himself against the piles of dirt, he lowered his body into the grave. Stretching out, he lay Johnny Miller into the wooden rough box. He gazed at the cloudless blue sky and wondered if he might have gone temporarily insane; but for the first time in two days, his spirit had found some sort of peaceful oasis. He rested where Annie would be resting, and it felt all right.

"Annie, this is where you will be until God reunites us. Someday I will be down here beside you, and we will be resurrected together."

Lying there where Annie would soon be resting had a calming effect on him.

"Okay, Johnny, it's time to get out of the hole you're in." He heard Annie's voice. And even in the numbness of grief, he recognized what a spectacle he would present to any passerby on Strawberry Lane if a glance across the countryside caught sight of a body ascending from a grave.

After a quick change of clothes, he returned to the living room, where questioning looks were cast in his direction but he offered no explanation.

Time paused at 4:32 that afternoon when a funeral car brought Annie back to them. The simple oak coffin built next door in the furniture shop now rested in the corner where John's desk usually stood. The hinged lid on the coffin folded back, revealing Annie.

There are moments in life that are so sacred, so inexpressibly unpredictable, that words fail humans. One such moment is when the body of a loved one is first revealed to a loving family. Reality at last meets unbelief. One's mind may attempt to disbelieve what has happened, but the presence of a body is an undeniable and potent dose of reality.

The Amish community is sometimes seen as staid and unemotional. Some parents never hug their children or tell them they are loved. Physical and verbal expressions are traditionally not their way of life, but this is certainly not an indication that love is lacking. They love in action, in working together and eating together. Theirs is a living love, not always spoken aloud.

But the Millers broke with tradition. They hugged one another and loved each other as never before. Their grief drew them into a tight circle around the coffin, and their circle drew in the Yoders. John wrapped his arms around Johnny and, weeping, told his son he loved him. The room behind them held its breath in silence, as friends respected the sacredness of the moment. The only sounds were those of grief … and the tick tock of time slowly passing.

40

Amish funerals are much like their regular church services. The service was held in the main house. Lines of wooden benches filled both the main floor and the basement. The coffin was moved to the space in the living room beside the steps leading downstairs. John stood by the stairs, near the coffin, so that his voice could be heard on both levels.

At the close of the service, everyone filed past the coffin for one final viewing, first friends and neighbors, then the family, who gathered around for their final goodbye to their Annie.

Then several men from the church gingerly folded the lid back over the coffin. As that cover slowly descended, Johnny dropped his head, keeping his eyes on Annie until the lid blocked his view. *Please, one last glimpse. Why speed up time now? Hold this moment longer. Please, just one more look.* The lid was closed, and screwdrivers were already fastening it down.

The family walked up the hill to the cemetery, followed by a special carriage bearing Annie's body. The procession of black buggies stretched up Strawberry Lane. Four pallbearers carried the casket carefully to the waiting grave, settling it onto straps that would lower it into the rough box.

As Annie slowly descended to the same space Johnny had

filled, the familiar Loblied began. Begun by one man who is the song leader, this worship song is used in every service. Sung slowly like a Gregorian chant, "Das Loblied" has four stanzas, each syllable held for an indeterminable period of time and moving up and down the scale. The leader's voice that day began with one single note that ascended and descended the musical scale like a vocal gymnast. Then everyone joined in.

Although the English translation of *Das Loblied* is *The Worship Song*, Johnny had always thought the singing of it to be poignant and sad. On this day, as they lowered his wife to her resting place, the words spoke of worship and thanks, but his spirit felt only the mournful timbre of the long notes.

> *Oh Lord Father, we bless thy name,*
> *Thy love and thy goodness praise;*
> *That thou, O Lord, so graciously*
> *Have been to us always.*

The words *love* and *goodness* floated through the air, reaching his mind weighed down by pain and loss. Like the viewers who had passed by Annie's coffin, they drifted by, then silently settled into place, finding seats in his mind beside grief and hurt. In his own time, he would decide the proper seating arrangement.

> *Put wisdom in our hearts while here*
> *On earth thy will be known*
> *Thy word through grace to understand*
> *What thou would have us to do.*

He was still here on earth. Where was Annie? He could barely grasp that Annie would not be here tomorrow or the next day or next week. What did God expect him to do without her?

An ash tree at the edge of the cemetery released a gentle shower of yellow and green leaves. Johnny watched one slender flutter of color slowly rotate downwards and follow Annie into the grave. It came to rest beside the casket, on the top edge of one side of the rough box. All his thoughts fixed on that wisp of yellow, knowing it would remain pinched between the rough box and the covering boards until the end of time.

As the top boards of the box were slowly placed over the casket, the leaf remained. He wanted to lean over, brush it away. Then, as one board came down to imprison the leaf in the grave, some small movement of air gave it a gentle push, and it fell onto the dirt outside the rough box. He felt a great relief.

Was grief sending his mind into a place of instability? Was grief itself a form of insanity? Why was it so important that leaf fall outside the rough box? What had compelled him to lie in Annie's grave? Was he losing his grasp on reality?

The shovels began to rain loads of dirt on top of Annie. Still the singing went on.

> *That we praise thee in our assembly*
> *And feel grateful every hour.*
> *With all our hearts we pray,*
> *Wilt thou be with us every day*

How could any man who was watching his wife being covered with dirt feel grateful for that hour? The grave slowly filled. He needed to comfort his wife, reassure her, be one with her.

It's okay, Annie, you will be fine there. I was there, too.

He could hear Annie's reply, "Yes, but they weren't hurling dirt on top of *you!*"

In spite of having such a short period of time together, he still knew exactly how Annie would reply.

The ground on both sides of the grave was carefully scraped, and the grave site was now marked only with a mound of earth. The singing stopped, and the crowd slowly dispersed. The Miller and Yoder families remained, one family in their loss and grief.

What happened next was so outside the Amish tradition that it broke through even the haze of Johnny's grief and astonished him.

"What has happened with our family this week is hard to understand," John began, "and we don't always understand the ways of God. We all loved Annie very much. In her short time with us, she reminded us how powerful love can be. She has changed our family forever. Let's make a circle around the grave, hold one another's hand, and I will pray."

Following his prayer, John gave each child a hug and a greeting of love. Johnny didn't move, too stunned to comprehend then the impact Annie had had on his father.

***

The day had ended. Physically, mentally, and emotionally exhausted, Johnny collapsed in the reclining chair, the same chair where Annie had spent her last night. A few short days ago, life was so full and promising; now, he saw only emptiness.

Beside the chair, the container with the chrysalis still stood on the little table. Annie had been intent on watching that chrysalis, but in the end she had chosen to cling to her notebook instead, writing her last words to her husband.

He reached over and picked up the jar. The chrysalis hung from the screen over the top of the jar. He pulled off the screen and held the chrysalis up to examine it. The creature had darkened since Annie had proclaimed that the butterfly birth would soon come. She had asked him to release this last Monarch.

He tried to recall her little songs about butterflies getting wings, but he was too exhausted to remember. Fatigue won out. His hands dropped, his head fell back against the chair, and he collapsed, body and spirit, into uneasy slumber.

The chrysalis rested on the back of his left hand. In the too-silent house, both slept.

II

The Wandering

41

The Monarch was completely exhausted, but something in her tiny brain told her she was almost home. Two generations before, her ancestors had left a pine forest deep in the mountains of Mexico and had begun the long journey. Each generation had continued northward, until, exhausted, they died along the way. They had, however, been careful to lay eggs so that their line would continue and the journey would be taken up by their offspring. This Monarch had hatched from one of those small, grooved ovals and she persisted in the northward migration, flying the third and final leg of the journey home.

Although she and her mate had left the southern part of the state only yesterday, he had not been able to finish the journey and had passed away in the afternoon, having lived to the ripe old age of two weeks. Together, they had covered close to eighty miles a day; and although several incidents had resulted in nicked wings and lost scales, they had had a good life together.

She was happy to have shared her days with him; and when he had faltered and had begun to drift downward, she had wanted to remain by his side. A stronger compulsion, though, kept her winging toward home, where she must prepare for the miracle of the fourth generation.

So she flew on, alone.

The Monarch's eyesight had always been feeble, but her antennae and brain told her she was nearing the Miller farm. Although she herself had never been there, her family had claimed that land far longer than the Millers had been farming the valley.

Many generations ago, the feathery parachute of a milkweed seed had drifted over hill and dale and settled gently on a tract of land. It settled onto the soil and sent forth small, supple milkweed shoots. This sticky, milky plant hosted Monarch larvae. Not only did the milkweed supply food for the newly hatched worms, but it provided protection from predators. The leaves on which the caterpillars feasted contained a poison which made the Monarchs repulsive, even toxic, to birds looking for a meal.

Momma Monarch traveled onward on her mission of propagation until she reached the home farm. Finally there, she alighted on a milkweed plant along a fence row and gently deposited more than one hundred eggs on the receptive green expanse. Many of those offspring would not survive, but the multiplicity of eggs would assure survival of at least a few.

Secreting a sticky substance, she attached her eggs to the underside of the milkweed leaves. The tiny Monarch worms would hatch here and have instant food. This would be the special generation. This fourth generation would live an incredible seven to eight months and was destined to go on a pilgrimage of several thousand miles.

Her life mission completed, the Monarch made a final drifting loop around the plant and settled softly on the ground. She slowly crawled to a nearby multiflora bush, where she hid herself, took her last breath, and joined her mate in the butterfly hereafter.

42

It was August, the height of summer on the Miller farm. In one egg attached to a green leaf, a tiny caterpillar developed. He awoke on the sixth day, feeling trapped by the sides of the small container pressing in on him. And he was hungry. Compelled by his voracious appetite, he chewed his way to freedom, then feasted on his first breakfast, the eggshell he had just abandoned.

Stretching out to his full one-eighth of an inch, he sensed he had entered a much wider universe. His mind gradually cleared, and some imprint on his brain shouted, "Eat like your life depends on it!" He did not yet understand the reason, but he followed the dictate to eat.

Not bad, he thought as he munched. *Perhaps a little milky and sticky.* His mouth never stopped chewing, but he was soon conscious of other newly hatched brothers and sisters emerging around him on his plant and also starting to devour the green food so conveniently provided.

Some siblings, thinking the plant too crowded, crawled away to neighboring vegetation. That was a fatal mistake; nasty insects and birds quickly ate up those who had left their leaf. As in any other family with over one hundred children, this family showed many different levels of intellect.

Sadly, some of his siblings were given no chance at life. While they still slept in their egg containers, an evil fly had discovered the eggs and pierced the covering around the larvae. The horrible insect had deposited its own eggs on the little worms; and when the eggs of evil hatched, they consumed the tiny Monarch larvae.

A shadow passed over the young caterpillar as some new presence moved with ease through the air above. The presence turned and fluttered back. Another momma butterfly was looking for an available milkweed for her own brood. She swooped low and encouraged the new larvae to eat without ceasing.

"Milkweed holds life for you," she said. "You will grow on its nourishment now, and a power in the sap will protect you from evil predators wishing to eat you after you get your wings. Eat! Eat! You are special; you are the generation that will live a long time and wander a great distance."

Her words sent reverberations through the tiny worm's body. He attempted to reply, but the words stuck in his throat, held fast by the sticky substance he was gobbling up.

Amazing! Incredible! he thought. *We are going to grow wings and fly!* He cleared his mouth of the milkweed and shouted to his siblings. "Good news, good news! We are only going to be worms for a short time. We will turn into things of beauty and one day fly on long journeys!"

Some laughed and said he was a dreamer. "Where are the wings on your back? You are a worm. You will always be a worm. Accept it."

"But that pretty creature told me I would fly someday. She also said to keep eating the leaves from this plant. 'If you must leave, find another like it,' she said."

Many unbelievers would not listen to him. He did not care who believed him. He trusted what the winged beauty had told him. Was it possible he could even become as beautiful as she?

**

For the next three weeks, he did nothing but eat milkweed leaves and eliminate what he did not need. He ate so much he could no longer contain himself. He outgrew himself and found it necessary to change skins. He would struggle out of old skin four times in his life; and each time, he paused in his chomping long enough to check for wings.

There was no sign of wings, but he had plenty of legs—three pairs of front legs and five pairs of hind legs. Sixteen legs made it easy to scamper from leaf to leaf on his milkweed home.

Two antennae at his forward end and two antennae at his back end were sensitive to any movement and told him about changes in his sphere. He was growing longer and fatter and, he thought, more handsome, with impressive black, yellow, and white colors circling his body.

Occasionally, a nasty bird still tried to sample one of the worms, but with every mouthful of milkweed, the caterpillars were becoming more toxic to the enemy. As a result, he was feeling quite safe, and thus was unprepared for what happened one day. His antennae and his brain had no expectation of this, no knowledge of the event, no memory that warned him or advised what should be done.

Another beautiful apparition approached his milkweed plant. This creature did not fly, although it had what appeared to be wings of some sort. Instead of sixteen legs, it had only two; and it approached walking upright on those two legs. The unfamiliar creature hovered over his milkweed home, and he sensed no reason for alarm.

The next thing he knew, he was falling, falling, dropping downward through air. The leaf he had been chewing followed him, and both landed with a thud on a surface he had never before felt. He did know that once again he was encased and no longer free to roam his plant. More milkweed leaves dropped into the container, and then came a small stick with little branches.

He had plenty of food, and that, at least, made sense. He had eaten his way out of the egg container, perhaps he would need to eat his way out of this one, too. Sweet sound waves came from the creature; he had no comprehension of the meaning, but he was soothed, nonetheless.

The unfamiliar container moved along, floating through the air. His antennae quivered, trying to gather information that would tell him where he was and what direction his legs must go to find his milkweed plant once again. But neither his brain nor his antennae held any understanding of what surrounded and held him.

The mystery deepened when he was taken into yet another container. The beautiful creature who carried him seemed to be returning to its own host site, a space that opened its mouth and swallowed both caterpillar and creature. This enclosure took away the sun, too, and the striped caterpillar was completely disoriented.

"This must all be part of getting my wings," he told himself. "I will know what to do when the time comes, I suppose." And he set to munching.

Day after day, more leaves dropped into his container, and he forgot that his movements were restricted. This life was actually better than roaming on a milkweed plant. Food came to him. He did not have to defend his leaf against hungry siblings. His antennae no longer needed to be on full alert; here there were no bad birds or other evil doers. All he needed to do was eat and shed his skin when the old one became too tight.

At last one day he could feel that something special was about to happen. He had grown to a full two inches in length and had shed three skins. The fourth set of clothes was feeling old and used up. His instincts were telling him what to do and when to do it, and that comforted him.

On that day, he climbed up the little twig and listened carefully to what he was to do next. "Attach yourself securely to the twig and wriggle out of that skin. Fall asleep for several weeks, and when you awaken, you will have your wings."

As simple as that?

He was so fat that he could hardly remove the last skin that bound him. He twisted in circles, frantically trying to pry it off. With great effort and at the point of complete exhaustion, he wriggled out of the last remnant of his caterpillar life and it dropped to the bottom of the container.

"Wow. That was hard work. I'll need that long nap to recover." He was too tired to look at his body. If he had, he might have been amazed at the jade green color that was nothing like the striped skin he had worn on the milkweed. He pulled all sixteen legs toward himself, and forgot about eating.

Resting, he felt the new green exterior hardening into a shell.

"What's this? Now I'm trapped inside again. Inside the inside that's inside. I'm going to have to do the escapes all over again, after my nap. When do the wings arrive? That creature with two legs has been looking out for me; I wonder if it will help me escape once I have my wings."

He drifted off to sleep, and the vibrations of sweet sound waves from the two-legged one was the last thing he heard.

For thirteen days and nights he slept. On the evening of the fourteenth day, a jarring blow roused him from slumber.

43

Confused and dazed, he felt a tremendous squeezing about his body. Where was he? What was taking place? Panic-stricken for several seconds, he listened and remembered that he was a worm who had been promised wings after a long slumber.

An uncomfortable lump pressed against his casing. He must escape this captivity. Pushing with all of his might, he managed to crack the confining walls. Slowly and deliberately, he pulled his body to freedom and lay gasping and wheezing on an unfamiliar surface. This was not milkweed, and it was not the container which had carried him away from the milkweed.

His antennae unfurled and swiveled about, surveying the landscape. The edges of the universe were dark; but directly above, a white light emanated from the gloom. This was not sunlight, but it was the only light his compass could find. The surface on which he wobbled about gave off several distinctive aromas, and he absorbed those into his brain. This was his birthplace, and he instinctively stamped it as a place of beginning, a place of safety.

Something was woefully amiss, though. As a worm, he had zipped to and fro across the milkweed leaves. Now he wobbled slowly, his balance precarious. He now had only three pairs of legs, and he had somehow lost ten of his scooters.

The wings! Swiveling his head to get his first look at the promised glory, he was sorely disappointed. The beautiful wings he had been anticipating were curled up and deformed. His dream was ruined. Had he slept too long, or not long enough? Were his disbelieving fellow worms right, after all? Were they all destined to be surface creepers forever?

While he lamented his misfortune, a movement on his back startled him. Swiveling his head again, he was surprised to see that the wings were beginning to straighten. An inner voice of instruction shouted, "Move your wings up and down!"

He felt a coursing of liquid in the wrinkled wings and, over the next hour, moved the unfurling flags up and down, up and down. He wobbled about, adjusting to walking on only six legs. The wings, growing stronger and more firm, compensated for the missing limbs.

"It's a miracle!" he exclaimed, although there was no one to hear. "I do have wings. See! It's true, it's true!"

Would these new wings actually work? He would trust his instincts. Everything he had been told had happened. Things he had not understood before were beginning to make sense. He was destined to be a wanderer and travel a great distance. His wings had surely been given to him to carry him over that distance, and when the time came to use them, he would know. For the moment, he worked at moving his new wings up and down, waiting for the next word.

Everything imprinted in the memories of all generations before him was now part of his own being. He added the experience of this unexpected place, recognizing that these smells and sounds and sensations were new and not part of the memories.

He had been chosen and brought here by the two-legged creature. Was there a special mission for him? But to fulfill his destiny, to go on that long journey, how would he escape this last confinement? There was no sun to guide him, only that white light pushing back the darkness.

"Whoever has brought me this far will not abandon me now." He was certain his inner instructions would answer his questions at the right time.

For now, though, it was time to fly. Scampering along on his remaining six legs, he hurled himself from his birthplace. And he was flying, flying ... and falling. He landed on a hard surface he did not recognize. He knew, though, it was nothing like the dirt under the milkweed plant he had once lived upon.

"That didn't work too well. Give it another go!" he shouted to encourage himself. With a wild flapping of the new wings, he cleared the hard surface. He was off! He was in the air! He was a flying worm! "I can't be a worm anymore; I am a completely changed being!"

He looped around the room in complete astonishment. The wings actually worked. Floating slowly back down to his birthplace, he saw the twig and casing lying where he had recently been born. Fully alert now, he once again explored and gathered imprints of every mound and recess of his launching spot. He would need to remember this place, but it was time to venture farther and deeper into the unknown.

Executing a perfect takeoff, he was airborne, and none too soon. He felt the vibration of sound as something smashed onto his birthplace. Flying higher, he developed a better sense of the world he now explored on wings. A two-legged creature rested below him. Not the beautiful one, but another, who moved restlessly.

Drawn to the bright light, he circled it several times, seeking the information his compass needed. The white light did not give him what sunlight bestowed, but he was so elated with his flight that he was not yet concerned about the light's inadequacy. He floated. He drifted. He glided. He could not wait to escape this confinement and explore the vast universe awaiting him.

The light moved and he followed it. He fluttered through the mouth of the enclosure, pursuing the light, and then two things happened: the light disappeared and a sharp coldness struck him.

The cold air almost paralyzed him; the strength he had felt coursing through his wings earlier now rapidly subsided, and he felt himself drifting with waning strength. He changed direction, circling back to return to the warmth and light of his birthplace. But there was only darkness.

He was trying to understand what the voice of instinct was telling him, but he only knew he must find a place to rest until warmth returned to the world.

Slowly he winged his way around a corner of the house and let himself sink downward toward the porch. He landed on a wooden board and crawled along its underside until his body bumped another creature hanging in the corner.

"Watch where you're going!"

He realized he could indeed have avoided the collision. When he was a worm, he had had six eyes, but none of them had worked too well. The world from the vantage point of his milkweed plant had been rather blurry, and he had relied on his antennae to give him information about his surroundings. Now, as a butterfly, he had eyes with thousands of individual light receptors. And even in the darkness under the porch, he could tell that his eyesight had improved and he could have seen the other Monarch hanging there, if he *had* watched where he was going.

He was more startled, though, that he had understood what the other creature was saying to him. Receptors in his new wings picked up the communication and relayed the message.

"Let me guess. You were just released from the inside."

"Yes." His body trembled. "It's so dark and cold out here."

"The warmth and light will come again. And it will go again, too. When that happens, I return here to rest. It's as close as I can get to my birthplace. I also came from the inside, a week ago."

"How did you get from the milkweed to the inside? Was it the creature with two legs?"

"Yes. I saw the creature out here several times after I was released, but lately it hasn't appeared. Perhaps it's only there to help us when we first get our wings."

His wings now felt heavy and useless. Somehow, the other Monarch knew his alarm.

"Don't worry. When the light comes again, the warmth will come, too, and your wings will be strong again. Then I'll show you all the best flower clusters, and you'll be eating delicious nectar instead of bitter milkweed.

"Rest now, and tomorrow when light and warmth arrive, you'll begin to realize the miracle of your new wings."

The dazed Monarch, hoping the promise was true, rested his new wings against each other in an upright position and slept the open-eyed sleep of the butterfly.

44

Light and color burst everywhere, startling Sabio, the butterfly, from his rest in the shelter of the porch.

"Follow me," called his fellow pilgrim as she swooped out into the sunlight. Her intense, beautiful colors were a banner against the sky.

After the frightening paralysis of the night before, the Monarch was now amazed at his mobility. He looped, swirled, drifted, and floated. Testing the limits of his new wings, he flew farther and farther. High in the sky he ascended, ecstatic with the freedom. An occasional air current brought wilder thrills. With wings spread wide, he glided on the whims of the wind.

Eventually, he landed on a brilliant flower, and instinct took over. Unfurling his tongue, he drank from the sweet nectar hidden deep within the petals. His friend joined him, and together they sipped from this wellspring of nature.

"How much do you know about us?" asked his friend.

Sabio told her what he somehow understood.

"We are destined to travel far from here. While yet a worm on the milkweed plant, I was told that we fourth-generation butterflies are the special generation. We will go on an extraordinary pilgrimage. Whether we return home here is unclear to me. We would be wise to build up our bodies with as much nourishment as possible, so we are ready to leave."

"Do you know when we will start our journey?"

"Not exactly. I am certain, though, that we will know when it is time to know."

Sometimes he heard other butterflies in the neighborhood talk about the pilgrimage. Every day, one or two departed, winging away in answer to some call; but no one left behind seemed to have details about when or how his own call would come.

So Sabio spent his days sampling all the flowering plants on the Miller farm. He frolicked and went on foraging trips with other butterflies. Some days he traveled with his porch friend; other days, he meandered wherever he pleased, alone.

He was growing in strength and vitality. When he found an air current pleasing to him, he often moved at speeds approaching fifty miles per hour. His strong wings could beat ten flaps a second when he really wanted to move.

Sabio couldn't resist a smooth pool of water. He studied his reflection and marveled at the vibrant hues created by the tiny scales covering his wings. He noticed his colors were slightly brighter than his friend's, although she was larger. His back wings sported several dark spots that her wings did not.

He also could not resist teasing a bird now and then. Most birds had learned that the bright colors he wore meant his body carried the noxious milkweed poison. A Monarch is unpalatable, causing violent sickness in any bird foolish enough to try a sample. Sabio sometimes lurked beneath a leaf, waiting for a bird to glide close to his hiding place. As the bird approached, he darted out and flashed his bright wings. The ambushed bird would wheel in panic and flee from the colors of terror.

"You've got an ornery streak," said his friend one day after she had witnessed the game he played. "How is it that you're named Sabio?"

He did not know how this name had come to him.

"It's a perfectly good name, I think."

"Yes," she agreed. "But in the land to which we will travel, that word means *wise*. Sometimes, I think the name doesn't quite fit you. I think I'll call you Sabe."

A ripple of irritation went through him. He was a special butterfly; of that, he was certain. He had been chosen and plucked from the milkweed by the keeper of the birthplace of all special butterflies. He had been born in a palatial container. He was gifted with wisdom other butterflies lacked.

But here was a surprise. Apparently she possessed knowledge he did not. She knew they would travel to an unknown land, and she knew the meaning of his name.

She was called Mariposa. He liked the sound of her name; it suited her. He often called her Posy. He watched as she collected dust and nectar, and he thought the posies looked more beautiful whenever she settled on their petals.

When the sun slipped away, they shared the porch place of rest. No matter where he wandered during the day, Sabio was always led back to his starting point under the board where he had first met Mariposa. He might be in the tall grasses of the meadow or deep in the woods hunting new wells of nectar; yet when he was called to fly home, he knew instantly which direction to take.

He began to notice a change in the light during the day. He had soon discovered that resting in places where the sun shone full on his wings would warm and relax him and strengthen his body. But the time came when even hours in the sunlight did not warm him as before, and the nights under the porch were growing colder.

Messages from within told him the time was near. He told Mariposa, as they hung side by side under the board.

"The time for our long journey has come. We must go. Staying here will mean death. Let's travel together to the faraway land waiting for us." Sabe had become quite fond of Posy. "We can look out for each other along the way."

He understood clearly that at the right time his navigational system would show the way. All they needed to do, now that their call had come, was to begin their journey.

Together they decided. When the light returned and their wings warmed once again, they would make a last visit to the wells of sustenance and then depart this place. Most of the remaining wells had dried up, and the butterflies had to burrow deep to capture the honey nectar.

As the first rays of morning broke the duskiness under the porch, the two released their grip on the board and floated into the day. Pausing on a remaining dahlia, they drank deeply and filled their small abdomens with life-sustaining fluids.

"The journey ahead will be long, and I hope to complete it with you," said Sabio. "We will take turns flying in the lead, and whoever follows must keep the other in view."

Sabe led and Posy followed, taking flight into the blue September sky. They did one loop around the familiar farm, getting a last glimpse of their birthplace. Memories of a time long ago flashed through Sabe's mind as remnants of the milkweed birthplace along the fence row passed beneath him. Taking a wider flight pattern than ever in his life, he looped along the edge of Milford. The landscape of his youth was still in his vision as he turned and locked in his bearings, heading in a westerly direction.

A short distance farther and at new heights, the wanderers boarded an air current bending in a southwesterly direction. They set about acclimating themselves to conditions aloft.

Somewhere over Pine Creek, Sabe glimpsed the gravity of the moment. The mystery he had been born to, what had been hinted at by a passing butterfly while he was still a worm on the milkweed, was now unfolding. He was leaving an idyllic life of flitting from flower to flower and flying into an unknown future that he had been called to but that was still a mystery.

Posy's presence comforted him. *Wandering with a friend is certainly better than going solo*, he thought, as the valley of his birth disappeared forever.

45

Sabio and Mariposa spent most of the morning adapting to the unique demands of long-distance flight. Wings spread wide, they discovered the pleasure of gliding along on air currents. With a little practice, directional changes became second nature. Dipping wings downward or sideways, the two Monarchs turned and swooped and looped in all directions.

Sabio had been right; his navigational system directed him to a determined corridor of travel, and he did not doubt the accuracy of this direction. Occasionally, currents took them outside the corridor and then a frenzied flapping of wings was necessary to return to the preferred route. Sometimes, happily, they found and boarded a fortuitous current flowing back to the solace of their corridor.

The first evening found them clinging to the underside of a brown leaf on a tree. Sabio had been vigilant for changes in weather conditions, and he kept several hundred eye parts scanning the landscape below for quick shelter in times of danger, preferably structures such as building overhangs or bridges.

Nevertheless, the easterly wind had caught them unprepared when it did what it had done for centuries and caused the sky to cry. Wet droplets hit the butterflies as they were descending for the day. Immediately, their wings grew heavy with the moisture.

"Keep moving your wings and follow me!" Sabio shouted. They were descending rapidly with no solid refuge in sight when he spotted the leaf still clinging to a branch. Their legs grasped the underside of the brittle shelter as the drops pelted their refuge. For all of their adult lives, their sanctuary under the porch overhang had been solid and stable, and this clinging to a shuddering, shaking, rattling leaf was an experience they did not enjoy. The two huddled together as water flowed over the edges of their protective roof.

The storm ended. In the waning twilight, Sabe and Posy fluttered to another branch and waved their soggy wings until they dried, then spent the night clinging to the underside of the limb.

The second morning dawned bright and clear. While waiting for the sun to warm them and speak its directions, the Monarchs dined on a clump of goldenrod. Back home on the farm when Sabe had burrowed into blooms in search of nectar, his legs often emerged covered with the flower's dust. Before entering another flower sanctuary and drinking, he would always rub his feet clean. Now he noticed there was very little dust on his legs.

"Are you ready, Posy?" he called, lifting into the air.

The previous day he had witnessed the playful spirit of his fellow traveler. The gentle air current on which they were gliding along had suddenly turned to rolling undulations. Sabe had spread his wings and plowed straight ahead, but he heard shouts from Posy behind him.

"Maaripohhhsa! Maaripohhhsa!" Posy was riding the waves of air with enthusiasm. Down and up, down and back up. She took each loop with the same exclamation. "Maar-i-pohhh-saaa!"

When he asked her about the shouting, she had said that it was always the word that came to her when she was thrilled or excited. Whether she had earned her name because of her exclamations or if the word came because it was her name, neither of them knew. Either way, it was quite all right with Sabe. She was his Mariposa, and he was happy she accompanied him in this adventure.

By the second evening, they had reached the southern part of Ohio and rested, unaware that they dined and retired for the night less than one mile from the tree where Sabe's father and mother had spent their last night together.

Entering northern Kentucky on a calm morning, Sabe and Posy headed in a southwestern direction. There was no air movement, so their progress slowed considerably.

"Perhaps if we go higher we might catch a better ride," suggested Sabe. They flew to such dizzying heights that Posy feared they would bump against the blue ceiling. Clouds passed beneath them. They boarded a current hurrying due west; and although Sabe knew this was a harbinger of bad weather, he decided that hitching a ride was preferable to exerting so much energy at lower levels.

He ignored, too, the warning of a sudden drop in temperature. Then came more undulations. He was enjoying Posy's shouts of "Mariposa!" and thinking of adopting her style of riding the dips and waves when a missile nipped the edge of his left wing, sending him into a tailspin.

He tried to right himself as he plummeted downward, but hard projectiles shot through the air all around the two wanderers. At this height, water droplets had frozen and he and Posy were flying in the midst of an ice storm.

He regained his balance but had to dart and dodge away from more of the falling ice. The missiles would kill them both. They had to get to shelter quickly.

With wings tapered backward, they dove downward. The ice pellets hurled past, hissing and crackling as they hit the ground. Sabe saw a bridge in the distance.

"There! Under there!" They sailed into the sanctuary as the skies let loose a heavy barrage of frozen missiles that rattled on the top of their shelter. One more minute, and they both would have paid the price for his recklessness.

"Sabe, your wing is hurt!" exclaimed Posy. A small corner was indeed nipped off. Several scales were also missing, but he felt fortunate to be alive.

He was mortified that he had ignored all the warning alerts and his carelessness had almost killed them both. This would be a long journey, and he must be more mindful of what weather conditions were telling him. He did not deserve the name he carried, and he wondered if Posy might think of giving him a new name, perhaps a name that meant *foolish one.*

"No more foolish chances; you have responsibilities and a duty to uphold," he told himself. He recalled the butterfly who had told him, while he was still a worm, that he was special. "You are fourth generation," she had said. Much was expected of him.

46

Days later, after Sabio and Mariposa left Tennessee and entered Arkansas, they met fellow wanderers from Midwestern states and Canada now entering the corridor of travel and blending with the eastern crowd. Although Sabe had no way to number the pilgrims, over one hundred million Monarchs had felt the call to migration. He also had no way of knowing that only one in every five of these millions would arrive at their destination.

"We'll need to stay alert, make sure we don't lose each other along the way," said Sabe one night as they rested on the same branch that dozens of other travelers had also chosen. He did not know the odds were against them, but he did believe that traveling with a companion enhanced the chances of survival.

Mariposa preferred to let Sabe take the lead, but he soon learned that she was better than he at keeping them on course. He rather enjoyed sensing his way through the corridor leading toward their goal. Since he was not a follower of the masses, Sabe tended to wander along the periphery of the intended route. While he sailed along daydreaming about what was to come, Mariposa efficiently calculated their bearings. At times, especially under overcast skies, she would fly along his right side and gently nudge him back on track. Her antennae were finely tuned to the sun's position in the sky, a skill passed from generation to generation.

With favorable conditions over Arkansas, they had been putting nearly eighty miles under their wings each day. As they approached Saratoga, in the southern part of the state, the days of intense traveling began to take a toll.

Sabe slowed his flight to a gentle glide.

"I'm famished!" he signaled to Posy. "I saw a good roadside spot down below. Let's eat and then find a place to overnight."

Along a highway filled with the roaring beasts that carried two-legged creatures, clusters of Joe-Pye weed dotted a field. Sabe had also caught the shimmer of Millwood Lake. Surely there would be a resting place nearby.

In his rush to partake of the promise of the Joe-Pye, Sabe glided into the path of one extraordinarily large and snarling beast. He felt himself pushed roughly upward and away from the gigantic head. As he tumbled sideways, he witnessed a horrible scene. The jaws of the beast had captured and flattened many fellow butterflies. They had not been as fortunate as he and would never go any further on the journey.

Sabe had only a second to try to understand what he had seen; then an incredible turbulence clutched him, rendering his wings useless and tossing and turning his body until he was dizzy. The beast had passed, but the maelstrom following it left Sabe lying upside down on the gravel roadside.

Breathless and scared silly, he tested each of his six legs.

"Are you all right?" Posy glided to a stop beside him. When she saw that he would survive, both antennae came down over her mouth, stifling her laugh. "Did you learn anything there?" she finally managed to squeak out.

"Yes, don't eat Joe-Pye here. It's protected by beasts and a fierce wind."

"You may not be as wise as I thought."

Still lying on the gravel, Sabe admitted sheepishly that yes, he had been careless. He flopped over and took inventory of body parts. Covered with grit from tumbling along the roadside, he found that he was missing a few more of the scales that covered his wings to keep them from breaking apart. Once lost, scales were gone for good; he could never replenish them. The damage would not end his journey, but he must use more discretion.

At least, the black spots on his wings were unaffected. He hoped his battle scars made him even more attractive to Posy.

"I am quite a resilient fellow, though, aren't I?" he quipped cheerfully as he shook off the dust and grit.

"Resilient, yes. I'm convinced you must be destined to complete this journey."

Several other clusters of butterflies were gliding in to find spots to overnight near the tranquil lake shore. Sabe and Posy swooped beneath the roof of a picnic shelter and settled in.

"I do believe that tomorrow I will lead and decide when and where we eat," said Posy.

Sabe did not respond. He was seeing again the jaws of the huge beast, the flattened butterflies, and the quick glimpse of his own possible demise. Thinking about the fragility of their lives, he decided that someone, somewhere, must be looking out for him and Posy as they journeyed.

***

In the morning, a heavy mist hung over Millwood Lake. The Monarchs had kept dry in the refuge beneath the picnic shelter, and Sabe was certain if they moved quickly they could ascend through the vapor to clear skies.

Their wings did grow heavier as they rose through the blanket of moisture, but soon they burst out of the fog and were welcomed by the blue Arkansas dome. The sun's warming rays skimmed across the top of the drifting gray expanse as the two kept climbing, finally reaching cruising height where they spread their wings to soak up the strength of the sunlight.

Posy's antennae found the rising sun and then the distant horizon. She made her calculations quickly, using the formula engraved on her brain.

"Follow me," she called to Sabe. The fog hid the landscape, and she did not want Sabe to take any chances as they winged their way into Texas. She knew they still had many days until they reached their destination, and her friend's wandering along the outer edges of their path not only delayed them but also exposed them to more dangers.

The following day, somewhere between Dallas and Longview, a stiff headwind met them, blowing in from the west. The corridor of flight was three hundred miles wide here, and Sabe decided to drift with the current for as long as possible. He was still feeling the effects of his encounter with the beast on the highway. They'd have a relaxing day; and if the wind cooperated, they could make up the difference quickly. Fortunately, the current he boarded also curled slightly south, and Posy's calculations showed they were only slightly off course.

Approaching Houston from the east, Sabe was intrigued by the vast body of water off in the distance. The air took on a different quality, filled with moisture from its journey across the gulf. The traveling would have been more difficult, but the air current pushed them back across the corridor where they wanted to be, and Posy's antennae relaxed.

As they drifted beyond Houston in a southwesterly direction, the air lost its moisture and flight was smoother. More travelers crowded the skies, as all routes from the eastern states converged. Sometimes Sabe lost sight of Posy as they mingled with thousands of other Monarchs, but she always found him again.

He almost lost her entirely one evening. They glided into a lovely spot with brightly colored flowers that promised a succulent meal. A two-legged creature much like the one who had chosen them walked among the blooms. With no reason to fear that creature, Sabe and Posy landed on blossoms nearby.

Sabe visited a yellow rose, and he had just unrolled his straw tongue and found sweet nectar deep within when a movement brought him to full attention. Turning toward Posy, he saw a black cat crouched, its yellow eyes watching his beautiful companion flitting happily in the paradise of lantana and alyssum and salvia.

"Posy! Cat!" he shouted. He was too late. A black paw shot out and smacked Posy out of the air. Posy landed on her back on the ground. Dazed, she flopped over and attempted to take flight.

Wham! Another blow smashed her down. The black beast crouched, waiting for her next attempt at escape.

"Posy! Don't move!"

Desperate to save her, he swooped so close to the cat's head that he brushed a whisker. The yellow eyes followed his flight. Sabio darted back, tantalizing and taunting. Black haunches coiled, ready to spring. Sabe danced away from the brute, who had forgotten the motionless Posy.

"Here, kitty, kitty," called the two-legged creature. The cat bounded away, and Sabio, with all senses on alert for more danger, winged back to find Posy, who lay dazed beneath a columbine.

"What happened?"

"A cat. Are you all right?"

"I think so. Nothing seems to be broken or missing. I think I might have landed on my right antenna. It's got a little bend in it."

Sabe acknowledged Posy's superior navigational abilities, but he did wonder if this might take her skills to a new level. Pointing one antenna toward the sun and one toward the distant horizon, she might make even more efficient calculations. But since he really was growing wiser, he kept that bit of humor to himself.

47

The two Monarchs adjusted their course slightly and descended into Hebbronville. Sabe spotted a flat field where orderly rows of rocks jutted up from the earth. A few scrubby trees scattered among the stones might give refuge for the night, but his attention was drawn to the flowers draping many of the rocks. He glided into the Old Hebbronville Cemetery with Posy following.

Disappointment filled him when none of the blooms offered even a drop of nectar. He sensed none of the usual pleasant aromas, either; and as Posy lit on one rock beside him, he signaled his dismay. "Looks like everything is dead in here."

They would not invade the town. Neither wanted to tangle again with a garden beast. Looping around the fenced area, they discovered several patches of mist flowers and a drift of partridge peas. Soon their hunger and thirst were sated, and they clung to a twig on a yaupon tree for the night.

On their final morning in Texas, they fluttered into a clear blue sky. Posy's bent antenna continued to calculate directions splendidly, and they covered 52 miles by midafternoon.

Soon they would cross the Rio Grande River and enter the country last seen by their great-grandparents one year before. Their fragile yet strong wings had propelled them southward for three weeks; they had been traveling longer than most generations of Monarchs lived.

Yet the dancing flight must continue. They were not yet home.

They found lodging near the Texas border town of Zapata, where a dam created the Falcon Reservoir. Fingers of water carved inlets along the shore, and trees and bushes lining the banks seemed an ideal place for overnighting. Many other migrants were already clustered on branches, and Posy suggested finding a place in the rocky promontory overlooking one inlet. Fissures in the rocks gave shelter and still held the warmth of the day. The two wanderers squeezed together in one cleft and spent a calm and peaceful night.

The night turned chilly, and butterflies in the trees and bushes huddled together, shivering. Sabe and Posy, though, were warm the entire night. They departed the next morning, rested and refreshed.

The sun's warmth came quickly as they winged their way toward Guadalupe, Mexico. In the early afternoon, Sabe surveyed the jagged mountain peaks of the Cumbres de Monterrey National Park. Pulled by the promise of adventure, he drifted downward with the intention of exploring forests and canyons.

Posy hung back. She sensed that they were nearing the end of the journey, and she did not want to delay. Sabe convinced her to at least explore with him, and the beauty of the park did look inviting.

"This would be a great place to stay," said Sabe, as they drifted above lush vegetation covering a mountainside. "Why go further? This seems perfect."

Posy objected. She did not want to stop short of the goal.

"Let's at least spend the afternoon and night here in the park," argued Sabe. He thought perhaps she would reconsider and agree to remain with him at this beautiful spot.

It was indeed a stunning place. They descended, detouring around a cloud of mist rising from a waterfall, and entered a deep canyon that was sliced by a river and lined with towering cliffs.

Gliding to a stop on the riverbank, they found themselves in the company of many other butterflies. The low music of the placid current welcomed the wanderers.

That this place might also hold great danger for them never occurred to Sabe.

Planting his legs against a smooth rock that jutted into the stream, he unrolled his proboscis and drank deeply. With no warning sign and in a split second, he lost his purchase on the rock surface and tumbled into the grip of the waters.

Posy heard his muffled cry. Communication flowed primarily through their wings, and Sabe's outstretched wings were caught fast by the water. Posy scampered as close to the edge of the rock as possible. Sabe lay stretched on the waters, helpless.

"Move all your legs as fast as you can," she advised. With all six stompers paddling furiously, Sabe turned his body bit by bit toward the bank. Posy could do nothing but watch and call out encouragement.

Exhausted and frightened, Sabe dragged himself at last onto a root reaching from the riverbank into the water. For an hour he rested on the branch, drying his wings. Posy sat quietly beside him. Finally, she saw his wings begin again to move up and down.

Posy crept a little closer to her companion. They were quiet as they watched two other butterflies dancing above the stream. The dance must have been a game, a dare between the two to see who could fly closest to the water without being caught by the flow.

On one particularly low swoop, the larger butterfly misjudged and his wings grazed the peaceful-looking waters. That slight brush with the perilous danger cost him his life. He lay pasted to the water, held by its grip. Before he had time to attempt to free himself, a ripple appeared on the surface of the river. A burst of water ... and the floating butterfly disappeared.

His companion, in foolishness, drifted back, seeking his playmate. In a flash, the enemy rose from the watery underworld and snatched the second Monarch from the air.

Sabio was shaken; he had seen enough.

"You were right," he admitted. "This place, although appealing to the eye, is not where we should be stopping. This is not a safe place for butterflies. We should never have let ourselves be distracted from our goal."

Posy wanted to remind Sabe she had been against this expedition from the start, but then she remembered how he had saved her from the garden beast. She did appreciate his adventurous spirit, but this trip was not about adventure. At stake was the survival of her family. This canyon, with dangers lurking in lovely settings, was not where they had been called to stay.

**

Over the next several days, a veritable traffic jam filled the skyways. Anticipation ran throughout the vast clouds of butterflies; everyone knew the journey would soon be finished. The crowd now numbered in the millions, and Posy relaxed her constant monitoring of direction; although she still occasionally checked their position, she was content to follow the waves of orange and black, all headed to the same destination.

The congestion presented new challenges. Every directional change had to be carefully thought out lest they bump into a fellow traveler, and Sabe and Posy sometimes lost sight of each other in the crowd for hours. The flapping of millions of fragile wings reminded Sabe of the soft pattering of rain drops on the porch roof of their early days.

Posy saw it long before Sabe did. She found him in the crowd and winged to his side.

"There!"

She took the lead and swooped downward toward the town of Angangueo. They floated over whitewashed homes with tiny but lovely back yards. Shops lined the cobblestone streets, and many two-legged creatures went to and fro. A cluster of small two-legged ones waved banners and danced along the streets as they welcomed the Monarchs home. Surprised, Sabe understood their words.

"Mariposa! Mariposa! Mariposa!" the children shouted.

"Why are they shouting your name? How do they know you, among all these millions of wanderers?" Sabe was more convinced than ever that he was indeed a fortunate butterfly with an incredibly special companion.

Posy gave him her sweet butterfly smile. "In this country, my name means *butterfly.*"

There was more shouting, but this clamoring was in all parts of his body. His directional beacons overrode every other signal and said, *You're almost there!* This message was so clear and so powerful that he ignored the flowers that had been draped everywhere in the town to celebrate the coming of the Monarchs.

The two wanderers, along with millions of others, wove through the streets, around buildings, over trees. Through the town they flew, over cornfields and patches of brilliant wildflowers, up the canyon toward the mountain that stretched nearly 10,000 feet toward the sky and called them home.

"Nearly to the top. That's where we must go," said Posy, breathless from excitement. Sabe followed as she ascended again.

A piney scent engulfed them. Hundreds of tall oyamel fir trees rose from the forest floor. Many of the trees were covered with what appeared to be beautiful orange and black flowers. As he winged through the forest, Sabe realized these were not trees with flowers but trees completely covered with fellow butterflies. In a hushed and reverent tone he spoke to no one and everyone.

"Amazing, incredible, glorious," he intoned. It seemed as if all the butterflies in the universe had come home.

Carefully flying around tree branches already heavy with Monarchs, Sabe headed for the periphery of the forest. It was far too crowded at the center of butterfly universe. Posy followed him without comment. At the edge of the masses, they chose a tree branch with a good view of the surroundings and joined several thousand others also settling in.

"Posy, lock this branch into your being. Wherever we journey through the day, we will always come back here. Whatever our future holds, we will meet it together." Side by side, they nestled into a peaceful and much deserved rest.

Sabio did not know this was the same branch his ancestors had called home three generations before.

48

The sharp scraping sound jerked Johnny away from a vision of Annie. She often walked through his dreams, laughing, vibrant, and very much alive. This dream left an ache, though. She had suddenly appeared as he rounded a corner of the house, and they stood face to face. She was smiling at him.

"Annie, how are you?" he blurted out.

"I am fine, Johnny, completely fine."

She drifted away before he could say anything else, and he walked on, hearing his own voice saying, "She's dead, you know." She had been gone four months, and reality was finally crowding into even his dreams.

At times, he almost believed he could somehow mend this splitting apart of his life. Perhaps moving back into the big farmhouse, back to the comfortable home of his youth, would close the cleft that had opened between unscarred boyhood and stable manhood. Maybe those few years after Annie showed up in his life could be sealed over, moved out of his psyche, so that the gash would heal and his life would once again feel whole.

Those thoughts were soon banished because, try as he might, he could find no way to deny that brief slice of time. He knew that nothing he could do would eradicate all the consequences of loving

Annie and then losing her. His life was forever changed. But what had it been changed to? What was his life now?

The February weather matched his mood. The first week had been damp and dreary. Even a smidgeon of sunshine would have improved everyone's dispositions; but it was winter in Ohio, and asking for sunny days was asking for quite a lot.

The cows were mooing impatiently. He must get out of bed and get to the barn. Then he recognized the sound that had interrupted his dream. It was the scraping of a shovel. Throwing back the curtain, he was surprised to see that the previous night's drizzle had turned to snow and ice; and now his dad was clearing a path to the barn.

Ten years before, Johnny would have been thrilled to see the blanket of snow. He would have built snowmen and gone sledding with friends and counted the snowfall as an exciting gift. Now, snow meant only work and misery. Had this change come, too, when he lost Annie? He could not remember a time when he was happy and excited about life; every step he now took was drudgery.

Mandy and Naomi greeted him as he walked into the barn. He heard them, but did not respond. That was becoming a habit. He did not intend to be rude or distant, but life was not the same, and he was having a hard time going on with old rituals. Sometimes he stood apart from the rest of the world and watched life go on as if everything was normal. No one realized, it seemed to him, that it was impossible for life to ever be normal again.

Naomi had the feed scoop in her hand and was scattering the cow's morning nourishment in the trough. That was usually Johnny's job, but he felt no guilt. He did not care. He slumped down on the one-legged milking chair and settle into the routine, listening to the white swishes of milk hitting the bucket with a hypnotizing, rhythmic beat.

Milking was one of the few times when the numbness seemed to lift and his thoughts broke free of paralysis. He had always enjoyed this chore, and now its familiarity and repetitiveness allowed his mind to be brave enough to wander down paths he had ignored for a time but had never quite forgotten.

The old questions were back. Was this farm his life? When he and Annie were dreaming about children and growing old together, he had been content to accept this place as his future. He had even welcomed such a future. But Annie had vanished from that future, and with her went his anchor and all his dreams. Now he was right back where he had started, wondering if he truly was Jonas's John's Johnny, born to fit neatly into this lineage and continue the Amish heritage as the fourth generation of Miller farmers.

The one thing he did know was that he was slowly dying even while living. The desperation sometimes threatened to suffocate him, as surely as if he had lain at the bottom of Annie's grave and they had thrown the dirt on top of him that day.

Something had to change. He needed to find some direction, find some way to heal the restlessness, find something that would fill the hole in his life. In his desperate searching, old fancies had been rekindled, and now the man still had to deal with the boy's doubts and dreams.

He toyed with the idea of a move. But the move might bring a fate similar to death.

The consequences of his actions would open Pandora's box; he knew that. He was now baptized, a member of the Amish church, and leaving the church would mean he would be ostracized by his family and friends. If he did this thing, he would cease to exist in the Amish world.

Would his parents honor such a brutal dictate? Would he be banned from their table, unwelcome in the family circle? The Miller family had been known to break with tradition; and with the passage of time or perhaps the understanding of the bishop, the ban was sometimes occasionally lifted. But the bishop was now his father, and Johnny remembered well John's insistence that he could not sign for Johnny's driver's license. It would not have been right, John had said, to require one thing of the people in his church and not follow those requirements with his own family.

Johnny stood up, lifting the pail of warm milk. He would soon find out what his family would do with a wayward son.

***

"Johnny? Johnny!" Naomi's voice pushed into his thoughts at the breakfast table. "Are you listening to me?"

"Ummm … no, sorry."

"And I called to you in the barn twice this morning, and you didn't seem to hear me," Mandy chimed in. "What's on your mind these days?"

Johnny knew that his mother thought his moods and distraction were caused by memories of that terrible September day. Or perhaps she had guessed what was truly burdening him, since he had never been able to hide much from his mom.

"I'm thinking of leaving," he answered.

"Leaving? Leaving what?" Mandy was clearly shocked. So she did not suspect, after all.

"Here. Home. Everything. I have to do something … different. I can't go on here, sad and depressed and lonely."

"But we're here for you, aren't we? That will be enough, we will get through this time somehow …"

"That used to be enough, Mom, but Annie changed all that. And now, I don't know where my life should go or what it should be. I really need to find some kind of direction, and I can't seem to find it here."

John's deep voice spoke up for the first time.

"What are your plans, Son?"

"I'm thinking about going on a long bike ride. I've always wanted to see the West. I'll take the bus to the West Coast, then pedal across the country and give myself some time to try to think through things, sort things out. Maybe I'll end up in Florida. Maybe I'll find a job there."

He did not say it, but yet he had said it. He was leaving the farm. And now he must say the next sentence as gently as possible.

"And I'm thinking perhaps I should leave the church."

There was silence around the table. He was afraid Mandy would cry, and Naomi looked like she was working out a puzzle, trying to read his mind.

"Have you really thought through the consequences of such action?" John's words were stern, but his face was sorrowful. He did not have to enumerate everything Johnny would lose. Everyone around the table knew exactly what this decision meant.

"I've already lost everything important to me. This is no longer enough." Johnny knew the words would hurt them, but it must be said. "I don't know what my life is now. Allow me to go figure it out."

Mandy started to speak, but quickly pinched her lips shut. They sat in silence, no one eating.

Mandy finally stood. "I'll pray it is God's will to bring you back home." And she began to clear the table.

49

The next weeks passed quickly. Johnny was surprised to find that finally making the decision to act had lifted his spirits.

What was his life now without Annie? What was his future? As far as he could see, there were no answers to those questions. The unknown did frighten him, but he would face it head on instead of drifting around in fruitless circles.

Did he want to remain Amish? Did he want to be a farmer? At this point, his answer to both questions was *No*.

It was far easier to deal with questions of preparation for his trip. He briefly entertained the idea of buying a new bicycle. The bike of his boyhood days, purchased with the egg money, was now outdated; bicycle technology had advanced since the day he had first pushed it up the street in Stevenson. However, he knew the bike was dependable and virtually maintenance free. It had opened up life for him so many years ago, and perhaps it would help him rediscover life. It would be like having the comfort of an old friend along on the trip. He would take his boyhood bike.

A trip to the welding shop turned the bicycle into a touring bike. It was no longer a thing of red-and-chrome beauty, but it was functional. The front basket was still solid, and those items that must be readily available he would stash there in front of him.

Another wire basket was welded to a frame and attached to the rear fender. His tent, sleeping bag, and clothing went into that back basket. Fully loaded front and back, the weight of his entire ride was almost seventy pounds. But the bike frame was sturdy, Johnny was strong, and there was no timetable for his journey.

Included in his stash was a last-minute addition he took from the tree house. Old memories had drawn him many times to the hideaway in the tall oak, and he sat there one afternoon and let the flood of recollections pierce and warm him. Each wall and corner held memories, some visible, others only a remembrance tucked away in his mind. The curtain and the rug underfoot were reminders that Annie had been here, and now she was gone.

On a whim, he grabbed the transistor radio. Perhaps he would want a noise box at times when thinking became too painful.

***

Early on the first day of March, Johnny pedaled away from everything he knew. The difficult goodbyes had been said. He promised Mandy to write often, and he heard his dad once again say, "I love you, Son."

Annie's notebook, holding her thoughts from the summer of joy and also the letter with her last words to her husband, was packed carefully among his belongings. At the times that he felt he could bear to read it, her handwriting on the page brought her voice back to him.

In that notebook he had also discovered a letter to Christine. He had no idea if Christine, sometime in the future, should ever see this; but he thought that perhaps he would add to the notebook for Christine his own memories of her mother.

Darkness still covered the valley when a solitary man wearing a dark blue denim jacket closed with hooks and eyes, a black hat, and barn-door pants pedaled away from his Amish existence.

Johnny had plenty of time to reach the bus stop in Stevenson.

He had left the farm early enough so that if he met other morning riders or was recognized by farmers choring in barnyards, the darkness would blur the details of his burdened bicycle. He could imagine the speculation that would rage through the community if he was spotted pedaling along on such a strangely outfitted and fully loaded bike. Folks for miles around would be wondering what Johnny Miller was up to now. He could imagine how the tongues would wag in shops and mills, or at quiltings and auctions.

At least for a short while, their talk would all be speculation. He was fairly certain that neither John nor Mandy had told anyone outside the family about his plans. He suspected that his parents hoped he would soon miss home and would return before many folks realized he was gone. Naomi, of course, had told Paul. Johnny would have, but she had seen Paul before Johnny had a chance to tell his best friend his plan. Paul came by one night to say his goodbyes, but things were awkward between the two.

Eventually, word would hit the grapevine that he was headed to Los Angeles, California, and from there he planned to ride a bike across the Southwest to Florida. That would perplex folks.

"He's an Amish man, what's he thinking?"

"Didn't you know? He's left the Amish church."

"How can he put his parents through this?"

The John Miller family would be news for miles around, at least, throughout the Amish communities.

Johnny slowly got the bicycle up to speed. His Red Wing work shoes still carried some reminders of barn chores at home. That, too, would wear off, he thought grimly.

The bike's headlight cast a small yellow circle on the highway ahead, and the red blinker on the rear flashed a goodbye to his valley of birth, his boyhood home, and the life he had known.

50

Past the Valley View School he pedaled with a ferocity meant to ward off any ambush of memories. Soon after, he was rolling through the deserted streets of Milford. The dark windows of the hardware store reminded him of the day he had purchased those jar lids for Mandy, the day his family had tricked him into meeting the new schoolteacher.

As he rounded the hilltop at the edge of Stevenson, faint light touched his shoulders and announced the arrival of the morning sun. The row of buildings stretching out along Main Street was dimly outlined. It seemed a lifetime ago that he had pushed a shiny new bike up the sidewalk and then pedaled this very hill out of town to freedom. It *was* a lifetime ago, he thought. And that life was gone. What was his life now?

The sandstone courthouse towered over the downtown, and he cringed at thoughts of another time he had caused shadows of shame and embarrassment to fall on his family. But that was the old Johnny. He had become a new creature and mended his ways. Still, here he was again, bringing pain to his family and putting them at the center of local gossip.

Was he making a grave mistake that would doom him to a lost eternity? That thought haunted him. He knew there were people who believed that, and he was desperate to resolve his questions and doubts for himself.

He had several hours to wait for the arrival of the Greyhound bus. He had never seen the streets of Stevenson so deserted or the stores so dark and quiet. The barber's pole revolved in the early light, the red and white stripes endlessly circling and climbing to the top where they mysteriously vanished, only to reappear at the base of the column and begin again to circle and rise.

The shop was already lit. An early customer was being sheared. Johnny paused and took in the scene. The man sat in an elevated chair, like a king wrapped in a royal garment. The barber shuffled about behind the throne, cutting and snipping with precise movements. Scissors and comb seemed to work as one instrument as the master groomed the elevated one.

The barber's shop had always fascinated Johnny. Mandy always wielded the scissors at home; and as a boy, Johnny could not understand why some people would have their hair cut here instead of at home. He had never been inside a barber shop, but he had wondered how the world outside looked from the perspective of that kingly chair.

Behind the glass door at Kauffman's Five and Dime, a hand appeared above the CLOSED sign and flipped it over. With nothing else to do, Johnny propped his bike against the wall and ventured inside. As he wandered through the aisles, the creaking of the old wooden floorboards seemed unusually loud, and he felt conspicuous and out-of-place.

Perhaps he had made the decision days or even weeks before, but only now did he acknowledge it. Here in Stevenson, he would leave Amish behind. He knew he was still an Amish man, but he would strip himself of the outward signs. He picked up a pair of jeans, several shirts, and a colorful windbreaker jacket and laid the pile on the counter by the cash register. Another thought came, and he returned to the shelves and brought back a double-edge safety razor and a can of foamy shaving cream.

He had plenty of time for metamorphosis. Back at the courthouse, he leaned the bike against the rail that led down worn sandstone steps to the basement level and carried his bundle to the old restroom. There, an Amish man stared back at him from the mirror above the sink.

"Who are you? What are you?" Johnny asked the image.

There was no reply.

Both sides of the double blades sprang into action. He thrust and stabbed, and his beard slowly disappeared. With one final scrape and a brisk splash of water, the transformation was complete. A quick rinse of the lavatory, and Amish went swirling down the drain.

The man in the mirror slipped into new zipper pants and the flashy jacket. He bundled up the clothes he had discarded. Pausing at the door, Johnny glanced once more at his image and the strange combination of his new clothes and the black hat he still held. He cocked his wrist to flick the hat into the waste container, but at the last moment pulled back. Something within halted the impulse. *Take it all with you*, it said.

Perhaps he did need some reminder of who he once was. Perhaps he could not part with the shirt, pants, and jacket because he could still see Annie's head bent over her sewing machine as she stitched them. Whatever the reason, everything was stuffed into the plastic bag in the rear basket of his bicycle. Why he had obeyed that voice, he did not know.

51

The man in the mirror had reminded him also that he had one more vestige of Amish—his bowl-shaped haircut. The barber's chair was now empty, and the master was busy sweeping the floor, unaware of the audience standing outside his window.

The door squeaked as Johnny stepped inside.

"Morning, young man. Need your ears lowered?"

Johnny gave a brief and businesslike nod.

"Have a seat, and let's round off those corners for you. I've never seen you in here before, where you from?" The barber did not wait for a reply. "My name's McMillan. Mac the Barber, they call me."

Johnny slid into the chair and did feel very much like royalty. Mac cranked a hand lever on the side of the chair. With each crank, Johnny ascended higher. Grabbing a large towel hanging from a nail on the wall, Mac gave it a snap and, with a flourish, floated it across Johnny's body and fastened it behind his neck.

"You know, I started doing this when I was about your age. Never thought then that I'd be here this long." Mac pulled scissors and comb from a drawer and with the concentration of a surgeon snipped away at the bowl of hair.

"My father took over this shop from his dad. I never wanted to be involved in it myself; my goal was to be a doctor. Then I went off to the war, and that changed my mind. I saw so much of death that I never wanted to be anywhere near hurt and dying people again. I came home from the war in '45 and took over this chair." Mac waved his scissors, blades snipping the air, toward another chair that was nearly hidden by stacks of shampoos and creams piled on the seat. "Dad had that other chair over there, and we worked side by side for the next fifteen years. One day in '60, he keeled over right in the middle of giving a man a haircut. He lived several more months, but never set foot in here again."

He paused for a moment, and Johnny managed to get in a few words. "Was that in November of '60?" He had noticed the calendar on the wall was frozen in November of 1960.

"Never got around to changing it back then; now I can't. It reminds me of the best fifteen years of my life. I always hoped someday my boy would take over Dad's chair and we could work side by side and have those good times Dad and I did. But these days, a small shop won't give two living wages. Folks don't care about grooming like they used to. Oh, yes, the old timers still do; but there are fewer and fewer of them. Too many hippie types these days, with that long and untidy hair. Seems like they don't care what they look like.

"See those cups lined up on the shelf? Shaving cups, one for each of our regular customers, each one with its own brush. The ones on the far left are retired; their owners are gone now. Seems the row of cups in use gets shorter and shorter each year. Only about a dozen there now. Used to be, the whole shelf was full.

"Say, what's your name? Where did you say you were from?"

Finally, Mac the Barber did pause and wait for an answer.

"I'm Johnny Miller from over by Milford."

"Well, that sure doesn't narrow it down much. Isn't everybody over there named Miller?"

There was no point in telling Mac that his customer was Jonas's John's Johnny.

The old chair, having seen three generations of customers, had slowly lost its pressure and drifted back to floor level. Several pumps of the hand crank brought Johnny back up to Mac's eye level. The barber turned away for a moment. When he came back to his task, a shining single edge razor dangled from his fingers. The polished silver caught the light and looked cold and merciless.

"I'm going to shave the back of your neck and around your ears, no extra charge. For an extra buck, I would have shaved your face; but I see you've already done that."

Johnny could have saved money by letting Mac remove his beard, but he had had no idea that was a possibility.

Mac swished a brush through the soap in a cup. After carefully covering the back of Johnny's neck with warm foam, the barber brandished the weapon. Johnny tensed, and Mac chuckled.

"Haven't cut anyone too bad yet. Of course, there's always a first time for everything."

"Where is your son?" Johnny asked, trying not to think about the sharp blade.

"He's over there in Vit Nom. That war's been dragging on for too many years." Mac was silent for a moment. Then, in a different voice, "Too many of our boys are gone."

Johnny felt a tug of guilt. Because he was Amish, he had been relatively unaffected by the war in Vietnam. In fact, he had thought little about that conflict on the other side of the world. Amish religious beliefs had created an insulated life, and he had been protected from many things other folks in the world must deal with. Now here he was, turning his back and walking away from that life, but before he had even left Stevenson, he was confronted by difficult issues of life in the outside world.

His head and neck felt chilled and bare. He rubbed his ear. Mac noticed, and grinned.

"Yeah. This haircut won't keep you warm, that's for sure. You need a hat." He nodded toward a row of baseball caps hanging on the wall. "Customers leave 'em here all the time. I let 'em hang there, hoping people will claim their own. Go ahead, pick one and take it with you."

Johnny was a grown man, married and widowed and off to meet the world, yet his heart jumped at the offer. He had spotted the dark blue cap with the grinning Indian almost as soon as he had climbed into the chair, and now he took it down, ran his hand over the red bill, and settled it over his short hair. He could not suppress a delighted smile as he looked in the mirror; for the first time in his life, he was openly displaying his allegiance to the Indians.

"Take a look at you now," exclaimed Mac. "Has anyone ever told you that you look like Paul Newman?"

"No," Johnny replied, and wondered how Mac knew the third-grade teacher back in Milford Elementary. He peered more closely at his image. Mr. Newman was old and pale and heavy. Johnny really did not think he resembled him in any way.

A snarling roar rolled down the street as the bus downshifted.

"Bus is right on time today," observed Mac.

This bus would stop in Columbus, Ohio, early that same afternoon, after making stops in other small towns. In Columbus, Johnny would have to find the next bus headed west. That was his only plan—head west.

His ride into the unknown choked the street with exhaust fumes. The driver helped him stow the bike beneath the bus. He took the sandwiches and cookies Mandy had packed and settled into the seat behind the driver. Johnny was hoping the driver would talk to him as he drove; he needed to mine as much information about bus protocol and terminals as possible. And also, he admitted to himself, he was not yet prepared to be alone with his thoughts.

The driver ground the gears and gunned the engine, and Stevenson and life as Johnny had always known it disappeared behind the hills.

52

Johnny had always thought he was a pretty bold fellow, ready to take on almost any challenge. Now, though, the security and sanctity of home and family was no longer within easy reach. He was facing an unknown future head on, and somehow he would have to grapple with the uncertainties that had landed him on this bus. He had left his safe haven of home only a few hours ago, and already even more questions were floating through his mind.

A picture of the barber's son fighting in Viet Nam rose up beside an image of himself plowing fields and pitching hay. He had automatically registered as a conscientious objector; it was what the Amish and Mennonite boys did. But he had never given much thought to exactly *why* he did that, other than to repeat what he had been taught about peace and violence. He was Amish; therefore, he would not enlist in the army. The choice had been made for him, and he had never questioned it. He *had* wondered, though, how people who say they loved peace could tear families apart by banning some members from their circles.

Now he was walking out into the world in English clothes—and he felt unexpectedly exposed. His beard and plain garb had somehow protected him from having to deal with difficult questions. Now his clothes and beard were gone, and he wondered if he had actually been hiding behind the word *Amish.*

What did it really mean to be Amish? Was it a tradition? Was it a religion? Did shaving and changing clothes mean he was no longer Amish? If that was true, then being Amish only meant dressing in a certain way. He still had his barn-door pants and black hat; if he rotated his clothes, could he be Amish one day and English the next? He felt silly for entertaining such absurd thoughts. There was more to it all than that.

If the image in the mirror were accurate, he was looking quite English. His beard was gone; he no longer had that silent declaration of the reason he was not in Viet Nam. Who was he in this new life?

These new questions came and took their place alongside the old questions that had haunted him for months. Did God really mean for Annie to die when she did? Johnny had heard preachers say that God controls all events in our lives; and if a person's time is up, then he's gone. An Amish neighbor had fallen off his roof, broke his neck, and died a few weeks after Annie's funeral. It was his time to go, it was God's will, the preachers had said. What if the man had taken more safety precautions? Could he have avoided the tragedy? Apparently not; it was his time.

And where did Annie go when she died? That answer, too, he had heard time and again at funerals: We have hope that she arrived in heaven. What did that word, *hope,* mean? Could he only wish and long for the best? Was there no way he could be certain that Annie was safe and at peace?

Already, he missed his father. Johnny wanted to relive a conversation he had begun with John once about death and hope and life hereafter. John was an Amish bishop, but he heard questions. Johnny knew his father preached not from tradition but from his search for the truth in Scriptures. Johnny sat on the bus as it rolled through the hills, and he wanted to talk with his dad. Why did he not have that conversation before he left? With a grim objectivity, he looked back over his life. First, he had been too young to think about death, then he was too rebellious to listen to the church or Scriptures, then he was too happy, and eventually, too full of grief. Now, stripped of all his life thus far, he came face to face with his doubts and questions. He wanted to talk with his dad about *hope*.

But it seemed he had missed all opportunity to do that.

Why was he on this bus? Why was his beard gone, his head cold under the baseball cap? Why could he not have been content to be a good Amish farmer, accepting all that life entailed?

He knew how all this would look to friends and neighbors back home. This journey that he hoped would find him peace and answers to his questions would seem to others like a flight from the church and, they would say, from God. They would expect him to feel guilty; they would *think* him guilty. He did admit to a few twinges of guilt. Still, he believed his motives were pure. He hoped the Scriptures were true, and that God saw his heart and understood his confusion.

When he had decided to follow Jesus that day in the tree house, his decision had been born of more than desperation at the possibility of losing Annie. He realized that following his own ways had led him down paths that were only destructive and chaotic. Unless he gave Jesus control of his life, he would never find peace.

So he needed to find answers. He needed to settle some things. How should he follow Jesus now, in this confusion and blackness and void?

And what if following Jesus meant he must leave his family and church? *Could* it mean that? Would God ask that of anyone?

53

All of the questions, new and old, were too much for Johnny's tired mind. He had slept little the night before, caught between the sadness of leaving his family and the excitement of finally beginning his search. So he closed the door on his jumbled and noisy thoughts and instead chatted with the talkative driver, trying to learn as much as he could about bus travel.

He felt swallowed up by the city. From his spot on a front seat, he watched as the driver maneuvered through the confusing maze of streets and merged with the steady stream of traffic. Tall buildings rose around the bus, and concrete had blotted out almost everything green.

The bus pulled into the terminal on East Town Street in Columbus. The driver had told Johnny this was a new Greyhound station, very nice, he had said. But even though the building buzzed with activity, the bare walls and rows of seats looked cold and unfriendly. Announcements of departures and arrivals filled the air. At the ticket windows, Johnny looked for the kindest face and asked for help in finding a bus traveling west. In a little over an hour, one bus would depart for Denver. There were other options if he was willing to wait, but he was anxious to be on the move. As long as it was going *west,* almost any bus was would do.

The route to Denver would take him through Colorado and the Rocky Mountains. He had never seen a real mountain and could not imagine an entire mountain range, although he'd seen plenty of pictures. He was finally going to see the West. Denver was twenty-four hours away, and then he would transfer to another bus that went to Las Vegas where yet another transfer would finally put him on a bus to Los Angeles.

An attendant helped him load the bike into the cargo hold. The man asked if Johnny had more bags, and when the answer was no, the man eyed the packs in both baskets.

"You need anything from here? Denver's a real long ride, and you might want something to cover up with while you sleep."

Johnny thanked him for the advice and dug out his old denim jacket, the one he had worn while pedaling out of the valley. The radio came with him, too; he thought he might need company in the lonely hours ahead.

He was happy that the earpiece was still intact; no one would be disturbed by his choice of music. And even though he was tired, he was far from sleep; and he was not yet ready to wade again into that maelstrom of questions.

From the window seat at the rear of the bus, he watched the landscape roll by. A sign welcomed him to Indiana and pierced him with sharp arrows of remembrance. Twice before he had traveled to this state. The events of those trips seemed as distant and faded as though they had happened a lifetime before; yet only a few short years had passed. Leaving Ohio had felt so adventurous when Annie was with him; now, even though he was eager to see what new life awaited him, everything was tinged with melancholy.

Several hours passed, and the bus arrived in Indianapolis, where the driver announced a forty-minute layover. If he wanted to stretch his legs he was free to do so as long as he was back in time to catch the bus. He decided to spend half an hour breathing fresh air and exploring.

The air was not as fresh as he'd hoped, and his exploring only reminded him how little of the world he had really seen. The bus station was on Illinois Street. A brisk stroll took him past Pennsylvania Street and Delaware Street. He wondered if all fifty states were accounted for here in Indianapolis. He filed the question away in his memory bank, to be researched someday with a map of the city in hand.

Back in his seat, feeling the bus roll into motion again, he realized that he was now adrift in the midst of all those states, farther away from home than he had ever been in his life, with no idea what awaited on the road ahead.

***

His stomach reminded him it was supper time. The first bite of one of Mandy's sandwiches turned all his thoughts toward home. They would be choring now. He had left John with all the farm work. Other family members had agreed to help with the milking until their wayward brother returned or until John decided to sell the herd. Johnny wondered how long his father would wait. Did he expect his son back home soon? Johnny remembered that his father had admitted to trying life in the world, but he had not found it satisfying. *Maybe he knows me better than I do myself*, thought Johnny, *and he is confident I'll be returning soon.*

He noted wryly that he already missed the routine of milking chores, the bantering back and forth, and the singing. But could it ever be as it once was? That was all lost to him, wasn't it?

The bus was somewhere between Effingham, Illinois, and Kansas City, Missouri, when darkness descended over the land. It was now impossible to see much of the landscape. With darkness came the realization of how alone he was on this journey, and the loneliness was as dark as the night. He was relieved that he had the radio with him. He twirled through the stations, looking for something that would keep his heavy thoughts at bay. The chatter of deejays offered tidbits of local color from stations he'd never before tuned into. Some of the music was comforting, with familiar voices singing familiar country songs.

He pulled his old jacket over his chest and arms. The coat smelled of home and a better time.

***

A humming sound woke him. His neck and shoulders ached, and he had no idea where he was. *On a bus, Johnny, much farther from home than you've ever been before.*

Morning light began to bring color back to the landscape, and Johnny marveled at the flat land and vast fields. What must it be like to farm such huge tracts with no hills?

"We'll be stopping for twenty minutes in Junction City, Kansas," announced the driver. What a relief. He desperately needed a break. He had never before been cooped up in a vehicle this long. "Another six hours, and we'll be in Denver."

Colorado! He looked forward to seeing that state. His long-ago dreams of the West had always been set in Colorado or Texas; and after riding the bus almost twenty-four hours, he had still not seen any area that was more appealing than what he had left behind in Ohio.

The twenty-minute break refreshed him. He bought a cup of coffee and ate two of Mandy's cookies.

When the bus started rolling again and he waited for the arrival of the Colorado mountains, he twiddled the radio dials. A preacher from all the way down in Oklahoma floated in on an AM station. The sermon must have been prerecorded, because the speaker had a full head of steam and was shouting vociferously. It was much too early in the day to be that excited.

The preacher, though, had worked himself into a frenzy, declaring that this day would surely be the last day salvation was available to some folks.

"If you died today do you know where you will spend

eternity? You can know without a doubt where you will spend eternity," he bellowed. "What does your salvation rest on? Are you anchored to the rock?"

Johnny gave the dial a whirl and muttered, "I have hope."

***

When at last, a sign proclaimed that they were indeed in Colorado, Johnny was disappointed. The land was still as flat as Kansas. Perhaps it was a good thing he had never come west with his cowboys. Far in the distance, though, loomed what he thought must be a mountain range. Maybe Denver marked the beginning of the West.

Shortly before noon, the bus came to a stop at 17th Street and Broadway. Johnny had arrived in Denver. The massive mountain ranges looming around this city were indeed a spectacle to behold. Most of the mountains still lay under a shroud of snow. *Surely no one can farm here,* Johnny mused. *That snow will not be gone in time for spring planting, even if one could plant those slopes. I doubt this terrain would support crops, and no cattle could graze on those mountains.* Perhaps the West of his dreams began on the other side of the Rockies.

The timing of the buses amazed him. They arrived in Denver within several minutes of the posted arrival time. He retrieved his bike and went in search of a bus marked for Las Vegas.

He had never had any desire to visit the one state in America that allowed gambling. But the quickest route to Los Angeles ran through Nevada. And at least he could add one more state to the list of states he had seen. He was certain, though, that he would never be back this way again.

Toward evening, the bus stopped at Grand Junction, the last stop in Colorado. Johnny had been fascinated and thrilled by the ride through mountain ranges and deep gorges.

The stopover was forty minutes, enough time to replenish his food supply. Mandy's last sandwich had disappeared earlier in the day. Johnny strolled to a nearby store. Close to the checkout, a rack displayed postcards boasting of the splendor of Colorado; and he purchased a few, unsure whether they were for friends or for his own collection.

It was soon apparent that the postcards were meant for him. By the time the bus reached Green River, Utah, all six cards were full of notes he had written to himself. He planned to transfer his thoughts to Annie's notebook later, when the bus stopped in Las Vegas. With home disappearing behind him, he was trying to focus on what he was searching for and what he wanted to achieve with this ride. Without a definite purpose, the long ride across the country could turn into nothing more than a frivolous adventure. He was not seeking adventure; he was seeking answers.

Crossing over the Green River, he remembered a geography class when the teacher had spoken about the Green River flowing into the Colorado River and together both rivers flowed through the Grand Canyon. The diverse landscape of Utah amazed him. He had had notions about what these western states looked like; but so far, nothing he had seen matched the country of his imagination.

Utah had magnificent beauty, but Johnny saw very little of agricultural value. What passed for parks and scenic vistas was really nothing more than the effects of extreme erosion.

54

Johnny slept for hours, through Cedar City and a quick five-minute stop in St. George.

He did awake, though, when the bus came to a halt at the Union Bus Depot. It was after midnight, but how much after, he did not know. Traveling through several time zones and being in such unfamiliar surroundings, he no longer had any clarity of time. At home, he needed no timepiece. Everything was regimented. Awake at a set time every morning. Go do the chores, eat breakfast, then tackle whatever work needed to be done. On the farm, he could judge the time within minutes by checking the angle of the sun or by a quick glimpse at the cows grazing in the field or a dozen other indicators of the time of day. In his previous life, getting something done was a matter of time and timing. Out here, with no responsibilities, time was only something folks wore on their wrists.

The Union Bus Depot was in a state of disrepair. The main building was being torn down, to be rebuilt as the Union Plaza Motel, a sign declared. The bus depot would then be part of the newest Las Vegas hotel.

Johnny would change buses here and had a one-hour layover before the final leg of the trip to Los Angeles. He retrieved his bike and propped it alongside the building. The radio went back into the rear basket; he planned to sleep the final six hours on the next bus. When he stuck the postcards into the writing tablet, several envelopes slipped to the sidewalk. Of course, it was Mandy looking out for her son. The envelopes were already stamped and addressed to his family at home. Standing on the gritty street in Las Vegas with garish lights flashing around him, Johnny felt loved and wanted.

With close to an hour to kill and knowing he would never pass this way again, he decided to explore and attempt to understand the allure of this city. Above towered a neon cowboy with lights flashing, waving his neon arm back and forth, welcoming all to this world. The cowboy stood atop the Pioneer Club, and the large flashing sign on the building advertised GAMBLING.

Johnny knew it was well past midnight, but he pushed his bike down Fremont Street in a glaring, artificial day. Everywhere, lights flashed names of hotels and gambling establishments. Folks poured out of places like The Mint, Golden Nugget, Binion's Horseshoe, and Four Queens. Traffic jammed the streets and bodies swarmed on the sidewalks. The city flashed and glittered. He felt crowded and oppressed. This city, like the mountains, was beyond anything he had imagined it to be.

A dry wind kicked up and sent waves of grit into his face and down his neck. While he was gawking through a window at spinning slot machines, his bike tire bumped a pedestrian.

"Watch where you're going, bum!" the man shouted. Johnny's face was no longer clean-shaven and his clothes were disheveled; he supposed he did look something like a bum.

Many unsavory characters lurked about. He was glad he had not left his bicycle packed with possessions at the bus station. A man with bleary eyes and slurred words asked him for change for coffee; the beggar addressed Johnny from a seat on the sidewalk.

Johnny mumbled an excuse and turned away.

He needed to get away from here, and fast. This was no place for an Amish man; this was no place for any man. He turned his bike to return to the station.

As he passed, a casino's doors swung open and roars of laughter mixed with shouts of jubilation or wails of dejection. He suddenly felt very sad and lonely. He had never before been in such a crowd and felt so lonely. Moving as fast as he could through the crowds, he tried to escape the noise and confusion. He knew for a certainty he would never set foot in this town again.

The noise followed him onto the bus. Any hope of sleep was lost once the bus was rolling toward Los Angeles. Every seat was full, and Johnny was surrounded by discouraged and broke gamblers headed home to towns scattered between Las Vegas and the coast. Many of them were drunk and were loud in their misery and laments. He understood little of the gamblers' jargon, but it was apparent that no one had won. Still, he was amazed at the common chorus he heard, "Next time, I'll win it back."

From Barstow to Anaheim, these eternal optimists departed the bus. With great relief, he left the bus at Union Station in Los Angeles.

"What a lot that was," he remarked to the bus driver while waiting for his bike to be unloaded.

The driver shook his head. "I do this run every night. I've seen so many people who have lost everything. But they keep coming back, convinced the next trip will make them rich."

***

The hour was early; the day was crisp and fresh. Johnny was lonely and tired and hungry. He desperately needed a place to rest and freshen up.

Pushing his ride into Union Station, he met humanity as he had never witnessed it before. Folks of all races and nationalities milled about. Many bearded and dirty folks slept scattered about in the rows of seats. Well, if he looked like a vagrant, he may as well sleep a few hours here himself. In a corner away from the stream of people, he lowered his bike to the floor and stretched out beside it with an arm on the front wheel and his legs draped over the rear wheel. It was the only protection he had against any broke gambler driven by desperation to thievery.

A huge city and a large country waited outside, but he had no idea where to go next. That decision would have to wait a few hours. He fell asleep and shut off all thoughts of bright lights and dim people.

55

Something bumped his foot, prodding him out of a deep slumber. He moved his leg, but the bumping followed, nudging and insisting, until he was pulled from sleep, immensely annoyed.

"Move along; pushin' broom here. All hippies, vagrants, squatters, must leave. Move or be swept away."

The broom bumped his foot again, insisting on action. His tired eyes opened far enough to see a black face leaning toward him. Johnny scrambled to his feet.

"My apologies for being in your way, sir. I'm not a vagrant, nor am I homeless. Just needed a short nap."

"Ah knows you isn't a vagrant, 'cause no vagrant would burden himself with so much baggage as ya'll is carryin'." The man behind the broom chuckled.

"Where you from, young fella?" The broom paused, and the man peered intently at Johnny. "Why're you runnin' from home?"

"I'm from a little town in Ohio called Milford, and I'm not running from home."

"Thas down in Amish country! Lots of them Amish folks drivin' buggies down there. Ah'm from Clevelun myself. The missus and ah enjoyed an occasional trip to Amish Country."

"I am Amish myself."

"Young fella, ah knows what Amish is, and you isn't it."

"Really, sir, I am Amish. I left home several days ago and took a Greyhound bus out here to ride my bicycle back toward home. I cut off my beard and changed my clothes, but I still have my Amish hat and shirt and pants."

"Well, ah nevah heard such nonsense. Ah left Clevelun thirty years ago fer a betta life. But you surely had a wunnerful life back in Ohiah. Why'd you leave?"

"I did indeed have a great life. I'm trying to decide if that is the life for me, though. I was in Cleveland one time to watch the Indians play, and it seemed like a good place to live. Why did you leave there, sir?"

"Came outta the service in '42, ah did. Had seen too many warm places in the worl by then and Clevelun was too cole. Didna have much family there no more, 'cause my mama passed while ah was ovasees."

"What about your father? Doesn't he miss you being around?"

"Pappa was not allus aroun'. Only thing he evah gave me was his name."

A large black hand extended a greeting. Johnny shook hands with a black man for the first time in his life.

"Name's Leroy L. Jackson, Jr. My daddy was Leroy L. Jackson the First. Ah promised myself to wear my daddy's name well. You's name is like ennythin' else, you can either wear it well and take care of it or you can destroy it. Got married to a great lady, name of Mildred, ah did. Give me three chillen, she did. Two girls and one son. She passed on five years ago, yes, she did."

A faraway look entered the man's eyes as he recalled former days. Johnny took the silence to interject his own story.

"Leroy, that's why I am out here on this ride. My wife died recently, and her death turned my life upside down."

"The Lawd gives und the Lawd takes."

"Do your three children live near you?"

"They does, and they is gettin' school learnin'. Myself, ah quit afta sixth grade to help Mama. Grew up on the streets, ah did. Did sum things ah'm not proud of. My lovely wife Mildred insisted on the chillen gettin' a better eddacashun than ah did. She allus say ah only use half the alph'bet when ah speaks. She made fer sure the chillen learned proper grammar.

"She worked so hard, Mildred did; an' ah worked two jobs gettin' those chillen that learnin'. The oldest girl is in med'cal school, goin' to be a doctor. The boy gots a free ride to college ona football scholarship. Youngest is still in high school. Looks like about fo' or five mo' years of workin' two jobs, and my work'll be done. God rest your soul, Mildred," he says, looking upwards. "Those chillen is wearin' the Jackson name well."

"Where is Leroy L. Jackson the Third going to school?"

"You's a smart one, young fella. Ah never did tell you his name, but you figgered it out. That's from eddacashun. Leroy, he plays fer the Unversity of Suthen California, he does. He one of the best college football players there is. Looks like he be a high pick fer that Nation'l Football League this year. When they picks my son, evahbody in 'merica gonna know who Leroy L. Jacksons, the First, Seconds, and Thirds is.

"Son, whatevah you do, make your father proud. Do nuthin' to hurt your family name."

Johnny wondered what Leroy would say about how he had worn the Miller name thus far. He said nothing.

"Say, where you off to frum here?"

"I don't know. Can you give me directions to the ocean? I want to see the beach."

Leroy gave Johnny a big grin, and Johnny guessed that he was in for some surprises in this foreign country.

"Son, there is miles of ocean and beaches in both directions. Which way you headin'?"

"South, toward San Diego a ways, then across Arizona."

"Best way is to take South Alameda Street outside the station here and just run 'long it till you reach Highway One near Long

Beach. Be verra careful. Traffic is horrible out there. Even more dang'rus are sum of the characters ya'll will meet. You will sure need the Lawd. Get yourself a map, too. Stop at the Standard Gas Station a block down South Alameda. They's free, you know. Get a city map, too, or you might nevah find your way out of this town."

Johnny thanked him for the advice and left reluctantly, knowing he would never see this man again. Friendly faces had been few and far between.

Leroy called after him as he pushed his bike away.

"It's been a pleasure meetin' you, young man, and may the Lawd be with you."

***

Out on the sidewalk, a hippie with a long moustache and hair to his shoulders called attention to his wares. Each arm was heavy with watches, and more timepieces were pinned to the long, full white shirt. He wore pants covered in bright flowers that flared out below the knee like a woman's dress. Dancing and skipping in circles, he shouted, "Time for sale. One dollar apiece."

Johnny watched, waiting for the huckster to trip over his big pants; but Johnny did need time, and he paid the one dollar for a broad-banded watch with large numbers.

Other street vendors hawked an array of goods. What they all had in common was their uncommonness—at least, to Johnny Miller's eyes. All wore colorful garb, and there were many weird hats and dark glasses. Unusual seemed to be the norm; Johnny thought that if he still had his beard and put on his Amish clothes, he would blend right in with the crowd.

Except for a few black and white images in newspaper photos, Johnny had never seen a hippie. He walked slowly, pushing the bike and staring—probably to the point of rudeness—as he scrutinized the dress, antics, and demeanor of this strange crowd.

Then he turned his attention to the city. He'd never seen so many streets going in all directions, and he had never smelled anything like Los Angeles. Even bushes and trees were foreign. The shape of the straight, tall palms fascinated him, as though they were stretching upward through the stench, gasping for clean air necessary for green growth. Every now and then, a sweet aroma of blooming flowers did drift across his path.

Before mounting the bike, he gave himself time to try to adjust to this new world. Leroy's voice came back to him, reminding him to be careful, blessing him with "the Lawd's protection."

He would not soon forget Leroy. A man with nothing, he had worked hard to make something out of his life. He then passed his name on to his children, confident that they in turn would add to the good. Johnny's family had done the same for generations. Even when there was little in the way of possessions to grant children, they at least passed on a name. With the help of the Lord, he must discover what it meant to be Jonas's John's Johnny.

56

Even before Johnny asked for the maps, the gas station attendant seemed to know that this young man on a bicycle didn't belong here. The attendant also told the bedraggled traveler where he could find a good eatery. Johnny thanked him.

I need a good, solid meal at Mom's table right now.

Johnny's gaze went everywhere, taking in the massive buildings, those palm trees, the strangely-dressed people, the terrifying traffic. Yet, not far from the gas station, he happened to glance downward and see a wallet resting against the curb. Braking to a stop, he bent over and picked it up.

The folded soft brown leather was stuffed with cash. One compartment held small cards with phone numbers and addresses. The name on the driver's license matched the name on several of the cards. Samuel Cohraine, Attorney at Law, lived in Malibu, according to the license; but he apparently had an office on the same street along which Johnny was now pedaling.

Great, Johnny thought. *I can drop the wallet off at his office and be on my way to lunch and Long Beach in five minutes.*

The errand was not quite that simple. In the distance of only a few blocks, Johnny was assaulted by much irate honking; and more than one car had passed at such close range that the rush of wind threatened his balance and left him shaken. He was beginning to wonder if he would escape this city alive.

The South Alameda Office Complex was easy to find. From the looks of the expensive cars in the parking lot, Samuel Cohraine, Attorney at Law, and the five other law firms listed on the sign were all doing quite well. Rows of luxury cars on this concrete field brought a momentary longing for Johnny's old horsepower-packed transportation, the feel of the leather in his hands, and the smell of horses and springtime on dusty roads ...

But that was the past. This was his present.

He dropped the kickstand and parked his bike between a gleaming red sports car and a more sedate black sedan. If anyone was looking out a window, he supposed there would be some chuckles at the juxtaposition of an old, loaded-down bike with the fancy cars. Then again, instead of amusement the sight might cause consternation, since the ragtag look of his transportation might label him as a vagrant. He would deliver the wallet quickly, before anyone called the law to remove him from the doorstep of this obvious wealth.

A receptionist behind a desk asked how she could help him.

"I have a wallet belonging to Samuel Cohraine. I found it lying on the street. I'm here to return it."

"You did ... you are ..." Her businesslike voice stammered as though she did not have a standard response for such a visitor.

She picked up the telephone. "Mr. Cohraine, there's a young man out here who says he has your wallet, and he's here to return it." She paused. "So you *are* missing it?" She looked sideways at Johnny as he stood waiting.

After a short conversation, she put her hand over the speaker and asked if the contents were intact.

"It's full of money and lots of phone numbers and names. I didn't count the money, though, so I could not say if everything is still here," replied Johnny.

She relayed this information, listened to the voice Johnny

heard only as a low rumble, then said, "Mr. Cohraine is very relieved to have those contacts returned and says to keep the cash and leave the wallet and the rest of the contents with me."

"Oh, no! I could never keep this money. It's not mine. I'd like to return it, please."

She stared at him, as though he were turning into an elephant before her eyes.

"Mr. Cohraine … ah … the young man asks if he can *please* return the money." Her voice dropped. "I don't know, but he looks like Paul Newman."

Before she could return the receiver to its cradle, a door opened and a tall figure emerged.

"Nancy, what time is my next client this morning? If she arrives before my conversation with this young man is over, offer her a cup of coffee and ask her to be patient. An honest man in a law office is someone I must meet." He chuckled at his own humor. "Please, come in."

57

Johnny followed the attorney down a hallway leading to a number of offices. A brass plaque attached to an elaborately carved wooden door announced the domain of Samuel Cohraine, Divorce and Family Law. The lawyer settled into an enormous leather chair behind an equally enormous desk that, for all its work area, held no papers or files of any kind. Johnny did not see even a pen or pencil. Cohraine motioned toward a chair, and Johnny felt the attorney's eyes taking measure of this stranger who had landed in his office. But Samuel Cohraine's smile was quick and easy; and in spite of the foreign surroundings, Johnny felt comfortable with the lawyer.

"Thanks for returning my wallet. I didn't even realize I'd lost it until Nancy called. This morning, I stopped at the station and went inside to make a purchase. When I returned to the car, I paid the attendant for pumping the gas, and I noticed a small spot of dirt on the passenger door. I now remember laying my wallet on the roof of the car while I cleaned off that spot, and I must have driven off with it still on the roof. How fortunate you happened along. Most folks would have taken the money and tossed the wallet."

"I couldn't do that, knowing it didn't belong to me."

Samuel Cohraine was younger than Johnny's father. He had salt-and-pepper hair and skin that said he spent as much time outdoors as he did in this richly furnished office.

"Wow! You do look like Paul Newman!" he said suddenly with a laugh. "Is the Sundance Kid waiting outside with your horses?"

"I'm … not sure I understand." Johnny had no idea who the lawyer was talking about. He could, though, explain how he had found the wallet. "I arrived in town this morning. Came from Ohio on the bus, and I'm intending to ride my bicycle across the country toward home. I stopped at the gas station to pick up a map so I could find my way out of town; and not too far from the station, I spotted your wallet in the street. I didn't even take the money out to count it, but I assume it's all there."

"I'd be happy if you'd keep it, to thank you for returning the rest of the contents."

"I want nothing in return. Except … well, will you tell me who this Paul Newman guy is? You aren't the first person who's said I resemble him."

"You really don't know?" Johnny could tell Cohraine was suppressing a smile.

"No, sir, I don't."

"Newman is a very successful movie star here in Hollywood. The Sundance Kid was his sidekick in his latest movie. It was a big hit; anybody that likes western movies or horses loved that movie. You really do look like a younger version of him. The ladies here in Los Angeles will absolutely love you."

Johnny could feel the flush rising up his neck toward his face.

"You're looking at one Ohio Amish man who's never heard of that Newman fellow."

"You're Amish? I've read about your communities, but I've never met an Amish person. Excuse me for saying this, but you don't look like I expected an Amish man to look."

Johnny laughed, but there it was again—the way he looked did not match the label he had given himself. Was that all there was to being Amish? Was it simply presenting certain outer appearances?

And had he just said he was an Amish man?

Johnny knew nothing about the obviously affluent lawyer or his life in Los Angeles and Hollywood; yet, for some reason, he liked Samuel Cohraine. The attorney knew nothing about the life Johnny had left behind, and he was both curious and respectful. They fell into an easy conversation, and Johnny found himself telling the lawyer about his upbringing in an Amish family and describing many of the things that Samuel's world considered necessities but the Millers lived without. Johnny could see the amazement on the older man's face.

"In your community, I would have a difficult time making a living. It sounds like families stick together, so there are probably not too many divorces."

"I don't know anyone who's divorced. I've never even met anyone who is divorced."

"That is truly amazing," replied Samuel. "In my line of work, I know very few people who have not been divorced. I'm not sure that I'm proud of it, but I'm the most sought after divorce attorney in Los Angeles. This is not what I set out to do when I first began studying law; but somehow, it's what has taken shape over the years. Marriages falling apart have made my career."

He pointed to a wall filled with photos, most of them marked by scrawling signatures, and he recited names of famous actors he had represented. Some of the names Johnny did recognize.

"You would be amazed at how much wealth I have split between warring spouses. Of course, a great deal of that money stays with me."

"But how do you know which side to take?"

"Usually, neither party is more to blame than the other, so the first caller gets my services. Whoever hires me knows they will get an equitable split. Sometimes both parties sit here in the office and we work it out. I'm an equal opportunity offender. It doesn't make much difference to me which side I'm on … or against.

Johnny sat in the luxurious office and wondered how someone

could build an empire on the tragedies of other lives. But Samuel Cohraine had been direct and honest with him, so he asked the question that was burning in his mind.

"We believe … that is, the Bible says that what God has put together, man should not separate."

"Believe me, Johnny, God did not put together the marriages I help take apart. Oh, there are some Hollywood marriages that stick, but they are few and far between."

"Are you divorced?"

"No, I've been happily married for almost thirty years."

"So how have you survived? What causes all those divorces? What's the secret?"

Cohraine looked thoughtful, and Johnny saw not a rich divorce attorney but a man who had kept his vows for thirty years when everyone around him had cast aside such restrictions.

"Johnny, it's really very simple. When I married my wife, God did join us together. I know this sounds strange coming from someone who has built up a very healthy bank account dealing in divorces, but folks that truly put God first in their marriage will not get divorced. Both spouses must put God first. I love my wife more today than the day I married her.

"Selfishness, Johnny. That's what wrecks marriages. Listen to the attitudes of today: 'I want things my way. I have a right to be happy, and if you don't make me happy, I'll find someone else who will. This is my life, and no one can tell me how to live it. The most important thing is for me to find satisfaction in life.' The selfishness song goes on and on.

"It's a disease, Johnny, and we've all got it. The only Person who can cure us is God."

That sounded like something Annie would have said. "My wife was the most unselfish person I've ever known," Johnny said. "She … died last year. But she always said she was a worm God had turned into a butterfly."

"I am truly sorry for your loss, Johnny. If you find love again someday, the best marriage advice I can give you is something I heard a long time ago. It has worked for me, and every man should hear it. *If you want to be treated like a king, then treat your wife like a queen.* I guarantee it works. If everyone did that, I would be drawing up wills and setting up trust funds, not divorces."

Samuel Cohraine sighed as though he did have some regrets, then he pushed back his chair and stood to his feet.

"I need to get ready for my client. You probably don't watch television, but if you did, you would know her name. It's just another couple million dollars to divide."

He walked across the big office with Johnny and at the door again expressed his thanks for the return of the wallet.

"There are not many honest folks like you left, Johnny. Please, take this money as a thank-you."

He opened the wallet and handed Johnny five twenties. This thank-you was exorbitant, and Johnny was ready to again protest and refuse when a firm impression closed his mouth. It seemed as if he heard Annie saying, "Take it. It's a gift from a grateful heart. Take it and give it away. You will know when the time is right to offer it."

So Johnny accepted the money and thanked the lawyer; but as he turned to go, Samuel Cohraine had one more question.

"So, if you were raised Amish, you probably know horses pretty well?"

This was a surprise. What was behind that question?

"Yes. I grew up handling horses," he said. "Plowed fields with them. Drove a buggy horse named Joyce. They're amazing animals, much smarter than some folks believe."

"Look, I raise horses on a farm out in Topanga Canyon. I need an honest man like you to run errands; and if things work out, I could use your help in training my thoroughbreds."

58

Johnny felt as though his heart had stopped beating. His childhood dream might be right here—the West, a job working with horses—all in one neat package.

But this was only the first day of his ride; he had not actually started his journey yet, and already he was faced with this temptation and decision. Could his search already be over? Before it began? *No*, he told himself, *this is not what you came here to do; this is not what you left home for.*

"How determined are you to continue your bike ride?" the lawyer was asking.

Johnny grinned.

"Since I've only pedaled close to a mile thus far, I'm still quite determined. That is, if I get out of this city alive."

"How about considering my offer?"

"It sounds tempting, but I really must continue with my plan."

"At least come out and have a look at one of my horses. He's a three-year-old that's won a number of races and has been nominated for the Kentucky Derby. He's favored to win the Santa Anita Derby in April; and even if he finishes in the top three, he's a cinch for the Derby. I think you'd really appreciate this horse. Please, come out for a visit and tell me what you think."

Now the temptation was not only horses, but a possible Kentucky Derby winner! Johnny could no longer resist. What harm could one day's delay do? He was not on a timetable anyway. He had a chance to look into the eyes of and put his hands on the chest of a potential Kentucky Derby colt.

"I'd love to see that horse, but I have no idea where Topanga Canyon is or how to get there. I was heading for Route One, near Long Beach. Is your farm anywhere near there?"

Johnny could see that the farm and his horses were Samuel Cohraine's passion. He was no longer a smooth, sophisticated lawyer, but a man as excited as a farm boy who gets a new bicycle. He stepped back behind his desk and reached for the telephone.

"Here's what we'll do. I'll send you to my house; you can get a shower and we'll find you some clean clothes and then you can go out to the Canyon and see the horse. I live in Santa Monica, about fifteen miles from here. It's a bit north of Long Beach, but Highway One is not too far from my house. When you're ready to get back on your bike, the Santa Monica Pier would be a great place to start your journey.

"I'll draw you a map to get you through town, maybe route you through Hollywood and Beverly Hills. You'll get a taste of the wealth of my clients, some of which, of course, they'll bring to me. Let me make a quick phone call home."

He was talking rapidly and already dialing, and Johnny felt as though he had been hooked up to a powerful engine that was racing down the tracks with no thought of stopping for anyone or anything. No wonder this man was such a successful attorney.

"Hello, Audrey, dear. Is your mother there? Have her call me as soon as she gets home. We're having a guest for supper...You'll be at home all day? Good. Show my friend to the guest house and have him clean up a bit. Then I want you to take him out to Topanga Canyon to the farm and show him the horses. He especially wants to see Sun Dancer."

He hung up, and the excitement still lit his face. Johnny was to make himself at home at the house, and Cohraine's daughter would take him out to the farm to see the horses.

The phone rang again.

"My client is probably here," Samuel Cohraine said as he picked it up. Instead, it was Nancy, announcing the arrival of an officer of the law. "He's responding to several calls about a loaded bicycle out front." Samuel grinned at Johnny. "Come, let's get you on your way."

Officer Smith and Attorney Cohraine seemed to know each other well. Johnny was introduced as Mr. Cohraine's friend.

"If that overloaded bicycle is your share of a divorce, then my friend Samuel is losing his touch," joked the officer.

"He's a richer man than appearances suggest," said Cohraine. "Say, Tom, I have to get back to a meeting with another client. Can you sketch out a route to my house for Johnny here? Route him up around Hollywood and Beverly Hills, then pick up Route 2 over to the house. Which reminds me—it's time to get your fellow officers together and have another cookout at my place. Thank the men for looking out for us."

"Sure thing, Mr. Cohraine."

"Maybe you could get on the radio and ask other men in blue to be on the lookout for young Butch Cassidy here as he rides through our city?"

"Of course. Hey, do you have any hot tips on the Santa Anita Derby?" The attorney was already moving away, headed back toward his office building.

"I'm not a gambling man, Tom, but Sun Dancer could make you very happy," Cohraine called back. "See you tonight, Johnny."

***

The city that he had thought might kill him suddenly opened up and welcomed him. Johnny followed the route outlined by Officer Smith, and as he traveled, police cars honked a friendly hello. Officers rolled down their windows and greeted him. He was in the city of celebrities, and for a while, he felt like a star himself.

At a busy intersection, a cruiser pulled up beside his bicycle.

"Hey, there, Johnny. I probably shouldn't do this, but stay right up close to my back bumper and let's have some fun." The siren started wailing, lights flashed, and the cruiser and bicycle wove through the congestion. Mercedes and BMWs and a few Rolls Royce limousines pulled to the side as Johnny sailed by on an old red bike.

The officer finally pulled to the side of the street and motioned Johnny around his car. "This is as far as my patrol goes. On the sidewalk over there is the Hollywood Walk of Fame, in case you're interested. Your next stop is Beverly Hills. They're expecting you."

Johnny had never heard of the Walk of Fame, but he suspected it was nothing he needed to see. The sidewalks were filled with tourists taking pictures of the concrete.

Beverly Hills boggled his mind. Massive mansions hunkered down behind walls of lush vegetation and palm. Most also had fences, sequestering the rich and famous away from the common folk. Mr. and Mrs. Movie Star expected commoners to pay homage to their stardom and celebrity; but when any admirer did show up, he could only stand at the end of the driveway.

The gawkers pressed their heads against grilled fences or stretched their necks attempting to catch a glimpse of their idols. Johnny wasn't certain which side of the fence was most in need of a good dose of common sense.

Riding down Route 2 toward Santa Monica, he glimpsed the Pacific Ocean for the first time. At last, he was nearing the edge of America! Perhaps tomorrow he would finally walk the beach and splash in the waves of the ocean.

The directions were accurate and he easily found the beautiful ranch house with a circular driveway. One extension of the sprawling building was a three-car garage. As he approached, he caught a glimpse of a pool and the roof of what must be a guest house hidden in the gardens. Although this neighborhood was not up to Beverly Hills standards, it was still a very wealthy community. And Samuel Cohraine's house was not walled off from the rest of the world.

Johnny stood at the end of the driveway and gazed at the distant views of ocean. What would life be like if one could look at this every day? Would a person finally take it for granted and not even see the majesty? He remembered marveling at the panorama below his tree stand. He had never grown tired of watching new scenes unfold in their valley. Had he given up forever the riches of farm and family that he had once possessed?

59

"You must be Johnny. Daddy told me you were coming."

Johnny had seen no one when he paused to admire the view. Now she stood before him with a hand extended and introduced herself as Audrey. "How was the ride through town? It's hard to imagine anyone riding a bike through Los Angeles."

Should I tell her I had a police escort? Should I tell her how glad I was to see that blue water? Should I tell her my name? No, she already knows that. What do I say next?

His mind fumbled about, looking for an appropriate response. He was not normally so tongue-tied, but something about the girl smiling a welcome struck him deeply and turned him into a pile of mush. Suddenly conscious of his appearance, he now did feel very much like a vagrant who had wandered in from the street.

"Ah … ummm … I'm sorry, I was expecting … that is, I wasn't expecting …" He took a breath and tried not to look straight into those eyes. "Let me start over.

"Yes, I am Johnny. This morning I was sleeping on the floor of a bus station and now here I am in your front yard with the Pacific Ocean in sight and it's all so surreal that I don't know what I'm thinking or … saying."

She laughed, and he heard Samuel Cohraine's laugh in hers.

"That's all right. I agree, this is a far cry from a downtown bus station. Take a few minutes to adjust. Let me show you the guest house. You can relax for a bit and get cleaned up."

She led the way around the house, and he followed without a word, past the pool and down a flagstone walkway to a small guest house tucked into what seemed like a secret garden.

Audrey swung open the door and ushered Johnny into the little cottage. "There's a washer and dryer here, too, if you want to do any laundry ..." She stopped when she saw the look on his face. "Is something wrong?"

"I just realized that I've begun this long trip, and I've never done laundry. My mom or my wife always did it for me."

"Oh. You're married?"

"Was. Annie passed away recently. That's why I left home, to give myself time to try to put everything back together again."

"I'm sorry for your loss," she said quietly. "But it's not possible, you know—putting things back together. You can't go back; you can only go forward."

She was not only strikingly beautiful, she was also intelligent. Johnny wondered how she had gained this wisdom. Had she lost someone dear to her?

Audrey opened the door to a closet in the hallway. The shelves were filled with neatly folded clothes, both men's and women's.

"If you want something fresh to wear, you'll probably find something in here that's your size. Give me your dirty clothes, and I'll wash them for you."

She was a worker, too. Not a spoiled rich kid.

"This afternoon, I'll take you out to the farm and show you around. Dad wants you to see Sun Dancer."

"Your dad sounds very excited about him."

Audrey smiled. "Yes, he is. We all are."

Johnny's stomach growled ferociously, reminding him that he had not eaten breakfast or lunch. For that matter, he could not remember when he had last eaten.

"Come in to the house whenever you're ready, and I'll make you a sandwich or two ... or three. Did Daddy tell you dinner is at seven? And he's planning on you staying here for the night."

"No, he didn't mention that. But I suppose it's futile to argue with him."

"Yes, that's my dad."

Audrey left, and Johnny rifled through the stacks of clothing until he found a suitable outfit. His three-day-smelly clothes went on a pile for the ... the ... well, there was only one word that came to mind ... the *princess*. The king of this place treated his queen well; and quite naturally, their offspring was a princess.

He ran the water as hot as he could endure. A bottle of something promising relaxation of tired muscles stood on the edge of the tub, and he dumped a generous amount into the hot water.

Dropping his body into steam and soap, he decided the first order of business was to put back into place the pieces of brain matter that had been dislodged in the last half hour. Sliding low in the bathtub, he welcome the warmth of the water engulfing his body, up to his shoulders and chin.

What had just happened? How could some woman he had never met before shake him so? Those eyes, that smattering of freckles, the hair flowing down over her shoulders ... yes, Audrey was a beauty. But there was something else about her, some indefinable quality that broke through everything else and insisted that he notice her.

His eyes closed as he sank lower, until the water covered all but his nose. He could not escape the feelings and questions bombarding him.

What happened back there?

I love Annie. I can never replace her. It's too soon to notice other women, to even think about another relationship.

His body slumped even further, and the water covered him completely; he held his breath as thoughts raced onward.

Who says when it's time? You didn't ask for this pain and loss.

But it had only been six months. He must grieve Annie for at least a year.

A year? Says who? Many Amish men marry quickly after losing their wives.

Audrey was definitely not Amish.

Maybe you're not Amish, either.

Then why did he keep thinking like an Amish man?

How do you know what an Amish man thinks if you're not sure you're Amish?

Hadn't he identified himself as an Amish man that morning? And who was he arguing with, anyway?

Too many questions without answers.

He did what any man in such a situation would do. He raised his head and gasped for air before he drowned.

***

The grime and grit of the long bus ride came off as he soaked in the tub, and both the unpleasant memories and the weariness were likewise banished by the astonishing beauty he met as the events of the afternoon unfolded.

He walked back to the Cohraine's house through the gardens, densely planted with all kinds of shrubs and trees to create a private oasis. The three fat sandwiches Audrey made were things of beauty themselves. Johnny savored them as he enjoyed Audrey's company. He could not ignore her beauty, but their conversation was so lively, he had little time to stumble and stammer. She was obviously curious about the Amish man who had appeared in her home; Johnny was curious about her life, too, and their conversation never lagged.

Then it was time to head out to the farm, and when Audrey pushed a button and opened the garage door, more beauty took his breath away. Sunlight flashed off red and chrome.

"My twenty-first birthday present," Audrey said. She was

grinning at him while he stared, speechless, at the Mercedes-Benz 280SL convertible. He had never ridden in a convertible, and now he tried to picture himself in his Amish clothes driving down a California highway in such a car. It seemed a ridiculous picture. Besides, his hat would probably blow away. He had the feeling that Audrey's grin was not so much pride of ownership as it was amusement at his astonishment. He wondered if she guessed at the pictures in his mind.

The calendar and magazine pictures he had seen of the Pacific coast did not adequately depict the magnificent ocean views as they went skimming along the coastal highway. Audrey pointed out where he would be connecting with Route One when he continued his ride. Turning off onto Route 27, they headed north through the Santa Monica Mountains. From ocean views to mountain ranges blending into more mountain ranges, the vistas in all directions piled beauty upon beauty.

Old Topanga Canyon Road veered off to the left; and with tires screeching, the red convertible took the turn at breakneck speed. Audrey advised him to hang on.

"No sense having all this power and not using it." Hugging the curves and jumping at any touch to the accelerator, the sports car did what it was built to do—perform. "I'll let you drive home."

He was already on sensory overload from the scenic beauty. The car was a dream car, the kind of vehicle most young men could only dream of owning.

Oh yes, he might as well admit it, the beauty behind the wheel was also quite a distraction. The soaking bath had given him time to reflect on matters of the heart and mind. After emerging from the water, he had found himself in an imaginary conversation.

"She is quite cute, isn't she?" came the familiar voice.

"Annie, what are you saying?"

"I saw your reaction when you met that English girl."

"Well, she does remind me of you, with those freckles and ..."

He wasn't sure how to go on.

"Yes? And what?"

Those conversations still came to him, even though he knew Annie was gone. Though they had had too short a time together, he had known her well; and he could still hear exactly how she would respond in these conversations. Would she walk in his mind forever, questioning and commenting?

He sat pressed into the back of the seat, his heart beating furiously. One hand gripped the "Oh, my goodness!" door handle while the fingers of his other hand counted the months since Annie had passed. Six months. It had been almost one-half year; should he even be having such thoughts about another woman? He knew men who had married that soon after losing a spouse. Until this day, he had not even desired to entertain thoughts of finding another wife to replace Annie. That would be impossible. But now a strange jumble of unfamiliar and unexpected notions burst through his brain and left him shaken. And he had only met Audrey a few hours before!

Wait, did she say I could drive this car on the way back? Does she not know anything about our people? What did her dad tell her? Amish don't drive. Of course, Amish don't typically run off and do cross country bicycle rides, either. What would she think about my way of life? What does it matter, I don't even know what way of life I want right now. Furthermore, there is no way anyone that fine would be interested in me. But ... Annie found me desirable, why not an English girl?

"Because you're Amish, that's why," replied the sweet voice of Annie.

"Get out while you can, Annie, this girl is a race car driver!"

"Ah, perhaps it's you that's in a precarious situation. I can leave anytime, but it looks like you're in for quite a ride."

60

Johnny was convinced that the safest and surest way to arrive back at Samuel Cohraine's house would be for him to drive.

He had done what many other young Amish men did; he had retained his driver's license even after selling his car and joining church. Some men renewed their license as a document of identification. Others kept them, he was sure, as a reminder of a life given up. Some liked the idea that a valid driver's license with their name on it still existed. Perhaps the thought of living a preordained lifestyle where rules were outlined for each life was why some of them hung on to their passport to the past. A silent act of rebellion, holding onto the thought that "I could drive if it really became necessary," appealed to some. In that speeding sports car winding through California hills, Johnny still had the right to drive tucked in his wallet.

"Yes, I'll drive home," he told Audrey as they careened around another curve. She grinned, but didn't take her eyes off the road. Her hair was pulled back into a ponytail that was now flying out behind her head. Johnny's own head was bare, swept by the wind; he was still not accustomed to the short haircut.

The red convertible swung into a lane on the right and soon drove through an open gate.

"Looks like Pedro is here. He's the trainer; I think you'll enjoy meeting him."

Majestic oaks lined a driveway leading to a stable topped with spires. Off to the right was a dirt track, and several thoroughbreds grazed in a fenced area.

Johnny's attention was drawn, like lightning to a rod, to a golden chestnut colt grazing alone in one paddock. He was obviously a horse among horses, the reigning hero here at this ranch. Tall, powerful, and confident, he carried an aura that spoke of greatness. As the two walked toward the stable, the colt threw up his head and watched them, ears flicking forward and nose quivering with curiosity.

"What a horse," Johnny said. "That must be Sun Dancer."

"Yes. That's him. We'll find Pedro first and maybe he can convince Sun Dancer to agree to introductions. That horse doesn't cooperate with anyone other than Pedro and his jockey. Even Daddy gets no respect from him."

The sight of the horse quieted the frenzy of convoluted thoughts about Annie and Audrey. Odd, how comforted he was around horses. At the Miller farm, horses had always been a part of life, almost a part of family. Johnny had never once felt animosity toward the horse that had struck out at Annie. It was a horse; it did what came naturally to horses.

The stable was as clean as Mandy's kitchen. Several horses in the stalls stomped and whinnied. One brown mare thrust her head over the lower portion of the stall door, stretching her neck as far as possible to watch Audrey and Johnny approach. The metal name tag beside the door told Johnny this was Lucy in Disguise.

"This is Lucy, Sun Dancer's mother," said Audrey. Johnny reached out and stroked the mare's nose.

"You must be so proud of your son. I hear he's going to win the Kentucky Derby," he crooned. He cupped her head between his hands and gently laid his forehead against hers, whispering to her in Dutch. In answer, Lucy whinnied softly and nuzzled his chest.

"She likes you," Audrey said, watching Johnny woo the horse.

"More than that. She's in love," Johnny murmured, more to the horse than to Audrey.

"It's a horse, Johnny, not a girl! You aren't going to be asking her out, are you?"

"Oh, she's both. Horses are amazing creatures, Ann ... Audrey." He hoped his recovery was quick enough. If Audrey noticed, she gave no indication.

Lucy and Johnny spent a few more minutes in communion, like old friends who had not seen each other for a long a time. Audrey walked through the stable, looking for Pedro. She returned alone, and the two left Lucy and headed outdoors.

"What was that gibberish you spoke to Lucy?"

"It's Pennsylvania Dutch, a dialect we Amish use. Basically German, with some English words mixed in."

They were at the fence encircling Sun Dancer's paddock. Audrey scanned the field and surrounding buildings, looking for signs of Pedro. Johnny's eyes were on the magnificent horse. Alert, ready, and quite unperturbed, the colt watched the two visitors.

Johnny slipped through the fence. Sun Dancer tossed his head and pranced sideways. This visitor was taking audacious liberties. The red-gold neck and flanks gleamed, reflecting the sun's rays like a bright penny. Delicate legs danced a sort of ballet. The king of the ranch was showing off and proclaiming his sovereignty.

Johnny stood and waited. Sun Dancer stopped dancing and also waited, nostrils flaring and lips constantly moving. Then, remarkably, he moved toward his visitor, tossing his head. He was still the boss, but he had decided Johnny deserved a greeting.

Johnny reached out a hand, palm upward, wishing he had asked Audrey for some treat. The colt took in Johnny's smell, took measure of the human's confidence, and decided he was worthy. When Johnny laid his hand on the chestnut neck, the skin rippled but the colt did not move away. Horse and man had a private conversation—this, too, in Dutch—before Sun Dancer tossed up his head, wheeled, and trotted off.

Audrey had given up looking for Pedro and watched, fascinated by the exchange between Johnny and the horse.

"How did that happen? What were you two talking about?"

"Oh, nothing much, just some talk between us boys." Johnny grinned at her and felt himself flush under the admiration in her eyes. He turned away, watching Sun Dancer, and hoped she would not noticed the red creeping up his neck.

Pedro was nowhere to be found. They no longer needed him, anyway. Sun Dancer and Johnny had met and connected without the trainer. Johnny stood at the fence and watched the red colt, imagining him flying over the Derby finish line, alone and far ahead of the rest of the field. He wondered how it would feel to be astride such horsepower.

Then he took on another kind of horsepower. As they turned to leave, Audrey tossed him her keys. The engine jumped to life. Johnny respected the power of the horse. But the power of the car made him feel invincible.

He was transported back to the day he first drove his little blue car. It seemed like so long ago, yet it was only several short years. Then he saw himself in a buggy on a country road with Annie tucked in beside him. One foot was on the dashboard, and three small, dark-haired children in the back of the buggy pressed faces to the rear window, taking in the world around them. That's what his life should have been.

He was ambushed by the next picture his imagination presented. A happy family in a convertible headed along a winding road to a white California beach along a shining ocean; Audrey sat beside him in the front, and three little children wiggled in the back seat. He shook his head.

Get back to reality, Johnny. There are too many cultural differences to even consider it.

"Your dad says you have a sister; is she also in school somewhere?" He decided to stick with safe subjects.

"She's in Florence, studying art and visiting all the museums over there in Europe. Daddy's on a museum board and supports the arts. He believed studying in Italy would advance her career."

Johnny wondered what Daddy had planned for this younger daughter. Did she have great opportunities awaiting her? What would it be like to have so many options? Only a few roads had opened for his life. Eight years of school, then life as a farmer or perhaps a carpenter or furniture builder. Audrey's career path, with her dad's money and influence, would probably take her to the top of some organization.

"So what degree are you pursuing? Will you be following in your sister's footsteps?"

"Not a chance. Dawn and I are as different as two people can be. She is more like Dad; she has his drive and desire for achievement and recognition. I plan to be a teacher somewhere. Maybe in a poor foreign country. I love children, and I want to change the world, one small person at a time."

An admirable goal, Johnny thought, but what could Audrey know of poverty and need?

"I've seen the difference one person can make in the lives of young girls," she went on, and although he couldn't take his eyes from the road, he could hear that her thoughts were far from the red convertible and the California mountains. "Ever since I was a little girl, I've gone with my mother to orphanages in Central America. I know I could make a difference. I have the good fortune to have wealth and status that can be used for good. I'm going to be a teacher, and someday a substantial portion of my parents' wealth will come my way. My plan is to give as much of it away as possible. I've seen the results of too much money in people's lives, and it won't happen to me. I'll get the most out of my money by helping those less fortunate than myself."

Johnny had met Lucy in Disguise back at the stable. Could this girl be Annie in Disguise? Annie's young charges had admired her and she had loved being their teacher. Johnny would never have believed it possible he would meet another girl like Annie. But here, in the most unlikely place and circumstances, he had somehow met a familiar heart and spirit.

Pulling into Samuel Cohraine's driveway, Johnny had a compelling sensation that he should run to his bicycle at once and pedal furiously and never look back. Instead, he sat alone in the gardens and remembered Audrey's smile as she waved and said, "Come back over to the house at seven for dinner."

He wondered if she thought he looked like Paul Newman.

61

Supper was remarkable in its similarities and its differences. Four people at the table, just like home. A mom and a dad, a guy and a girl. It could have been Mandy and John and Naomi and Johnny. But one choice had brought him here, instead, to the opposite end of the country, eating with a family who could not imagine living as the Millers lived.

He had spent the hour before the evening meal sitting in the gardens, listening to a small waterfall, trying to sort out his thoughts. So many of his choices in life had had consequences that reverberated for years. Now, he sensed a huge choice of paths awaited him. What kind of world did he want to live in?

At supper, one road widened and welcomed and tantalized him. Samuel Cohraine wasted no time in putting an opportunity before Johnny.

"Son," (he addressed Johnny just as Johnny's father did) "Audrey tells me that you and Sun Dancer seem to have some kind of connection. I've been thinking about this today, and after hearing about your afternoon, I've made up my mind. I want you to work for me."

Johnny felt as though he had been grabbed by some strong unknown force and resistance would be futile.

"You're an honest man; I know I can trust you. And you have a way with horses. That's enough for me. We'll start you out running errands and helping out on the farm. You'll have a special assignment to work with Sun Dancer, and we'll see where that leads. If you are who I think you are, you could be leading that horse down the walkway at Churchill Downs in a few months. Like that picture, Johnny?"

Johnny had already imagined being with Sun Dancer at the Kentucky Derby. His dream, though, had them both in the winner's circle, with the garland of roses draped over the powerful red neck. But the life Samuel Cohraine now offered him was beyond any of Johnny's most elaborate dreams.

"You can stay in the guest house, at no charge. You'll have a pickup to drive, plus I'll pay you $10,000 a year. Once you're established as part of Sun Dancer's team, you'll get a portion of his winnings. Give us a try. Stay, and see where this could take you."

How could anyone offer that kind of money to a complete stranger? But what would happen if he abandoned his bike ride and stayed right here?

Samuel Cohraine saw Johnny's hesitation.

"Let's make that $15,000, the vehicle, no rent, a percent of winnings, and a percent of future stud fees. I'll give you all that, if you'll give this a chance and it all works out. And I believe it will. I believe we could have great success, working together. You could make quite a difference for us, Johnny."

The offer was enormous. Exorbitant. Everything he had ever hoped for or dreamed about had just fallen into his lap.

He stared at Samuel.

"I ... I would need some time to think about that."

"Breakfast at six tomorrow. Give me your answer then." Samuel Cohraine was a no-nonsense, take no prisoners, get-to-the-bottom-line-now kind of man. He apparently had full confidence that Johnny would not be able to resist such a generous offer.

Late into the night, Johnny tossed and turned, attempting to find sleep. His own thoughts competed with other voices; conversations clamored inside his head. Every family member offered advice. John was adamant; there was no question what the choice should be. Naomi was more sympathetic. Mandy simply said she had all the confidence in the world that her son would make the right decision.

What would Annie tell him to do? But could he even ask her? There was Audrey ... and she would be part of his life if he stayed here. How could he turn to Annie for advice while Audrey was standing there smiling at him?

Annie did not wait for him. Her voice came through all the rest of the clamor.

"Remember when I told you about Jesus coming into my life and giving me the Holy Spirit as a guide? Seek His Spirit within you, dear. You've tried everyone else, now try listening to Jesus."

"Oh, Annie, how I miss you! How do I still always know what you would say?"

"I was going to tell you to pedal away from that place as fast as your Red Wings could pedal, but I decided on a better plan."

"You're a funny one, Annie."

"You were always the funny one, Johnny."

"I love you Annie."

"I love you forever, too."

Did other spouses who had lost loved ones still have these conversations? Or was he losing his grip on reality?

He slipped out of bed and knelt by the bedside and begged a higher power for help in making the decision. In the stillness of the night, the answer arrived.

Son, you're not home yet.

***

Audrey was not at the breakfast table. Johnny was relieved. He was also disappointed; they had not said a proper goodbye the night before. But perhaps this was just as well. They would never see each other again.

He explained his reason for turning down the lucrative offer.

"Mr. Cohraine, I appreciate the opportunity, but if I don't continue my ride, I'll always wonder what might have been."

"I expected that answer, although I'm disappointed." Samuel Cohraine seemed to be assessing something else, but he only handed Johnny a sealed envelope.

"Audrey asked me to give you this, if you turned me down."

Gripping the envelope in one hand and shaking the attorney's hand with the other, Johnny took his leave. Coasting down toward Route 1 and the unknown, he fought an immediate and ferocious barrage of *what ifs*.

***

The road rolled away beneath Johnny and he wondered if he would ever find the freedom he longed for. Who could possibly feel free here, hemmed in by more traffic than he'd ever seen in his life? He caught glimpses of blue Pacific, but he paid little attention. At the moment, staying alive was more important than enjoying the views. So he concentrated on staying alive.

Even the constant danger of heavy traffic could not make him forget the letter that had added weight to his ride. Tucked in a zippered pocket of his windbreaker, the envelope both warmed and burdened him.

Away from city traffic, Highway One snaked along the mountainsides, high above the ocean pounding the beaches. He wanted to feel the sand on his bare feet, but he could see no convenient route to the water's edge.

Near Venice, the road finally veered closer to the ocean and the edge of the continent. A pier jutted out, like an arm extending from the land. Johnny pulled off the road and propped the bike against the wooden walkway. Boats groaned in their slips, tossing tall masts against the sky; water sloshed and slapped the pilings. The sounds were of a life far removed from his farm.

His Red Wings came off. The sand slipped through his toes, caressing his skin. A motor on a fishing boat sputtered to life. The wind played with several sailboats farther off shore, filling their canvas with the early morning salt air. Two yachts anchored nearby amazed him with their size and majesty. How, he marveled, do such enormous things stay afloat?

With his back to the city and traffic, he saw only water and sky. Back home, the many hills and trees cut the view of the heavens. Far, far out, the ocean and sky met; and Johnny wondered what mysteries lay beyond that thin, shining line.

He was finally standing at the end of the continent, and already he was curious about the next horizon. Would he always feel such restlessness? If one of those yachts were to carry him over the westward waters, would he find some enchanted island that finally satisfied him? Or would he continue to wonder what was out there, beyond his sight, and thus continue to wander; until one day, rounding a hill, he'd walk into Milford again and see the Miller farm in the distant valley? Then what? Would that be the end of his journey, or another beginning point?

The wind molded the windbreaker to his body, and he felt the shape of the letter in his pocket. *Maybe that was the enchanted island*, he thought, *and I've sailed right by.*

62

Now he squinted at the watery horizon and wiggled his toes in the sand. Had he just narrowly escaped? Or had he passed up an incredible opportunity that could have turned all his dreams into reality? The letter was still in his pocket, unopened. Would he be wise to put more miles between himself and *her* before he read it?

His curiosity won the debate. He slid his finger under the flap, breaking the seal.

Dear Johnny, the small, neat handwriting began. *I was sure you would turn down Daddy's offer. I am both impressed and sad.* She went on to describe the characteristics she found favorable in him. She also expressed feelings that he had already suspected.

Put on your Red Wings and go back to her, you dummy, argued one part of his brain.

But the answer he had begged for the night before had come so clearly that he could not ignore it. He could not look back. Home was still somewhere out ahead of him.

Audrey had included maps she thought would be helpful. She had obviously worked late into the night to list suggestions on where to stop, restaurants, diners, and places to camp. She gave him alternate routes around the busy interstates all the way to San Diego and even included names of family contacts along the way.

"Better get back on that bike and start pedaling, while you still have a bit of willpower," he said aloud.

In the next twenty-four hours, he lived more than he had in the last four months. The day was filled with amazing sights, sounds, aromas, and people. Everything was novel and unexpected. He wondered exactly what he had expected of the California coast; but he knew his imagination had fallen far short of what he was seeing. How could he ever describe all this to his family at home?

Toward evening, he arrived at Long Beach, his goal when he had first pedaled away from the bus station. He had stepped off the bus only yesterday, but it seemed like weeks had already passed between his first smell of downtown Los Angeles and this exhilarating ride between mountains and sea.

To his dismay, he found Long Beach quite congested. Audrey had made a notation about good camping at another beach several miles farther, so he pedaled on. Her directions and knowledge of the area were concise and accurate, and three dollars got him a choice camping spot in a tree-covered area on a bluff at the edge of Sunset Beach.

Assembling the tent poles and erecting the canvas took much too long. This project was so much easier when a friend was helping out. After much arranging and rearranging, his home away from home sat by a rock outcropping that looked like a giant stone chair and commanded a view of the long sandy beach.

Behind his campsite, a wide concrete walkway ran through the trees and campground. He sat atop his stone chair, between the beach and the walkway, and simply watched the constant parade of humanity. Then, as the crowds thinned and the sky slowly changed, he witnessed his first spectacular ocean sunset.

Only two days had passed here in California, and already he had been offered a passageway out of his old life. He had been easily distracted from his mission. He remembered the scribbled notes to himself on the postcards, written from a sad and lonely heart as the bus rolled through the night. Sun Dancer and Audrey and a red sports car had looked so good, and all of his being had wanted to stay. Still, something had told him this pathway would not lead him home.

Another pathway glowed on the waters. The orange sun hung just above the horizon and threw a red-gold corridor across the ocean waves to the shore. He walked to the shoreline, mesmerized by the shimmering avenue of light. No matter where he stood, the golden pathway lay directly in front of him. Even when he tried a sidestep and leap to the right, the beckoning glow still lay at his feet wherever they fell in the sand.

"Doesn't matter where you are, that road will always be there. Line up a million people on this beach, and each one will have their own path, right out to the sun."

The voice startled him. Concentrating on trying to sidestep his own path of light, he had not noticed the stranger who now sat in his spot atop the rock. Embarrassed by his obvious naiveté, he explained that he was a stranger to the ocean.

"Where are you running from, young man?"

"I'm not running." *Why did people think that?* "I'm taking some time to contemplate my life."

"You're too loaded down to contemplate. Most of what you carry with you is baggage, young man. Unburden yourself, if you really want to see life."

What was this man talking about? Johnny looked at his tent and bicycle and the few possessions in the carriers.

"A man's got to have a place to sleep."

"What's sleeping got to do with carrying your house with you? Sure, a turtle does it, but a turtle has no choice. Man needs to get out of his protective shell and live. What's your story?" the stranger asked again. "What are you running from?"

63

Johnny wanted to shift the conversation. He was finding it more and more difficult to explain why he was wandering about on an old bicycle so far from his valley in Ohio.

"Where's your home?" he asked the strange figure.

"Right now, home is right here on this rock. This is my rock, but you're welcome to use it. Name's William. Some call me Wandering Willie."

"I'm Johnny Miller. So you're ... homeless?"

"Oh my, no. My home is so large, it takes half a year to cover it. The southern wall is San Diego, and the northern wall, well, the northern wall gets pushed farther north every year."

Johnny was beginning to wonder if Wandering Willie might be a little crazy. He was not making sense. His home was hundreds of miles of the West Coast, and he had no possessions? As a matter of fact, Wandering Willie *looked* a little crazy, with long, dirty hair, a wild beard, and a yellow and orange shawl draped over his shoulders as he sat, ramrod straight and cross-legged on Johnny's rock—Willie's rock. A black hat on the man's head reminded Johnny of his own, squashed at the bottom of the bike carrier.

"But where do you sleep?"

"Home is much more than where you sleep at night, Johnny.

Tonight, there are at least five places within a mile of this rock where I can sleep, if I choose. Depends on the weather, if it looks like rain or not. If the weather's good, this beach will do nicely. Rain or a bit of a chill, and I'll find more shelter. One soon learns which storage buildings are unlocked or which restaurant docks put out a welcome mat.

"More important, I prefer to live in the back of the house. Most folks only use the front door in life. They see the façade, deal with whatever front is presented to the world. They never see real life—folks working behind the scenes, cooks and janitors and maids, all those folks who provide service to the masses. That's where I live, wandering behind the scenes where the real, down-to-earth folks work. The rich industrialist sits in the fancy dining room eating exotic food off exquisite china and knows nothing of the living behind that perfectly appointed dining room. I eat the same meal off a paper plate, pay nothing for it except to offer the chef whatever gustatory gossip I've picked up lately. I know these people; they know me.

"Believe me, boy; I'd rather sleep under a restaurant kitchen than in the most luxurious hotel room. There's no more soothing sounds than the clatter of china, the rattle of silverware, and the banter of workers."

Johnny had heard of people like this—people who lived on the streets. But he could not imagine such a life.

"And you carry nothing with you? How do you survive?"

"You're carrying too many possessions," Willie replied. "How do you survive?"

Johnny had no answer. He didn't even understand exactly what the man was questioning.

"Get rid of most of your stuff, and see what happens. Folks are tied to their stuff, as surely as if they have a ball and chain locked on their ankles.

"Hello, Lizzie," Willie called, giving a wide wave toward the walkway. Johnny looked up to see a lady pushing a shopping cart.

Lizzie returned the wave. She shuffled along, eyes to the ground, stooping now and then to pick up something from the sand. "Even folks with as little as Lizzie, there, can be desperate if they hang on too tightly to what they have."

"And you've held on to nothing?"

"Oh, I was almost caught in the trap. My path was going to be straight to the heights of the American Dream. I was on my way. An engineering degree from a prestigious university landed me a job where I worked on a project that was going to take me right to the top. The job consumed my entire being; I had no time for anyone or anything else. But it seemed a small price to pay. I was going places and, supposedly, getting what I wanted.

"So I'm not quite sure why I was at the beach one day. But I walked along the water and rested on a rock much like this one. I baked in the sun and let the surf hypnotize me. Time stopped. I realized that what I was feeling, briefly, was peace. I was somehow in tune with the universe.

"Do you believe in visions, Johnny Miller? I certainly didn't. But in those seconds, the universe—or something or someone— gave me a glimpse of the future. The technology I was working on would not free man; it would enslave him, trap him more tightly than ever before. I knew it was true. *How* I knew is still beyond me. But that brief time was the most sacred moment of my life."

Johnny wasn't sure exactly what he believed about visions, but apparently this man's life had been changed by whatever insight he'd been given.

"There was only one thing to do. I quit my job and started walking, in a quest to find more of that inner peace. I started out with a backpack, but that stuff bogged me down and kept me tied to the old life. So I sold everything and gave away the money. I was the poorest philanthropist in the world, but also the happiest.

"I've been walking for five years, and sometimes I can recapture that feeling of freedom. Sometimes, instead of walking, I just sit. Those moments of frozen time when I become one with the universe can now last for hours. That's freedom, Johnny; that's when I find pure freedom!"

The figure on the rock threw arms toward heaven and held a silent, motionless pose. Johnny had no response to the chant on peace and freedom, and becoming one with the universe made no sense to him. Silent, Willie looked like some Biblical character raising arms in supplication, but Johnny had to wonder if the man knew a God that actually heard prayers.

Then Willie dropped his arms and voiced a question that cut through Johnny.

"What path are you looking for, my friend?"

64

Johnny had no answer, so instead he told Willie about his life in Ohio, his growing-up years, finding Annie, and losing Annie. He tried to explain why he was biking a highway so far from home, attempting to describe to this stranger, an English man, the choice that must be made between the Amish church and the world. Willie listened intently.

"Man, you're caught in two rips."

"Rips?"

"A rip current. Some folks call it a rip tide, but *current* is a more accurate term. Watch those waves out there come in and break on the beach." He motioned toward the surf. "The water runs back out to the ocean; more waves come, break, retreat. Nothing, you think, will ever stop that rhythm of rushing and receding.

"But what's going on beneath the surface? Sometimes obstacles like sandbars create a barrier and the water can't flow smoothly away from the shore. Then it seeks other passageways, and often forces its way through narrow channels at a strong and rapid rate. That creates a rip current. You can't see that on the surface. Swimmers are caught unaware, and many people have died when they're surprised by a rip current."

"You mean … if you're caught, there's no hope?"

"There's hope, Johnny. Fighting the forces of nature can be disastrous, but you can outsmart a rip. The key is not to fight."

"But if you don't fight it, won't you be washed away and drowned?" It only seemed logical to fight through. "How else do you escape, if not by fighting your way out?"

"Here's the key, Johnny. Folks try to fight a rip and die from exhaustion. You need to stay calm and allow nature to take you on its ride. At the same time, use your head. Watch for the edges of the rip. Only when you get to the weak outer part of the current will swimming move you in the direction you want to go."

The sun had slipped below the horizon, but its light still lingered on the beach and in the gray-blue sky. Wandering Willie and Johnny watched the crashing waves in silence. Johnny wondered what dangers lurked in those currents. Willie had said he was caught in not one but two rips.

"So I'm caught in two rips. I'm guessing you meant my grief and all my questions about the church. How do I save myself?"

"Stop struggling so much."

That seemed impossible to Johnny. He had to find his way out of these questions, this confusion, and the desperation.

"Grief is part of our natural world, and it is overpowering. People try desperately to fight it. They naturally want to find a way out of it. But often that leads to making strange or abrupt choices when they're not thinking rationally. Go ahead, let the grief overwhelm you; let it carry you along on its current, taking you to the outer limits of its power. If you do that, you'll find a place where you can start thinking rationally again. You might lose some ground occasionally and get swept back into the current, but you'll know that you can survive."

Yes, Johnny knew what it was to be swept into churning currents that overwhelmed and threatened to drown him. He wondered how it was that Wandering Willie understood so much about grief. What else had he lost when he left behind his old life?

Before he could form another question, Willie went on.

"The church is a powerful current, too, much bigger than you. Flailing about and fighting it will do you no good; you might even put those who try to save you in peril. Instead, look for calmer places where you can think clearly."

Johnny suddenly wished for a long hour in his tree stand. And isn't this what he was doing on the bike ride? Wasn't he looking for a place where he could think more clearly?

"Learn everything you can as you navigate the waters. When you get back to shore, you may see that the current has indeed taken you to where you want to go. Or you may find a way to dig a new channel, and turn the flow of water in a better direction."

That didn't seem likely—that if he simply watched and learned and waited, his life would turn in the right direction.

"Stop struggling so much," Willie repeated. "Wait. Find the edges of this current and make your way back home, wherever that may be. What you learn now as you float along will determine where you wash up on shore."

For all of the long conversation, Wandering Willie had been sitting cross-legged on the rock, wrapped in his bright shawl. Now he rose, stretched a long and bony body, and climbed down to the sand beside Johnny.

"If you're going to be on the road, I have two more pieces of advice. You're traveling too heavy. Get rid of everything you don't need. And dig deeper, Johnny. Things aren't always as they seem."

"Dig deeper? What do you mean?"

"You'll know it's time to dig when it happens."

Johnny took a deep breath. "Okay. Don't fight the rip. Lighten my load. Dig deeper." He was wondering, though, how much of this strange man's rambling was actually good advice and how much of it should be ignored and discarded.

Willie turned to leave. The woman with the shopping cart passed again on the walkway above them, this time headed in the opposite direction.

"Lizzie!" Willie shouted. "I'll walk you home!"

"She has a home?"

"No. Elizabeth's great career depended on outward beauty, so job offers dwindled away when her looks faded. She lost what little she had saved to an unscrupulous agent. She'll be sleeping tonight at a homeless shelter."

"Do you sleep in those shelters?"

"No, of course not. Those are for homeless people. I've got another mile to go before reaching my home for tonight. It's getting dark; I'll walk Lizzie to the shelter first."

Willie reached out a sunburned and wiry hand. "I hope life's current washes you up at a peaceful place, young man."

Johnny remembered the money in his pocket. "Willie, please let me buy you several meals." He extended his hand with one of Samuel Cohraine's twenty-dollar bills.

There was still enough daylight that Johnny could see unmistakable disbelief and revulsion on Willie's face. Was he going to refuse the gift?

Willie reached out and took the bill. "If the advice I gave you is worth twenty dollars, then I'll have to accept it."

Johnny knew at once that he had done the wrong thing, but it was too late to take the money back. Willie walked away, dangling the bill from two fingers like one might carry a dead mouse by the tail, and Johnny saw that his gift was toxic.

Lizzie was waiting for Willie. She gave him a hug and he tucked the twenty-dollar bill in the pocket of her over-sized shirt.

"I could have told you this was not the time."

"I know, Annie. It seems it was the wrong thing to do. But it's this rip I'm trying to escape. My mind sometimes malfunctions."

"What's a rip? That girl who almost caught you?"

"You're funny, Annie."

The rhythm of the waves breaking on the sand lulled him to sleep. In his last moments of consciousness, he thought he was beginning to detect where the rip ended and the safety of the journey home began.

65

The same sounds that lulled him to sleep woke him in the morning. Waves lapping at the shore told him he was not on the farm. Even though it was early morning, there were no cows waiting to be milked. Back home, he would be thinking about the day's work even before he was out of bed. Here, everything about the coming day was unknown.

Shortly after dawn, he took a barefoot stroll along the corridor where the water washed the sand. Alone on the beach and deep in thought, he reflected on chance encounters and how they had already changed him. Or perhaps these were not chance encounters at all. Perhaps divine providence was setting up these meetings for his well-being. He knew his mother was at home praying. Did God have a hand in these meetings? And if God did, then should Johnny have given more consideration to Samuel Cohraine's offer?

No. He had been right to leave that behind. The answer that had come to his prayer had been clear.

His stomach sent out distress signals, and a quick check of Audrey's recommendations showed the location of what she said was a favorite café. Riding through the campground, Johnny noticed how free the ride was without all the additional weight of his tent and equipment he had left at the campsite. Willie was right;

the weight did slow him down. He decided to go through his possessions and determine what was not needed on this journey. He would carry only the absolute necessities.

The population of the campground had swelled in size since his arrival the previous evening. Tents had gone up and many campers had parked throughout the campground. A few sites looked like permanent residences, with wash lines stretched between trees and piles of belongings stacked under tarps, plastic, and even large pieces of cardboard.

Long days of travel and little sleep had blurred events in Johnny's memory, but now he realized this was a weekend. City dwellers were escaping to the beach. He counted his days on the road; almost a week had gone by, and he had yet to turn his bike eastward. On the next day, he would get serious about pedaling and put more miles behind him.

Several blocks away from the beach, he found Sam's Diner. How had Audrey ever discovered this place? What would a girl like that be doing here? The small eatery was crowded and noisy, an amalgamation of humanity gathered there in what seemed like a family reunion. Johnny was drawn in by the aroma of frying bacon and eggs. Sam himself was behind the counter, flipping pancakes and greeting customers.

Johnny had rarely eaten in restaurants. A few times when he had joined his father in timber buying, they had stopped to eat at small diners, and he always enjoyed watching the camaraderie of folks at these establishments. A small restaurant had recently opened in Milford. He had taken Annie there once, for the novelty of the experience, but even though the meals were good, none of the food rivaled Mandy's cooking.

Spying a vacant seat at the counter, he slid in beside a young man about his own age.

"Welcome, my friend. Haven't seen you here before." Sam's greeting drew Johnny into the family reunion.

A row of green tickets fluttered above Sam's work space, and his grill was loaded with orders of eggs, home fries, and bacon and sausage. Plating orders from the jigsaw pattern of foods on the grill and maintaining four separate conversations seemed impossible to Johnny, but Sam made it look effortless.

"Hippie Chick will be right with you," Sam added.

"Order up, Cindy!" Sam slid several plates onto a side counter, and a young lady skipped around the corner carrying two empty coffee pots. Her tattered and faded blue jeans were topped by a multicolored tee shirt embellished with hand-painted slogans. At least a dozen braids sprouted from her head, sticking out in all directions, with bits of brightly colored fabric woven throughout the entanglement. Her head reminded Johnny of a flower garden with weeds growing tall amid the blossoms.

"Young man over there, good-lookin' dude, waiting to order." Sam stretched out "duuuuude," and the flower-garden girl rolled her eyes at him as she picked up the full plates.

Sam turned back to Johnny.

"She's just back from a coupla months at a commune. Looking for enlightenment." He grinned. "We're waiting to see how successful that was. What's your name, friend?"

"Johnny Miller."

"Well, Johnny, I'm Sam, and if you need information or advice it's free right here and guaranteed to be true. This is my buddy Ron, right here beside you."

Johnny turned and reached to shake Ron's hand, but the young man simply rose from the counter stool, picked up his bill, and turned away without a word. Sam stopped scrambling eggs for a brief moment and watched Ron go.

Johnny was astonished to see an empty sleeve where Ron's right arm should have been. How had he missed that?

Sam went back to the eggs.

"Sad. We were so happy to have him back home and relieved that we hadn't lost him, but in a lot of ways, we lost more of him than just an arm."

"What happened?"

"Hand grenade. Nam. That's what happened to his arm. But I can't tell you what all must have happened over there to our friend Ron. He's wounded and hurt in ways we can't imagine."

Viet Nam. Again. Johnny was reminded that he had had no part in the war that had consumed most of America. He also felt that strange sense of nakedness—he was standing in front of the world's eyes as an English man. The beard and hair and clothes that might have warded off questions about his non-participation in the war were gone.

"Hey, dude," interrupted a cheerful voice. "You're doing some heavy thinking. I'm getting heavy vibes from you." Hippie Chick was standing in front of him. "I'm Cindy. What can I get you?"

Johnny ordered bacon and eggs and one pancake and then commented on her unusual shirt.

"My friend at the commune made it for me. Sydney's the most talented clothing designer ever. He made all our clothes."

Sam shook his head.

"Still can't understand it. Why would a designer be in a commune? Is he hiding from something?"

"Sometimes folks need to get away from *society* and get back to the basics."

"I don't dig that, Cindy," answered Sam. She grinned at his attempt to use her slang.

"You're learning, Sam. You'll be ready for a commune one of these days. You'd be a great cook!"

"I *am* a great cook," Sam answered with exaggerated dignity.

Hippie Chick was gone with both hands full of plates.

Sam nodded toward the door.

"Is that your bicycle parked out front?" Johnny nodded. "Which way you heading?"

"Tomorrow I'll head toward San Diego."

"Just back from Nam?"

There. The question had come. It hung in the air above the

counter, and Johnny wished he could wave it away.

"No, sir. I haven't been ... that is, I'm Amish. I haven't been part of the war."

Was it his imagination, or had the folks at the counter and tables around him suddenly quieted? Sam stared at him.

"You don't look like what I thought Amish looked like."

"No," Johnny shifted uncomfortably. "I don't look like most Amish. At least, not right now. I cut my hair. Changed clothes."

"So the Amish don't serve at all?"

"No. We register as conscientious objectors. We believe that Jesus taught us to love our enemies instead of killing them."

Sam seemed to be weighing something in his mind. He smacked several pancakes with a flipper and shoved a pile of bacon onto a plate with such force that two pieces slid to the floor.

A man with bushy gray eyebrows was sitting on Johnny's left and now spoke for the first time.

"Son, let me tell you what happened to Ron's arm. He was riding in a convoy of half a dozen vehicles. He and some buddies were in the back of one truck. They passed through a village that seemed peaceful enough. Then a little waif of a girl in a white smock came racing around the side of the truck. Her arm was raised, and they were shocked to see her holding a grenade.

"That's what they're doing over there. Using little children. Threatening families, holding parents hostage, forcing little kids to do terrible things."

Almost everyone in the diner was quiet, listening to the story.

"What do you do? Shoot children? But it's kill or be killed, I guess." He shook his head. "Terrible mess. Terrible.

"Ron's buddy Shelly was the commanding officer. But he never gave the command to shoot. Ron says Shelly had two little girls of his own at home. Maybe Shelly was thinking about them.

"Instead of shooting, Shelly pitched his gun aside and threw himself on top of that grenade when it landed on the truck bed."

The bushy gray eyebrows met in a deep frown.

"He was blown to bits. For his men. And because he couldn't shoot a child sent to kill him."

The entire room was quiet. Johnny could hear the bacon sizzling. Hippie Chick, leaning against the counter, ignored the tears that were sliding down her cheeks.

"Ron got hit by some of the shrapnel. They couldn't save his arm. At least, we got him back alive. But I know there are days he would rather be dead. That's what our boys are dealing with. And when they come home, they're treated with contempt and hatred and are called baby killers."

Johnny had no words to offer. Men were dying in the war; even those who lived were being destroyed. While he was plowing fields and courting a beautiful girl. He stared at his coffee cup.

Behind the grill, Sam cursed the Vietcong, then jumped as gray smoke started rising from the bacon. Hippie Chick ran around the counter to wave a dish cloth through the smoke, trying to dispel the cloud.

The man with the bushy eyebrows said softly, "That's what the enemy is doing to us. I don't think I'm going to be loving them."

He picked up his bill and headed toward the register.

Johnny dropped his head into his hands, and stared at the Formica countertop. He tried to imagine war like that coming to his valley. His little nieces and nephews, used to ambush the enemy. What would he do?

Talk at the tables had started again, but in more subdued tones. Hippie Chick was again carrying plates to waiting customers. Everyone seemed to ignore him. His eggs were cold. His appetite was gone. Sam had said nothing more to him.

He picked up his bill and went to the register. Hippie Chick appeared behind it and took the slip of paper and his money without looking at him. He turned to go.

"Wait," Cindy said. He looked at her. She seemed to be trying to decide what to say and what to leave unsaid. Then she shook her head slightly, and she went on with a light tone.

"I heard you say you were headed to San Diego. You'll see my friends from the commune. Every Sunday they come out to Huntington Beach to sell things we grow and make on the farm. They'll have produce from the garden, and Sydney and the seamstress girls make shawls and shirts like I'm wearing. You really can't miss them. You'll hear them before you see them. Say hello to Sydney and Lisa for me. Tell them Hippie Chick Cindy said hello. And if you need anything—help, information, anything—ask them."

"Order up, Cindy! You do have other customers," called Sam. With a long and loud sigh meant for her boss, Cindy turned. "Bummer. Conforming to the man can be such a drag."

66

On his ride back to the campground, Johnny saw none of the scenery and was unaware of the traffic around him. He could not forget Ron's story. And he could not forget that he had no answers to the questions.

He had wished for his beard and plain clothes. He had wanted to hide behind one word: *Amish.* Was that the only reason he did not fight? Because he was called by a certain name?

Wandering Willie had told him to dig deeper. Johnny had not understood everything Willie meant by his strange comments, but he did know that it was time for him to go deeper than clothes and a lifestyle. Was he a conscientious objector only because he was Amish and that is what Amish men did? If he wanted to follow Jesus, how would he face an enemy? What did it really mean to follow Jesus? How did Jesus expect anyone to love enemies who were out to kill you? And if he had declared he would follow Jesus, would it make any difference if he were English or Amish?

As he neared his tent site, he passed a man rummaging through a pile of assorted tools and miscellaneous hardware. They exchanged greetings and Johnny remarked that it appeared he was planning to camp there for a while.

"We're not camping. We're living here now," the man replied.

A small girl poked her head out of the tent and watched shyly.

"It's okay, Debbie, you can come out," said her dad.

They had been living at this campsite for almost a year, he told Johnny. When his construction business had collapsed, they had lost almost everything, including their house. He worked around the campground to pay the site fee, and his wife helped with laundry and cleaning the camp buildings. Now and then, he picked up small construction projects. Without a word of complaint or whining, the man expressed the hope that he would find enough work so they could get back on their feet financially and find a place to live.

Small mounds of possessions covered with plastic cluttered the campsite. A lady emerged from the tent and apologized for the appearance of the place.

"We barely have enough room for the three of us to sleep in there, and we need to keep our clothes and tools and cooking equipment outside."

Johnny introduced himself and explained that he was riding across the country on his bike. "I'm sorry you folks are homeless."

The man smiled.

"We may be homeless, but we're sure not hopeless. If you look around, there are folks everywhere without hope; they're the ones that are truly homeless. We know if we keep working hard our hope will bear fruit someday. This camp is only temporary."

He spoke with a positive assurance, and Johnny believed him.

"Does your daughter go to school?"

"There are more families here in similar circumstances. We walk our children to a school bus stop so they won't fall behind on their education."

"I always liked school. Do you?" Johnny asked Debbie.

She was still shy, but she told him, "I like my teachers, but sometimes the other children make fun of my clothes."

Her mother sighed and motioned toward a pile of clothing. "I keep them patched and clean, but she hasn't had a new dress in several years and she's growing out of what she has. I know the day will come, though, when she will go to school wearing new clothes. I know it will."

Johnny admired the unity of hope this man and woman shared.

"Now!" rang a voice in his mind. "Now is when you need to dig into that pocket and give."

Grinning to himself, he reached into his pocket, squatted down in front of young Debbie, and handed her a twenty-dollar bill.

"A lady I love very much wants you to have this. She says to have your mom buy you some new dresses."

"Is it real?" wondered Debbie. He nodded, still grinning. Then, in a quick motion, her small arms encircled him with a hug.

"Hope and pray. Pray and hope. You see, it does work," the woman said to her husband with tears threatening her voice. "Thank you, thank you. God bless you, Johnny."

Light of heart, Johnny pedaled back to his campsite. How could such a small act of kindness make a person feel so good?

"How did I do, Annie?"

"You did great; except, I shouldn't have to remind you."

He spent the next hour sorting out everything he did not need. An extra shirt and a coat and three pairs of socks. Cooking equipment. Picking up the Indians ball cap, he hesitated for only a moment. The tops of his ears still itched with sunburn. He had discovered that a ball cap did not protect his head as well as his Amish hats. The cap was thrown on the stay-behind pile. Keep the sleeping bag. What about the radio? Did he need it? He postponed that decision.

The beach and the walkway were soon swarming with activity. He decided to walk and explore. A veritable circus had materialized, with folks on roller skates, bikers, jugglers, musicians, and peddlers selling their wares.

Back at his beach campsite, he relaxed, lazing about in the sand and sun. He did feel a bit guilty. His father had modeled a strong work ethic and drilled it into Johnny, too, and now it shouted, "You should be working!"

The radio helped to shut out the accusatory guilt. Lying in the sun, giving in to the hypnotism of the waves, listening to familiar country songs and sometimes fiddling with the dial and sampling more rock music than he was used to, he whiled away the afternoon hours.

But something was amiss, and the problem was not his lack of work. Entertained by the radio, he had approached no one and no one approached him. He had isolated himself, alone in the world created by the radio, and he decided he did not like the loneliness.

The previous night's encounter with Willie, the morning's story of Ron, and the hours he had spent on the beach watching people—all had opened his eyes. In his valley back home, he knew almost everyone, knew their families and their history. In only a few days, he had met new faces and heard new stories. For some reason, at home he had never thought much about human wants, needs, and hopes. Back home, the Millers and their neighbors were who they were; and they were certain the world outside was nothing like them. Now Johnny had met all these new faces, all looking quite different than the people he had known—and all the faces had their own stories to tell. Yet in so many ways, they all shared so many things.

He felt he had been torn away from his past. He had lost the one he had loved the most. And then he had voluntarily given up what he might have kept. Very little, it seemed, of his past life remained. He looked at the radio. That was also a part of his past, and he was still holding on to it. When he hid behind it, he quit digging deeper—and he was lonely.

The radio was added to the too-much-weight pile.

***

The next morning it was not the ocean but sounds of people scurrying about the campground that wakened Johnny. The flurry of activity fed his own excitement, and anticipation of the unknown journey ahead pulsed through him.

As he was packing up, he caught sight of the homeless but hopeful carpenter several sites down, already out browsing through a pile of tools. From another pile, he pulled out a garment of some type and handed it into the tent.

Johnny had a possession this family could certainly use. He strolled along the campsites and stopped at the carpenter's home.

"Look, my tent is a burden to me," Johnny began. "It's too big and so much extra weight to carry. Do you want it?"

"Are you serious?"

"It's yours. You could live in this larger tent and store your stuff in your smaller one."

The man stared at him.

"You're giving us this? You don't know ..." The man's voice faltered. "It's an answer to prayer! Let me tell my wife."

He disappeared inside his tent.

Soon mother and daughter were chattering excitedly as they inspected the interior of Johnny's tent.

"It's so big, I could almost bring a friend along home!" exclaimed Debbie.

"I can actually stand up in here," said her mother. Turning to Johnny, she asked, "Why are you doing this for us?"

"I'm Amish, and ..." *Wrong, Johnny.* He started again. "When I became a Christian, I decided to be a follower of Jesus. He changed me. He changed my heart from one that always wanted more things to a heart that wanted to give. And I was raised Amish; it is our tradition to help people in need. I'm leaving these things here. It's all yours, too, if you can use it. I've already packed all I need." He saw that Debbie had discovered the radio and was twisting the dials in delight.

The family looked dazed by their turn of fortune as Johnny pushed his very light bike toward the walkway, wondering how many additional miles he would be able to put behind him on this day because he had lost all that extra weight.

"Wait!" the woman called after him. "You've left your razor and shaving cream here."

Johnny called back over his shoulder as the bike picked up speed. "I won't be needing it. It's too much extra weight."

To someone else he said, "It's just you and me now, Annie."

67

Many times on the morning ride, Johnny commended himself for heeding Willie's advice. Losing unnecessary weight made pedaling the coastal highway much easier. The road climbed and descended, curving around cliffs, hanging above crashing waves, and sometimes dropping to harbors and soft sand beaches. The traffic, constant and fast, demanded that he stay alert. He breathed a sigh of relief after navigating safely through each beach community or busy town.

He was thankful for his black hat, once again perched on his head. Though a bit crumpled, it offered more protection than the ball cap he had left behind in the tent. Here in California, no one would know this was an Amish hat; here, anything and everything was in style. As a matter of fact, it appeared that the more bizarre an outfit, the more it fit this coastal culture's sense of fashion.

Highway One would end at Dana Point. Johnny looked for a place to pull off the road so that he could study Audrey's map for routes to San Diego.

Hippie Chick had been right. Johnny heard the commotion before he understood what he was witnessing. Singing accompanied the pulse of a drumbeat; actually, the sound was more of a primeval chant. He could not understand the words, but his body could feel the deep throb of the drum.

A school bus that was no longer a school bus was parked in a pull-off area. Hand-painted flowers, rainbows, peace signs, and slogans festooned every side and a few of the windows. A table in front of the bus held neat piles of fresh produce; another table offered clothing and blankets in bright hues. Cindy's friends from the farm commune had set up their wares.

The red strawberries looked delicious. Strawberries would not be ripening in the Millers' patch at home for almost three months. Johnny browsed through the pile of clothing, but reminded himself that he wanted to carry only what was necessary.

"Hey, man, I love your hat. Can I take a look at it?" A slender young man with long hair pulled back to a ponytail stood behind the table of clothing. Beside him was a woman with sparkling dark eyes and a ready smile. She was wearing a shirt that Johnny thought must have included every color known to man; a headband stitched with an intricate pattern of beads held her long dark hair away from her face. She was tall and looked strong; the man was of average height, but unusually thin. Both of them were Johnny's age or younger.

"Sure." Johnny removed his hat, brushed off some dirt, and handed it across the table to the designer. The young man's long, slender fingers gently explored the surface, measured the brim and crown, and tested the strength of the felt. His inspection reminded Johnny of Mandy's examination of quilts, studying and storing away all the fine details of composition.

"Hmm," the man said. "Hmm. Umm."

"What do you think of it, Sydney?" He looked at Johnny with raised brows. The tall woman looked at Johnny, too, as though she expected an introduction.

"And you must be Lisa."

"Do we know you?"

"No, you don't. But yesterday I met your friend Cindy at Sam's Diner. She asked me to say hello if I met you."

"Cindy! She's a bright spot of sunshine, isn't she? We certainly miss her at the farm."

"So you all live together on a … commune?"

"Folks call it that. I suppose it is, except that most communes around here have disbanded and our place is a sort of haven for the last remnants of those who still want to live this lifestyle. We have eighteen people in our group."

Johnny looked at the table with produce. "Do you farm?"

"We live on a piece of land about forty miles inland, just outside Wildomar. There's one hundred acres there, but we haven't been able to do much with the land. Most of our vegetables are grown in greenhouses." Lisa grinned. "Not many of us ever learned to farm, not even to garden. Those who tend our crops have had to learn by trial and error."

"It looks like you're doing some things right," Johnny commented, gesturing toward the produce.

"Do you know anything about growing things?"

"I'm a farmer … I was a farmer."

"If you're heading our way, stop and visit us. Stay awhile; give us some pointers. I'm sure Collar won't mind."

"Collar?"

"William Collier. He's the *de facto* leader of our group. An ancestor of his founded Wildomar, and his family owns the land we live on. No one had farmed it for many years, so there was no objection to our moving in. Nobody pays much attention to us."

Johnny had been seeing cities and beaches and mountains. He wondered what a farm in this part of the world looked like. "My plan is to go south to San Diego, then head over to Yuma. Would your farm be along that route?"

She thought for a minute, and Sydney spoke for the first time.

"No, we're south of Lake Elsinore. You'd have to turn east right now. But not too far from our farm, you could pick up Route 79 in Temecula and that will take you in the direction of Yuma. If I were you and traveling on a bicycle, I'd avoid San Diego."

Johnny only heard half of what Sydney said, because he was caressing the shawls of rich color stacked on the table. Wandering Willie had carried a similar shawl.

"Do you make these?"

"I sketch the designs. Lisa and a few of the other girls do the cutting and sewing."

"You must be quite talented."

Sydney blushed and said nothing, but Lisa jumped in to remark that Sydney had worked for a designer shop in Hollywood.

"And he ended up on a farm?"

Lisa's eyes sparkled when she smiled. Johnny thought he saw something more, though, behind the sparkle. Regret? Longing? He was not certain what he saw.

"We do have some interesting stories at our farm. If you decide to stop in and you have the time, we'll gladly tell you more." A customer was handing Lisa a shirt. "We'll be back to the farm by four this afternoon. You can't miss the place."

She turned away to take the customer's money.

***

Johnny touched the shawls one last time, then eased back onto the highway, merging again with the traffic.

In San Juan Capistrano, he was faced with a choice. Either he would follow Audrey's directions toward San Diego, or he would go it on his own. He was beginning to suspect that, while the route Audrey had outlined for him might be quite practical for her sports car, she had never pedaled a bicycle along the same route. Johnny, on the other hand, was on a bike. He had seen several signs marking bike paths along the coastal route, and now he wondered if those paths might have been more enjoyable or, at the least, more safe.

And there was something else to consider: He was pedaling someone else's route, not his own. Following directions mapped out by someone who knew the area did feel comforting and safe. But in doing so, he was tethered to a plan not of his own making.

He pulled up to the first trash bin he saw, gathered all of Audrey's maps and notes, and severed his safety net. Her letter dropped into the bin, too. It was unnecessary weight.

He checked his own map and started pedaling northeast toward Lake Elsinore. A slightly frightening sensation of being adrift in the unknown rose in his chest.

68

Johnny told himself that by now he should not be surprised that nothing was as he expected it to be. Still, he was surprised. He knew that somewhere he would meet the desert, but the part of California that he was now pedaling through was still green and mountainous. On the narrow highway, he wound around sharp turns, climbed and descended, only to again be faced with another uphill stretch followed by a curvy coast down into another valley.

Signs told him he was going through the Cleveland National Forest on the Ortega Highway. Some hillsides were draped with a rich orange cloak of poppies, and one meadow was a sea of yellow and blue wildflowers he could not identify. Two deer stood like statues in the trees and watched him coast by. Although the endless Pacific Ocean was impressive, this slice of California was much more appealing to Johnny. He wondered what it would be like to farm here. If the commune's land had these lavish wildflowers, he would ask what they were.

Finally, a long valley opened up and Lake Elsinore lay below, mirroring blue sky and pillars of white clouds. The town crowded around the lake's shore, as though drawing life from the waters.

Johnny followed a sign promising that the town of Wildomar was only nine miles away. Soon a honking horn and friendly shouts prompted him to pull off the pavement and stop pedaling. The hippie bus pulled up, with heads and arms dangling out the windows. As the bus slowed to a stop, Lisa called out from beneath a mass of wind-tumbled hair.

"So you decided to visit us? Great!" She gave orders to someone else in the bus. "Grab his bike and load it up." It was apparent who was in charge of this tribe.

Johnny offered no resistance, and let the flood of merriment overwhelm him and take him in. The bus rattled into motion again, and Lisa made introductions. Johnny was welcomed heartily, and when he settled into his seat, he heard a few girlish giggles and an "Oh, he's so cute!"

"All right, ladies, I found him first," said Lisa. Johnny had first thought she and Sydney were a couple, but now he doubted that conclusion.

The bus turned onto a dusty and bumpy road lined with placards and odd artistic creations. They crested a small hill, and Johnny tried to mask his shock at the first sight of the commune.

There was no house in sight, only a scattering of weather-beaten outbuildings that most farmers back home would not even use for their animals. Several vehicles were parked at odd places, looking as though they had died years ago and no one had bothered to remove the carcasses. Very little grass grew here; the scrubby trees looked thirsty. Johnny remembered what his father had said about being stewards of the land, and he thought to himself that no one had cared for this land in a long, long time.

It was difficult to believe that Lisa lived here. Her speech was almost free of the slang he had heard everywhere the last few days. She carried herself with confidence; her clothes were clean; and she seemed to care more about her appearance than the other girls in the bus. He realized she was watching his reaction to the farm, and was obviously waiting for a comment. He had better say something.

"Where do you all sleep?"

"There's a chicken house with some bunks. It's fairly comfortable."

Johnny noticed the smattering of chickens scavenging in the dirt. Several goats and two dogs rounded out the menagerie. To his eyes, the entire compound looked tired and dirty and beaten.

"Let me introduce you to Collar, first, then I'll show you around," said Lisa. "Collar is a little strange. Just agree with everything he says, and it will be cool."

***

Collar was more than a little strange. The glazed look in his eyes brought back memories Johnny had already sorted and filed away. He had seen that look at the quarry on the weekend the Indiana boy was killed, and Johnny had hoped he would never see it again.

"What it is, man," he said when Lisa introduced Johnny. Collar's words were drawn out, every sentence slow and finished with *man.* Johnny explained his situation in as short a fashion as possible, guessing that none of his story mattered much to Collar.

"Bummer, dude, that's heavy, man."

"Johnny was a farmer. I invited him to stay here and help us with the farm. Is that all right with you, Collar?" asked Lisa.

"You were raised on a farm? Far out, groovy, man. Can you milk goats, man?"

"I milked cows, but I suppose I could milk a goat, too. I can't stay here, though; I need to continue my ride tomorrow."

"Sydney needs to get you other threads, man. Those jeans look too uncomfortable, man."

Collar had totally missed Johnny's mention of leaving the next day. Johnny almost laughed, though, at the comment about his clothes. To all appearances, Collar himself was wearing a dress. Surely Collar did not expect their guest to put on similar threads?

"Sydney makes all our clothes," Lisa interjected. "Some of the men enjoy the freedom of an outfit like Collar is wearing. It's patterned after Scottish kilts."

"It does look comfortable," Johnny remarked, understanding that Lisa wanted nothing to upset Collar. *But*, he thought, *there is no way Sydney will get me into a dress.*

69

"Let me show you around, and we'll find a place for you to sleep tonight." Lisa said.

"I gave my tent away and was planning to sleep in my sleeping bag."

"Oh, there will be room in the chicken house. You can park your bicycle over in that storage shed."

The storage shed was full; the bike barely fit into the small open space in the middle of the floor. Some of the tools had been used, but most of the piles and stacks of odds and ends were covered with dust. Johnny took a closer inventory and realized there was quite a lot of pipe—pipe that could be used to irrigate this thirsty place. No one had touched it, though; the dirt and debris covering it told him that no one even realized what they had here.

Two long, glass-covered greenhouses still stood, but several window panes were broken and one door sagged on a single hinge and was propped shut with a board. Through the glass, Johnny saw long rows of green.

"We grow our strawberries, lettuce, and tomatoes here."

"Do you irrigate your plants?" Johnny could see a concrete water trough, similar to the one in John and Mandy's basement back home. Theirs cooled watermelons and Johnny's Stroh's, but this one had children splashing in it.

"We carry it down from the pond." Lisa noticed his glance at the water trough. "That's where we bathe and wash our hair."

"Right here? Out in the open?"

"Yes." She gave a small smile and said nothing more as they walked past the outdoor bathtub.

"Looks like dinner's almost ready," She waved toward two women arranging dishes on a rough table set up beside an abandoned bus. "Everyone has their own assignment here. Some prepare meals; some work in the greenhouses; Sydney and I make the clothes."

A group of three girls had corralled a goat and were attempting to milk it. The milking was nothing like the Millers' milking routine. One young woman perched behind a nanny goat while another held the uncooperative critter. The goat bleated and kicked and squirmed, and the girls squealed and shouted threats. The bucket was kicked over, and the weak streams of milk went in all directions. Those girls needed practice; there was no rhythm to their milking, no proper squeezing technique. No wonder the goat was upset.

Johnny could not help but laugh at the circus, and one of the girls threw an angry look his way.

"Think you can do better?"

"Ah, yes, I think I can."

"She's all yours."

Johnny had never milked a goat, but he could milk a cow in his sleep. How much different could this be?

He crouched behind the goat and thought that this was really only half a cow; only two teats instead of four. He grasped them with authority, and a wave of homesickness grabbed him. He missed his cows. He remembered how Annie had laughed at herself the first time she tried to milk.

Johnny had only a second to think of home; then the goat looked back at him and gave a good kick. The girls giggled.

Johnny grabbed both of the goat's legs and lifted up the entire back end and thumped it back down on the ground. He patted the nanny on the flank. "There's a new sheriff in town, girl.

"Give her some grass," he told the young woman at the goat's head; and while the goat was chewing he began again, sending two straight streams of pure white milk into the bucket. It seemed like years since he had milked, but the rhythm came automatically and the bucket began to fill.

"Far out," said one girl. "You are really good. Groovy."

Back home, he had always liked to lean his head against his cow, but here—well, he was sitting at the business end of this goat and decided that pillowing his head was not a good idea. He did talk to the animal, though. She calmly chewed her grass and conceded his authority.

The milking maids pressed closer, watching the motion of his hands, and then asked him to teach them. He was now their hero. No one had ever taught them to milk; they had tried to learn on their own and had little success. Johnny felt sorry for the goats.

Supper consisted of vegetable soup and a crusty bread baked in an outdoor brick oven. Still warm, the bread was delicious, even though there was no butter or jam. The talk at the table was all about the girls' new milking skills. With Johnny's coaching, they had picked up the technique quickly.

As the group finished supper, talk turned to carrying water the next morning. Most of the tribe was needed to carry enough water for the greenhouses, cooking, and bathing; and they told Johnny the water-carrying chore would take most of the morning.

He remembered the stack of pipe in the shed and asked why they did not run pipe from the pond down to the greenhouses. Everyone looked at him as though they had never heard of irrigation. Everyone except Lisa, who suddenly lit up and sparkled.

"There's enough pipe out there?"

"I saw quite a stack. And boxes of fittings and gate valves. It looks as though someone planned to irrigate at one time and bought all the materials, but never got the project done. It seems simple enough. Run the lines from the pond, and let gravity do the work for you."

They looked at Johnny without a word, and he knew they had no idea how to start this project. How did this tribe ever hope to survive out here? He had to admit, though, the cooking was good. He helped himself to another piece of the crusty bread.

"I'll help you do it tomorrow. We'll lay irrigation pipe to the greenhouses. You already have all the tools and material you need." Johnny was beginning to see how much his father had taught him, and he wondered what the fathers of these men might have passed on to their sons. Certainly not agricultural or construction skills.

"Does that mean you'll stay here awhile and teach us to be better keepers of the land?" asked Lisa.

Once again, the temptation. Could this be a wonderful opportunity? He already had ideas for making this a more productive enclave. Collar might have the title of leader, but everyone looked to Lisa as the strongest and probably the smartest person on the farm. Together, Johnny and Lisa might actually turn this place into a productive farm. Collar would not have to be dethroned; he had already abdicated his position by retreating into another world. He was not at the supper table, and Johnny had not seen him since the introductions.

Johnny was intrigued by the challenge. Still, if he wanted to run a farm, he knew where one waited for him, one in much better condition than this land that had been neglected too long. He suppressed a smile. That beautiful farm, though, had no fawning pixies willing to flatter him. Then he decided he must also suppress his vanity.

"One day. I'll stay through tomorrow and help you set up the irrigation system. Then I need to be back on the road."

70

Long after the others drifted away, Lisa and Johnny sat at the table and talked. She came alive when the conversation swung to her plans and hopes for the farm. She explained that the commune had three distinct groups, the clothing group, the garden group, and the egg and milk group.

"Most communes have one common group where everyone shares everything," Lisa told Johnny. "We believe in individual enterprise here. Sydney makes clothes for everyone, we all eat the vegetables, eggs, and milk; but when we sell our products, each group keeps the proceeds to buy more material or feed or seeds. You see, we're smart enough to know this won't last forever, and someday we will all be doing our own thing anyway."

Johnny wondered if this organization was Lisa and Sydney's doing. Collar certainly could not think about or plan for the future.

"How about Collar? Does he care at all about holding this group together?"

"You spoke with him; did you see any survival skills? His parents have money, and they're actually glad he's not at home to embarrass them. Besides," she smiled, "he has his own private garden hidden away back in the hills. That's really the only thing he cares about. He spends most of his time back there."

"His own private farm? But what does he grow?"

"Marijuana," Lisa explained to Johnny. Johnny had heard of it, but he had never met anyone who actually cultivated such a crop. "Some of our family here do drugs, but neither Sydney nor I ever touch the stuff."

"You and Sydney—how did you end up here?"

"I moved to Los Angeles three years ago from the Midwest. Had big dreams of an acting career. But it wasn't long before I was so repulsed at the shallowness of the Hollywood crowd that I was ready to return home. I met Sydney at the boutique shop where he worked, and we struck up a friendship. We're as different as two folks can be, but he had similar observations about the people he was dealing with.

"I saw how talented he was, so I offered to help him establish his own business. He's so creative—but he has no head or backbone for business. On his own, he would get eaten up by the business world. A shop patron had a daughter living at this commune, and Sydney agreed to come here for a year and work on designs if I accompanied him. Our plan was to stay a year and see what happened to our dreams. It's been close to two years now; and although it's been a laid-back life, I know it's time we took steps toward our goal of opening up a shop. You need to see Sydney's little sewing room. I'll show it to you tomorrow."

The chicken house, happily, had been thoroughly cleaned before it was turned into a bunkhouse. Johnny unrolled his sleeping bag on a hard and narrow bunk that had its own little window framing thousands of stars pinned on a dark sky. Listening to a few hens clucking goodnight, he felt like a ten-year-old in the chicken business once again.

***

At least, no one had tried to put him into a dress. In the morning, he remembered Collar's remark about his jeans. Collar had been right; the jeans weren't all that comfortable. The men on this farm all wore loose outfits, ranging from kilts to baggy pants with homemade suspenders holding them up. If Johnny was going to work here, he would dress the part.

In the shed, he dug out his barn-door pants, slipped out of the jeans, and pulled on the familiar feel of home. The shirt Annie had made him, of her favorite blue color, went on next, and he hitched up his suspenders over it. His very short haircut changed the way the black hat fit, but he settled it firmly on his head and ambled over to the group gathered for breakfast.

"Groovy, man!" Admiring comments greeted him. "Wait till Sydney sees that outfit; he'll freak out," said one of the girls.

Collar was again absent from the meal, and neither Lisa nor Sydney appeared at the table.

One of the girls was trying to talk another into trading chores. She was too clumsy, she said, always breaking eggs when she gathered them. Johnny could not resist interjecting his own opinion and wisdom.

"Perhaps it's not your fault; perhaps the eggshells are too fragile. Do the shells seem to be hardening properly? Are you adding any oyster shells to the feed?" Blank stares greeted these questions. "Egg shells are calcium. So are oyster shells. Adding several pounds of ground up oyster shells to the chicken feed will increase the hens' calcium intake and harden the shells."

"Outta sight," mumbled one woman. "That guy's a genius."

Knowledge had given him power here. Were these people so desperate for a leader that they would accept him because he could milk a goat and feed chickens properly? Johnny knew he was only one step away from commandeering the whole operation, if he chose to do so. Even Lisa would not oppose him; she knew how much they needed help, and she had asked him to stay. The power was his for the taking. The realization both confused and exhilarated him.

71

After breakfast, eight of the men stood shoulder to shoulder, huddled together, listening to Johnny as he outlined the plan for the irrigation pipes. He gave each one a job, and they scattered, a few almost trotting to their assigned work. The mood was enthusiastic and hopeful; they had a plan to better the farm, and they were ready to dig in and work. Good. Perhaps all they really needed was someone to direct them.

Sydney finally emerged from a small, ramshackle building. Lisa had not included that building on the tour the day before. He started toward Johnny, then froze and stared. His eyes were on Johnny's "new" pants.

"Those pants are amazing!"

"My pants? My wife made these. In our Amish community, all the men wear these."

"What are they called?"

"You mean, do we have a name for them? *Pants*, maybe?" Johnny laughed. He had never considered these pants stare-worthy. "Sometimes we call them barn-door pants."

"Follow me," Sydney's voice, usually gentle and quiet, now took on a tone that demanded unquestioning obedience.

"Where?"

"Back here to my shop, I want to sketch those pants. They are absolutely genius!"

Johnny stepped through the door of the shack and forgot he was in the middle of an isolated and dusty wasteland. Sydney's shop was vibrant with color and texture. Large windows were scrubbed clean, letting in the sunshine. What looked like a fabric jigsaw, with dozens of small pieces waiting to be fit together in a pattern, covered one long table. Scissors, pins, tape measures, and sketch pads waited for Sydney's creative hand. In front of the largest window stood a Singer treadle sewing machine.

"Wow, so this is how you do your sewing. I wondered how you managed it without electricity. My mom has a machine like this." Johnny could see her, with head bent over her work and fingers guiding the fabric while her foot moved the treadle.

"Those pants are simply amazing. Do you mind if I inspect them more closely?"

"I suppose … within reason …"

Johnny hoped Sydney did not expect him to take off the pants and hand them over, as he had done with the black hat when they first met. But Sydney was simply circling around him, looking closely, sweeping lines onto his sketch pad, and talking to himself.

"Buttons across the front. Flap resembles a barn door. So simple. Why didn't I think of this?"

Sydney sketched the design for his new line of pants. "I'll call these Johnny BarnDoors. And if they sell, I'll give you half the profit," he promised.

"No need for that."

"You have my word on it. You can't possibly know how much you've inspired me. This may be the big break I've been waiting for. I know the hippie community will love them; we'll have to see if they go mainstream, too. Johnny BarnDoors for kids. Johnny BarnDoors in all colors and sizes. Maybe even winter and summer fabrics. The possibilities are endless."

"Sydney. *Sydney.*" Johnny spoke firmly to pull the designer from his daydreams. "Remember to take care of Lisa if you strike it rich. She's brought you this far, and she seems to really respect you and your talent."

"Lisa deserves her dreams, too. She would have been a great actress if she could have tolerated foolishness," Sydney replied.

Lisa walked into Sydney's studio then. He showed her the sketches and outlined his plans for a new line, the Johnny BarnDoors. She caught his excitement, and Johnny decided it was a good time to slip away and see how the irrigation project was coming along.

***

The men worked hard that day, and the physical labor exhilarated Johnny. The system they rigged up to carry water from the spring-fed pond to the greenhouse seemed simple to Johnny; but there were shouts of amazement and celebration when the valve was opened in the greenhouse and the first water gushed from the pipe.

Lisa smiled and nodded her head as she watched the water fill a bucket. Then she turned and congratulated Johnny.

"Thanks so much for all you've done for us." He heard the gratitude in her voice. "I would try to talk you into staying, but I know you have dreams you need to follow. I hope we meet again."

"I'm not leaving yet. I want more of that wonderful bread and one more night in the chicken house," he joked.

"You're more than welcome," she said warmly. "You're leaving in the morning then?"

He nodded. "Probably early. I like traveling before the rest of the world wakes up."

"Remember, you've got a long, dry desert ahead of you over in Arizona. Make sure you carry plenty of water."

"Could I borrow some of those plastic jugs? I'll keep those full. I have room, since I'm not carrying much else with me. My sleeping bag is the only thing that takes up much space."

After supper, Johnny rolled up his sleeping bag, jeans, and shirt. His wallet went into one pocket of his Johnny BarnDoors, and the three twenties still waiting for adventure went into another. Then he picked up his bundles and visited Sydney in the studio.

"Hey, Sydney, would you consider trading one of those shawls for my sleeping bag? I'll even throw in a pair of too tight jeans and a shirt."

"Gladly," said Sydney. "Take your pick."

Johnny chose a blanket with bright yellow and orange patterns because it reminded him of Wandering Willie.

First, he checked with Annie. Then he dug into his pocket and pulled out one of the twenties.

"Since you've agreed to include me as partner in your new venture, I want to present this seed capital for the Johnny BarnDoor pants. Use it to buy the first bolt of fabric. And when you make your first sale, thank Annie."

Sydney wrapped his arms around Johnny and tried to blink away tears.

"Some things are meant to be," he whispered.

That night Johnny wrapped himself in his new shawl and slept in the chicken house as a bright moon rose over the landscape.

Early in the morning while the farm still slept, he rolled his bicycle away from the buildings. The water jugs, filled from the bubbling spring on the hill, had replaced most of his other belongings, but Annie's notebook was still tucked carefully into one side of a basket.

He was now carrying the minimum necessities for survival. He had given up more things he did not need, to make room for an absolute essential on his journey through the wilderness.

Pushing his bike up the dusty lane, he stopped at the top of the hill and looked back at the moonlit landscape. This had been a rewarding stop. Never had he been with folks so simple in so many ways and so pure. Not once had he heard anger or jealousy expressed (except, perhaps, when he had laughed at the goat milking circus). This was just a group of folks trying to live together in harmony.

"Farewell, Amish hippie land," he murmured, getting back on the bicycle.

He pedaled toward the approaching dawn and thought to himself, *Wow. These pants really are comfortable.*

III

Wandering Home

72

Sabio and Mariposa had found life on the edge of the oyamel forest sublime … at least for a while. On warm days, Sabe floated on air currents high above the fir trees, sometimes accompanied by his Posy. The beauty of nearby streams and waterfalls compelled him to visit often, but he had learned his lessons well and approached bodies of water with extreme caution.

Even a slight dampness could be fatal here on the mountain. At these high altitudes and quickly cooling temperatures, moisture could bring freezing paralysis to the delicate orange and black wings. Then immobility would make him an easy target for the birds. Sabe had been dismayed to find birds here that were not deterred by the milkweed toxin, as the northern birds had been. These evil marauders swooped in twice a day to feast on the butterfly colony.

At night, the black-eared mice foraged for food on the forest floor. They collected the bodies of the dead or dying Monarchs and pounced on any live butterfly unfortunate enough to be caught on the ground.

As the days and nights grew colder, thousands of little corpses littered the ground under the oyamel firs. Even though the mass of butterflies clumped together ever tighter to conserve and share what little heat remained, hundreds succumbed to the cold. Sometimes a snowfall would both dampen and chill them, and Sabe and Posy huddled with others on the evergreen branches now wearing heavy cloaks of orange and black.

The colony was a large one, and many branches were overloaded. Occasionally a loud crack resounded through the forest as a branch broke under the massive weight of the butterflies. The unfortunate Monarchs hanging on to the underside of the branch met with instant death as the weight of their winter home fell and crushed them.

The winter was long, and Sabio and Mariposa's life became quieter and quieter. They rested, conserving the food and energy still stored in their bodies.

On days of sunshine, though, Sabio was not content to spend quiet hours immobile on the overloaded branch. With any warmth of the sun also came a restlessness. Was it possible that this place was not a permanent home? On those days, he fluttered from limb to limb, seeking the wisest among millions, but no one had an answer for him. In the end, he could only rely on what he felt within. Something was happening, something he could not quite grasp. He was missing something, longing for something.

And then one sunny day in March, he could name what was happening to him. The spirit of wandering was upon him again, and he was longing to go home.

**

Sabe hesitated to tell Posy of his decision. For the last few days, she had refused to join him in his forays into the surrounding countryside. His vivacious Mariposa had been more subdued than he had ever seen her.

Finally, he was overwhelmed with the desire to begin another long journey. Their last journey together had been a pilgrimage of survival. Now some internal clock told him it was time to leave the oyamel forest and go home. He had no question, hesitation, or doubt. It was time.

"Mariposa," he began one evening, "I have come to understand that this is not home. This was only a temporary resting place, necessary for our survival."

"Yes," said Posy, speaking more strongly than she had in days. "We need to leave soon, for our own well-being and for our children and their children."

"We will give birth to our family at the same place we were born! It will be great to be back beneath our porch and to drink sweet nectar from those beautiful flowers. We'll leave first thing in the morning."

"Yes," agreed Posy, "we cannot delay. We would be wise to start ahead of the masses."

The following morning Posy and Sabio pushed away from the branch that had been their sanctuary for nearly five months and joined a procession of like-minded wanderers also reacting to the tug of home. Drifting above the streets of Angangueo, they looked down on whitewashed houses and shops, but the crowds that had so joyously welcomed them were now absent. Side by side, Sabe and Posy silently winged their way ever higher until they finally found a suitable air current.

Something did not seem quite right to Sabe. Climbing to this height had required a considerable effort. Perhaps his strength had waned because he had spent so much time at rest on the oyamel trees. But, he thought, the quiet time should have refreshed their bodies and prepared them for another long journey.

He watched Posy gliding ahead of him; she had lost much of her intense color and seemed unusually pale. He would not alarm her by mentioning it, though. Perhaps, once they had settled into their traveling routine, both of them would find their old vitality once again.

Mariposa, for her part, was well aware of her condition. She was also concerned for Sabio's well-being. The luster had drained from his beautiful bright colors. She had once thought the nicks and dents in his wings, medals of misadventures on the journey south, added a rugged look to her friend; now those scars only called attention to the fading of his beauty. She decided not to alarm him with her observations.

Navigation on the journey home would be a cinch; they would travel north, following as closely as possible the path they had taken south.

The ease of navigation and the excitement of being on the road toward home overshadowed their weakness, at least for a time. Both made frequent stops at flower clusters, building up energy; but much of that energy was burned rising back up to flying heights. Sabe noticed they were traveling shorter and shorter days. Every night, they dropped to a resting place with their energy completely sapped.

73

Living beneath the wide open skies was easier than Johnny had expected. Willie had been right. Possibilities for sleeping arrangements were everywhere as long as he kept his eyes open to see them. During a few thunderstorms, he found shelter beneath overhangs of buildings; and several nights he slept in structures that he supposed were barns, although they looked nothing like the barns in the valley back home.

His journey gave up more delightful surprises. The Arizona desert, which he had imagined to be flat and sandy and dry and desolate, was soaked with color. Carpets of orange poppies covered slopes of the foothills. Bristly cactus wore splashy pink, purple, or white blooms. A spindly plant called ocotillo waved tales of bright crimson at the end of each branch, and the homely Joshua tree was decked out in what looked like frosty white pine cones.

Every now and then on lonely days of pedaling through the desert, Johnny did wonder if he had been foolish to bring his old bike. But his apprehension never bore fruit in reality; the bike's tires rolled along with no sign of rebellion or exhaustion. Many long stretches offered no roadside stop for food or water, but it seemed that an oasis of rest always came along when he needed it.

Eventually Arizona and New Mexico were both behind him. Texas, however, loomed bigger than Goliath.

He had no complaint about the landscape through which he was traveling. The scenery was both beautiful and intriguing. He was astonished at the first sight of immense fields of peppers and beets. At another place, he stopped to watch a tractor pulling a wide cotton planter down rows that stretched into the horizon. What would it be like to plant twelve rows of seed at one time, in a field where he could not even see the boundaries?

Nor was he bothered by loneliness. He was seeing the world beyond his own valley and had much to think about. He had neglected writing down his thoughts for several days. As he pedaled along Route 90, he decided it was time for a day of rest and catching up on his journal. He wanted to capture details of events while they were still clear in his memory. Yet he could not seem to stop. Instead, he pedaled from early morning to late in the evening, sometimes even eating a sandwich on his bike, as something compelled him onward.

The problem with Texas Route 90, he decided, was the distance that must be traveled without arriving anywhere. He pedaled the undulating road, fighting the wind that constantly tried to push him off course, and wondered if there would ever be an end to the vast state. Checking his map frequently, he sensed that he was only creeping across the expanse that was Texas.

No one had asked him lately what he was running from. Perhaps that was because he was no longer running. In fact, he knew that the war that had raged inside him for so many years was now almost over.

Another reason he had not written down his thoughts lately was because he had not quite sorted them out. One question still troubled him. What had happened to Annie when she died? Where was she as he crawled across Texas? He had watched her body being lowered into the waiting grave, but he knew Annie was not in that box. At times he heard her voice in his thoughts, and he wondered if her spirit hovered nearby. Had she watched him pedal all these miles? Did she know what he was doing?

He had opened her notebook and read her last note to him. She had written of Jesus calling her and of God telling her it was almost time to go home. How could she have been so certain of that? Could Johnny know without a doubt that she was with Jesus, with the One she loved more than she had loved even her husband? How could he, too, have such confidence in heaven?

Johnny replayed, over and over, a conversation with his father shortly before he had left home.

"Dad, do you believe Annie is in heaven?"

"We have a hope that she is," Dad had replied.

"But, Dad, must we go through life only *hoping?* I want more. I want to *know* where she is."

"Son, *hope* is a word like *love,* with many different layers of meaning. Our hope of heaven is more than a wish or a desire; our hope for eternal life is based on trust in what Jesus said, and we have confidence that God does not lie. You know that Annie believed Jesus with all her heart, and He promised that anyone who does that will have eternal life and be with Him in heaven."

Our hopes are based on what Jesus said. God does not lie. Johnny was beginning to see that everything depended on trusting Jesus. *Having faith,* his father had called it.

***

Maybe he needed to have more faith in Route 90. There seemed to be no hope of getting anywhere in the vast open spaces. But he had to believe this road would eventually lead to his destination, even though he still did not know exactly what his destination might be.

His mind kept urging him to sit still for one day and gather all his thoughts into a neat package. Maybe then the last few corners of questions and ponderings could be caught up and tucked into place. His mind needed time to stop and consider the honest answer to Willie's question: *What path are you looking for?*

His body, though, did not want to stop; there was a peace in the constant movement. The hum of tires on tarmac and the endless rotation of pedals and chain were the sounds of freedom. He was caught up in the rhythm and movement.

But both his body and his mind knew that this could not last.

74

Early one morning, the Rio Grande River shone in the distance. Memories of a night spent wedged in the cleft of a rock flooded through Sabio. That day on their journey south, they had flown many miles and still had the energy needed to cross Falcon Dam before nightfall.

Now a stubborn wind blew the two Monarchs slightly off course, and they lacked the strength to struggle back to their previous path. They were east of Falcon Dam near Rio Grande City; but, fortunately, the river here was a mere ribbon and they crossed it easily. More good fortune visited them when the strong wind blowing due west gave way to a gentle breeze from the southwest. They struggled mightily to reach a higher altitude and then allowed the breeze to carry them miles into Texas.

Few words had been spoken in the first days of their journey. Both of them directed all their energy into flight.

Several times Sabe observed Posy glancing at him with a pained expression. He wondered if the pain was her own debilitating fatigue or if she had noticed the changes in his appearance. Something was happening to his body that concerned him greatly. His strength ebbed quickly, and the coloration of his wings had changed to a drab, light brown color. He could feel his wings and body drying out and turning brittle.

How he could ever reach home in this condition concerned him. He was certain that Posy's agitated look meant that she had noticed his decline.

Posy had noticed, of course, but her urgency sprang from other unexpected changes. She had mentioned it several times before, but Sabe had not given her suggestion much thought. As they settled for the night on a large branch with several dozen other travelers, Posy spoke her concern again, this time with such firmness that Sabe took notice.

"We must find milkweed, and soon. The babies will need it."

"But we are not even close to home," Sabe lamented.

"Tomorrow," said Posy, ignoring his objection. "Tomorrow we search for milkweed."

***

Home had been on Johnny's mind. Every family scene he glimpsed tugged at his heart and reminded him of his own loved ones. Every ranch and farmstead he passed brought back memories of the sounds and smells of his own farm in the springtime. Enormous fields turned and planted made him long to be caring for the earth again.

Texas was the land of his dreams. The landscape through which he pedaled was exactly as he had imagined as a youngster dreaming of the wide open West. Yet everything whispered, *Home*. And this was not home.

He had been on the same highway for 500 miles as he approached Uvalde. He had studied his map so often that he knew each day what towns were ahead and could visualize the web of highways without taking out the map while he traveled. In Uvalde, the logical route to Florida would have been to continue east, through San Antonio and Houston.

But at an intersection where Route 83 turned south toward La

Pryor and Crystal City, Johnny suddenly swerved to the right and took an unplanned route.

Why he obeyed the impulse, he did not know. Something deep within had prompted him to turn away from the sensible but increasingly mundane route. He had discovered that the unknown road sometimes led to great discoveries, and he wondered how often in life he had missed out on unknown adventure because he took the safe, least difficult route.

Now he followed a prompting in his spirit and unknowingly headed off in the direction of home.

75

Perhaps it was curiosity that suddenly swerved the old bicycle onto a new route. What kind of place deserved the fascinating name of Crystal City? Johnny had once heard a preacher in an English church describe heaven as a crystal city. The minister had drawn a vivid picture of jeweled gates and bright lights emanating from within. The light glistening off those gates, the preacher had said, would blind a person unless he had been given a new body capable of withstanding such beauty.

Johnny was looking forward to pedaling through Crystal City, but he was expecting no jeweled gates.

A vast building sprawled over many acres, stretching out beside Route 83. As Johnny drew closer, he was astonished, not at the size of the huge complex but at the bright red letters on the side of the building that proclaimed it to be McCollum Equipment Company, "Makers of Quality Farm Implements for 100 years." Smaller words told him this was the Laredo Plow Division. Below the company name, a series of vignettes painted on the wall depicted the history of the plow, beginning with a single horse and a one-bottom plow and ending with a large tractor pulling a massive sixteen-bottom plow.

He braked to a stop and stared. The Miller family had used

Laredo plows for three generations. "Laredo means quality," John had often said. When they needed a new disc and planter, there was no question that it would be Laredo. Now Johnny stood right in front of the plant where their farming equipment had been made.

He studied the mural and grinned. Apparently, Laredo now also made a piece of equipment that combined the functions of a plow, disc, and planter in one amazing contraption. The Miller family, however, still cultivated their ground with horses and the old one-bottom plow.

***

The sun had climbed well into the sky the next morning when the sharp edges of hunger reminded Johnny that he had not eaten breakfast. Up with the first rays of sun, he had begun pedaling immediately, hoping to get many, many miles of Texas behind him that day. But on the north edge of Crystal City, the Oasis Drive-In sent out aromas that suddenly made food more important than miles. He swerved into the parking lot.

He propped the bicycle against one side of the diner. The stucco wall was painted to look like a tropical forest, and a colorful parrot glared at him from a tree limb. A large OPEN sign hung on the door facing the sidewalk, and several late-model cars were parked on the other side of the diner. Two old air conditioners hung from windows, and an ice bin growled away as it tried to keep bagged chunks of ice from melting. Johnny wondered how hot it would be before the end of the day, and he wished for his summer straw hat rather than the black one he was still wearing.

The place was empty except for a group of well-dressed men lingering over coffee at a round table in one corner. Johnny chose a booth away from the group, but the place was so small that the conversation from the round table drifted over to his corner.

"Looks like March sales will set records again," said one man.

"Those overseas sales are really going to put us over the top," observed another. "Bill says if China ever opens up to the outside world, we'll need to expand manufacturing again, perhaps even open another factory in Europe."

A young man entered the conversation and commented that Bill had been talking a lot lately about Asia and China. "He's got connections in Washington; he probably knows more about those possibilities than most people."

"He's more interested in getting Bibles into China than selling farm equipment there," another said with a laugh.

Johnny could no longer contain his curiosity.

"Do you gentlemen work at the McCollum Company?" Several answered in the affirmative. "Our family back in Ohio has used your equipment for generations, and my dad's a loyal customer. He'll be so interested to hear that I actually rode by your plant yesterday."

One man with gray hair and a moustache looked at Johnny with a puzzled expression. "You look Amish," he said. "Although your hair and beard are not quite what I would expect."

This took Johnny by surprise. He had seen no signs of Amish communities since he had left Ohio. How did a man in Texas know what *Amish* was supposed to look like?

"I am," he said and decided not to explain the short haircut. No need, either, to tell them why he was wandering all over the country, so he kept to the subject of farming equipment. "You may find this hard to believe, but we still plow with horses and your one-bottom plow."

"That one-bottom has been discontinued for years!"

"Yes, but in our community we can still get parts for it. Dad wouldn't miss an issue of your newsletter, either. When it arrives in the mail, he reads that before the daily newspaper. He often talks about how much he admires your owner's spirit of giving to help needy causes."

The gray-haired man nodded thoughtfully. "Bill takes good care of his employees and gives away most of his profit."

"Folks would be amazed if they knew Big Bill's philosophy on giving," added another.

"He must be in his seventies by now. Does he ever stop at the factory?" Johnny asked.

"Almost every day. Our main factory is in Laredo, but this plow division is where his life changed, so he spends most of his time up here. If he's not at the factory, he's out at the cross."

"The cross?"

"Yes, the cross. That's his love. If you're traveling south toward Laredo, you can't miss it. About ten miles out of town. As a matter of fact, Big Bill will probably be out there today, if you want to stop and meet him."

76

Johnny downed his breakfast quickly, forgetting that he had been hungry. There was a chance he could meet the man whose company values and personal philosophy had touched their Amish life far away in Ohio, and he was also wondering what cross it was that the man loved so much. In his anticipation, he also forgot that he wanted to explore Crystal City. The highway skirted the town, and he was soon pedaling south, scanning the horizon for a cross.

Nearing an intersection, he could see it off in the distance. But to reach the cross, he would need to leave his well-defined route toward Laredo and veer off in another direction. Plans for a big-mileage day vanished with one simple turn of the handlebars, and he entered a small country road that led toward the cross rising from the landscape.

The landscape was rolling, and once or twice as the road dipped he briefly lost sight of the cross. Then it came into view again, standing atop a small knoll like a beacon, compelling wondering folks to pay a visit. It tugged at his spirit.

He rolled to a stop. The cross stood several hundred feet away from the road, set apart from a small parking area by a row of trees. Made of wood and about sixty feet tall, it was situated on a raised platform. Long steps led up to the foot of the cross.

He had stopped by an ordinary mailbox at the side of the road. Printed on the side of the box, where an address would normally appear, were the words, STEPS TO A CHANGED LIFE. Johnny opened the box and found a stack of cards inside. He took one and read a hand-written note from Bill McCollum.

> *Friend, you are not here by accident. You were drawn by the sight of the cross. This cross is only two planks of wood and is powerless in itself. It cannot change you. It is only a reminder of another cross. What took place on that cross has power to completely change your journey in life. When you arrive at the foot of the cross, you will have a choice to make.*

Johnny placed the card back in the mailbox. No need to carry more weight with him. He propped the bicycle against a tree and started toward the cross.

The steps were made of granite and almost ten feet long, running deep but not high. As he put his foot on the first step, his eyes fell on the large word carved into the polished gray stone: REPENT. After that came these words:

> *For all have sinned and fall short of the glory of God. Romans 3:23*

Large letters on the next step spelled out BELIEVE, and the words below it read,

> *For there is one God and one mediator between God and men, the man Jesus Christ, who gave himself as a ransom for all men. 1 Timothy 2:5-6*

He moved one step closer to the cross, where CONFESS was carved into the granite.

That if you confess with your mouth, "Jesus is Lord," and believe in your heart that God raised him from the dead, you will be saved. Romans 10:9

The last step encouraged him to RECEIVE.

He who has the Son has life; he who does not have the Son of God does not have life. 1 John 5:12

Johnny walked slowly to the base of the cross. There, one more line in the stone at his feet presented the choice everyone must make.

Everyone who calls on the name of the Lord will be saved. Romans 10:13

Kneeling, Johnny pressed his forehead against the cross, felt the warmth of the sun-soaked wood, and whispered, "I believe. I am calling, Lord." He remembered the day in the tree stand, when he had begged God for help and decided to give his life to following Christ. The warmth from the cross seemed to spread to his soul, a warmth of peace and joy.

Rising from his knees, he tilted back his head and looked up at the cross. The cross Jesus died on was empty. The tomb in which He was buried was empty. Jesus was alive. Although Johnny wandered alone somewhere in the vastness of Texas, he no longer felt lonely. Jesus Christ had promised to be with him always, until the end. He might have been far from home, but he was not traveling this journey alone.

And he was not alone at the cross. Glancing toward the row of trees and the parking area, he saw a man at the picnic table. For a moment, he thought it might be Bill McCollum; he had forgotten, in his pilgrimage to the cross, that McCollum was the reason he had first come here. Then Johnny saw the battered truck and noted the faded pants and shirt, and he felt sympathy for the unfortunate soul who must have had a breakdown or run out of gas at this remote spot. The truck was older than he was; so old, in fact, that Johnny did not recognize the make or model.

The man's head lay on the table between outstretched arms, and he did not hear Johnny approach. Two twenties still waited in his pocket. It had been weeks since he'd been prompted to give one of those away. Here was a perfect opportunity to give a gift to someone who could not possibly repay him.

Johnny cleared his throat and shuffled his feet a bit as he walked, hoping to awaken the man.

The man jerked upright and looked around.

"I didn't hear you drive in."

"I'm on a bicycle," Johnny told him. "It looks like you have a bit of trouble with your truck, sir. Do you need gas? Can I help in any way?" He laid a twenty-dollar bill on the table.

The stranger seemed surprised, then smiled, and finally rolled back his head and laughed heartily.

"My wife will love this. Does my truck make me look that desperate?" He reached out and took the bill. "I'll take your money for one reason. You are a man with a good heart, ready to help a complete stranger in trouble. It's hard to find folks like that anymore. But we'll put your twenty to good use."

He reached a large hand across the table and introduced himself as Bill McCollum. Johnny surprise came out in a stuttering explanation. "I thought … yes, your truck does look … I believed you were …"

McCollum was smiling in a good-natured way. Johnny took his hand and said, "Johnny Miller," and then finally blurted out, "Are you really the owner of the Laredo plow? I mean, the McCollum Equipment Company?"

"One and the same."

"That truck isn't quite what I expected you to be driving."

"Sit down, young man. You look as though you have a story to tell. It's not every day that an Amish man on a bicycle arrives here. Tell me your story, then I'll tell you why I'm driving that truck."

Bill McCollum seemed like such an *ordinary* person and he listened so attentively that Johnny was soon comfortable telling him about losing Annie and leaving home to look for answers in matters of his own faith.

"Those verses leading to the cross comforted me," Johnny concluded. "They assure me that I really do have eternal life."

"You'd be amazed at the power the cross has to draw people to it. Long ago, a cross was constructed as a killing device. But what took place on it is so incredibly amazing that simply the symbol of one reminds believers how important Christ's death and resurrection are. A cross right here at this spot changed my life."

Bill McCollum went on to tell his own story, and more than once there were tears in his eyes and voice.

77

Big Bill's great-grandfather had started the company. At first, he made only plows. The business was successful, and he and his son, Bill's father, continued to expand the line of equipment.

Bill was the first of the family to get a college education. When he came back home and joined the business, he thought his book learning qualified him as an expert in everything, and he soon made some choices his dad disapproved of. A pattern quickly developed—when major decisions needed to be made, Bill and his father were usually at odds. Then the elder McCollum suddenly passed away, and Bill was the man in charge. And charge he did.

He borrowed a great deal of money to expand and update the factory. Unfortunately, other manufacturers had entered the market and were undercutting his prices, so he started worrying a great deal about the competition. He had kept Steve, who had been his dad's right-hand man for many years; and Steve advised Bill not to meet other competitors' low prices. He would tell Bill that their company had the best product on the market, and folks would always pay for quality. Bill didn't listen to Steve's advice and insisted on pricing his products ever lower.

Actually, he did not listen to much of anything Steve tried to tell him. Bill didn't make it easy for Steve to stay with the company, and he hoped that Steve would give up the battle and leave on his own. But Steve stayed. Bill was determined to do things his own way, and he consistently ignored the experience and wisdom of his dad's trusted advisor.

He not only ignored wise advice, he also sometimes ridiculed it. Bill's father had always given 10 percent of the company's profit to charities. Bill discontinued that practice. Steve was really upset with that move. He was a born-again believer and was not ashamed of it. "You honor God, and He will honor you," he often said. Bill thought such an idea was ridiculous; the company couldn't afford to be giving away money.

Bill had been raised in the church, so he had heard the truth preached often enough; but after high school, he quit attending. College offered so many distractions that he never had room for a relationship with God.

Somehow, though, he managed to marry a woman who was a Christian and attended church every Sunday.

"Without that lady in my life," Bill told Johnny, "I would not be here today. She never begged me to go to church with her, but I often heard her praying for my salvation. She'd leave me notes saying she believed in me and that God loved me. She kept on loving me even while I grew hard and bitter and unlovable. We had two children, and I was on the verge of bankruptcy, getting more desperate every day."

He needed a hiding place from the mounting problems in his business and his life, and he found it in an old highway rest area that the county no longer maintained. That spot was right where he and Johnny sat talking. He would come out to the deserted roadside park and bring along a bottle to blot out his despair.

"I was here one night without a drop of liquor in me," Bill continued. "I'm not sure how it happened, but I was completely sober. And I was at the very bottom of the pit. I was convinced that everyone—the business, my wife, and my family—would be better off without me. I was dragging my family and my business under.

"I parked right where the truck is now. That old thing had lots of holes and leaks and rattles even back then; and I sat there with the motor running, thinking that I really should turn off the engine because it was probably cranking all kinds of dangerous fumes into the cab. But you know what? I didn't care. I didn't care what happened to me. There was no hope in my life, no light at the end of the tunnel, no reason to think there could ever be anything good in my life again. I couldn't think of one good reason to go through one more day.

"I fell asleep. It could be I was breathing the exhaust. I'll never know. I only know that when I fell asleep, I slumped against the door. That door has always had a defective latch, and next thing I knew, I'd tumbled out of the truck and was lying in the dirt. For a few seconds, I wondered if I was dead and in hell; but I soon recognized my surroundings. I lay there, looking at the sky and wishing I could disappear in some black hole of the universe."

Out near the road, the power company had strung new electric lines. The insulators on the cross ties reflected the moonlight and caught Bill's eye. Then the light shifted, as though God Himself had moved the moon in the sky, and one pole changed into the shape of a cross. As Bill looked up at it from where he lay on the ground, that very ordinary electric pole seemed to melt away and transform into a cross.

"In all those years I went to church as a young person, I'd heard plenty of sermons about the cross. I knew its significance. Jesus died to pay for our sins. Because of His death, we can have our sins forgiven, be at peace with God, and live forever with Him in Heaven. The cross has the power to bring us from death to life.

"I knew then that if there was any hope for me, God was my *only* hope. I crawled to the base of that electric pole, crawling to the base of the cross. The weight of my guilt and shame was such a burden. Face down on the ground, I gave up and asked God to rescue me. And my life has not been the same since that moment." God took the guilt, and gave Bill peace.

When Bill finally left that cross, his truck had run out of gas. So he either had to sit and hope that someone would come along—which was not likely—or he had to walk the ten miles back home to Crystal City. He felt so lighthearted, he decided to walk home. Along the way, every crossbar on an electric pole reminded him of Christ's cross. He talked with God all the way home.

"On that walk home, God began to change my heart and thinking, and I was convinced that the first thing I needed to do was give back to Him His 10 percent of the company's earnings, just as Dad had always done. I'd been greedy and had robbed God of what was His.

"I made God a promise that night. If He would allow the company to somehow survive and once again be profitable, I'd give Him not 10 percent but the 90 percent, and I'd run the company on the remaining ten."

The company was making nothing at the time, and 90 percent of nothing was nothing, so Bill wasn't sure his vow was much of a faith promise. But he made the promise to God with sincerity and intended to keep it.

It was almost four in the morning when he returned home, but he had to wake his wife and tell her what had happened. She was overjoyed to hear his news. Then she told her husband about being awakened around one o'clock with a prompting that he was in trouble. So she had been praying for his safety until she finally had a peace that he was all right.

"Her prayers saved my life, Johnny. I believe that. I believe I could have died in that truck."

Bill told his wife about the promise he had made to God. She laughed aloud. He thought she was laughing at him, that she thought his promise to God was ridiculous. She explained that she was laughing in joy.

"Bill, you have no idea where God is about to take you and your company. I believe our 10 percent will be more than enough."

Now Bill had some hard choices to make. Steve knew the

company better than anyone, and his advice had proved to be true. So on his advice, instead of lowering prices, the company upped them and grew their reputation for a quality product. The competition then raised their prices, and it became a strange price war—attempting to stay above the competition's price. The strategy was contrary to everything Bill had been taught in college. But the farmers and ranchers who had trusted the company with their business for over one hundred years were happy to see quality brought back to the forefront. And they were willing to pay for it.

Bill promoted Steve and in a short time made him president of the company.

"That was my best move, I think. Dad probably intended to do that, too, but he died too soon," Bill reflected.

In the next two years, sales doubled and the profits started rolling in. Bill honored his commitment to God, and the 10 percent he kept for the company was more than the company had ever made when his father kept 90 percent. Bill learned a valuable lesson: He could not outgive God. The more money he sent to missions and charities, the more money the company made.

The company expanded their buildings in Laredo and in Crystal City and now had factories in five states, one in Europe, and several more on the drawing board. Steve had long since passed on; Bill was still chairman of the board, but his son Will was running things from the corporate office in Laredo.

"This spot has been a special place for me," Bill continued, looking around. His gaze stopped, resting on the cross rising above the countryside. "Over the years, I occasionally returned here to think and renew my promises to God. About ten years ago, when I was thinking about my decision to turn the business over to Will, I came out here early one morning.

"Sitting here, looking around, I was sad that the roadside park had been abandoned for so long and was now in complete disarray. Then an idea came to me, a thought that I believe was placed in my head by the Holy Spirit: *Build a cross here.*"

Bill had felt a little bit like Noah must have felt when God told him to build an ark. He was certain people would criticize him and think he was crazy to build a wooden cross out in the countryside. The idea really made no more sense than giving away most of his profits. But he decided to obey what he was sure the Holy Spirit was telling him to do.

"It's been ten years, now, since I built the cross. Many days I sit here for a few hours over lunch and read my Bible and talk with God. He sends people here who have been wandering from the truth. You'd be amazed at the stories I've heard and the lives that have been changed because they came to the cross."

78

"Many days, no one shows up, but then I spend my time fueling myself with God's Word," Bill McCollum told Johnny. He stood up. "I want to show you something."

He led Johnny over to the truck. Johnny wondered why someone so successful would drive a pile of junk.

"See how old and worn out the body of this truck is? Look, the door still doesn't latch properly. You'd almost think this old relic would not even run. But take a look at the engine."

The hood of the truck opened from the side. Bill pulled up the hood to reveal a gleaming chrome and black engine.

"This truck is like you and I when we accept Christ into our lives. We receive a new power source. We may still appear old and decrepit on the outside, and we may still have to deal with the consequences of our wrong choices before we met Jesus. Yet if He is our power, we can conquer any mountain or slog through any deep valley.

"And this truck won't take me anywhere without fuel. Our fuel is reading God's Word and prayer. Many Christians go through life barely running on fumes because they are too busy to fill their spiritual tanks. Then they wonder why they feel no power in their lives, no victory over evil. They're out of gas."

"I sometimes doubt," Johnny admitted. "I've wondered how I could be certain Jesus has saved me."

"Have you ever considered that the devil is the one whispering that question?" Bill asked.

That was a new thought for Johnny.

"Think about this, Johnny. When you were out drinking and partying before you were saved, did you ever question your status with God?"

"No, I knew what God thought of the way I was living."

"That's true of most folks. And the devil has no need to bother lost folks with questions about their salvation. He already has those souls. He wants to bother the folks who are saved. The best remedy for ridding yourself of old Beelzebub's testing is to be so read up on God's Word and so prayed up that the devil can't stand being anywhere near you.

"Don't misunderstand me, the old evil one is powerful. But he is no match for a born-again Amish man ... or any Christian man or woman." Bill grins. "He is, of course, quite upset by this cross, since we've snatched many folks away from him here at this spot."

One of the verses Johnny had read on the steps was still echoing in his head, almost as though someone was speaking it. *Everyone who calls on the name of the Lord will be saved.* The devil wanted Johnny to doubt that, but that was the Word of God!

Bill ran his hand lovingly along the hood of the old truck. "I do have a new truck back at the factory that I use to drive back and forth between Laredo and Crystal City. My wife's embarrassed to be seen with me in this one, but it always reminds me ..."

He looked at his watch.

"I need to be back in Crystal City soon. If you're headed to Laredo, I may see you again. I'll be coming down that road later today. We keep the company jet at the airport down there, and I'm flying to Washington tonight for a trade meeting. Those folks in Washington think I know something about business." He chuckled. "Since most of them don't, it's not too hard to appear intelligent."

"You have your own airplane?" Johnny was astonished. He had never flown and never would, but here was someone who owned a jet.

"You'd be amazed what 10 percent of a God-owned company can accomplish," said Bill. "Johnny, I'd like to get to know you better. Are you going to be in the area for a while? Would you consider flying with me to Washington? We'll be back tomorrow night; you'd only lose a day. That twenty dollars you just donated would buy the ticket." He grinned.

"That sure does sound tempting, but we Amish are not permitted to fly."

"I certainly don't want you to do anything against your beliefs." Bill handed him a small green card. "Here's my business card; if you ever change your mind, give me a call. Remember, you've got a $20 round-trip ticket to anywhere in the world."

Johnny took the card, but knew he would never take advantage of such an offer.

"If you're not going to Washington with me, would you like a tour of the factory in Laredo? It's about eighty miles from here to our main office. How long would it take you to bike that far?"

"If I leave here now, I could be there by noon tomorrow."

"I'll call my son and tell him to expect you. The address is on the business card. Ask for Will. He'll give you a tour of the factory, and I think you'll enjoy it." Bill climbed in and slammed the door. "I have a feeling we'll meet again," he said through the open window. "And if you'd ever consider working for us, look me up. We could use a man like you."

The old truck roared off, and Johnny was alone at the cross.

**

It was as though every part of Johnny's journey had pointed him in this direction and led him here to the cross. Had God arranged all those meetings for him?

His head was spinning, but deep inside there was a new peace. At last, he had the certainty that had eluded him for so long. *Everyone who calls on the name of the Lord will be saved.* There was the assurance he had searched for. It was the Word of God, resounding a firm answer to Johnny's doubt.

He was drawn back to the cross, unwilling to leave. He slowly took the steps once again, sat down on RECEIVE and stretched out his legs over CONFESS.

The afternoon sun spread warmth through his body, and he rested against the base of the cross. Closing his eyes, he imagined that he heard the sounds of the crucifixion, heard the gasps of pain as nails were driven in and Jesus' mother wept. Jesus looked down at Johnny, then, at the foot of His cross, and Johnny caught a glimpse of how deeply Jesus loved him. And as life ebbed away from the Savior, His blood dropped down on the wanderer at the bottom of the cross and washed away his sins.

Jesus died, and Johnny was cleansed.

There beneath the cross, Johnny was stunned by what God's love had done. Like a river, love poured over him and into him, alive and unending.

79

With great reluctance and feeling as though he was breaking a sacred hour, Johnny left the cross. As he rode down Route 83, his mind was still held by the events at this place, and a song began in his head. First it came only as a memory from long ago, the sweet memory of evenings spent with family and friends singing together as Fiddle Bill fiddled. Without fail, the evening was brought to a close by singing several songs without Bill's accompaniment. One of those was "Amazing Grace," the song that always left Johnny's father wrung with emotion. The second song was the one now ringing in his head as he pedaled and sang aloud.

I must needs go home by the way of the cross,
There's no other way but this;
I shall ne'er get sight of the Gates of Light,
If the way of the cross I miss.

The way of the cross leads home,
The way of the cross leads home;
It is sweet to know, as I onward go,
The way of the cross leads home.

The words of the old hymn meant much more to him now than when he had sung them as a boy. He felt tears on his cheeks and realized that they were tears of joy and not sadness. How long had it been since he had felt joy? That river of love he had felt beneath the cross had turned into tears of joy, flowing outward.

Glancing to his left, he could still see the cross away off in the distance. *A beacon for weary wanderers,* he thought.

> *I must needs go on in the blood-sprinkled way,*
> *The path that the Savior trod,*
> *If I ever climb to the heights sublime,*
> *Where the soul is at home with God.*

> *The way of the cross leads home,*
> *The way of the cross leads home;*
> *It is sweet to know, as I onward go,*
> *The way of the cross leads home.*

There was a third verse, but he couldn't quite recall the words. They would come back to him, he was sure of it.

***

"I'm here to see Will."

The young receptionist did a quick survey of the disheveled visitor standing in her lobby and looked skeptical.

"Is he expecting you?"

"I believe he is. The name's Johnny Miller."

She grabbed the phone and pressed an intercom button.

"Mr. McCollum, there's someone here who claims he has an appointment with you." She lowered her voice and whispered to the phone, "He looks like a vagrant. Maybe homeless."

Mr. McCollum must have had a question for her, because she replied, "Not shaved in weeks, I'd say. Wrinkled shirt. Dirty hat that looks like it was used for a pillow. Should I call security? Yes, he did say his name is Johnny Miller." She listened, her eyebrows went up, and she turned back to Johnny. "Mr. McCollum will be right out to see you."

Johnny's old ornery nature kicked in. "Thanks, ma'am. And yes, I did use this hat for a pillow last night. Slept in a field beneath a cattle shelter. Best night of sleep in weeks. I probably need a bath, too." He looked down at his shoes. "Hmm. I knew that aroma wasn't the natural odor of your lobby here."

"Johnny, welcome to Laredo!" boomed a deep voice. "Dad told me to expect you."

Johnny extended his hand, but Will ignored it and wrapped him in a bear hug. Johnny saw the shocked receptionist look away.

Will led the way down a wide hall and chatted as though Johnny was one of the family. "Dad says your family still uses our one-bottom plow. I suppose you know that we've diversified since that plow, and now we manufacture many types of agricultural equipment. Some folks say we are outstanding in our field, but I like to say we're out working in our fields."

Will opened a door leading into a room with dark paneling and plush carpet. A long mahogany table anchored the room. Johnny ran his fingers along the wall, admiring the grain and rich color.

"Whenever I walk into this room, I feel the essence and backbone of our company. These men have led us to where we are today." Will stood at one wall, in front of a row of framed portraits of the company's presidents. Jedediah McCollum, the founder, looked like an Amish man. Through the next one hundred years, one McCollum after another had taken the reins of the company.

Johnny's eyes were drawn to one position in the parade of presidents. The line of white faces was interrupted by the portrait of a black man. The name plate identified Steve Richardson.

"Is this the man your dad made president years ago?"

"Yes, that's Steve, the man that saved our company. Dad did a lot of things wrong early in his tenure, but the smartest thing he ever did was putting Steve in as president. There was some resistance at first to a black man leading the company and some idiotic comments, but people soon realized their paychecks were good only because of this great man, and it was about green, not black or white. I had the good fortune to work with him for several years before he retired."

On another wall, a banner proclaimed, TO GOD BE THE GLORY. Below the banner hung photos of orphanages and other buildings and villages around the globe.

"This is what we call The 90 Percent Project. I'm sure Dad told you about his deal with God. This is part of what God's 90 percent is doing."

One photo showed an aircraft. Johnny pointed to it and asked, "Is this what I would have flown in if I would have gone to Washington yesterday?"

"Yes, that's our Gulfstream GII SP. Dad uses it to fly around the world and visit all these projects." Johnny admired the sleek design of the airplane. On the tail section was a logo that looked like the globe, and the words painted along the fuselage read, TO GOD BE THE GLORY.

In one photo, Big Bill stood alongside a young black man in a pilot's uniform. Will saw Johnny studying the picture.

"That's Josh Richardson, Steve's grandson. He returned from Viet Nam an experienced pilot and we hired him. He and I are great friends. He was determined to go into the ministry, but Dad had other plans; and Dad can be very persuasive. He had been leasing aircraft and pilots for all these mission trips, but he convinced Josh to get his commercial license, and we purchased the first company plane. Last year we upgraded to this Gulfstream. Josh is with Dad in Washington today. Actually, Josh is now the one who oversees the dispersal of God's 90 percent, and I handle the remaining 10 percent.

"Let me give you a tour of the factory. That's what you came to see, I believe."

There was nothing like this back home. Johnny was astonished at the assembly line churning out products. The factory used all the latest technology, according to Will. Overhead conveyor belts brought the correct parts to the correct station. A chassis began its journey down the line and finally rolled off at the end as a completed combine. The combine itself was amazing, having little in common with the horse-drawn machines used on Miller farm.

After the tour, Will escorted Johnny to the company's guest house near the factory.

"You're welcome to stay as long as you want. We have more than enough accommodations here for sales people and other visitors. Any food you find is yours. There's a washer and dryer there, if you want to clean up." He grinned at his guest. This was the first indication Will had given that he had noticed Johnny's appearance. His hospitality and graciousness left Johnny with a longing for the warmth of his own home.

80

As dawn filtered through a heavy cover of clouds, Johnny left the guest house. He had expressed his gratitude and said farewell to the younger McCollum the evening before. In return, Will had echoed his father's invitation—Johnny was welcome any time, and if he was ever in need of a job ...

In spite of the clouds, Johnny's mind was clear, as sharp as it had been in weeks. During the last two days, his entire being had been cleansed, everything from his soul to his socks.

He was quite proud that he had conquered the faulty washer in the guest house the night before, even though it was apparently not sealed properly and mounds of foam bubbled out as it washed his clothes. A second and third wash without detergent had rinsed away all the extra foam. Clean clothes, a full stomach, and a good night's sleep all made him eager to start pedaling again.

There was something else that added to his energy and brightened his outlook. He had tossed about on the soft mattress for over an hour the night before. At first he thought it was only the bed that kept him from sleep, so he had moved to the floor with his clean shawl covering him. Still, he lay awake.

Then he had finally acknowledged the only thing that would give him rest. He took a sheet of stationery from the desk and began his letter to Ohio. He signed it, sealed and addressed it, and breathed a sigh of relief. Sleep had come immediately.

He was going home.

***

He had asked Will about the best route across Texas and headed northward.

"You really only have two choices. Route 59 stretches all the way to Houston; that's over 300 miles. It's a busy highway and will be quite congested around the city. A less traveled route would be Route 359 over to Hebbronville, then pick up 285 all the way to Highway 77. From Corpus Christi you can take lesser highways along the coastline."

The second route seemed the better choice, and the distance from Laredo to Hebbronville was a little over 55 miles, a perfect day's ride. Johnny had looked at Corpus Christi on the map, thought it looked like a good-sized town, and surmised that it would surely have a Greyhound bus station.

As he pedaled down route 359, the song about the way of the cross still floated through his mind. He could not remember the third verse; that was the only blemish on this perfect day. Bits and pieces came to mind, but he could not put that last verse together.

He stopped several times at small outposts on the Texas prairie. In late afternoon, a sign welcomed him to Jim Hogg County, and he was soon in the outskirts of Hebbronville. He rode past the Jim Hogg County Jail and the Jim Hogg County Courthouse, a stately building with tall white columns.

He was hungry. Surely there would be a Jim Hogg diner or restaurant. But apparently Mr. Hogg had never ventured into food service; the only eating establishment in view was a small diner named Frank's. Perhaps the proprietor was Frank Hogg. As a matter of fact, Johnny thought, he would enjoy a good ham dinner.

One thing could be said about Frank's: It was the kind of local hangout where a good meal and local information was always a sure thing. At the counter, Johnny chatted with the server while he enjoyed fried potatoes and a thick slab of ham.

"What do you mean, you're Amish? What does that mean?" the waitress asked.

By now, Johnny had learned to give a quick overview of his background and beliefs in a few brief sentences.

"It sure sounds idyllic. Why would you have left that?"

"The truth is, I'm heading home." Saying it aloud flooded him with warmth.

"Those sure are odd looking pants you're wearing."

"Cutting edge of fashion. They're called Johnny BarnDoors," he deadpanned. "I need information. I'm looking for a place to sleep tonight. What's available? Is there a cemetery near here?"

The server nearly dropped her coffeepot at that question, and he added quickly, "I enjoy visiting cemeteries, and it's still quite early. Thought I'd take a look."

"There are two," she replied. "There's a real old one on the edge of town up on Route 359. It's full. In other words, no vacancies. But the newer one on Route 285 does have openings." Johnny had to laugh at that one. She laughed, too, but from the looks she gave him as he finished his meal, he knew she was wondering why he would want to wander about cemeteries.

He would not even try to explain to her that he was quite serious about spending this night in a cemetery. It had been one of his goals for the past several weeks, and he had been looking for the right resting place. It was surprising how many cemeteries were enclosed by high fences.

Dusk was settling in when he spotted the opening in the black wrought iron fence surrounding the old Hebbronville cemetery. Making a quick check of traffic north and south, he pushed the bike past ancient stone monuments with names faded and forgotten. Some stones marked the graves of Civil War veterans, their years cut short when they joined the Confederate cavalry.

Toward the rear of the burial grounds was a red brick mausoleum holding the remains of Jim Hogg himself.

Johnny parked the bike behind the small structure and unrolled the bright shawl that had become his security blanket. The aroma of lavish soap suds still lingered. From this vantage point, he was invisible to anyone passing by, and he doubted the old soldiers resting around him would have visitors that evening. When he craned his neck, he could make out the corner of Frank's Diner. He was already looking forward to a hearty breakfast there.

The night was calm. Brilliant stars shone on all those gathered above and below ground. He nestled close to the sun-warmed bricks enclosing Jim Hogg, who rested in undisturbed slumber.

81

Sabe and Posy had struggled along for days, and no milkweed had appeared. Afternoon was fading into evening, when the two landed in an open field with waves of wildflowers. That day they had floated along on a cushion of air; yet even the minimal exertion required to remain aloft had exhausted both. They landed nearly twenty miles southeast of the cemetery in Hebbronville, Texas, where they had rested one night on their journey south.

That evening, as they sat side by side on a gently swaying flower, Posy remarked that perhaps they were intended to give birth to their family here and then continue on home alone. "Did you ever see your mother or father?" she asked thoughtfully. "I have no memory of mine."

He had been so certain that going home was the best thing for both of them. Now he wondered if he had been mistaken. "Nothing makes sense any more. I do remember that back in my youth an adult flew over my milkweed plant and told me I was part of the special fourth generation. Perhaps that was my mother."

"What if we are not intended to return home?" wondered Posy. She had a look in her eyes that he had never seen before. "Maybe this is home for us, and our long life will be completed here. We are quite ancient, you know."

Sabe could not comprehend an ending that did not conclude at the place of his birth. He did admit, though, that he had no strength left for the journey.

"Posy, I don't know if you noticed, but I am not the butterfly I used to be. I am pale and colorless and extremely weak. How could you still love such a fellow?"

She waggled her antennae at him in that way he had come to love. "I didn't fall in love with colors; I fell in love with Sabio. Yes, your color was stunning; but there is more to us wanderers than color." Her own colors looked faded in the evening dusk. Her wings came together in gentle repose. "All this talking has completely worn me out. Find a suitable branch somewhere; and while you're at it, search for a milkweed plant. I am quite sure tomorrow we will be parents."

***

The gray dawn stillness was broken by the chirping of one bird. Then another joined in, and soon a cheerful chorus pulled Johnny from deep slumber. The first rays of sunlight streamed through the branches of a tree along the cemetery fence. Watching a new day arrive, he wondered if there were still more encounters ahead or if it was time to end his journey.

The previous evening, the server at Frank's had looked up a number for Johnny, and he fed the pay phone outside the diner and called the Greyhound station in Corpus Christi. A bus to Nashville left every afternoon at four, and a route out of Nashville would bring him to Columbus in two days. The third day could see him pedaling from Stevenson to Milford and home.

Home! Could he perhaps be home even before his letter arrived? He took pleasure in imagining his homecoming. He would ride up the road toward the Miller farmhouse. The valley would be spring green, and he would smell the newly turned ground. Mandy might be out planting the garden; maybe John would be plowing with that Laredo plow. Or would he already be planting? Everything depended on the weather. "We partner with God," John often had said, "when we care for the land."

His letter did not give details about why he was coming home. How could he begin to list, in one short letter, all the ways he had changed? How could he explain that everything he had experienced had worked to draw him closer to home? How could he tell his family in a few scribbled words that he had discovered he was a farmer and he was an Amish man?

Would they be surprised that he wanted to stay in the Amish church? His father had been right when he said Johnny would find nothing in the outside world that satisfied more than the life they had in their valley. Wandering far from home, Johnny now saw all the good things that their life held. Most of all, he believed their traditions were meant to keep him close to God. Some things still frustrated him, things he wished would change; but he believed he would gain far more by going back home than he would lose. It was the best way for him to live.

Johnny suspected that his mother would not be surprised to see him returning. Somehow, it had always seemed that she could read Johnny's mind, and maybe she could even read it from a thousand miles away. Mandy would not be surprised; she would just be overjoyed that her son was home.

82

Every parking space at Frank's was full, both in the lot and on the street. Pickups and cattle haulers mixed with big luxury cars. One car sprouted a pair of longhorns from the hood.

Inside, Frank's hummed with a mix of people even more fascinating than their vehicles. The previous evening, the place had been filled with families and couples enjoying a quiet supper. This morning the crowd was laughing and boisterous, decked out in large hats and big belt buckles.

Johnny slipped in between two ranchers seated at the counter, and in no time he was talking with them about cattle and ranching. When he explained how his family made a living farming just over one hundred acres, the rancher on his right laughed and remarked that he had that much acreage for each cow he owned.

"A thousand-acre ranch is quite common around here. Today I'm on my way up north to the King Ranch, near Kingsville, to pick up some cattle. That's one of the biggest ranches in the world at 825,000 acres." Johnny did the calculation and tried to imagine one ranch the size of 8,000 farms like the Miller farm. "The King Ranch covers parts of six counties," continued the rancher. "Are you riding up that way?"

"My plan is to head over toward Corpus Christi and from there either continue biking or catch a bus ride home. What's my best option for a ride to Corpus Christi?"

"That would be 285 out past Falfurrias, all the way to Route 77. That goes through Kingsville. You could visit King Ranch."

Johnny finished his breakfast, thanked the men for the information, and stepped outside into a gorgeous Texas morning.

He noticed the change again this morning; there was a new clarity to his thoughts. On some mornings, things happened in slow motion, but on this morning his mind was crystal clear. He saw things he would otherwise pass by. On mornings that his mind was clogged with thoughts and problems, he tended to miss the beauty and wonderment of small details. But on this day, everything was in sharp, clear focus. A sign at the car lot advertising the best deals around hung askew. At the edge of town, he noticed the symmetry of the rows of gravestones in the newer cemetery. A duck slowly made its way to the center of a small, placid pond, trailing the soft ripples of a wake that expanded smoothly in each direction. Johnny marveled at the intricacies of God's creation.

In the cemetery the night before, he had finally pieced together the third verse of the hymn. Perhaps it was because he was sitting among graves (it does give a new perspective on everything); or, more likely, it was a result of this clarity of mind that he had had the last few days. Maybe his mind was freed because he had decided to end the journey in Corpus Christi and board the bus for home. He was also still filled with the wonderful feeling he had encountered at the base of the cross. Perhaps it was that feeling that had brought back the words.

As his tires hummed down Texas Route 285, he sang with joy that old song.

I must needs go home by the way of the cross,
There's no other way but this;
I shall ne'er get sight of the Gates of Light,
If the way of the cross I miss.

The way of the cross leads home,
The way of the cross leads home;
It is sweet to know, as I onward go,
The way of the cross leads home.

I must needs go on in the blood-sprinkled way,
The path that the Savior trod,
If I ever climb to the heights sublime,
Where the soul is at home with God.

And, finally, the words of verse three rolled out:

Then I bid farewell to the way of the world,
To walk in it nevermore;
For my Lord says, "Come," and I seek my home,
Where He waits at the open door.

He heard a vehicle come up behind him. There was the toot of a horn, and he was brought from his sacred thoughts back to Texas. A cattle hauler passed, and an arm waved from the window. He could see only an arm, but he thought it must have been the rancher he had talked with at breakfast. The folks in the great state of Texas had been kind and considerate.

This was where he would have wanted to be if he had followed his dream to go west. How would his life have been different if he had acted on that dream? He would never know. His choices had shaped his life, and those choices had brought him here, to this road on this day.

An hour out of Hebbronville, he pulled off the road for a break. He remembered an apple he had picked up at the Laredo guest house, and he dug that out and leaned against a fence, munching the fruit and watching a herd of longhorns slowly lumber across a field. The apple was firm and crunchy and of exceptional flavor. Juice dripped down his chin. He wiped it with his sleeve and tossed the apple core into the field. The pale yellow missile landed near a cluster of blue wildflowers bending in the prairie breeze. A butterfly with faded colors landed on the discarded core. It resembled the Monarchs Annie had released, but its colors were far less vibrant.

Come to think of it, he had seen numerous butterflies over the past several days. He tried to recall if Annie ever mentioned that Monarchs were native to Texas. He did remember her talking about their long migration journey. Perhaps these Monarchs were like Johnny, just traveling through.

Pushing off again, he picked up the pace a bit. The distance from Hebbronville to Corpus Christi was exactly 100 miles. He could get 70 miles in on this first day, and that would give him enough time on the next day to stop at King Ranch and still arrive at the bus station in plenty of time to buy a ticket and start home.

An uneventful hour passed, with the occasional cattle truck rattling by. About twenty miles east of Hebbronville, the highway undulated in moderate ups and downs. This suited him just fine. Easy uphill climbs, followed by restful downhill coasts.

83

Sabio and Mariposa sat silently awaiting the morning sun. Finally, the yellow warmth appeared over the horizon. They moved slowly from flower to flower. "We need to load up on nectar so we can get some distance in today," said Sabe.

"We won't be flying far today," Posy told him weakly. "And you need to find a milkweed plant quickly."

Their flight was low that morning. Sabio's thousands of eye parts were scanning the ground for a plant suitable for birthing. Posy plodded slowly along, trying to stay aloft, while Sabe flew long, looping circles in search of the elusive milkweed.

Ahead, a straight highway ran all the way to the horizon. A dusty lane used for farm implements crossed the road and stretched in opposite directions. At the intersection of the two, the lane had widened from years of farm traffic. This morning the widening was just a lonely, barren area of dust in the middle of nowhere.

But could it be? Several species of scrubby bushes were determined to live in the dust at the edges of the lane; and interspersed among the bushes, tall green plants reached toward the morning sun. Sabio recognized the plant that had turned him from a worm to the handsome creature he once had been. He winged lower and saw many more milkweed plants.

Hurrying back to Posy, he told her of his discovery. "Follow me. I found the plant for our family's birth."

"You did great, Sabio. And just in time."

They landed softly on a milkweed leaf, and Posy immediately began making preparations for her babies. She ignored Sabe completely, and with no idea what was expected of him, he took to the air again. He had seen a few blossoms on other low-growing plants. The food here was limited, and he saw no sign of water. Posy, though, would not be flying any farther today.

Something else had caught his eyes before he had found the milkweed. Far away, a very small object was moving down the highway, moving toward the milkweed patch, slowly growing in size. Whatever it was, the object set off feelings in Sabe that he could not interpret. He fluttered ahead to inspect it.

The object met and passed him. Recognition coursed through his antennae and body. The messages he received didn't quite make sense, but there was only one way to find the truth. Turning as abruptly as his diminishing strength would allow, he fluttered behind. The object was moving along at a speed he could have easily surpassed in his youth. Now, he fought to catch up.

Sabio came in for a landing and made a discovery that sent vibrations of exhilaration and shock through his entire being. Then understanding flooded through him. He had been wrong about home, after all. Now truth was upon him, and he recognized it.

They were finally home. He must tell Posy.

***

Topping one gentle hill, Johnny felt a slight touch. Then it was a distinct tickle. He glanced down and to his left, and grinned with pleasure. A butterfly had landed on the back of his left hand.

His hands inadvertently followed his glance and turned the handlebars. The bicycle drifted away from the shoulder, much too far out into the lane of traffic.

The blast of horn and screech of tires slammed into him.

Johnny felt nothing, but he knew something was amiss. He was not pedaling; he was flying through the air. His mind told his legs to pedal, but his body and mind no longer worked together.

He landed on the side of the highway and the air was crushed from his lungs. A second later, he heard the rattle of his bike hitting the pavement.

Get up! his mind yelled at his body, yet he could not move. *Why can't I move? I feel no pain. I must be all right.*

Someone's hand was firm on his back.

"Don't move. Stay still. My partner's driving to the next ranch to call for the squad."

Why would you do that? What happened?

"I'm sorry. I'm so sorry. We couldn't stop. We came over the hill and there you were, right in front of us. Just hang in there. Help is coming."

***

"I've discovered home!" Sabio was breathless from hurrying back to Posy. She had finished positioning her eggs on the broad leaves of the milkweed.

"You've what?"

"Home. My birthplace. Follow me."

Posy was very tired.

"No, Sabe, this is where it ends, here on the milkweed plant. I have realized for a while now we were only intended to reach this place to reproduce, and then to die. It is over for us."

"That may be true, but I assure you that home is just a few short flutters away."

Humoring her friend one last time, Posy tried to follow him. Drifting only a few feet above the ground, she struggled to keep up with Sabio, but fell at last in the dust, completely exhausted.

"You go on. I can't," she gasped.

"No, we are almost there. See out there, lying by the roadside … that is home."

"No, Sabe. Unfortunately, that is not home."

"I insist," he urged frantically. With the very last of her strength, she pulled herself up to follow her mate. They wobbled along the ground, wings dragging and fragile legs stumbling. "We are almost home," he said excitedly. "Beneath here! Follow me!"

Spent, the two at last found sanctuary beneath Johnny's left hand lying motionless on the sun-warmed pavement.

84

He swam out of the blackness and tasted blood in his mouth. His body seemed to have been detached from his mind, but he managed a few words.

"Am I hurt?"

"Yeah, I believe you are, but help is on the way."

He tried to move his hand to his face to wipe away something that was clouding his vision, but his left arm would not move. He was not even sure where his other arm was; he could not feel it. The thin wail of a siren grew larger. It took him back to that long, long ride with Annie, racing to the hospital with lights flashing and siren keening and his wife so quiet and pale.

More people were now beside him. More voices.

"Hang in there, buddy, help is on the way."

A new voice said in low tones, "This guy's a goner."

***

"Posy, Posy, we are home! Can you not detect the aroma of our birthplace?"

Mariposa leaned against Sabio, completely exhausted from the journey and the efforts in propagating her future family.

"No, Sabe, I can't. But I feel safe and at peace here."

Her frail wings folded in rest, and she was the first to lose life.

Sabio now understood something he had not grasped before: Going home meant returning to the place where he had been given life. Every one of his senses told him he was finally home.

In one instant, he knew this. Then he followed Posy into nature's hereafter.

***

Johnny could not see anything except his hand resting beside his head. A trickle of blood slid along the pavement toward his fingers, but he could not move his arm. The clouds blocked more of his sight, but he was certain he saw, huddled under his cupped fingers, a butterfly. Or perhaps even two.

His body felt nothing. The world turned, and he saw bits of blue sky through the clouds in his eyes. He felt himself lifted. *What happened? Why will my legs not pedal? Why can't I move my arms or my feet?*

"Did anyone check his pockets for an ID?" They found his wallet. And a single $20 bill.

"His name's Johnny Miller. Looks like he's from a town in Ohio called Milford. No phone number. Business cards. One from a Samuel Cohraine in California. One from Bill McCollum."

Voices. "Can you hear us?" "Hang in there." "We'll be to the hospital soon."

The voices faded away, and soon there was no sensation at all. He was floating through a corridor of some kind, turning from side to side with no effort but a thought. A brilliant white light appeared and grew larger and larger, and he suddenly burst out into an area shimmering and pulsing with light.

From out of the light appeared a being that stopped his heart— if it was still beating, which he was beginning to suspect it was not.

"Annie! Annie! Is it really you?"

"Yes. I came as soon as they told me you were on the way."

"Annie, what happened? Did I really die?"

She smiled at him, that same tender smile that he remembered and missed so much.

"That's one way to look at it, dear. Up here, we see it as really coming to life."

"I was riding my bicycle … I must have had an accident. The butterfly! A butterfly landed on the back of my hand. Was that you, Annie, in that butterfly?"

"Oh, Johnny, I did often wish I could have been a butterfly, but neither of those two was me. Sometimes a butterfly is just that, a butterfly."

"Annie, I've missed you so much; it's been such a long time that you've been gone."

"A long time? I just arrived in Heaven this morning! Let's hurry and go inside, so I can show you around before the rest of the family arrives later today."

"I can't believe this is really happening, Annie. Pinch me; make sure I'm dead."

She giggled and reached over to give his arm a gentle pinch. Then, grabbing his hand, she said, "Come. We're going home."

Annie suddenly stopped, as though listening to someone.

"What?" Johnny said.

She looked at him with a clear, strong look in those lovely dark blue eyes, a look that held no sorrow or pain, and she said, "Not yet."

"What do you mean?"

"Not yet, Johnny. It's not yet time for you to stay here. I've just heard: You will need to go back."

"No! I'm here with you now. We're together, and I don't want to lose you again. I don't want to go back! I won't go back!"

Epilogue

On the first Saturday in May, a small figure hurried along a path through a field on the Miller farm, headed for the woods on the hilltop. Simon, the son of Johnny's sister Martha, often showed up at the Miller barn around chore time to lend a hand. At Simon's age of ten, Johnny had already been doing a man's work, but times were changing. Many Amish families no longer farmed, and Simon only volunteered to help when it suited his schedule.

Today his schedule did not allow it. The boy could not be in the barn this evening. He had become quite helpful to his father in the furniture shop, so it wasn't that Simon was averse to hard work. Something far more important called him to the woods.

The tree house hidden in the tall oak at the top of the hill had been taking up more and more of the boy's time. Simon's Uncle Johnny had built the hideaway, and the boy had been told by his mother how important that retreat had been to his uncle.

But Uncle Johnny had grown up and gotten married; and in the summer after the wedding, Simon had sneaked up to the stand several times. He admired the weathered walls and old roof, and he sat with legs dangling from the deck, looking over the countryside in quiet awe and soaking up the panorama below him. He poked about inside, browsing through the few books and magazines, reading the scrawled note hanging on the wall, and wondering about the scraps of paper inside painted beer bottles.

One day last summer, he had been startled to find his Aunt Annie there, writing in her notebook. But most of the time, Simon felt quite cunning in his ability to sneak in and out of the deer stand undetected, often approaching from the woods and scampering up the back set of rungs.

He did not know that Johnny had often spied his nephew trying to stay invisible as he slipped through the trees. Johnny only grinned, recalling memories of his own boyhood, and he never revealed his knowledge to Simon. He was actually quite pleased that someone else found his thinking stand appealing.

Johnny had other interests that summer. The farm took most of his time, and he wanted to spend every spare minute with his lovely Annie.

A year later, on this day in May, Simon had no concern of being seen. His much-loved aunt was buried on Strawberry Hill, and his uncle was lying in a hospital somewhere in Texas. Simon's only concern was that he might miss a few words of commentary about the horses entered in this greatest of horse races. The coverage started at five. His steps quickened to a trot.

Simon had a love for animals, and he especially admired horses. He pored over everything he could find about each colt in the Run for the Roses. And this year, for the first time ever, he would hear everything as the horses pounded down the track.

He situated himself facing the woods. He did not wish to have the sound waves from his new transistor radio float down toward the barn. As he skimmed across the dial, the little transistor came to life. Simon propped the radio against the wall of the stand and relaxed, soaking up every word that created the scene in his mind. The announcer was already describing the massive crowd.

"What a splendid evening for a horse race! There are close to 135,000 people here at Churchill Downs for the running of the Kentucky Derby. It's quite a field we have here today, thirteen of the finest three-year-olds in America. Many are anxious to see the big chestnut colt from California. Sun Dancer struggled a bit in his last race but he's still the favorite. This could be the year we see a colt break the two-minute barrier in the world's most important horse race!"

Simon knew no horse had ever run the long, one-and-a-quarter-mile race at Churchill Downs in less than two minutes. There was even talk about Sun Dancer pulling off the nearly impossible feat of winning the Triple Crown, taking all three of the biggest horse races for three-year-olds.

"There's another big red horse we need to keep an eye on today," the announcer was saying. "Secretariat's had some impressive wins, but many wonder if he can go this distance. Well, folks, the horses are being led into the starting gate."

Sun Dancer was the last horse into the gate. He paused and pranced and pawed before agreeing to enter. Then they were all out of the gate and the race was on.

Three horses quickly charged to the front. Sun Dancer ignored the speedsters as they passed him. He settled in about midpack; it was a long race and the colt liked to make his move after others tired. Simon knew Sun Dancer had won races coming from a spot dead last. The horses passed the first quarter mile, and Sun Dancer was still stuck in the middle. Passing the half-mile marker, he drifted to the outside, where he could improve his position without interference from lesser horses.

Simon's tense body leaned toward the radio. His palms felt sweaty, and he held his breath, not wanting to miss a word.

The announcer was now very excited, and Simon heard the swelling roar, the crowd screaming and cheering. The announcer shouted into the microphone as the horses rounded the far turn and entered the long homestretch. Sun Dancer was on the move, picking up speed as though he never tired, passing horses that dropped away one by one.

"Oh, but look at this! Here comes the other red colt, Secretariat. He's only half a length … they're neck and neck … heading for the finish … but now Secretariat's pulling away! It's

Secretariat by two and one-half lengths! Secretariat comes out of nowhere to beat Sun Dancer! What an incredible race!"

Simon heard the time announced and the roar of the crowd. Secretariat had done it; he had set the world record and won the race in under two minutes. His official time was 1.59.40. It had never been done before. The greatest horse ever had just won the Kentucky Derby, and Simon had heard every second of it, as it happened! He sagged against the wall, dazed with happiness. Secretariat had just broken the record, and he had heard it all.

In second place, Sun Dancer had run the second fastest time in Kentucky Derby history with a time of 1.59.90, only one-half second off the winner's pace. Simon's heart was still pounding, as though he had been in the saddle of one of those big red horses flying down the stretch. He drifted into a daydream about riding such a horse, feeling the power and speed beneath him.

Someone was interviewing Sun Dancer's owner.

"Your horse just broke through a time barrier, yet you lost the race. How do you feel about that?"

The owner's voice came through the radio, strong and steady.

"You race your horse to the best of his ability, but sometimes you simply get beaten by a better horse. Quite like life, I say. Some days you win, some days you lose. I have won more times than lost, and I'm a fortunate man. But the truth is, this is still just a horse race, and there are more important things in life than racing."

The microphone moved on to speak with someone else, and what Simon could not hear or see was Samuel Cohraine turning to the beautiful young lady who fidgeted by her father's side.

"Now that the race is over, Dad, how soon can we leave for Corpus Christi?"

Johnny's story continues in

WANDERING HOME

"The doctor's here."

They hurried back to Room 3404, but the still form lying in the bed was the only person there. The bleeps and whooshing of the mysterious machines and devices attached to Johnny seemed all the louder in the stillness of the room. Naomi had never seen her brother so motionless and silent, so lifeless. No, she would not use that word.

The doctor came through the door.

"Dr. Schmidt, this is Johnny's family, the Millers."

"Your son is lucky to be alive," began the doctor. "His body has suffered quite a trauma. He has three broken ribs which will just have to heal on their own, although they'll give him quite a bit of pain in the meantime. His right hip is broken; we'll do surgery to pin that in a few days. Our greatest concern right now is cerebral edema, which is swelling of the brain. That causes a buildup of pressure which in turn can cause damage to the brain cells. Right now, we've got to stop that swelling and relieve the pressure. We've done surgery and inserted a ventric that will drain the fluid, and we've got him on medication to reduce swelling."

"And is that having any effect, Doctor?" Samuel Cohraine went straight to the bottom line.

The doctor hesitated just long enough for Naomi to catch the extreme danger gripping her brother.

"No, he is not progressing as I'd hoped. Even if we save his life, we do not know how much brain damage there has been. We've done everything we can. I'll be honest with you. We need a miracle."

- Now available -

Made in the USA
Coppell, TX
10 November 2019

11168780R20213